Originally from Chicago, Elizabeth Reeder has lived in Glasgow for over fifteen years. She writes fiction, essays and for radio and teaches on the prestigious MLitt Creative Writing at the University of Glasgow. Her first novel, *Ramshackle* – which Alan Warner described as '. . . knowing, wry and affectionate' – was published by Freight Books in April 2012. Her essays and short stories have been published in *Chapman*, *PN Review*, *Kenyon Review*, and *Gutter* Magazine.

D0533545

FREMONT

Elizabeth Reeder

KOHLPUBLISHING

First published by Kohl Publishing Limited 2012
Glasgow

© Elizabeth Reeder 2012

First edition

Elizabeth Reeder has asserted her right under the Copyright, Patents
and Designs Act 1988 to be identified as the author of this work.

ISBN 978-0-9573308-0-1

The paper used in this book is recyclable. It is made
from low-chlorine pulps produced in a low-energy,
low-emissions manner from renewable forests.

Printed and bound by
CPI Group (UK) Ltd., Croydon, CR0 4YY.

Cover illustration and design by Emily Chappell

Typeset in 10 point Adobe Caslon
by 3btype.com

For my mom

&

for ARTT

MANIFEST DESTINY

THAT DAMN MAP

In a Midwest state that will remain nameless, in a place offering up tipping cows and crackling cornfields, stands a small town, one man's ever hopeful claim to fame. Just a ways north and west of this town, originating from an unseen source, a thin creek breaks ground and gurgles a course past the only hill in this otherwise pancake-flat place. Now up on the hill, in a mock-antebellum house that is falling down around the moving mass of bodies they call family, live the Fremonts, and on the rather dull, scuffed wall of their entrance hall, is a map. This map, handmade and huge, has been and will always be, incomplete.

Secured to the wall and painted with care, this map represents the somewhat united states of the Fremont family. Each state, made up of carefully carved and painted plywood, is attached to the others and to the topographically detailed wall with superglue and is about the size of a dozen finger-painted hands. Texas, being slightly larger by nature, is the size of big men's hands.

And although the story lives here, above this moody creek, as Hal and Rachel and their kids go about the business of being a family, the story starts in the diner where Rachel Roanoke and Hal Fremont, in a fated moment, meet.

MANIFEST, DESTINY

Rachel has been husband-hunting for months. Across the street from the diner where she works, they're building an Opera House with its west side perched on a steep cliff that edges the Pacific Ocean. Each day she watches the builders come and go and she keeps an eye out for a man who will move her deep down where she needs to be sure, but no one has, so she flirts in a way that is good for business but never brushes their hands or shoulders, and lets proffered phone numbers fall to the floor to be snatched up by Caley, a low-maintenance bottle blond who isn't nearly so discerning.

At her breaks, Rachel stands where the diner's building turns the corner into an alley and she realigns herself with the movement of the tide; she remembers Menatauk, the island where she grew up. Cosseted between the mainland of a different coast and the barrier islands of the Carolinas, it's a place she's never seen on any map. As a kid she used to climb to the top of the hill that cleaved the island in half and from there she'd take in the view of the Island's secure ‹‹‹ shaped coastline and the protective surrounding water that would take her to the mainland when her father banished her into the waiting riptide.

Here, leaning against the roughcast of the diner, just a hint of coastal coolness to the hot air, a single strong gust of sea-wind makes Rachel blink. She lowers her head, a hand across her forehead like a visor to protect her face, and clears the lashes from her eyes.

When she looks up a slim figure walks along the scaffolding, his easy body stretching like a continent across the watery blue of the sky, each steady step finding the steel beam while he looks out to sea. She has to cross her legs to keep the riot under control.

This man, who she watches carefully from behind the counter at lunch, is hers and he'll have perfect skin when she strips him down.

At lunch he doesn't take his eyes off Caley but Rachel knows he'll notice her in time. His name is Hal Fremont and his dad built a town somewhere in the Midwest. His parents died in a car crash just a few weeks back, and him just past twenty, or so the crew said at lunch when she slipped in a question about the new guy who went back to work more promptly than the old-timers who sat drinking coffee and asking for refills.

'That one's looking for a wife,' says Bill the foreman. 'That's what I think.'

'Those virgin bones sure could use a seeing to,' says Caley, watching Hal's legs cut a fine line through his jeans as he crosses the street back to the site.

'Don't you dare, Caley. That one's mine.' Rachel blushes, but stands her ground.

The boys invite Hal for a lunch of chicken-fried steak, mashed potatoes and gravy at the diner across the street from the site and he notices the pretty, wispy blond waitress. But when he goes back for dinner it's the manager, a dark beauty, who catches him up.

Rachel has her sleeves rolled up and her long black hair is pulled back off her face. With arms like that he knows she'll be able to handle an army of boys. Her body is strong and the slow red of her lips puts Hal in the mind to pursue her.

Luckily for them both, Rachel does the work for him. She doesn't wait to hear what Hal thinks of the world. She doesn't think about whether she'll be happy or content or whole. Instead she wears her sensible black flats so she won't fall head over heels before him.

Coffee pots in hand, one black-rimmed, one orange, she banters with the regulars, keeping her body neatly at a distance as she pours decaf or regular into basic cream-colored mugs. Leaving the weak-ass decaf behind she refills Hal's mug, cutting the distance between them. Her hand on his bare arm. When she falters, Hal steadies her; the whole room sees it, something rare, perfect. Men loosen their shirts at the collars, women fan themselves with the menus, and pat their faces with tissues which, when pulled from their purses, are white as doves.

He doesn't let go of her arm after she swoons. He stands, picks up his hat and puts it on his head. Then he takes both the bill and Rachel to the cash register. The room stretches around them, people lean in to hear the pace of their breath. It's steady but stronger than before.

In front of the cash register they manage to pry themselves apart. It's a force of will. They can't do the sorts of things they want to do, on the floor, in the middle of a packed diner. Or can they? Rachel slips behind the counter, smoothing her skirt and trying to find the earth beneath her and beneath that, the water.

He grins and this steadies her.

'Would you like to get married?' she asks when he hands over twenty bucks to pay for his dinner.

'That's the plan,' he says. 'Someday.'

'Does tomorrow suit?'

His smile isn't so much slow in coming, as luscious. 'Well yes, I suppose it does.'

Hal and Rachel exchange only phone numbers and, on the next day, on their first date, they go to the registry office. If they'd been different people they'd have had a satisfying screw in the long alley behind the restaurant and gone their separate ways. But they aren't different people, they're family people.

'Do you take this man?' asks the justice.

'Mmmmmm,' says Rachel.

'Excuse me miss, is that your answer?'

'I do,' Rachel says, the three daisies in her bouquet, bright yellow with ruby centers, doing nothing to distract her from her man. His dark eyes, a hint of tight curl to his buzzed black hair. The smell of him, her knees aren't joints but rivers. He looks at her, but quickly. She can't see the slim fine lines of his hips and thighs but she knows, knows, how it will feel to place her hand, just there, in the small of his back and pull him to her.

The distance between them sears with heat and her dress, a cheap, light cotton sundress borrowed from Caley, ripples in the ocean breeze which tries to cool what might ignite.

Hal stands, hat in hand, and is still. The breeze lifts his hair and he licks his hand to smooth it down. It's too much, what he sees of her, and she smells like rain coming on and making everything dance.

They don't touch. They'll falter if they do. They both know it.

'I do,' Hal says. 'For better, worse, richer, poorer.'

The smartest, most ridiculous thing he's ever done: he's going to bring the most beautiful woman in the world home and they're going to build things.

'You may kiss the bride,' says the justice.

Hal and Rachel don't move. The room bends in, they're pulling the water from the air, loosening the wooden joists of the beams which stretch across the ceiling.

'You may kiss the bride,' repeats the justice of the peace, taking a step back.

But they don't kiss. Rachel places her hand on her cheek to cool the flush. Hal reaches back into his wallet and pulls out two twenties to tip the justice and the organ player.

'Thank you, ma'am,' he says, first to the justice, and then again to Rachel when they climb into their car.

'The pleasure will be all mine, I'm sure,' she says. 'Well, maybe not all mine.'

And it's Hal's turn to blush.

Out of the city soon enough and Rachel sits in the passenger seat and looks ahead, out the side window. She loosens her hair, rolls down the window. Hal turns on the radio, moves his hands over the wheel. He's a good driver, quick, of course he's quick. They need to get where they're going. But he's never reckless. Rachel likes this.

They don't talk. There's no need. She could tell him about how her family, the Roanokes, tolerated her until she came of age and then they didn't care if she survived or the water took her; she could tell him about her time in the water. He could tell her about his childhood, the death of his parents, how loneliness had driven him to the coast in search of a wife. Sure. But what good would it do?

She is going to have girls, a boatload of girls, and that's not been done before. What they are doing, going to do, hasn't been done before.

Hal drives. Everything fades behind him, already myth. When operas are sung in the new opera house that overlooks the sea, no one but them will know why it was really built. It was built to bring them together. He carries everything he needs right beside him in this car and if they touch too soon, the wrong land will be consecrated. He has to be able to tell his first born, his son, when they stand one day in the magnificent hall shoulder to shoulder: 'You were conceived here, right here.' And with his son he'll gaze out through the open door at the town beyond and he'll say, 'All this is yours.'

The newlyweds drive on through the mountains with the full moon rising, and when the sun takes up its journey in the east, they drive towards that and the land starts to stretch with its palm open. The landscape changes from arid to desert to mountainous and becomes rolling prairie settling into flatness.

Rachel's heart races as she sees, imagines, what is before her. 'It's such a vast country,' and she dares to reach over and kiss the spot where his jaw meets his neck.

'Yes,' he says and puts his foot on the gas.

Hal and Rachel drive on, talking about the songs playing on the dio, but mostly staying silent, the car swirling up dust and storms t the horizon rising up behind them hides from their view.

At the end of the next day, Hal crosses a rickety bridge over a creek, drives up a small hill, swings the car into the drive, and parks so Rachel can admire the house and the landscape beyond. Unfolding herself from the car, she leans back against it and takes everything in. Hal stands beside her, a tentative hand on her bare arm. She tries to stay in the moment, but oh how she wants the moment to be more naked.

The house looks like it belongs on a cotton plantation and she half expects to see slave quarters out back, unmarked graves across the road. Columns support a dark roof and two porches, open to the elements, hang off the house like a fringe. In need of a new coat of paint, even now the white of it shocks against the blue of the endless sky pancaked to the sunken earth, which stretches out as far as the eye can see. Behind them lies a neat cemetery rowed with granite tombstones and then the hill falls down past sixteen houses, only to end, rather anti-climactically, at the gas station at the low end. The house lies so far inland it makes Rachel dizzy and she searches for signs of the water she can just about hear beyond the pounding of blood in her ears.

'My dad built most of those houses,' Hal says and his eyes go slightly distant. He shakes his head, shakes himself free of something bound. 'Well missus, let's see if we can't make some trouble,' and he slides his hand down his wife's arm, around her waist and picks her up, like the bride she is. He jiggles her a bit when he has to unlock and open the door, but he is all suave and knows it.

He places her on her new homeground and they stand side by side in the massive hall. 'Just think, soon this house will be filled with our children and everyone in this town and beyond, will know the Fremonts.' His open hand slaps the wall, bang on center—Midwest, here, home—and a few pieces of crumbling plaster fall to the floor.

'Come here, Hal.' Rachel wraps her legs around his narrow waist, forcing his hands away from the wall so they can support her hips and without knowing a thing they start to build a map. This blesse this hopeful, this damn map.

HOMEGROUND

'I'm off to work,' Hal whispers in the dawn half-light, kissing her and almost tempting her from sleep, but he's unwrapped himself from her and the sheets and goes off into the day. Rachel wakes a few hours later to strong sun coming in through the window. Hal has left a tall glass of orange juice on the bedside table and he's cleared out a chest of drawers and half the closet and carried her bag in from the car.

She straightens her pack against the wall and out of habit feels the side for the familiar presence of her maps and the small leather pouch she's carried all the way from the Island. Slipping into a summer dress and pulling on a plaid shirt of Hal's over it for warmth, she takes the back stairs down to the kitchen and heads out into the backyard with its oak tree and the creek beyond. The door swings within a short sturdy frame and a tight screen door slaps shut behind her. She pulls the shirt to her face, the smell of him is close, her husband, and this is their house. Wide planks, roughly laid and pitched, make up the porch and the four stairs down to the yard are sturdy, thick, mud-crusted. An old picket fence defines the yard but boys have a way of ignoring borders and it's broken and part-mended in half a dozen places. With its gate propped shut with a big rock, it's something Hal will need to fix before the babies they're planning to have start walking. In the far corner of the yard, there's a good patch of worked earth, some beans, rhubarb and potatoes growing, and plenty room for expansion. A little ways beyond the fence, the thin creek's path is marked by cottonwoods clinging to its curves.

Rachel turns back to the house and has to duck to fit through the low-slung doorway. The house still holds a faint smell of homemade bread and to her right sit floor-mounted, crammed-in, dented white metal cabinets, the line of them broken by the stove and fridge. A small window above the sink looks out over the nearest neighbor's house as it stands just slightly down the hill. Open shelves line the walls above the long Formica countertop and support neat rows of ns and canisters: flour, sugar, cornstarch, and coffee. A glass cabinet he end holds glasses and plates. Rachel does a slow 360° turn on the linoleum floor. To her left, tucked under the back stairs, sits the utility room that holds a big ceramic sink and an old Maytag washing machine but no dryer. Must be lines out back for drying.

On the Island, when the weather was on the turn, her Aunt Shirley would yell to her as she played outside. 'Bring in those clothes, Rachel. There's a nor'easter coming and the salt will crust 'em.' There'll be no salt here, just dust and pollen in the folds of their clothes, but Rachel's ready for that.

A round fold-leaf table butts against the utility wall and gives a clear view out to the yard for those lucky enough to face the wide and white-crossed windows. On the windowsill sits an empty pie tin and a dead spiderplant, its brittle babies scattered on the floor. Beyond the table, the door leads to the main hallway and on the next wall a swing-door leads into the dining room; a quick peek and Rachel shivers at its dark wood hutch, faux marble floor, and the long oak table stretching the full length of the room, then she steps back into the warmth of the kitchen.

Rachel makes her way through the house. At first she keeps to the middle of hallways and rooms and the house holds itself back. She runs her hands over the walls, the banisters, the doorframes and when she pauses on a step or in a doorway she begins to hear the rush of this house's life, how it breathes in the wind, how the creek gurgles and echoes in certain corners. She tries all the doors and none are locked to her. She opens windows as she goes, letting in light and air. Sheer curtains, pulled back at the sides, frame most windows and their views, although some remain unadorned. There is an unfinished quality about the place that makes any future possible.

At the top of the house sits a simple turret, with windows on all sides like a lighthouse, and when Rachel closes the door behind her, she's claimed it as her own.

Upstairs there are five bedrooms and stand-alone clawfoot cast iron tubs dominate the three bathrooms, leaded glass mirrors hangin
above the sinks. There are a few cracks here and there but it's a gra
house, with a welcoming heart. Outside, the farmland that use
be prairie stretches to the horizon, like the sea but less bea

This house makes sense to her: a bold statement, and also intimate, practical.

However, throughout her explorations one room eludes her: the entrance hall, with its massive vaulted ceiling and regal staircase. It dominates everything and yet often she cannot find it. She discovers that if you don't stay alert, you can miss it completely. Rachel pays attention, promises she will always pay attention, and then she stands for a long time in that elusive hall.

At the end of the long day, Rachel feeds her man: fried chicken, plain ol mash, string beans from out back, planted by his mother and harvested by her, his wife. Hal ignores the napkin folded on the table and licks his fingers. Then he reaches over and licks hers too.

'You sure are delicious,' he says as he lifts her to the counter and pulls the ties of her apron free.

During his first week back at work, Hal approaches the owners of the half-caste houses his dad had built. Fremont Construction was responsible for most of the houses in the then burgeoning town. The clean-lined, cut-out, prairie houses were solid, easy to throw up in a matter of weeks; but Lawrence, his dad, had liked to add a flourish to the houses he built, he liked to mock this and mimic that, and when he pitched these wild designs to first time homebuyers they believed in his broad shoulders and the glint of excitement in his eyes. Within a quick few months they found themselves living in houses that had started with grandness but transformed half-way through into hybrid houses: a casita morphed into a prairie-styled house at back, as did the mock-Tudor house Lawrence built just two houses down from his own fully realized mock-antebellum.

As he got older, Hal saw the point at which each of his dad's projects transformed into disaster. When a curved wall cracked two days after being built or when specially cut beams didn't fit the intended ceiling, he knew how to fix these things. He knew how to build on the spark of originality in the designs. But when he tried to talk to his father, Lawrence swatted round his ear like there was a buzzing and ordered his sons just to finish the house. Then he'd return to his drawing board to create his next flash design to dazzle the town.

Now, with his father gone, Hal needs to make things right and support his wife. He approaches the homeowners, hat in hand, a roll of designs under his arm.

'I'm sorry to bother you,' he always says right off the bat. Through the cracked-open door he notices how they've tried to make the best of a bad lot: carpeting over uneven floors, hanging wallpaper instead of painting the crumbling walls, trying to make the color scheme consistent even if the building is not. 'As you may know, my folks died not so long ago, and well, I've been left with the job of taking care of unfinished business. May I come in?'

Doors close politely with Hal still standing outside, until he decides to bring along the architect he's hired to confirm and strengthen the re-designs. One or two doors remain open and over coffee he shows his plans, calmly explaining the facts of a solid build, where his dad had gone wrong, and where he, Hal, will get it right. Hal needs a new contract, he needs to convince homeowners to fork over more cash, so he gets Taylor Brooks, the town's banker, to offer a good rate on a re-mortgage for the upgrades. The signatures, eventually, arrive in bunches. Within months he's re-building three of his dad's houses and has been approached for fresh designs for two more houses and an extension to the community hall.

He hires a whole new crew, an administrator, and his workdays naturally lengthen. And yet, Rachel always waits and eats dinner with him.

Rachel and Hal make the most of their weekends. He often comes home early on Friday and they get reacquainted wherever he happens to find her and then they reluctantly separate to different chores around the house and garden, occasionally finding themselves within the same room or just barely hidden spot and allowing themselves to get distracted again.

'The house is yours, do whatever you like,' is what Hal says fr that first day. 'It's ours now.' And he picks up a hammer to sort of the window frames that have become angled at the joints and so rattle a bit in the wind. Rachel cleans out the kitchen cabinets and the utility room and starts to get the garden ready for autumn planting. Hal builds them a compost bin and repairs the hoe and sharpens the secateurs and Rachel keeps the fridge well-stocked, a pitcher of freshly squeezed lemonade always ready. As a wedding gift to themselves, they plant a sturdy maple sapling in the far corner of the yard, giving it plenty of room to mature. She makes him wholesome food according to recipes she carries with her as memories, and makes plans to plant Shirley's heritage seeds too, century-old crops from the Island. Hal makes sure they always have a few six-packs of beer in the fridge in the garage, a bottle of vodka in the freezer, and in the evenings they drink beer or strong lemonade on the back porch, their bare legs intertwined, talking about their plans for the house. They make a lot of noise in these early days, Hal's laughter booms and Rachel's deep, almost dirty laugh matches his own in volume and generosity, and the neighbors are known to do some talking about the young couple often glimpsed or heard at all hours, out on their land, skinny-dipping in the creek.

A few months on, Rachel stands barefoot in the hall. Beneath her feet weave the cool threads of a utilitarian cotton rug, and beneath the floorboards, the cellar, and the dark earth holding the house close, presses a heartbeat of water. Her belly asserts a new roundness on the world and throughout the house she keeps the windows open and sometimes lets the curtains fly in the breeze; up here on the hill they're all exposed and the house often sways in the winds. With her jeans riding low, her shirt a bit high, she rubs her hand over her belly and stares at the arctic white expanse of the wall in the hall.

A gust of wind enters from the east and redoubles back. A tumult of sky and dust obscures the hall for a minute until the cloud moves ɔ the upstairs landing, and out through the open windows. Before ː, the wall shimmers with a wave that breaks over its expanse and it settles. The wall. Exposed for what it is.

Rachel blinks, steps back to get a better view. Bright infinite blue stretches to the east and west, and at its center, from floor to ceiling, a cartography of land emerges with its weaving, intricate, uneven, rushing pathways and pools. If she hadn't grown up surrounded by sunlight on water, she'd have had to turn away. Don sunglasses. Instead she understands what she's seeing: a map, their map.

The wind billows around her. Her blood rushes; she knows these places, has known them since the first time she entered the Island's waters, since she'd learned to read the maps her Uncle Walt stole for her. Her palm to the wall, it blue-beats a pulse through her. So, this is the reason.

She presses her body to the wall with eyes closed. The wall embosses itself against her and she notices the tiniest break in the blue directly to the east, a familiar dare of homeland that, as soon as she notices it, flickers and goes out. Her past. She follows the pulse down to the south and feels a clearer, nascent place, a jut to the far southeast; such a strong foray into the wild blue, a peninsula dusting out into an archipelago that risks everything until it peters out into impossibility and becomes blue too. This is her daughter—a thin finger of land pressed by the ocean on either side, brackish waters which clear as she walks along the riverbanks heading north. The sky scrapes clean above her, the land murky, changing beneath her feet, and when she looks within at her daughter's heart, she sees that it's true and destined to be broken. She doesn't yet have a name for her baby daughter, but now she has a place and time to discover it, to walk through her lands, ride her rivers, climb to her high ground and eventually Rachel will know enough to name her.

Rachel steps back and the rush of the day stills. The wall hides itself once more to the world, but never, not once, to Rachel who now knows everything, and nothing at all, about her children. She puts on a jacket and heads down to the hardware store for the materials she'll need to get the job done. She won't start it, not until she's discussed it with Hal, and it's nearly ten before he pulls into the driveway and takes the back stairs in one bound.

'Rachel!'

She's standing in the kitchen, the small bump pushing at her apron.

'My love,' he says, his arm sliding all the way behind her back to rest on her belly. She turns and places a hand to his face: a hot, full press. He holds Rachel with one hand, in his other he grasps rolled paper.

Her thumb traces his lowest rib, a concave cage protecting his heart. 'Hal, I want to show you something.' She leads him to the hall and he nearly trips on cans of paint, blue paint.

'What's this?' he asks.

'I'm going to paint the wall, something vibrant, for the kids. I was thinking of painting it with something like this.' She releases his hand and on the surface of the wall she traces the shorelines of a familiar country, part of a continent, starting high up in the right corner and Hal enjoys the curves of her as she bends down towards the skirting board.

He's seen this shape before in the moonlight, when he kisses her, but never known what it was. 'A map?'

'Exactly,' she says and smiles, 'a map of our family, our kids.'

He recalls the lines she's just drawn and he sees her plan so clearly. 'States,' he says, 'we'll name them after states. I like the sound of that.'

'Sort of, but not that…specific.' She rubs a finger at her temple.

Hal walks along the wall looking for the place where their house should be. It's pretty central but he can't quite pinpoint it. He takes a step back, 'We'll have a whole country. That's kind of cool.'

'I suppose so,' she says, hesitating. 'They'll be of places which hold rivers and mountains and…'

'And towns. Towns I'll build.' He turns to her. 'I've got something to show you too.'

With a flick of the wrist he unfurls his town plan across the floor. He uses a doorstop to weigh down one edge of the paper and his knee weighs down the other. He'd hired a helicopter and taken an aerial view of the town and the surrounding land and then meticulously worked out houses, re-builds, acquisitions, new builds he'll pitch to individuals and committees, and impressive county buildings he's decades away from being able to realize.

Rachel turns away from the wall which, in being named, feels slightly disappointed, and kneels down beside Hal.

'This is it. This is the town I'm going to build.'

She draws a finger along the bottom of the gridded plan. His is a solid vision with clean lines. Her thigh against his, he leans against her even as his arms move beyond their space into the air, into this place he's going to build.

'For our sons of course, I'm going to build this all for my boys.'

'Our children. You mean our children.'

'No, Rachel. Us Fremonts have boys. Lots of boys. Always have.'

She places her hand on his knee to steady herself. She's been here before: the stubborn, unchanging Roanokes and their freakish genetic proclivities to have generation after generation of boys; how they'd gotten into the habit of stealing brides from the mainland who had boys too... Until she came along, and then the Island and its community bucked her mother off first, days after Rachel's birth, and then her, days after her sixteenth birthday, into the water to preserve the only way of procreation they'd ever known. Hand to her belly where her child, another daughter of Roanoke, flips she asks, 'What if it's a girl?'

'Well, that's not going to happen.'

Rachel wipes her forehead, eyes shifting toward the door. She's ready to go, it'll be easy, she can make a run for it as he sleeps. She's traveled safely through flatlands and can easily do it again. But she has to be sure and faces Hal, 'Only boys?'

Hal sees a familiar look in Rachel's eyes, it's the look his brothers had before they'd abandoned him and their inheritance. Tread carefully. He clears his throat, his lungs ache. His palms start to sweat and he wipes them on his jeans before reaching out to touch her hair. He places a gentle kiss on her lips, his hand on top of hers on top of her belly. 'But if it's a girl and she's at all like her mother, I'll love her at first sight too.'

'Promise?'

'I promise.'

His breath races shallow, swirling, his lungs sharp with pain. He won't survive her departure, he knows it.

She searches his face, as if she could see in his still smooth skin, not only the lines and wrinkles that will emerge over time, but his integrity too. A hand to his cheek, a breathed-in kiss on his lips, 'I promise, I'll try to give you a son.'

'Just the one?'

'I'll do my best, Hal. Let's see what mother nature has in mind for us.'

Hal buries his head in her neck, the oxygen of her; she runs her hand over his arm, the truthful intention of his promise.

Together they smell of spring and sawdust and the possibility of sex and neither is surprised when they lie down on top of the paper plans, the hall cozy for all its grandeur, and yet again lose track of time and end up eating a cold dinner together, out on the porch, well after midnight.

MENATAUK

Rachel's dreams are memories, her history no guide to her future, and yet this is the place she spends most nights.

Standing on the westside of her Island ankle-deep in ocean water, at sixteen this is as far as she's ever made it. This short cove, the distant mainland.

When she was five the water had felt like this but hotter. Back then her small legs had reached the cove beach by navigating the thin, thorn-riddled path that cut down a steep embankment. The stretch of water between her small island and the big Carolina-land was smooth on the surface, but held dangers her aunts warned her about all the time. She slid into the water and let her legs and arms float out and heard her Aunt Shirley yelling down.

'Rachel Roanoke! Get out of that water this minute!'

Shirley sounded far away while the water's whisper was closer and more persuasive. Rachel floated, arms open like an angel and breathed in blue sky and it seemed to her that if she were to breathe in the water it would turn to pure air, salty in her lungs. Waves rose to meet the shore and curled under themselves: come, come, come. The water teased her body round, feet to the shore, and the riptide started to take her.

Her Aunt Shirley was a big woman, and fast. Down to the shore in two licks, she'd yanked young Rachel from the water, lifted her free of its pull and planted her well up the beach near where the brush took over from the sand. Rachel dripped and the dry air snapped the drops up, and the new scratches on Shirley's arms beaded with blood.

Shirley crossed her arms over her belly and her eyes had tears in them. 'Don't you ever, you hear me, ever, do that again. We lost your mother that way.'

Rachel knew this story well, both from tellings and imaginings. Her mother, Susan, had entered the water not long after her birth and she'd not been seen again. It had been a seismic moment in the Island's history for the Island had a habit of collecting women, not losing them; it might have been something in the water, or in the air, which meant that generation after generation of Island men begat boys, and these boys ran wild, and when they came of age they slid quietly into the slipstream and romanced girls from the mainland coastal villages, towns and cities, and brought them back home. Brides for brothers and cousins and second cousins, and the imported Island women, seduced by the men and Island in equal measure, bore son after son in some mythic inevitability.

Rachel's father, Trevor, was a charming man, head of the Island's council at twenty-two, and Susan had been a newly qualified nurse who lived in a northerly coastal town outside Boston. They met in Old Joe's Bar, which sat on an opportunistic street around the corner from the shiny new hospital and across the dock from the harbor. Old Joe served cold beer and greasy thick-cut fries to sailors and doctors alike. Known for its cracking conversation and wall-breaking brawls, a gentrification was taking place and both sides welcomed the pretty nurses.

Susan only accepted one drink from this man who seemed to

neither crewman nor doctor. Trevor quietly, respectfully, offered to buy her at least three dry white wines, and although she refused the generosity, she agreed to meet him at the same place the next night. Trevor came for the next six days, and Susan didn't overlook how the cuffs of his jeans were always damp, or how he brought her bunches of wild onions, lavender and flowers. On the seventh day he presented her with a simple gold band sitting atop a blue silk pillow. He was groom and ring bearer all in one.

He was charming, this man with wet jeans and a handmade ring. Smooth lines on his youthful brown face and his ways were unlike any of the boys at college or her thin-chinned, reliable high school sweetheart Charlie, or any of the white-coats who lurched towards her in the hospital halls. He talked about home like some guys talk about beer.

'Take me there,' she said.

'Where?'

'Home,' she said as she slid the ring onto her finger.

Out of his pocket he pulled its partner, thicker, even more roughly shaped, pounded into a circle with a small hammer, but it fit his finger and the deed was done. Not once on that boat-trip to an island or during the coming months did Susan doubt her man or her decision. This Island, the jut of land that was everywhere and nowhere, had a way of producing honest, handsome men, men like her Trevor who was both out of time and clearly, right here and right now, perfect.

'Divorce, divorce, divorce,' Trevor shouted eleven months later as Susan held her newborn daughter in her arms. 'She's no Roanoke,' he said, and his brothers and cousins crossed their arms and made their faces somber behind him. 'Roanokes don't have daughters!'

'It could have been any one of us,' Shirley whispered into Susan's ear as she steered her almost imperceptibly to the edge of the meeting, towards the clear path to the sea.

'Odds were bound to win out at some time.' Susan smiled, flicking her eyes back to her handsome husband who had pounded his chest twice and thrust his arms wide and was opening his mouth again.

'Whore!' Trevor shouted and there was something in the straight line of his shoulders that sobered her.

Susan didn't understand the change in Trevor. At Rachel's birth, he'd cried, touched her tiny hands and toes, her thin brown belly, her shock of black hair, peanut skin, green eyes. 'She's smooth and dark like my father, and those eyes are Virginia Dare's,' he'd said. 'That's where we come from,' Trevor said, the lightest of touches on Rachel's soft crown. 'A tribe and a colony came together to populate this island: the colony at Roanoke and a tribe called Menatauk. At risk from starvation and attack, we made a pact, worked and traveled together and made this Island home.' He kissed their daughter.

A few days later he stood, egged on by his brothers and cousins who had shiny new crossbows slung across their backs, and he was a changed man. The pressure of history? A slight to his manhood? Susan didn't know and it didn't matter: it's like they'd sworn to themselves that they, as men, had to protect the integrity of the Island and they were panicking because not once had they ever thought that future would include baby girls and the dangers they might bring.

'Divorce can get messy on the Island,' said Shirley, 'we better get a move on.' Menatauk didn't need scarlet letters, it had riptides.

It was broad daylight when Susan ran. Her heart was broken, her breasts still full. She couldn't carry Rachel while she swam and so she handed her daughter to Shirley. 'Protect her.'

'With everything I have.'

In those first days Shirley and the other women fought for Rachel's right to live on the Island until she came of age. A nod. And as she grew up Rachel's father would greet her with a half-raised hand, give her herbs or fish to pass on to Shirley, but he never had words to offer his daughter.

'Your mother will come back,' Shirley always told Rachel. 'She will. No one looks that way and doesn't come back.' But it'd bee sixteen years and they both feared Susan had been taken by the se

Rachel knew these waters from their feel on her ankles and from the maps Shirley's husband, Walt, generously stole from fancy libraries on the mainland. (A single thin razor dropped into the cuff of his trousers, and whisked out when the dainty librarians dropped their eyes to stop staring at this thickset, handsome man.) Maps were discouraged on the Island but Walt loved the details they held, the reminder that however imperfect, they proved places existed beyond what he'd seen.

Rachel liked the historic wisp-thin paper marked by Lewis or Clark's scrawled notes: *camped here April 24th 1805; salt lick marsh; beautiful plain 21–26 August 1804; killed first turkey on October 12, 1804, Caution Island; and as the Fork of the Blue crosses over the Platte, our halt on the Blue.* These were places people cared enough about to record for others. Currents traveled, weather survived, and people defined direction and land in relation to their own changing perspectives, their own lines of sight.

'What's this?' Shirley asked of the map Rachel had spread on the kitchen table.

'It's what they used to think the Mississippi looked like.'

'I barely recognize it.'

'Look at this one.' Rachel reached out and found another map, a thin parchment with slightly curled edges, the serpentine path of a remembering river thinning towards the edge. She turned it so Shirley could see.

'That's water?' Shirley asked.

'Yup. It didn't need to be blue, since early explorers traveled mostly by water it was assumed. In their maps, the edges of water always define the land.'

Shirley slid out a map of the Carolinas. She turned it, and again, smoothed her hand over a short stretch of coast. Nothing.

'Where's Menatauk?'

'It's not on any map,' Rachel said. Shirley rolled the parchments nd hid them behind a false wall at the back of the broom cupboard.

's time.' She and Rachel made their way outside to where boys

 roughhousing and kicking and cursing around the edges of the annual gathering. Trevor made a low rumbled call and a restless still swept over the community. He held his hands open, palms up and looked at Rachel. Shirley pushed her forward gently.

Rachel's hair reached her waist and her back was relaxed and straight as she walked slowly towards her father, her eyes never leaving his face, which softened then toughened as he looked at her. It was as close to love as she'd ever seen in him. He flipped one hand up to halt her. She paused. The sea felt close, riding the same thermals as the sky and the island knew her and her whole body felt its strength.

'We have nothing more to give you. You cease to bear the name Roanoke and must leave the island.'

A hush shuddered through the community. Rachel reached out and touched her hands to his face, felt his muscles contracting in his jaw. She lowered her hands, took a few steps back and focused only on her father. 'I am the first daughter of Roanoke, but by no means the last.'

The held breath of the Island, now released. A proclamation? A threat.

Rachel felt Shirley and Walt at her back, they're her parents, the ones who loved her tough and perfect. She felt that love right beside her, not strong enough to prevent the coming disaster, but there.

'Take her!' Trevor shouted.

'Run!' Shirley yelled, opening a gap in the circle for Rachel. 'Go!'

Rachel ran while the men and boys took their time organizing themselves into a chase, opening the weapons store. Where could she go but the coast? Everyone knew her line of Roanokes couldn't swim. Her mother had proved that well enough.

She made it to the water and there were no edges to her, never had been. 'It's a gift,' Shirley always told her. The water moved through her like a pulse. There were shouts up at the top of the cove, sounds of breaking branches. They were coming after her and there was no surprise in it. Rachel walked until the water reached her waist and then she slid under in a smooth dive. This time the ripping tide took her off the godforsaken Island.

She filled her lungs with blue and green and salt and exhaled grief.

She was salty and filled up and floating in ocean. Rachel lost track of time and sometimes the mainland seemed flat, too far to reach. The water grew cooler as it became deeper, faster. Familiar currents carried her places she hadn't aimed for, and these ancient currents altered behind her. As sun and stars traded places overhead she swam and floated in turn.

At first she held tight to a grief she felt for a place she loved and yet, with the water strange and strong around her, a heat grew at her center, and she found she had no rush towards land, she wanted, needed, to become her own ocean.

Eventually a passing trawler picked her up and the men fed her fish chowder out of a tin. They were nice guys but desperate, seafaring, often absent men and she learned she'd need to be discerning in her quest for a man and all he could bring her. She learned that not all men were safe harbors; some were simply fleeting moorings and so she played: fumbles on the deck, fishy kisses down by the ice-stored catch of the day. Once on shore with saltwater phone numbers written on her arms and hands like roads on a map, she found herself a job in a resort prepping food in exchange for room, board and pocket money. One quick hot shower left her without courtship obligations.

Not long after, she took a train to St Louis, built herself a coracle, and traveled the Missouri in a meandering, riparian way west to a different coast, for a different future; riding currents for as long as she could, portaging when the water wouldn't carry her. When she hit the mountains she leaned her boat against a tree and walked through the peaks, camping, stopping in towns, and working to gather enough money to make the next leg of the journey. Geological eras, rifts and congregations of pines; such crashing, whispering colors. She had maturity, a strong, travel-lean body, and a level-headed capability, and when she reached the coast she'd aimed for, she snagged herself a job at a greasy spoon diner that became so clean you could eat food right off the counter. And this fine view brought to her this man with his honest intentions, his raspy sleeping breath, and, well, he'll take her right to the heart of her destiny, her children, her map.

Rachel sleeps late and in the rose-cast of morning the wall holds more blue than is possible; the shape of it so familiar, unmistakable. Hal has plastered the wall and she presses her hand to its center, the heartland.

Her stomach arches away from and then back to her body, in a bid towards freedom and safety, and in the hall Rachel paints the ocean, listening to the currents and habits of her child. Her belly floats up towards her diaphragm; the pressure strong, like the baby has plunged her to the bottom of a deep-sea trench. She becomes a diver, inhaling and holding a deep breath, taking in enough oxygen to last the whole pregnancy. Sometimes with her first girl in her belly, Rachel thinks her lungs might burst but they never do. Humidity skates over her skin and she understands the beauty of the wetlands and of sinkholes and she feels small beneath wide skies with a fear of hurricanes rising in her. She stands on a limestone plateau layered with silt, shells and bones and craves brackish estuaries and sand dunes; she longs for, is full up with, this thin stretch of land that reaches out into the sea like all that is solid and good and full of hope.

She paints the hall and the eastern, western and southern borders become bright and blue, marking the expanses of oceans and gulfs. To this Rachel adds contours, continental shelves, ridges, trenches, depths and shallows. She paints all the major bodies of water: the Great Lakes, Salt Lake, the mighty Mississippi, the muddy Colorado running clearer since the dam created Lake Powell, Chesapeake Bay, Long Island Sound, the Hudson, the Missouri, the Platte, the Arkansas. Defining bodies that indicate the movement of time and possibility. Slowly the hall becomes mostly water, lapping around corners and over doors: cartographically accurate, elixir of life exact.

Rachel imagines the northern continuation of these lands (Saskatchewan, Quebec, Nova Scotia…) splashed across the wall upstairs (Alaska bending towards the ceiling) and the landscapes of Central America over the floorboards. In their daily comings and goings her family will splash in the Gulf of Mexico, traverse Costa Rica on their way to the kitchen, and stop for a bit of peace in the Bahamas as they grab their coats off the hooks.

Hal works hard too, as he waits for his firstborn. He builds a crib, a guard-rail for the top of the stairs, and a mini workbench with tiny, real tools. 'For our son,' Hal says, and Rachel counters, patiently, 'For our child, our children.'

FLORIDA

A jubilant dawn chorus enters Rachel's window and starts this spring day. Out in the garden, she opens the leather pouch and takes out the packets of Island seeds Shirley had carefully collected and marked for her, which Rachel had carried with her this whole time. She's expanded the garden, hoed the ground, and worked in compost to make it ready. Her belly is huge and she's too big to be able to kneel down and push them into the earth and stands, contemplating tossing the seeds and hoping that'd be good enough, when her waters break. There's a release and a different pressure and her knees are just a bit weak as she steps her bare feet from the soil onto the lawn. She's looking towards the neighbor's house considering shouting for help when she hears Hal's car skid around the corner at the bottom of the hill and struggle up the drive. He leaves the car running as he unfolds his long legs from the driver's seat, strides towards the house as he raises a hand in greeting towards Rachel. Within a minute he returns, stooping through the low doorway between the kitchen and the porch, with her packed overnight bag hanging easy by his side. He has a pair of her shoes held nonchalantly by two fingers of his other hand. He puts the bag in the trunk, all the time so obviously aware of his very pregnant wife standing there, and runs a nervous hand through his wild hair.

They walk towards each other, the air warm and full of spring. He places the shoes on the ground, so she can easily slide them on. Which she does.

'Ready, beautiful?'

'Absolutely.'

He kisses her and she blushes. Out the driveway and down the hill and he drives to the hospital with care and speed, with one hand on the wheel and the other hot on her knee.

'Does he have ten fingers and toes?' Hal asks the midwife.

In fact their daughter has arrived long and pink with untouched islands for toes. 'She's beautiful,' says the midwife and she hands Hal his daughter.

The baby has impossibly tiny hands and makes small, disconcerting noises. Where is his boy? Hal's face turns red, he can't get her comfortable in his arms. A patch of perspiration floods across his shirt. He looks around for someone to save him. Someone, help him. Rachel extends her arms and he pours the baby into them.

'Hey you, welcome to the world, Sweetwater,' Rachel says, lightly moving the blanket aside to reveal her daughter. Looking up, she catches his eye.

She knew, the whole time she knew. A girl. He breathes, slowly, like he does at work when faced with a problem. The solution is easy. 'Florida,' he says, naming her. A good place to visit, but he wouldn't want to live there. He leans over and kisses Rachel, confirms the baby's name with a nod, and does not think himself gruff when he asks Rachel how soon it will be before they can try again. 'For a son this time.'

Thinking, a boy, a boy will be better.

But he's promised, and it's a promise he needs to keep, and a few weeks later he emerges from his basement-workshop with a meticulously carved state: elbows, arteries, fingers and ribs which he edges up to the blue; proud borders, the delicate risky coasts of his daughter. Rachel stands, Flo in the crook of her arm, her other hand spread on his back as Hal fixes Florida to the wall, the first proof of their union.

TEXAS

Flo is a skinny little thing, with pink stick legs and arms, a smoo round belly, and a squashed face and Rachel could sit and just wa her for hours. She fattens quickly and Rachel has work to do, so with Flo swaddled to her back she plants the garden and tends to it as the weeds threaten to push out the seedlings. Flo's a content baby, easygoing and alert and in no time Rachel's ready to try again.

They both agree they want loads of kids, although Rachel doesn't believe she'll have any sons. However, when Hal mopes around the house, dragging his feet past the map, she thinks it can't hurt to do what she can to make it happen.

She consults books, follows folklore, grows, brews and drinks herbs; she does everything she can and is rewarded when she conceives a son. From the moment of conception, she feels as if she's eaten dirt—her waters do not run clear as before, but meander murky and foreign. And yet, still, often, in her bare feet, one hand on her belly, the other hand on the rough clear surface of the wall, she runs her finger along Corpus Christi, up the defining Rio Grande, and down the middle of the Colorado. In bed she takes imagined forays in the dark along the Pecos, Neches, Sabine and Trinity listening to the water around her, the small slaps of sound as it hits sand and rock and sometimes, occasionally, her heart, and she knows who her son will be. He has enough coast to satisfy any Island girl and because she holds her early doubts high in her head, Tex will never know that for those first few months his mother doubted she could love him.

Weighed down by the pregnancy, still breastfeeding Flo, Rachel falls behind in the housework and orders pizza from Tino's with staggering regularity. Flo wears clean all-in-ones and has fresh food on demand, while Hal often wears the same shirt to work two days in a row, unwashed. He tries hard not to complain, but occasionally brings home some prime rib for Rachel to cook, or carries his shirt out in front of him, an offering to the laundry goddess.

'You're getting a son,' Rachel says, her shoulders unassailable, her jaw set, and he backs off, once or twice cooking the meat himself; throwing the shirt in the machine, turning a handle, and tossing in a quick bribe of laundry soap.

Sure enough, after forty long, tired weeks, a stout, heavy boy appears. Hal takes him from Rachel's arms. 'Well done, Rachel,' he says as he checks his son's tackle.

'Texas,' she says and falls into a short, deep, well-earned sleep.

Hal walks with his son at arm's length like a loaded diaper. Then, making one of the most courageous leaps he's ever made, Hal decides to hold his son close. His shirt gets in the way so he sweeps it aside. His knees weaken and he sits on a chair with two thin crosses for legs and places the baby against his warm skin. Father and son are quiet and calm and at ease.

Upon waking Rachel finds her husband, and more worryingly, her son, missing. Nurses fan out like a well-trained military unit. An orderly runs at Hal and brusquely tries to take his son from his arms. Hal resists and clings to Tex, so she drags them both to where Rachel sits ready to feed her son.

She's given him his first son and he lets his wife coax the baby from his arms. She begins to feed him as nature intended and as Hal grasps his son's perfect foot, a spell of dizziness comes over him and his lungs tighten and itch. Briefly, Hal has known the intimacy of holding a son, and yet he is relieved when his son is taken from him and placed safely, firmly, out of reach.

This feeling of being trapped by his children will not lessen as Flo, who has been standing for a month or so, totters and then walks in a matter of days. Within a week she runs towards him as soon as he gets home from work, tugging at his jeans, holding her arms up for him to catch her up in a hug. His heart flutters, then pounds and the feeling does not lessen as he makes Texas and affixes the state to the wall with the care and attention only a proud father can give such a grand and intimate task; it will not dissipate as Tex turns from a newborn into a fat-cheeked baby. Will not lessen as Rachel places light kisses on his neck, maybe a small bite, after a long day's work and starts to make short lists of household chores he's fallen behind on. She places one list on the fridge with a magnet, next to his daughter's first finger painting, and thumbtacks another to the basement door. Each signed with a lipstick-kissed lip print in the corner.

His work has been demanding so much of his attention. They

get the contract for the re-fit of the town's water processing plant, and Hal starts to implement plans for more houses on the north side of town. He has to hire more men, and there's always training and daily meetings to ensure they work up to his standards. He's hired another architect on retainer and an accountant, and has plans to pitch a design for the new town hall, when the time is right. A tour de force, that's what people will call him. His houses springing up all over: his designs with the architects' stamps of approval, little tweaks.

Fremont Construction has a small office, the one his dad bought on the main street and on occasional nights Hal sleeps on a camp bed he'd picked up cheap from one of his workers who moved on to the big city. From his office he sees scaffolding and diggers and cranes and beyond them lie fields and a small forest. He's been spending Saturdays at the office and on Sundays before dawn he slips out to the car where he's already packed up his travel chair, walking boots and binoculars, and he goes birdwatching.

But it's a Tuesday and Hal rushes to finish the Jones' extension before the storm he can see coming arrives and he gets it done just before noon. He decides to go home early and spend the afternoon with Rachel and the kids and he sees a peregrine on the way home. That bodes well for the week ahead and the storm seems to have moved to the south. The dirt on his boots is thick and dry and he takes them off on the back porch before entering the house. All is quiet in the kitchen and after he washes the dust and dirt from his face and hands he finds Rachel lying on their bed, one child on either side, all hot with sleep. Their sleep has taken the oxygen from the room and Hal stretches his head back to get some cool, rich air from the hall. His body soon follows and before he knows it he's down by the creek, binoculars around his neck, walking, following the water east to the small marsh a few miles away and the rest of the world could rise up and a storm could wipe it all away and he'd not hear it.

The sun is bright and nearly setting on this cool day and Rachel stands on the back porch. Tex is asleep at her feet on a blanket, full of a rare day of napping, possibly fighting off a cold, and Flo, running in the yard, nearly trips on that rock that holds the gate shut. Rachel goes over and scoops her up. Her girl giggles and her cheeks are bright red and shiny. Shoving the rock aside with her foot, Rachel walks through the broken gate, another item for Hal's growing to-do list, her daughter on her hip.

In all directions, fields stretch broken only by sad clusters of trees that protect distant farmhouses from the plain winds. So much flatness, day after day, and she'd love to walk for miles and ride rivers and swim in the ocean but she spends all her time alone, in this house, with her kids, and the change has been sudden, or so it seems, and she wants to be out there, with her husband, with or without the kids. She misses Hal. She'd settle for a small family outing, a Sunday together, a BBQ in the backyard, and the mess of the house wouldn't feel so much like something that was hers alone but rather something they've neglected together.

Flo makes noises like she's hungry and Rachel turns towards the house, the oranges and pink of the sky make the windows look like paintings, the roof and columns like a frame. She puts Tex on the floor of the kitchen on a rug, with a rattle, and Flo stands on a chair and helps her make pancakes.

Hours later when Hal comes home, Rachel is at the door waiting, the kids already in bed. 'Hal, maybe you could take Flo birdwatching with you. Out in the woods, spending time with her dad. Maybe next week?'

He shifts his bag on his shoulder. 'She'd scare the birds,' is all he says to close the discussion and he takes to slipping out earlier and earlier, every day of the week, avoiding rooms from which he hears dawn-child noises.

Rachel pulls everything together. She has dinner ready for him and lets him know it with a call to the office and he tries to get home in time to eat with her and the kids. Sometimes he goes back to the office after, but as often as she can she pulls him to her and he's more than happy to stay. The land is still flat and she's lonely, but she's thinking about the next child and the ones after her and about wh she needs to feel happy. One night as they're rocking together, whispers, 'Let's move, nearer the ocean.' Abruptly, mechanically calm, slowing but not stopping the movement of his hips Hal replies, 'My father built this house. I will never move.'

Later, running her finger along his arm, she asks, 'Were you born here?'

'No. Dad and Mom moved me and my brothers here when I was seven. Instead of brawling, he built a big house.'

'What would he have been fighting about? And why this kind of house?'

'You'd have to have asked him that. It's nothing to fret over, it's home now.'

But the word home pinches his lips and he turns his back on her to sleep. She ignores his snub and turns towards him, her body lengthening and bending as his does. When she's pregnant again she'll carry her own ocean with her and she's not from this flat place, nor from the south or the north, and neither are her children. They will be their own lands, cartographers of their own lives.

TOWARDS THE FOUR CORNERS

Florida and Texas are easy to draw, edged by the ocean as they are: the Gulf, all the rivers that lead to the sea. Rachel takes particular care with her first-born, painting the ocean and its delicate land-defining contours that oscillate around the tip of the state. She spends days caring for the intricate line of Highway I weaving its way out through the water to the end of the Keys.

With their first two children put to bed upstairs and a bright moon rising, Rachel calls out to Hal. He does not answer, nor does he come to her. A sudden wind blows a sandy gale into the hall; dunes form on the stairs. As she sweeps the sand out onto the porch, as she sits alone drinking raspberry leaf ice tea at her kitchen table, she doesn't know what all the signs mean but she knows they aren't good.

Sometime around midnight Flo wakes up and won't settle, Tex eeds feeding, and Rachel has a craving for ice cream as wide as a ather front.

'Hal!' she shouts and there's an edge to her voice not to be ignored, even after it's traveled through hallways and down two flights of stairs. He stomps up the stairs and at the top Rachel hands Flo to him and says, sharply, 'I need ice cream. Double chocolate chip. The biggest old tub they've got.'

Hal juggles Flo to the car, fumbles with the car seat. Flo cries the entire car ride to the store and then falls asleep, finally, in the shopping cart. Asleep, she can't remind him she exists. Hal arrives home ice cream in hand, a six-pack for himself, and baby-less.

'Where's Flo?' Rachel asks.

His eighteen-month-old daughter, well, she's still back at the store.

After a worried phone call, and another trip to the store he could've done without, Hal retreats to the basement to demolish the six-pack. Over his head are two children, and a wife. In over his head is how he feels.

His inexperienced hands could do such harm to these little, loud creatures (like wrens, the sounds they make are too big for their bodies) and who, like baby cowbirds co-opting warblers' nests, are always demanding more than he has to give. His almost irresistible wife becomes complicated overnight, needy without asking for a thing. She needs him to be true and helpful and there on demand. She needs him not to leave their children in shopping carts.

Beer in hand, he realizes he just wants four walls and silence; or the building site: definable, controllable; or the expanse of the yard leading off into the field and birdsong. He wants more birdsong.

He shoves a few things into a bag, slings it over his shoulder and, like his brothers before him, plans to head for freer territory. With this image in his head, his new destiny, Hal takes the stairs three at a time and mounts the top with a light footfall. He swings the door open and it takes him just two hopeful strides to arrive in the center of the hall where he's halted by a force bigger than his petty wants: his shoulder takes the heat of a different dream, one still within his reach. He can't resist. He looks at the map: there sit the two states they've created and all that land on which buildings can be built, monument

In the kitchen, Rachel sings lightly in clear voice. At first it's a pretty, undecided tune but soon it transforms into a sailor's song of the sea and his return home. The moon pulls, the earth moves; like an animal in heat Hal crosses over Central America, enters the kitchen and faces his wife.

'We're in this together,' he says.

Rachel grabs him in her tidal grip, her pull so strong he can't breathe until she kisses him into life again.

They stumble up to bed and he's asleep before she's back from checking on the kids. Rachel watches him sleep and it's the first time he's given himself over completely to anything in this house since Tex was born. Rather than an intimate whisper, her husband is becoming a sound she's straining to hear and that's not good enough.

Instead of sleeping, she cleans the house, moving quietly from room to room, dusting, straightening, putting things in place, so she's ready for a day off. Before dawn she wakes the kids, gently. 'Shhh,' she says, 'Mama has a surprise for you.' She puts Flo in Oshkosh overalls, with a mini train driver's hat to match, an outfit she found at Salvation Army, and she puts Tex in a baby-blue grow-all with tiny sneakers on his unwalked feet. She feeds Flo toast and peanut butter and jam, while she nurses Tex. The coffee is on and she's packed a lunch for them all.

Hal comes down the stairs so quietly she almost doesn't hear him. She imagines him out there in the field, so quiet, walking towards the birds, pausing, walking again and she wants to hold his hand amongst the grasses, feel the coolness of the air off the creek; she imagines Flo holding onto his back, Tex swaddled to her. The sky looks set to be blue, the day warm. September is a good month for passage migrants.

If he's shocked when he enters the kitchen he doesn't show it. He leans over and kisses Rachel on the lips, ruffles Tex's infant-thin hair and gets himself a cup of coffee. 'I was going to go over to Sorenson's patch, good for the wee brown birds, this time of year.' As he says this he bops Flo on the nose three times, wee brown birds, and she giggles.

'That sounds perfect,' says Rachel.

Hal carries Flo on his back and she's respectful and quiet. She points when she sees movement and Rachel thinks she's got a knack for it and surely Hal will see how easy it'd be to take her along with him. Tex is fussy and Rachel holds back a bit so they don't scare away the birds, but more than once Hal waits for her, walks back so they're all together.

'But he'll disturb the birds,' she says.

'Today's not about the birds,' he says, and kisses her, Tex pressed between them, Flo on his back making kissing noises, just one of many loud, vivid sounds all around them on the walk. Back at home the kids fall asleep full of fresh air and exercise and Rachel and Hal do not go to bed for some time. Hal falls asleep first into a deep sleep of a man exhausted by his life, but when Rachel wakes at dawn to feed Tex, Hal's side of the bed is already cold.

Hal works all the hours he can and tries to be the father his kids need, earning a living, creating a legacy. Sometimes he falls asleep at the office and he's sleeping on the camp bed late one night when the wife of his new architect walks in. Hal watches her slip her husband's office keys into her pocket. Small, moving quickly, she barely displaces the air. Yet, when she stops, she scowls, ruffles through folders and papers, moving the calculator, his penholder. She exhales, annoyed to be here leaning over her husband's desk looking for whatever forgotten thing she has to come to find for him, while he sits at home downing beer, Hal's thinking. Nothing else exists in the room: just her, the handprint of paint on her white painter's smock, the curve of her body so clear, even as it has to work to define that sack of a thing. When she looks up, she notices him. He doesn't know what she sees but she takes a step closer and he stands up.

'I'm Hal,' he says.

'Sandra.'

And for their first few meetings they really don't say much more than that.

It's quiet in her studio, only the sound of wind through the open window, only her light breath that passes over him, and it's easy he amidst the bright colors of her paintings. He lets it all go. They lie on her day bed, which they hastily cleared of her artworks, and he has paint on his shirt and hands.

'It's quiet,' he says.

'This is rest,' she replies and they sleep, briefly, in stillness and silence.

When he wakes, she's up and dressed standing before a large canvas and she pays no attention to him. Those vivid wild colors, he wants those where he lives and like the most capable of shoplifters he palms a few delicate brushes and small pots of bright paints and puts them into the generous pockets of his oilskin coat. This will become a habit and at home he leaves these paints for Rachel, who accepts them unwittingly, and they find their way onto the map.

❧

THE DESERT YEARS

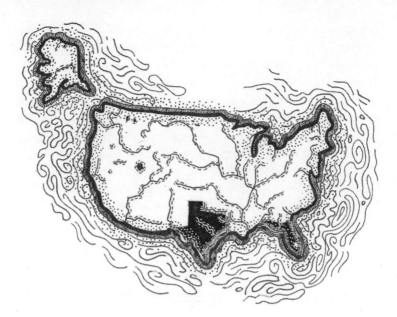

NEW MEXICO

Rachel had not planned to go this far west until she knew she could handle the searing heat. Hal has no such hesitation and takes his family to the desert.

This new baby in her belly barely has a drop of water in her. Hot and parched, Rachel moves as a foreigner unfamiliar with the land and its risks: pockets of water she can never find; the flash floods that seem to find her. Sand blows around the house, running up the stairs, mixing with the sugar and flour, clogging up the salt and pepper shakers, even creating pyramids of sand on the windowsills.

Rachel walks broom in hand, Tex on her hip, and two-year-old Flo toddling beside her grasping onto her maternity overalls. She sweeps away the detritus of the honeymoon period but it always seems to come back twofold. Soon she starts to collect the sand and put it out back in a big square sandbox with wingtips that she's had Hal build in the yard; she wets down the sand to keep it in place.

'It's the damn desert, Hal. What the hell are you thinking bringing us here?'

Hal's got no answer to that sort of crazy talk but he watches his wife circle moisturizer into her skin and her skin drinks it in and dries to snakeskin by the time she reaches the kitchen for her first cup of tea. Each night she carries a tray with a row of tall glasses filled with water and sets them on her bedside table. Empty glasses stand in the morning, small grainy rivulets having dried in the early morning sun. Sometimes, he'll bring her new glasses of ice water or orange juice, or offer to rub her belly with oil, her arms and legs with lotion. Rachel's thin body grows, pushing out into space away from the bed, away from him, as the months pass. And he wants to, but doesn't know how to, make it all right again.

Hand on her belly, this girl drops Rachel at the eastern edge of a high wide mesa. In the distance, the Sangre de Cristo mountains rise from the dusty expanse and Rachel travels west as the winds pick up, cumulus clouds come in from the north, dark and racing to meet her, and she starts to run, following the road, aiming to beat this storm to the safety of the hills. She pauses on a narrow metal bridge tensed over a deep rift canyon and the Rio Grande flowing far below looks insignificant, a delicate earthy thread weaving its way through her daughter, her hot heart. She's made it here to this bridge and lightning flashes, such lightning, and the earth rumbles and rain threatens but does not fall.

The storm clouds pass without gifting water and Rachel understands thirst for the first time and yet she never learns to wait until the night creek comes alive in the place where, during the day, only the lightest brush of growth signals the possibility of water. Rachel often finds herself in slot canyons where steep walls and sharp rims hide thunderstorms and their resultant confluence; water and rocks the size of couches, the size of fists, chase her down. She runs a lot in the desert; learning to climb to safety quickly. Her hands become calloused and dry with effort.

Children often surround her out here. They reach up to catch her hands as she walks; when she runs, she often has an infant swaddled to her back. Alone or surrounded, she's always aware of just how much she needs to protect.

Rachel keeps her emotions well enough to herself. It doesn't take a genius to recognize adultery: Hal's screwing some painter and his klepto hands bring her trophies like a cat dropping mice at her feet. These dusty reds burn Rachel's hands when she holds the small pots and singe her nostrils when she unscrews the tops. She starts to leave the bottles mostly unopened, lining a shelf above her desk in the turret. Her man will be faithful again, he'll come to his senses. He has to. Meanwhile, the paints gather dust and sand and every so often she cleans them off, lining them neatly in a row to remind her of decisions she still has to make.

Flo carries a cup filled with clear water precariously balanced in her toddler hands. 'Here Mama, drink.'

Rachel swallows it in one gulp, a wet kiss on her daughter's cheek. When Rachel reaches full term, Tex puts his hand to her belly and a strong pulse of water moves down to meet him, the Pecos leading down to the Gulf (flooding its banks in the summer) and the contractions start.

Naomi arrives as the first storm of the wet season. A brief breathless downpour. A drenched Rachel prays for it to last. But June has turned unbearably hot and dry that morning and any hopes she has of being able to escape to the sea evaporate as soon as they reach her lips. Naomi, tetchy that her mother could wish for anything but what she offers, grows silent and moody, waiting for her three dry, wry sisters with whom she'll share flat, hard-lined borders.

Hal sneaks downstairs just before sunrise, slips on the sand that seems to come from nowhere, and then rights himself. He goes to the basement and stays there all day, refusing food and refreshment, while he carves New Mexico. The house grows riotous then quiet above him, and he fixes his second daughter to the wall.

'There's still a lot of space,' he says to Rachel, when he slides into bed. She turns over, curling herself into him and whispers, 'Not for long Hal, not for long.'

He lies awake for hours, eyes open: all this water, all this land.

THE PAINTED DESERT

The new baby asleep in the bassinet, Rachel sits on the living room floor with Flo and Tex, painting their nails, singing on old Island song. A sudden gust of wind rushes the curtains up in a dance but, caught by the window, does not enter the house proper. The room itself is parched, as the whole house has been for over a year.

'My little man!' Hal exclaims as he enters.

Three-year-old Flo looks up at her dad but stays still. Tex scrambles to his feet, curls framing his face as he toddles towards Hal, and puts his hand out for a kiss, like a girl.

'I'm painted,' Tex says. 'Flo too.'

Tex loves it: the bright colors, the delicate feel of the brush against his nails. His mom and Flo and him all giggle and wiggle their fingers and toes at Hal.

'What the hell is this?' Hal asks, pulling Tex's hand roughly to show her. Rachel stands up grinning.

'Ouch,' Tex whispers.

'That's Tex's hand.'

'Don't even.'

'Hal, it's nail polish.'

'On my son!'

'Our son.'

'You might as well put him in a dress.'

'We've planned the dress-up session for tomorrow, dear. He has his gown all picked out, pink satin with a lace collar.' New grit between her teeth. 'I'm just trying to keep our kids happy, Hal. He loves the colors.'

Hal grunts and Rachel turns to their son. 'Look at him, Hal. He loves it. The color,' she repeats. 'The attention.'

'I want it off. Now.'

'Then you do it.'

'With what?'

'Nail polish remover.'

'And where will I find that?'

'I'm plum out. You'll need to go to the store.' Rachel crouches down and Tex puts out his hand, a neat bend to his wrist. She takes her son's hand, gives it a kiss, like he's a lady and she's his prince. 'Run Tex, go play hide-and-seek with your dad. You've got a good head start.'

Hal comes back from yet another unwanted, unplanned trip to yet another store, and is unwilling to humor this ridiculous situation.

'Tex! Here. Now.'

His son, still too young to be good at hide-and-seek, emerges from behind his hands and goes up to his dad. Hal pulls him into a bear hug, holding his son's arms tight in with one of his.

'Purty,' Tex says.

'You stop that. Now. No son of mine will have painted nails.' Hal takes Tex's left hand and starts removing the polish.

'I like pink,' says Tex.

'I like pink too,' Flo says to her dad, to her brother, to anyone who's listening.

Hal, intent on his task doesn't hear her; Tex grins.

'Pink is a girl's color,' Hal persists.

'I like girls too,' Tex says, flapping his trapped, still painted hand in Flo's direction.

'And I like my Tex,' she says.

Varnish stinks up the room and Tex squirms in his dad's arm, stifling, unsuccessfully, a sneeze. A wet arm. With the next onslaught, Hal releases him. Tex bawls. Deep, earthy, inconsolable gulps for air.

'Shhh, Tex. You'll wake 'omi,' whispers Flo when he toddles to her and she cuddles him. The baby's cries bring Rachel to the door.

'Enough, Hal. Come on over here, Tex.' Tex moves forward into her open arms. 'And you too, Flo.' Rachel embraces her kids, a fortress of love and consolation while Naomi lies in her crib, still crying but more softly at the sound of her mother's voice.

'Pink,' Tex whispers, his one still-painted hand wrapped around her neck.

'And beautiful,' Rachel kisses his forehead and then Flo's. Their breaths rising and falling together. Hal sits in his chair, legs wide. Rachel releases her kids. 'Sweetwater, can you take your brother to bed? I'll be in to read in a minute.'

'Flo room. Sleep in Flo room,' Tex pleads.

'Yes. Okay. For tonight.'

Taking Tex's unpainted hand, Flo leads him from the room, Tex swooping his pink fingers round and about in front of them as they go.

Hal starts in, 'No son of mine will be a sissy.'

'Or happy, by the looks of it.'

'He has to learn who he is.'

'It's just nail polish, Hal.'

'It's not: it's the polish; those damn curls of his; the necklaces; his love of pink.'

'He's not even two. He has an older sister who loves that stuff. At that age they mimic the people around them. He'll grow out of it.'

'And if he doesn't?'

'You obviously did.'

Hal notices the sweet upturn to her lips, her firm prettily manicured hand on her hip, 'Please don't encourage him.'

'It's just paint; you give me those little pots all the time.'

'That's different.'

'Oh yeah, you're doing the manly thing.'

With the kids asleep, the house a seashell to their ears, Rachel stands by the window in the kitchen, the full moon clear and then obscured as clouds shape-shift across the dusk sky; the landscape all a-light with bright burnished tones she's never seen before; rain pelting down and the ground shimmers with it.

'We didn't get the northern lights this year,' Hal offers. He stands behind her now. Close. Hands near but not touching her.

'Or perhaps we just never looked out for them at the right times.'

When she inhales his body stretches, the space almost broken. 'You can miss things if you don't pay attention.'

'Is that so?'

'Yes.' Rachel turns. Their bodies fit, perfectly. 'Tex will be fine.' So hot between them. 'So will Flo.'

'I just never thought it'd be this difficult.'

'You're making it more difficult.'

Hal knows she's right. It's just so big. Too big for them to handle. For him to handle. 'It's harder than I imagined. Too much to do. To be,' he says.

'Well, let's focus on the easy bit.'

A durable, obscuring rain beats against the roof. The inconsistent moon fades and reappears throughout the night, and yet the desert colors in the fields flourish. And both still annoyed, still agitated about their different opinions, about how to raise their children, they agree upon one thing.

HAL, IN A NAMELESS STATE

Hal was seven, in the woods out back of his parents' first tiny house in Kansas. Wind blew gently. The tips of the grass stirred, and then only just. Hal's dad stopped abruptly, held up his hand in silence, acutely aware of rogue movements ahead.

'A northern cardinal,' he whispered and pointed. Its body vibrant red and all still; its beak opened and closed and a disassociated song rang out before he flew beyond their sight. 'The female,' Lawrence said, pointing to another, more quietly-colored bird, beautiful in her subtlety. 'The male,' he said, cupping his ear to coax in birdsong.

A gust of wind rushed up taking the female cardinal with it, and they carried on, an unguessable father and his baffled son.

While angry hands of mud grasped at Hal's hand-me-down, one-size-too-big yellow galoshes, his father used big strides to cover the wet ground effortlessly. The low brow of the hill sank into the field and Hal's dad didn't even look back but assumed Hal would keep up. Hal's knees ached with the effort. He had none of his dad's grace and his boots knocked at his knees, making bending as difficult as fighting against the sucking mud. Heat bit at his arms and torso; his hands throbbed with cold.

His dad strode into the distance, his dark skin merging with the shadows of the trees, leaving behind his slow, rather timid youngest son. In the end, Hal couldn't keep up. And, in the end, he learned the lesson his father wanted him to: the world waits for no one.

Hal knew the way home and struggled with his head down. When a flutter cut through the air, he lifted his gaze, expecting to see a cardinal. But it was the swooping, swift flight of a common summer visitor he saw: a pretty barn swallow with its purple flash of a chest. It alighted on a low branch, twitching its long tail before flying off to winter in the southern hemisphere. A coming storm angled shafts of light and a corkscrew wind liberated leaves from branches. Hal lingered, knowing fall would come and go in a single flourish of water and wind. He let his feet sink into the mud and watched the flapping of a season pass him by. He noticed birds, the way the trees bent, he imagined the states the wind would blow through next, he took note of the shape and consistency of the clouds, and stored the information in his notebooks, next to the sketches of the things he wanted to build. When the rain started to drive rather than just fall, squelching and tugging with all his strength, he pulled his feet free and trudged onwards.

When he arrived home, hours after his father, Hal paused briefly at the doorway that marked the border between the harsh paternal lines of the house and his mother's space. Her delicate table, one leaf down, circled out from the wall, an old blue checkered tablecloth dropping over the edge. Looking up from her coffee and her stub of a cigarette, Cecilia saw her son and smiled.

'Can I have some hot chocolate, Mom?'

'It's too close to dinner,' his dad cigar-mumbled from the living room. 'Plus, you're too old for that. It's a pansy's drink.'

Three weeks after Hal's next birthday the family of eight moved to a flat excuse of a state and lived in a trailer until their house was built.

Hal's dad, who for years had been an itinerant builder, had bought five empty acres at the top of a slow slope of a hill (across from a small but growing graveyard) at the end of what would become a street desolately populated by houses and tolerating only dead-end traffic. He parked their trailer street-side of their lot. Along the west side, just behind and below the house, ran a weak trickle of water where the boys tried to fish at dawn, metal pails knocking against their legs, hands raw with the cold.

The day they'd arrived, after a run-in with a sharp-tongued local shopkeeper who used the n-word and refused to serve him, Lawrence, only ever his own man, raised his fist in retaliation but was halted by Jim Hegarty, Irish and a recent incomer as well. Normally as hot-headed and stubborn as Lawrence, Jim pulled him from the store and they got tanked over at Tom's Bar, where the local brew packed twice the punch of any bottle you could buy.

'The town needs men like us,' Jim toasted.

'This town needs to be raised up into this century.'

Lawrence arrived home in the early hours and pulled all his boys from their shared beds. 'Sons, we're going to make our mark here. Show them what the Fremonts are made of. We'll be our own men. Your grandmother earned her rights and we don't have to reinvent that wheel. I'm going to build a house that shows them exactly who I am.'

Yeah, a slave driver rather than a slave, thinks Hal now. But Lawrence's plan had been a good one: statement rather than violence; a building rather than battles. Quickly, with the help of all his sons, his own house rose from the ground, grand, impressive.

The columns stood proudly and the size couldn't fail to silence the locals living in their houses that kneeled so low to the ground. But as he grew up Hal started to notice how the walls of their house met at imperfect, too broad corners, just as he noticed the slight leaning of the stairs as he ran up them after school, but he kept his mouth shut, just like the locals who also took care when noticing, out loud, the things which set the Fremonts apart.

Hal and his brothers learned the construction trade whether they wanted to or not. Hal's oldest brother, Bill, even trained as a civil engineer, and Hal often read his textbooks, giving Bill some of his sketches to look over.

'These are good.' Bill checked some of Hal's calculations and his hand traced the lines of a three-bedroom house with a swooped roof. 'This reminds me of a bird in flight. This is really good,' he repeated, quietly, but Hal heard the pride in it. And then Bill rolled up the thin-papered designs and both brothers knew they'd never see the light of day, not at Fremont Construction. But Hal kept imagining houses, and then buildings, a city hall, a theatre he wanted to build, and he kept drawing. He kept these plans hidden beneath a floorboard he'd pried loose in his bedroom. First he'd be a trailblazer like John C Fremont, and then he'd come back home and build things. Building came easy to him. He had real talent, occasional genius. People said he had a knack for it, but his father never saw it. To Lawrence, Hal was a momma's boy, weak-minded, but good enough with a hammer to keep around. And besides, what else would he ever be able to do?

The family persisted with Cecilia's quiet attempts at love always ineffective in the face of Lawrence's dominant, vocal will in all things. One or two of his brothers found their own wills and escaped under cover of night.

When a fast rust took the bottom of the family car and it dropped out as Lawrence hit eighty-two miles an hour out on Route 147, the car and Lawrence and Cecilia careened into the lone ancient sycamore. Only twenty-year-old Hal walked across the street to see the earth foot-trampled over his parents' graves. High above the surprisingly sparse funeral gathering, a golden eagle pitched a call and Hal watched it ride the thermals until it was so high it merged with the sky.

After the funeral, Hal stood on the porch watching his brothers escape en masse. With haphazard bags slung over their shoulders, beer splashing in cases clasped under their arms, they walked away high-fiving each other, throwing back their heads and shouting, their voices infused with a finality and hilarity Hal couldn't fathom.

'It's all yours, Hal! Everything!' Bill shouted back. If Hal had been looking he'd have noticed how they discarded their father's expectations and left them cluttering the corners of the house, settling easily down into the foundations.

With his older brothers' departures, Hal inherited the business and the house and for the longest time Hal stood at the front door and looked into his house. It was deathly quiet. The vast hall spanned the width of the house and at this time of day almost seemed to shimmer like light upon water. This house, his house, was too quiet, too empty: it needed a family.

Now was his chance. He always dreamed he'd go on travels like John C Fremont had done, commanding men, naming things: peaks, plants, rocks, tribes of people. He closed up the house, gave a set of keys to elderly Miss West next door, and left the site manager in charge of the business. He slung his binoculars over his shoulder, slid his slim Audubon bird guide into his back pocket, and meandered his way to West Coast in search of a wife. At night he'd read of JC's adventures in the places he planned to drive through the next day. He was faintly disappointed not only that the landscapes didn't look as he'd expected them to, but as he drove through the Rocky Mountains he knew he did so as follower rather than as a trailblazer. JC hadn't been the first person to travel through most of those places, but he'd made them his own. Hal wanted to do this too, to make something his own, and he began to dream of his boys going out and helping him to make his mark upon the world.

In California he searched out to sea for signs of ospreys and pelicans and rare sea birds and found Rachel instead. Now she sleeps beside him, blithely unaware of how little progress he's making. How this house, this ridiculous house, has never garnered respect for the Fremonts as his dad had wanted it to, has never been the home Hal wanted it to be. He sits up and through the window a slow grey cloud passes through black sky and below and beyond lies a land so dark it's night too. He's going to have to build beyond this house, maybe even beyond this town, but he'll get the respect he deserves. He'll earn it brick by brick, son by son.

Sometimes instead of going straight to town to do errands, Rachel puts the kids in the car, gives them bottles, small containers of cereal, and toys, and drives out to where the highway merges with fields. There she does a three-point turn and takes in the entire town and the landscape it creates. Hal's houses grow from the earth whole. They make sense. They take the flat land and give it flight. They better be good, she thinks, keeping him from his family like they do. He has a light touch with the designs and a firm touch with his men.

As she walks along the main street, new residents, satisfied customers, approach her just to praise his work, his generosity and his way with people. If only he had the same graces at home, with his kids. Rachel notices how the long-standing residents listen in, making small discontented noises as they do, and how they then hold her gaze a fraction too long as she walks past. Sometimes their brief greetings turn from neutral to disapproving, and she doesn't like how their critical attentions then fall on her children before they pass too close, often knocking her shoulder before she's clear of their ill will.

ARIZONA

In the womb the next baby grows long and thin and moody, and Rachel dry-heaves at any time of the day. Naomi is teething and real fussy with it; Tex walks, but clumsily, and has a tendency to bruise easily and cry heartily; the house always needs to be cleaned and Flo, well, now that she can walk and talk, Rachel doesn't have to worry too much about her. She was born old.

Her relentless young children do not even let her go to the bathroom alone, or take a shower. Crowded on the bathroom floor, Flo sits with a book, Tex shakes his rattle, and Naomi giggles or cries in her bouncy seat, each of them gently sprayed through the space between the tiled wall and the loose shower curtain. For all this, she's abandoned. The new baby she carries shoves her feet into Rachel's ribs, and then she lifts her up to a high plateau and Rachel's grief soars and falls, toroweaping, mixing with the water from the shower.

Hal has secured the contract to build an annex to the court house, a few holding cells, and this is before he's finished his long list of rebuilds and new builds, or so he says on the rare nights he crawls into their bed. Designs fill his bedside table and cover the walls of the basement. She can only think what his office looks like. He's hardly ever at home and he keeps giving Rachel those damn paints.

It's hot, always too hot. Dry too. But like a gift, this girl in her belly brings water to the surface for her. As she gardens, as she walks, the sound of it murmurs towards her through layers of earth, and falls from the air. A rapture of water but it's inconsistent, unreliable. Middle of the night, Rachel is in bed, dreaming of the ocean, of what she understands, and a crash of thick muddy water rushes down on her with the force of a brick wall. Roughing her up in the debris, the surge tumbles and then discards her. She remembers reading of someone found alive, tossed high up onto a ledge by a flash flood in a slot canyon. He was found naked, clothes ripped off by the force of the water, mud packed up beneath his eyelids. That's how she feels: taken to the brink of death and destruction by what she most seeks out.

Rachel wakes with the bed covered with water, the baby coming fast.

'Hal!' The calm after the rush, the panic. 'Hal!'

But he's not there.

She yells again so loud that crotchety Miss West from next door hears her cries and brings towels, tells her to breathe, not to push, then to push, and with her three kids asleep in the next room she's alone with this old neighbor. Miss West puts a hand on Rachel's arm, her eyes checking the progress and she talks loudly so she can hear herself speak despite her own deaf left ear.

'So fast, this town is growing so fast. Much too fast, my dear. All these new people, they don't remember what's important. They don't remember where we've come from. It's important we remember who we are. That old Mr Fremont, before your Hal, his pa, well Lawrence here, he built something so he'd be remembered. But he wasn't from here. Not by a long shot. Push, my girl, push. Stop. Breathe. That's it.

That's right, Lawrence built this house and he built a place for him and his family and thought that'd be enough for us to overlook all the things about them that just weren't right. His wise kids got out of here. The smart ones leave, honey. Generations can still be incomers, no matter what they build. No matter what their desires are above their station. No matter what they call their kids. Push, my girl. Push.'

But Rachel isn't listening any more. She wraps her arms low around her belly and holds onto her baby. She closes her legs, keeps her breath as steady as she can, keeping it deep, moving the blood around her body. She has no power in her legs but she uses the old lady like a piece of furniture and she stands anyway. She will not let this hag touch her child.

'I want you out.'

The woman reaches out to stroke Rachel's hair. 'Push, my dear. Push. Squat if you must. I've heard that your people do that sometimes. Breathe. It's okay. She'll come when she's ready.'

'I mean you. Get out of my house. Don't ever cross this threshold again.' Rachel fires a look that even a Miss West cannot ignore. The old woman walks slowly, with as straight a back as she can manage, her disapproving looks scouring the place. 'Yeah, look around as much as you want to lady, you're on the way out. You can't stem the tide of change. This town needs a good shaking up. This town needs someone with a vision. This town needs us. And don't you worry, you'll be in the ground before you know it, and you'll not have to worry about how my family brings the tone of the place down!'

The front door never closes, the bitch has left it open. Rachel is in no condition to go and shut it. She leans against the wall, listens, and hears her three children as they sleep. She reaches for the phone, dials the operator, 'I need the number of a Mrs Cassandra Taylor's studio…' But the next contraction overwhelms her and Rachel drops the phone, yells, and there's no messing with a yell this deep and loud, that doesn't travel through the air but reverberates through the earth and to her man himself. 'Hal!'

The black of the night moves aside to let him speed past all who are wide-eyed awake in their beds, rattled by things they do not understand. Hal is half-dressed, his hair mussed, and he drives towards his house, racing, yes, but with a deep dread slowing his actions, thumping his heart. Sweaty and winded and smelling of another woman Hal closes the front door behind him and arrives by his wife's side, the baby's head cresting.

Hal moves to the end of the bed, and his wife locks her eyes on his. 'Wash your hands of that woman before you touch my daughter.' Which he does, coming back with a basin of warm water and clean towels. 'Catch her, you bastard.'

She gives him an even glare, her entire body flushed, her face set; she's in full fury. In any other situation Hal feels confident she would knock him out with a fine left hook. She would take him out. He eases his daughter into the world: she's a long beautiful child, a dark earth-red sort of beauty, with striding soles on the bottoms of her feet, already tough from her journey. The thin capable legs of a roadrunner.

'She's beautiful,' Hal says, gently wiping his daughter with a cloth dampened by warm water and then laying her in Rachel's arms. Arizona cries a short sharp cry and Rachel pulls her close. With a small body light against her own, she dreams of cupped palms of stone holding water, tinajas glimmering in the nearly unbearably hot sun, beacons of freedom and redemption.

Arizona won't be a tall girl, but rather muscular and lean; nothing spare on her. As a child she'll run for miles in preparation for running far away from the family, from this claustrophobic, caged place. She'll hone in on Rachel's constant inability to leave a land that doesn't suit her and at times it will be like they are crawling over each other trying to be the first to leave.

In the morning, Rachel calls the midwife so she can come and check on the new baby, pleased when she offers to stay for coffee and play with the kids. Flo and Tex are out back helping Naomi to walk and taking her around the yard, letting her fall down, picking her up again. Outrageous Miss West has opened Rachel's eyes to the truth of the matter—the truth being that this adventure is far more complicated than she'd ever imagined it could be and today, in the middle of the desert, two girls into the Four Corners, Rachel doesn't so much lower her expectations of Hal, but she changes her expectations, the goals, of the whole endeavor.

Hal calls Sandra from work the next morning and gets an earful. She's furious at him for being so foolish. 'It will only work,' she says, 'if you have your family.' She does not want a husband, nor does he want a wife, she reminds him. 'You already have one of those.'

Down on the site Hal borrows some tools and plywood and gets Arizona made. He speeds up the hill in the station wagon and the houses lean and lurch away from the road as he passes. Sliding to a stop, he unfolds his long legs from the driver's seat and loses packets of mud and dirt out of the creases in his jeans and the treads of his boots as he taps them on the steps leading up to the back porch. He clasps a bunch of bright daisies in one hand, which he has to put down to unlace and pull off his boots, slaps his legs a few times to rid himself of the worst of the excess mess and carries his apology to his wife.

Rachel, stirring a stout beef stew, has swept up her hair into a loose bun held together with a pen, and a perfect whimsy of black tendrils has fallen loose. He runs his work-rough hand down Rachel's arm and swoops the bouquet around under her nose.

She takes the daises from him and content with that he goes to the utility room where she keeps the lava soap ready near the big white ceramic sink, large enough to wash a toddler in. Flo and Tex slip-slide on the sand while they wait for their dad to sit down in his chair. Pipes clank and the house expands to make room for Hal and then it settles around the family, pulled down into the earth a bit more secure and just a little bit heavier.

Hal sits in his La-Z-Boy chair, flat-footed in his socks and still-dusty-from-the-site jeans. His kids clamber and slide and stumble and he smiles, ruffles their hair and roughhouses with them. They're sturdy enough, but his boys will be stronger, wilder.

Hal goes back out to the car and carries the freshly carved state of Arizona into the house. 'Come on kids. Look at that,' he says, 'isn't it amazing, beautiful, what's still to come?' And the kids buzz around the hall, 'Ari ri ri ri' and Rachel is at the doorway, holding the new baby. He slaps the wood up on the wall and although she's a bit rough around the edges, she'll do.

Outside the house there's a long stretch of fields crossed every so often by a road, paved or gravel, and the whole time the sky lifts up so light that this drought must end and they have a direction, many directions; their family has a map and they know where they're going, and no one and nothing, not even their own weak wills, can keep them from what they've set out to achieve.

MAGNET TO THE FACE OF A COMPASS

A few months later, Rachel and Hal get lost on the way to the All You Can Eat Barn and end up at what feels like the edge of the world and the light of the sunset fills the sky so they can't even tell which way is west, and Arizona cries and cries and cries and all of Flo's efforts to amuse her seem destined to end in an increase in volume, and Tex kicks the back of his father's seat and Hal reaches back and playfully grabs his leg saying 'aaaargggh, a monster has your leg' and the kids yell 'daaaaaaaad' in that slightly tired excited way kids do when they love a game, and then Hal turns back to the roadmap and he still can't figure out which way is up, and Rachel has this feeling, call it intuition, that the next one, Utah, they both know it, will be conceived tonight, on this lost turned around evening with children banging away in their rooms and the whole house heaving, feeling like it's been knocked on its side, and her and Hal laughing, possibly in hysterics, laughing because the whole darn thing is so funny and out of control and, in that moment, at the moment of Utah's conception, looking at it from the floor of the hall where they've fallen together, exactly what they both want.

UTAH

As Utah tosses and flips deciding how she'll be in the world, Rachel can't find the hall for days on end and sits in another unfamiliar room and weeps. Sounds of her children playing somewhere in this house come to her, but if she tries to follow them back to safety, she ends up in yet another oddly shaped room where she looks out the window and doesn't recognize the view.

Finally, she sits at the kitchen table, amidst a mess of papers and maps she's dragged down from the turret, and tries to find something that will root her in this next girl. The kids harangue around her, setting up and knocking over dominoes, making sandcastles, moats, and cliff-edged coastlines out of all the sand that accumulates daily. Arizona is in a bouncy chair and she bounces bounces bounces until she falls asleep, and it's in this stillness that a map catches Rachel's attention. It's a map of the Great Salt Lake and the directions are all wonky with north facing west and west south and the edges of the water lack distinction. It's basically useless as a guide. Right away she knows it's a body of water that can't actually be mapped because its shoreline changes so dramatically year on year. It's foolish to even try. So many of us are foolish.

This is how you lose yourself in a familiar place. The baby in her belly knows this and each night in her dreams Rachel stands in a red dusty land, blue skies slapping it flat a short distance away. She stands with her palm up in front of her holding a copper gyroscope, which is turning and tilting and always in movement.

After nine disorienting months, Utah emerges breeched and red and out of breath. She recovers quickly and once at home she's passed around from child to child by way of introduction.

'Arizona, Naomi, this is Utah.' Rachel opens the baby to each Corner so they can kiss her. She's familiar to them and they press their cheeks to hers and pat her legs with chubby toddler hands.

Rachel takes a risk and gives the newborn to Tex who sits cross-legged on the floor, and there, held near his heart, Utah opens her eyes. Tex's heart burns, beats like it'll burst out of his chest, a sweet sharp beating, and he lets his sister roll out of his arms and onto the waiting floor.

Flo bends down and scoops her up and sits with Utah protected in her lap. She moves aside the thin cotton blanket and checks for any damage. 'Fine,' she says, 'no bruises.'

But it's not strictly true. As Flo coos over Utah, Tex's heart knocks about in his ribs unable to find a reliable position and his heart beats itself black and blue in his chest.

ECHO CANYON

Hal notices the toddler sliding down from her chair, covered in smooshed peas. She's got a diaper-defined walk, big butt, unsteady legs, and Hal is lulled into thinking she's pretty harmless. She walks the length of the table, stops at his side, looks up at him, her knees slightly bent, opens her mouth and screams.

Hal looks down, holds out his hand in the universal gesture for stop. But nothing stops. Everything gets louder. This child's scream seems to allow the room to burst into pandemonium and all the kids start chattering and clambering and pinching and punching each other. He turns his head towards the kitchen and shouts, 'Rachel!' Nothing stops. No one arrives.

'Rachel! ... Rachel! ... Rachel!'

Holding an infant in her arms, Rachel walks through the swing door, reaches out and catches the screamer with a strong arm around her waist, presses her lips to the child's ear. 'My love,' she whispers, 'shhhh, my hummingbird. Who's my pretty Arizona?' The girl quietens a bit and Rachel looks up to the others, 'Now sit nicely and eat your dinner,' and they seem inclined to listen to her. Hal shovels in some mashed potatoes.

Still in Rachel's arms, the new baby swings her arms, giggling. 'Whoop whoop,' the screamer shouts. The house lurches like it's lost its bearings and the precarious calm breaks into riot and the older girl sitting at the table kicks her brother, twirls her utensils like t and bosses around another girl who sits looking as befuddled as Hal feels. He grips the table. The older girl stabs Tex in the thigh with a fork and he bursts into tears. Arizona, still covered in peas, is released by Rachel and toddles, stands, screams. And screams.

Rachel puts the screamer back in her chair and sits with Utah on her knee at the head of the table. Tex and Flo sit on either side of Arizona haranguing her with their dinner fingers. The quiet lost girl—Naomi, he deduces—sits trying to get to grips with her plastic spoon, getting it to do what she wants, when she wants, but her success is unpredictable, like the weather. When her siblings refuse to hush, she looks up, claps her hands and her clap is echoed by thunder outside and a powerful cold wind shoves the curtains into the room and Hal shivers. The screamer's bellowing crescendos.

Hal puts his head in his hands, closes his eyes, tries to breathe deep and slow. This changes nothing; his head spins. He opens his eyes: pandemonium. These wild girls should have manners, should respect the quiet he needs. At the end of the day, any day, all days, he needs clarity. He can just about handle the unfathomableness of his wife, but these girls can't even use their words and clearly have no sense of the importance of quiet or order or respect. The oldest girl gives him an impish look, kicks a sister under the table, twirls her fork, reaches over the screamer and stabs her brother again. Who is protecting his son from all this? Arizona inhales and then bellows the full marathon length of her exhale. She hiccups, inhales, and starts again.

'Out!' he casts a stern stare around the room. 'I want all of you out!' The pandemonium ignores him. There's no change in volume, nothing stops. Only Rachel stills; she stares at her husband who sits clutching his fork, his lips pressed to a tight white line where they meet. 'Out! Now!' he repeats.

'Shhhhh,' Rachel hushes the children.

It's clear that if he wants order, he'll have to impose it; he has to otect what little space he has. It only seems fair, historical even, ' he doesn't know why he hadn't thought of it earlier. His father

Lawrence and mother Cecilia passed their days in clearly demarcated rooms, why should he and Rachel live under different rules?

'Out!' Hal repeats and he glares at Rachel.

Kids clasp hands over their mouths and over those of their younger siblings. Rachel holds onto Utah with one hand and stands without asking anyone or anything for support. 'Come on guys, your dad is grumpy, let's go into the kitchen, give him time to think.' She starts to herd the kids towards the door.

'Not Tex,' Hal says. 'We'll be eating together in here from now on.'

Rachel tries on a loose smile, just for her girls, while her eyes are hard and sharp, just for Hal. She gathers her daughters together and kicks the swing door to the kitchen open with her foot, holding it open with her hip.

Through the kitchen window, the wide flat view is drawn long by the light and a flap of wings flashes orange in the setting sun. 'Look, there's a California gull,' Rachel says. Three pairs of hands hold onto the windowsill and watch the foreign bird looking to roost near a great salt lake, instead finding itself above a broad stretch of land where a whisper of salt-laden sand flies off the roof of a house.

Later Hal clasps her hand as she clears that night's dishes from his table. She pulls herself free.

'It's for the best,' he says.

Lifting his napkin, she notices it's still clean enough to use tomorrow. She pushes the door with her hip, and it swings, swings.

She tries to sleep in the house but it won't let her. She won't let herself. In the rocking chair out on the porch she sleeps wrapped in a blanket and in the morning on his way to work, Hal bends down, kisses her cheek and lingers, breathing close to her neck.

'I missed you,' he says.

The smell of him. Right to her toes. God damn these things she can't control. She touches his cheek.

'You better know what you're doing.'

'Trust me. Everyone will be happier.'

CARDINAL

Their garden is a strange beast. It's flat near the house where the kids congregate, and where that weird sandbox Rachel had him build sits overflowing with the damned sand, and then past the fence, the thinning grass slopes down towards the creek, which exists only as a dry trickle except in the wettest of years. Spindly cottonwoods cling to the hope of water and this is the place Hal targets with his binoculars. This is where he finds his birds.

Rarities can be seen flitting among the summer visitors, the passage migrants, and the just plain common. Over the last few years he's seen white-throated swifts, black-chinned hummingbirds, and a cactus wren the day they brought the last girl home from the hospital. It's become such a regular occurrence to see displaced desert birds that Hal wouldn't be surprised to see a roadrunner speeding along the sidewalk.

His favorites are the local, bright cardinals which nest in the rose bushes he keeps just for this possibility; or the robins that trust him enough to nest in his trees (and one year in the old fishing net Rachel left hanging from a stray nail on the garage); and the resident owl who Hal doesn't see much but who he hears, clearly, sounding out in the twilight.

Out on the edge of the rather haphazardly cared for lawn, out of sight of the house, on a Sunday, maybe a Saturday (if the job has gone smoothly and ends early), he'll pull out his field chair, push his baseball cap back from his forehead to give him the best field of view, and hang his ancient Zeiss 10x45s round his neck the same way he'd done as a boy. He identifies birds the old-fashioned way, by sketching what he sees, taking notes. He isn't world class, but he has a good eye for detail and his discerning ears can distinguish the high thin zee of the cedar waxwing, the clear whistle of the cardinal: wait wait wait cheer cheer cheer, and the fast changing mimicry of the mockingbird.

'And there, that's the mockingbird, Tex. You hear it? One after the other. His own song…' but Tex never sits long enough to hear. His son has a listening problem.

Behind him the seasons of the house come and go, and he tries, and fails, to keep ahead of all the repairs. Each of the back steps curves down in the middle from high use, a storm last autumn had bust up the gate so they keep it pitched open, the gutters on the west side of the house pour down a waterfall with each cloud burst, and from a distance the house definitely looks like it leans, ever so slightly, to the south. Like a dentist who ignores the state of his own children's teeth, Hal forgets to be vigilant about his own home territory.

Sure, Hal makes mental notes about repairs the house needs, and he not only sees but registers the to-do list Rachel keeps stuck up on the door down to the basement (years old, rumpled, yellowed, new things added, nothing crossed off). And yet, still, somehow, he forgets what he is obligated to do and finds himself once more with a beer in hand, sitting out back keeping his eyes alert to the flutter of wings or spending an hour with Sandra between work and coming home or going for a walk at the far side of town among the small cluster of trees they optimistically call a forest preserve.

His collapsible birding chair does not have the history of the chair he made during the first month of their marriage: this simple wooden chair he'd placed in the cavernous, map-less hall. In the early days he and Rachel fucked on that chair, the back knocking against the plaster, him taking Rachel's weight. Her fingers fanned in exaltation, pressed against the naked wall for support, his hands spread on her back. He misses the simplicity of that feeling. He misses that feeling.

Since the last girl was born Hal has taken to sitting in the chair facing the map, taking the whole thing in. He tips himself back and forth, rocking his head against the plaster of the opposite wall, balancing on two chair legs, then four, all made less secure by the sand.

Once in a while Hal runs his hands over the map (a spine straightening moment for any Fremont within a five mile radius) tweaking, rubbing off any scuffs from the states, erasing any marks he might have missed years before. Sure he traces the outline of Texas with his calloused finger and thinks he has quite an artistic flair. But never once does he think he could better his already perfectly acceptable work.

Still, sometimes after a few whiskies, sometimes completely sober, the states blur, shimmy out of his control like hot tarmac on a summer's midday. Sometimes he wears sunglasses, tilts in his chair, squinting behind the lenses, and watches the map, wills it to be still and clear, but it stubbornly remains in motion.

Eating in the dining room with five-year-old Tex never seems to live up to Hal's expectations. It's something he has committed himself to doing, like raising the kids Catholic or something, but his heart isn't in it. His clean face loses its shine and his hopeful eyes are so often disappointed when he looks at his son, who picks at things: his food, the beat up tong of his fork, morsels of Hal's attempts to be a father. If Hal had been able to describe how disoriented he'd felt since the last girl was born, if he'd been able to put that into words, or make that feeling go away, maybe he would have been able to make things right.

Flo serves her dad and brother in the dining room and gleans tidbits of knowledge from snatched conversations (stolen, because Hal stops talking when he realizes she's there). She has a series of black eyes and bruised ribs from all the fighting she's had to do in first grade at school, but she's learning what she needs to get to the top of that pile. She needs the same strategies at home, the same attention to details and opportunities: when she serves her dad and brother she stays exceedingly quiet, to blend in, and she learns a lot from her three-course forays into forbidden territory.

John Charles Fremont was a great man. A great man, Tex. Flawed. Sure. Who says great men can't make mistakes? In fact great men are more likely to make mistakes because they take risks. There was that messy business about the court-martial, to be sure, and he did lose a few men along the way. And he didn't always take responsibility for his decisions: there was that sunk boat on the Mississippi, for sure. But situations are complex and you don't always know what's gone down unless you've been there. Sure, Lewis and Clark didn't lose a single man to accident or incident. Only one to illness. Your mom prefers Lewis and Clark, of course she would. They never let anyone down. JC let a lot of people down. He called himself a trailblazer, and he was, he sure was. He was. He had exuberance, a vision, a fate. He had a fate to go west and he did. We all have fates, Tex. Mine is to build this town. You can see that can't you? Build this town. You and me and your brothers, we'll build this town.'

Tex squirms, his outcast blue eyes follow a hairy spider climbing up the dark wood. Hal slaps the table and Tex looks to his dad.

'You know I'm here for you don't you? Well, I am. JC was a man of questionable birth, a bit like myself. A bit like you. He never let that hold him back. He learned things that would set him free to make his own destiny. He adapted, didn't let failure quash him. Never let failure quash you. Or loss of equipment or men. What you build will always be greater than small losses. An iron will, unquestioned decision making, that's the skill.'

Tex lays his head on the table, still watching the spider's ascent.

'We're trailblazers, Tex, us Fremonts. We always will be. We're of the people too, imperfect, but everyone is. The difference is, we know who we are. We know who we are. We're Fremonts, Tex. Don't you forget it.'

And Tex nods, in sleep, the line of the table a weft in his cheek. Hal looks past his weak-willed son, sees Flo, just for a second.

'We're Fremonts,' he says. 'And don't you forget it.'

BORN FREMONT

Flo's a keen listener, an avid observer, and she sees how her father's eyes are clear and bright when he lowers his binoculars after a day of bird watching. These have proven to be vulnerable moments, if chosen right, and Flo has been known to slide her arm along his back, hug him soundlessly and disappear before he realizes he can't remember who she is.

Flo has few allies in first grade. School gates create a boundary, like a moat around a castle. They mark off a territory to be won over, defended, sometimes it feels like it's a territory that is always in dispute. Parents talk, kids listen, and kids call her names they hear in dubious company.

'Look, a Fremont mulatto.'

'Squaw.'

'Like your ma.'

'Incomer.'

'You should go home.'

'She's a Fremont. Get her!'

It has something to do with their last name too. That's what she doesn't quite get. Her dad talks about being a Fremont as a strength, but out here in this bad world, it's an excuse to punch her. While foes cement themselves together against her, she knows she has bigger battles than this puny playground. She has a whole stinking map to live up to. She pays attention to the punches and starts to fight back and before long she's wearing her black eyes and bruises like badges of honor.

Flo is on the porch shucking the corn. Six rips down on each cob, one for each year she's lived. In the driveway her dad's truck careens to a halt and high above the house, a whistle, distant and untouchable, screeches. Her dad's feet are huge in his large muddy work boots as he steps from the pickup, his footfall shaking the land like a giant's. His face holds the dust and sun and he strides past Flo without a glance.

Hal shirks off his boots and clumps of mud hit the ground like cluster bombs. He has paint splattered on his trousers like he's been dancing in a gallon of the stuff and inside he walks right past her mom who is feeding the baby in the kitchen and he stands by the laundry sink trying to remove the paint from underneath his nails.

Flo gets up and watches closely for sometimes, if she follows in Tex's shadow and doesn't do anything to remind her dad that she's a girl or a child, then she can climb up onto his lap and listen as he quizzes Tex, and sometimes he'll forget that girls aren't worth as much as boys and he'll talk to her too.

The other kids sit and wait inside, already learning from the briskness of his walk, the lack of music in the air, that he'll bypass them and head upstairs to shower. Rare are those days when one of them can catch his hand and pull him easily into the backyard to play. Today he takes no notice and leaves the kids to amuse themselves and her mom to swear with the effort of trying to remove the paint from his stained clothes. When Flo hears the shower start, she returns to shucking the corn.

COLORADO

On Christmas Eve, a new moon night, with one hand on her back, the other on her round belly, Rachel stands well wrapped up, with big fake furry boots, almost knee deep in snow and looks to the sky. The air runs thin through her lungs and the tough ground beneath the snow thrusts her towards the thick dark sky. She stands for hours, her legs holding her up out of sheer habit, while soon-to-be Christmas presents remain unwrapped inside on the kitchen table. She waits because Colorado has pressed herself to the very outer edges of her huge belly, with hands spread wide facing the ebony-defined cartography of space.

Rachel's pregnancy with Colorado comes fast after the other three and each of the four Corners, her desert girls, take her to dry, dangerous places and she'll survive because she has to. This girl loves the night and is only calm within it, so Rachel is cold and still and in need of sleep and she avoids spending too long thinking about Hal and how he imposes his will on the house, on the kids, on her; or about how he asks for a lot of tolerance, a lot of grace, but hands out very little in return. His damn foolish decision about the dining room; his damn insistence of solitude in his ridiculous basement; his shoddy work around the house. For the recent states he's guessed at borders, and used cheaper materials that are already threatening to disintegrate and yellow. His damn blindness about his kids and this damn house.

During the last four years, she has stood within the desert and has had to remain ever so slightly apart in order to stay alive. Too close within and you've become not the life of the desert, but the history of the desert. The cliff-laden plateaus of the southwest expose our history to scrutiny; each layer is a story, a girl too, and you can only survive this land by taking it on its own terms.

As one day turns into another the stars rearrange themselves and her and Hal's country appears in the night above her: stars for borders, planets for hearts. Her fourth Corner flickers, not yet born, but her other five children burn brightly. The North Star pulses undeniable in the sky and her urge is to use it as a reference point, to feel the rushed heat of it in her spine as she turns towards the south. As she turns the family south.

Colorado is born while her four sisters and one brother sleep in the rooms next door. Her dad is nowhere to be seen.

'She's a tiny one, but strong, look at those legs, she'll be crawling in days,' says the midwife. And this night creature stays awake until the sun rises and then, finally, she allows her mother to rest.

STATE OF DISGRACE

In the dry crisp cold of the January nights, Cole cries in her bassinet and Rachel lifts the small dark girl, with her bird-like legs and robust dark eyes that always look to the sky. She feeds her, walks with her, and eventually she wraps up warm and takes her girl outside. She moves the rocking chair to the driveway, covers them both in a thick wool blanket and with her daughter soft and light and full of breath on her chest, they both stare at the quiet of the sky. They come here every night and on clear nights or warmer nights, as spring approaches, some of her other girls join them and she moves the old bench out of the garage and over the yard and rests it against the fence. So, on many nights, there's a small cluster of intertwined girls and a very tired mother, swaddled in blankets and sleeping bags, safe under the stars. Some nights the Midwest winter is too cold and in order to appease Colorado, Rachel sticks glow-in-the-dark stars on the bathroom ceiling and will often fill the tub so her daughter has not only stars, but reflections of stars. She sets Cole's travel seat in the sink so the girl can see both and this, sometimes, gives Rachel a few hours of rest from this beautiful child who doesn't seem to have much resting in her.

It's grey and dismal and the house droops like an unwatered plant and the kids' moods are winter-exhausted and crinkly.

'Ari…want…out…side,' hiccups three-year-old Arizona, her face red and angry. 'Take. Me. Outside.' She gulps for breath between words, having been told not to go outside on her own.

'Not now,' says Flo, dismissing Ari and turning to Tex. 'That's mine, Tex. Give it back.'

He has a fire-engine in his vice-like grip, the ladder climbing to safety beyond his sticky palm. 'It's mine,' he says.

'I got it for my birthday.'

'Oh yeah?' Tex says as he tries to turn the crudded-up wheels. 'It's mine now.'

'You little…' And Flo goes after Tex with her newly polished fingernails. And Tex hits Flo with her own truck. She grabs for it and instead pulls off the ladder. The siren shrieks round and round. Brother and sister screech and tumble and claw. Grains of sand bite into their scratches.

'Ah! Ah! Ah!' yells Ari. Flo and Tex stop and stare. 'Out now,' Ari says calmly, pointing to her chest and then towards the door.

In her best bullying tone Flo says, 'If you want to go outside, learn how to open the door yourself.' Then Flo and Tex ignore Ari and dig in once more to their private battle. On her way to the kitchen, Arizona hits both Flo and Tex with an open hand on the back of their heads and goes to the back door to struggle with the handle. Eventually Naomi opens the door for her and they make it down stairs and to the sandbox where they lay their heads on the s frosted sand and listen to the soothing gurgle of underground water which rises up closer to the surface to meet them.

Flo and Tex emerge soon after, battlescarred, Rachel holding them both by the scruffs of their necks. Flo the clear victor, but Tex still holding the red truck.

'Now I want you both to tend to each other's wounds.' Rachel holds out a small bottle of Bacitracin and some cotton balls. Flo takes the bottle, Tex the cotton balls. Their mom's voice is cracked and fed-up. 'You are a disgrace to the word family.'

'Disgrace of a family,' whispers Ari from the sandbox.

MOCKINGBIRD

'It favors this great continent, Tex,' Hal lectures. 'This bird with a multitude of songs. Some people think that the mockingbird just mimics, but to the mockingbird the songs of other birds are just like notes to a musician. They're not like cuckoos tricking their way into another bird's nest, mockingbirds don't just mimic, they create. Although their nests may not be the sturdiest, they know how to protect their own.'

Six-year-old Tex chips the thick gloss stain from the underside of the table.

'I'd be a mockingbird,' Hal offers, 'I mean, obviously my first choice would be an eagle but if I had to chose a smaller bird, the mockingbird is a featherweight boxer, more than capable of looking out for itself.'

'Hmmmm,' Tex mumbles, peeling a good wedge of wax off with the jabbing action of his thumb. As satisfying as a productive cough.

'Son,' Hal says, looking about to make sure that neither Flo nor Rachel are swinging the doors or laying down or gathering plates, 'this might not be the prettiest nest, but it gets the job done. You now what I mean?'

'What?' Tex asks.

'And it's all yours, Tex.'

Tex looks around with disappointment. Even he can see that the house could use some attention, its ramshackle frame shakes when his dad walks and rocks when the girls laugh with their rowdy games.

'Do you understand? Everything you see is yours. And that's just the beginning.'

Hal grabs Tex by the arm and pulls him out into the hall. Flo, who has just flipped the door open with her hip, watches them go. She places the chargrilled chicken breast and rice down on the table where her dad should be sitting. She puts the SpaghettiOs where Tex had sat just seconds before. Curious and fearless she creeps to the doorway.

Out in the hall Hal arcs his arm across the mapped wall. 'All of this too, Tex.' He pounds the state of Texas with his open hand and something slips down, the corner of a revealing envelope. 'Remember this,' he says and like a magician Hal sleight-of-hands it back into place. Then he makes a ball in the air with both of his hands; fingers stretched like continents, a globe.

Tex nods blankly.

'It's what's up here that limits you,' Hal says, pointing to Tex's head. 'It's not just about land and property; it's about power and the natural inheritance of things. You have to realize this. It's what is given to our sort. You just need to realize what it's all about and take what's yours.'

Tex cranes his neck to try and see where the wall touches the ceiling of CANADA. He isn't reading that well yet and while he sees the bold black letters his mom has painted across the ceiling, he has no idea what they actually mean.

'Can I have my SpaghettiOs now?'

'In a minute son.'

Hal puts his hand on his son's shoulder and looks at the six states glued up on the wall. Tex tries not to shrug off the weight of his dad' hand and plays with a loose floorboard at his toe, which creaks w each kick.

The splintering of wood also hides the sound of Flo sn her way back into the kitchen. She's just heard a song, no remember and adapt. Putting her hand to her head, it's up here, she thinks, that's what limits us. And she knows that it'll be what will set her free too.

LONESTAR

Today is the first day of school. Their mom hands them their lunches in brown paper bags and Flo takes Tex's hand and smiles and waves to their mom as they walk down the driveway. She walks him to the school gates. The school's fence is tall and unassailable, and the schoolyard looks like a boxing ring, filled with bullies pressed into corners waiting before the bell. Flo releases his hand and shoves him forward.

Breakneck Biggins trips Tex as he crosses through the gate, stomps on his backpack and the crunch of pencils is clear even above his grunt. An unguarded Fremont: better than sloppy joe for lunch.

'Baby Boy Fremont. Like the curls. Do a dance for us? Are you sure you're a boy? I thought Fremonts only had girls, girly girls.'

'Hey watch it Biggins, you know what I can do to that puny neck of yours,' Flo yells but does not step forward.

Breakneck is joined by Greasy Jonny and they pummel Tex. Their thoughts move quickly and land hard like their fists. This kid doesn't even know what he has. His mother, she's an angel. They punch the boy and imagine what it'd be like to live in that house. It'd be nothing like where they're from. It'd be heaven, they're sure of it. It's only right that they teach the Fremonts about what they have. Stupid kids up in that house lording over the town, they don't even realize how they walk like they own the place. The Fremonts don't own the place. This place is ours. It's ours.

Flo stands in the crowd yelling, 'Fight them, Tex. Fight back. Do nething. Anything. Fight for yourself.' Tex hears his sister failing anything at all but yelp useless things at him. He closes his eyes, protect his organs. His head.

bell rings, kids go to their classrooms, and Flo is beside him.

'Stand up Tex. You're fine. Just a few bruises. You'll survive. You've got to fight for yourself, Tex.'

She looks innocent, like she's looking after him instead of letting him get beaten to a pulp. She looks so innocent.

'But you saw them. How do I fight that?'

She puckers her lips, squeezes his upper arm, hurrumphs her shoulders. Her grin is raw and mean. 'Are you saying you aren't going to be able to look out for yourself?'

Tex nods.

'And you want me to fight for you?'

He nods again.

'Well, Lonestar, that's gonna cost you.'

Every day he'll have to give her something in return for her protection. They shake on it. She holds out her hand. 'And for this morning…'

'But you didn't do anything.'

'Are you kidding? Do you have any idea how you'd look if I hadn't been here?'

He hands her his apple. It's a piece of fruit, not the world. The world is his.

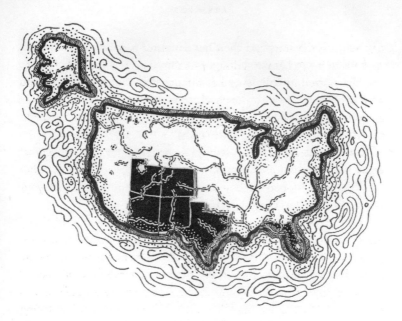

A CONTINENTAL DIVIDE

They are faithful people, Rachel and Hal: to each other, to the idea
of love, the idea of family. Even when Hal flirts with the idea of
individuality (even when he's having sex with another woman)
she's abided by his decisions. He's infuriating, inconstant, stubborn,
incredibly sexy. His arms all but bursting out of his shirts, how toned
all that building work makes him. The drawings he spreads on their
bed; his hands ever more talented, ever more, mmmmm, focused.
Even with the segregation, the sand piling up in the house, the plaster
threatening to crumble with the lack of moisture, Rachel loves Hal in
an unmentionable way, in an indecent fashion.

But now, eight years on, Rachel is stuck. She's exhausted. It's been
a year of nights spent with Colorado under the stars, and she's a child
who will not settle, and seems to want only the night. During the day
tetchy and restless and now that's she's crawling, you can't leave
one for a minute. Her sisters play with her, they seem to get on
t Cole's never truly happy until night falls and Rachel rocks

her beneath the stars and then her daughter is so at peace, she's so dark it's as if this baby girl disappears into the sky and Rachel has to reassure herself by following her infant's belly out to her arms and legs. She plants a kiss on her cheek, to make sure she's real. Her own gut churns, keeping her awake—she's still in the middle of the damn desert and doesn't know how to escape.

Rachel cleans the house, stomping, banging the vacuum against walls, throwing out clutter and mess, and the house rocks with her fury. She throws open the basement door and shouts. 'Just pick your crap up! Is that too much to ask?'

Kids press themselves to walls and she vacuums around them, barely seeing them. She hates this flatness, this thirst, this need for something else; she's tired of waiting, sick of her and the kids being so far down on his list of priorities, tired of pretending it's all okay.

She throws open the door to the basement and yells at her useless husband, 'It's just a list, Hal. A goddamn simple list. I'm just trying to stop this house falling apart. If you're so good with your hands then you can put them to work here. You can put them to work for your family!'

Rachel cleans and bangs and makes dinner and tucks the kids roughly into bed, Colorado included. 'Sleep,' she says, 'sleep. It'll be a new world order.' Hal knows better than to mess with her when she's in a mood like this and stays down in the basement with a few bottles of beer. It's still early when she falls asleep at the kitchen table, her head resting on a placemat.

When Hal finally emerges from the basement, he gathers her in his arms and leads her up to bed. The world sways, the dark need for sleep pushing in on her and Hal holds her whispering, 'Rachel. Sweetheart.' She hears him, but barely, he's far away and there's just the heat of bodies. 'I'll start on the list next weekend, I'll make you proud,' he says and the air is clearer, maybe he understands how she needs him to be. Maybe he'll come back to her with all he has. She doesn't know and can't hear anything besides the slow pushing of own blood through her arteries, the pounding of her head, and falls into a cool, endless and much needed sleep.

Cole is crying crying crying and her sister Naomi is trying to sleep beside her, waiting until their mom comes and lifts her out into the night, so they can all have peace. Naomi waits, Cole cries. Naomi waits, but their mom doesn't arrive.

The girls' bed is beside the window and Naomi pushes aside the curtain so Colorado can see the dark cloud-filled sky. This does nothing and she continues to cry. Naomi flings open her arms to push back the clouds and stars appear. 'Shhh,' she says to Colorado, climbing down from the bed. She picks up her sister. Colorado is a small girl, a good crawler but only able to walk if she holds someone's hands, and Naomi is robust and can just about handle her. 'Shhhh, if you're good, we'll make it outside,' and she's carrying her down the stairs and she's heavy and they make slow progress as Cole's head is craned back looking for the sky, and she whimpers, and Naomi keeps going, even as her arms and legs ache and she keeps having to shunt Cole back up on her hip, as she has a habit of sliding down her leg. The hall is huge and it seems to take forever to get across it and the wall is dark. Naomi can't see the map upon it and then they're through the kitchen and out onto the porch and down the steps. They stop and look up. Colorado claps her hands together, giggles, opens her arms, and then claps again. She squirms and on this moonless night her cheeks are bright and full of the light of the stars and Naomi's arms are tired and she puts Colorado down and she's so small, so tiny under the huge sky, and there's the dipper, her mom taught her that, and there's a familiar cluster of eight stars and there's no moon tonight, but it will be back again, that's what her mom says, sometimes it disappears but it always comes back and it's even there when we don't see it, and this is what Naomi turns to tell Cole but her sister is gone and there's a wind blowing clouds in from the west and Naomi looks to where the weather is gathering and she's leaning over and calling 'Cole, Cole, Cole' and the clouds blow in fast ·d they are pitched black and they dive the world into dark. Naomi ᵴ around the yard, through the vegetable patch and the flowers, he lawn, along the fence, calling her sister's name. She runs and and runs and shouts and the dark is really dark and peaceful when she stops running and stands on the fence and looks down the hill and clouds cover and uncover the stars, and the stars shine brightly in the shallow water of the creek, and she'd go down there if she could, to see them sparkle, but they're not supposed to leave the yard, for her mom says the water can be dangerous if you don't know how to swim. Colorado's a good crawler, even though she's new to it and Naomi thinks she could have gone back inside, to call for their mother. Naomi climbs the stairs and the kitchen door rattles shut behind her, the tiles of the kitchen floor are cool, and the hall feels like a cloud, it's fluffy and heavy and the stairs are tall and high and mighty and Naomi curls herself against the map and sleeps.

Rachel's sleep has been deep and when she wakes she thinks she might be pregnant again. Hal has already gone to work, which is no surprise, but the house is quiet, which is. Putting on a robe, she checks the kids' rooms, which are empty, and goes downstairs. In the cold, grey hall Rachel shivers, looks at the wall. The map isn't itself and that's when she starts to run, her bare feet on the floorboards, on the cold tiles of the kitchen, on the rough porch and out over the grass, past her girls standing there, and she takes note of how Flo holds Naomi, who is not to be consoled, and Rachel doesn't see an infant, and she runs through the wind-flung open broken gate. She runs over the rocks and the thinner earth, cutting her feet, and hearing only the thin run of water, this time of year. At the bottom she looks in both directions, but moves out of the shadow of the trees and finds Colorado. Her tiny, thin body within a wet, wrinkly all-in-one. Rachel scoops her daughter up and the world is dark and swirls. Her daughter is feather-light and slightly stiff, like a doll. There's a bellow in Rachel's head and the earth has no other sound. She does not know how to do this. The water eddies around her ankles, she could lie down too, in the pretty water, but her knees refuse to buckl and her chest won't heave. She has five children waiting for her by house and she clasps her daughter to her chest and walks up the

When Naomi had woken in the morning, Cole was beside her in the hall, real like how a cloud is real, she could feel her there, but when she tried to pick her up, there was nothing. Her sister looked at her and Naomi asked, 'Where did you go?'

'To touch the stars.' Cole's voice was brand new and alert.

'What are they like?'

'Dark and they move so fast, you'd not know it looking up, they're alive, Naomi, alive.'

And Naomi discovers that if she moves at just the right speed and holds out her hand, as if she could catch up the grasp of a girl just a bit smaller than herself, she can feel the wild, alive, pressure of a coal black sky in her palm. And she's out in the back yard, holding her sister's hand, showing her the exploding flowers of the goldenrod. Flo comes out and shakes Naomi asking, 'Where is Cole? Where is Cole?'

'She's here,' Naomi says, holding up her hand, 'she's here.' And then she sees what Flo sees: her hand is high in the air and it's empty.

Beneath Rachel's feet the ground is tough and sharp and at the top she sits on the bench by the fence and lets each child come and see their sister, touch her if they'd like. The oak tree bends down its branches and some of the girls cry, Naomi in particular, and the day grows darker, and a strong wind picks up, although the air blows dry and hot and the emotions in and around the house are steep and sharp.

The baby had not been in the water long, it seems, and there's no bloat. Up the stairs and into the bathroom, Rachel carries Colorado and the other kids follow her into the house and watch her as she washes the tiny body. She places Colorado in her bassinet in the hall, wrapped in a delicate cotton blanket. She needs something to bury her child in. Then she opens all the windows and doors and lets the nd blow through, encourages it to tangle the old air and the new, tertwine the dead and the living. Blankets cover the mirrors and ts on a black shirt, takes out her earrings and ties back her hair. d hoped the rage would go before she made the call. But it doesn't and she calls him anyway. 'Cole is dead. She drowned in the creek.'

Hal hears the wail of the wind, the clatter of the phone on the floor, the sound of tires on the road outside. An infant, a rattle, small footsteps. His wife might have hung up, maybe she's waiting for him to say something, he doesn't know. He's fallen to his knees and then further. It's the gate. He should have fixed it years ago. It's second on the list, which now, granted, is quite a bit longer than it used to be. All the other kids managed to stay in the yard just fine. He didn't even know she was crawling. The damn broken gate.

He moves out of his office and past Kitty without a word and he's at Sandra's and his knees hurt, his worn jeans are now torn. People have kept steely eyes on him as he's passed; they must know.

'It's over,' Sandra tells him through the door. She's sobbing, low down like she's slid to the floor. 'Go home to your family.' And her crying is close in, just the other side of the door and further away he hears the wailing from the hill. He knows what he has to do, but he's not ready for all that. He's thinking that even if he's not there, he can still help and so he drives into town and gets everything they'll need.

Rachel'd slept the sleep of the dead. She heard none of it. Not Colorado's nightly cries, not the clumsiness of her girls on the stairs, not Naomi shouting her sister's name. Not the storm and the wind, nor the clarity of the sky after. She didn't hear the clarity of the sky or the evocative calling of those true bright stars.

The infant's dress is cut to a simple design and when she has the dress mostly made she allows each child to press a few stitches through. Tex takes his time and his stitching is perfect. They stick twinklin sequins onto the finished dress and Flo makes Cole a tiny tiara rhinestones that will look pretty and bright against Colorado's of black hair. The wind whips around and about and the kid games and include their absent infant sister as if she's there, s running like they have an infant on their hip, bouncing her to quiet her as they always used to have to do, and telling her that night will be there soon and it would all be okay then.

At different times kids will drop out of the game to go and watch their real dead sister inside, hoping she'll wake up, even though their mom has explained, more than once, that she will never wake up again.

Rachel hears Hal's truck approach; it's hours since she called him.

'Stay off the driveway,' Rachel says to her kids, as she tosses tacks onto the blacktop of the drive.

Hal drives slowly alongside the house and up to the garage. Rachel meets him out back, and watches as he drives over the tacks. Hal sees them, but too late, and he swears and slams the car door.

He strides over and slaps her.

One or two of the kids gasp. Rachel takes the force of the blow, protecting her family behind her. He's just another person. She recovers and stands, looking like she'll simply take it, but it's a ploy and her punch comes out of nowhere. He absorbs the punch, touches his cheek in surprise. The air resolves.

'That's some hook you've got there.'

'I had lots of brothers.'

Their cheeks are on fire, neither has lost or gained ground, but now there's this between them. The tires deflate behind Hal.

'What the hell have you done, Rachel?'

'I'm making sure you stay home tonight.'

She wants to punch him again. And to fuck him. And to yell at him. And to be held and not have to say anything at all.

'She's dead, Hal. You didn't fix the gate.'

'You didn't hear her cry.'

'Neither did you.'

'That's not my job.'

'It sure as hell is.'

She has her hands balled into fists, at her hips. There could be a between them somehow, that slap and that punch, or a full scale ould be stirred up between them, and they have to choose. All of their kids have stopped playing behind them, standing still while the wind hasn't stopped but rather comes in gusts and eddies around and through the house and yard.

He has lengths of wood in the flat bed. There's neatly folded silk on the passenger seat too, a rich burgundy. She lets her hands open and soften, drop to her sides. 'That's just what I was thinking, we could make it ourselves.'

'That's why it took me longer.'

'You should have called.'

'I know. I should phone more. Be here more. Fix more.'

She touches his cheek, 'Let's not do that again.'

She looks at him, he's changed his shirt, has on clean jeans but his hair is mussed up, probably from driving with the window open. His eyes are red and his cheeks look dry. His eyes are sober. She should have looked at him, given him the benefit of the doubt.

'We've failed,' he says, 'you and me.'

She nods and he kisses her, a single long kiss and pulls her into his chest. He looks to their kids who start to play again in the yard. 'I failed you,' he whispers.

'She's inside,' she says and Hal goes over to each and every one of his children and hugs them, kisses both cheeks, hugs them again and goes into the house.

It's some time before he emerges again and when he goes to take the wood down to the basement, she asks him to do it in the yard. 'We hide none of this from them.'

He gives a plank to the oldest two and even the younger ones want to help, so he lets them hold onto an end each while he walks, hunched over, bearing the weight of the wood. And out back he builds the coffin for his daughter, the one he didn't protect.

Before bed the kids stand on the little stools in front of the bathroom sink and brush their teeth; Rachel climbs a ladder behind them and takes the stars off the ceiling of the bathroom. The youngest girls, the Corners, cry.

'We'll find a better place for them,' Rachel says, cupping them her palm, 'don't you worry.'

When they're done brushing their teeth, they all trail downstairs and press the stars into the inside lid of the coffin and Naomi lets it fall shut.

Rachel allows the kids to sleep wherever they like, in this bed and that, the wind still bellowing around them. Hal sits on the stairs and calls the police, the funeral parlor and the local newspaper but everybody already seems to know.

The Sheriff peers into the coffin, shakes the baby gently, being careful not to muss her up. 'I sure do wish you'd called sooner and not moved her from the scene,' says old Sheriff Bob, who keeps touching his face, wiping away a tear.

'My wife wasn't quite right, as you can understand. She wanted to get her ready.'

'I do. We never know how we'll react in these situations. It's not like you're in the habit of killing your kids, that much is clear.'

'So, are we square?'

'It's a domestic accident. Unavoidable. She's a young one, how did she get down there?'

'You'll not believe it, but she crawled.'

'Listen, I once found my eighteen-month-old son in a low branch of a small tree. I'll believe babies capable of just about anything.'

'I wish I'd known that. I'd have fixed the damned gate. I sure appreciate you coming out this late at night.'

'Give my best to your wife. I look forward to meeting her, hopefully under better circumstances.'

'I will, Bob. Sleep well, you hear.'

Rachel descends the stairs and she and Hal sit side by side, with the small coffin before them and the map needing attention. Together they paint Colorado a deep blue black, which they allow to dry, and then they paint a small family of stars. The hall is pitch black when they're done and they can only see each other. Rachel kisses him, ssses him to the wall off the eastern seaboard, and with a roughness that has never been between them, they fuck there until they are sore and bruised and there's room for nothing else but sleep.

Of course they can't drive to the funeral parlor the next day with all the truck's tires flat and it blocking the front of the garage where the station wagon is parked. Instead they walk, Rachel and Hal carrying the small casket between them, low so the kids can help. Rachel carries Utah on her back, and Hal carries Arizona, although she often wants to be put down so she can walk, like a big girl. Rachel, in her way, believes that this hands-on approach to the whole thing will mean it's resolved for the kids, for the family, because they can't change mistakes already made, they can't bring the dead back to life.

People of the town come out to their stoops to watch them pass. Later, in their houses, with the blinds snapped shut, they'll say what they think.

'She killed her daughter.'

'God's punishing him for his infidelity.'

'I hear it was one of the girls. Held her sister down into the water until she'd drowned.'

The Fremonts put Colorado in the ground in the new cemetery out behind the brick factory. They walk back home, singing songs of lonesome cowboys and lost loves that Hal conjures up from his childhood, when his brothers and him had to rake the whole yard. Rachel adds a few sailor's songs, island dirges, and when they get to the top of the hill, Hal barbeques burgers out back while Rachel makes potato salad and they wait until night falls to eat all together as a family on the grass underneath the stars.

Over the following weeks the Corners continue to talk to Colorado and include her in their games and conversations. Over the years it often seems as if they're asking her questions and as if they get responses too, and it's not something Rachel will question, because it seems to her to be a perfect way to deal with the whole thing.

She's got nothing, not in the bright sunlight, not during the lo[n]g nights she spends underneath the stars. Not with the wild ro[w] couplings between her and Hal. She hears nothing and cannot find the sleep she needs, the peace. Her daughter does not chastise her, nor does she forgive her. Cole is simply dead and the whole time Rachel knows she's pregnant again and that should be exactly the right thing but it's not and then one day Hal comes home, mid-afternoon, his arms all loose and difficult like he's been drinking, but Rachel doesn't believe it because Hal's not a drinker, not like that.

'Come and play with your pa,' he yells, 'come and play with your pa.' And Flo is bold and brings a Nerf football, and he throws it to her, without any coaching, and she misses it once, then twice, and then he uses her as a target practice.

'Hey!' Flo yells. 'Play nicely.'

'Play better,' Hal yells back. 'Play better.' And he slams the ball down on the ground and gets back into the car. Rachel hears nothing from him that evening. Nothing that night. Or the next day. Until the Sheriff pulls up to the curb the next evening with her finally sober husband sitting beside him in the passenger seat.

'He slept it off in a cell,' says Old Sheriff Bob, who is nearly eighty and long since past retirement age, as he hands her the keys to Hal's truck. 'It's only because of knowing his dad all those years that I didn't press charges for DUI. Keep a better rein on your man,' he says.

'I will Sheriff, I promise. Where can I get the truck?'

'What's left of it is in the salvage yard. He wrapped it around a telephone pole.'

She looks at Hal, who doesn't have a scratch on him. 'He's one lucky son of a bitch, that's for sure.'

'He sure is. Now Hal, this is twice in one week I've been up here, let's not make it a habit.'

She waits on the sidewalk while Hal gets out of the car and says thanks to the Sheriff, who then pulls away and swerves down the hill. Hal looks fragile and a bit broken but she doesn't care. 'I will not be married to a drunk. You've got a week to pull yourself together.'

He goes inside, takes the list off the basement door, and gets started. When he fixes the gate, Rachel sits inside and watches from upstairs window and she cries and cries.

About six weeks after Colorado's death, Rachel's alone in the garden (with the older kids at school, the younger kids napping) when she feels the cramp and the pull towards the earth and she lifts her skirt. As she hunches down, she weeps, mourning the state they've just lost. When Arizona and Utah start to cry for her to fetch them, she buries her failure, uses the garden hose to wash her thighs, and goes to take care of her kids. She is sore and empty and has no time to stop.

Hal does what he can, but the kids cry when he tries to get them dressed in the morning, refuse the food he attempts to make, and wait stubbornly for Rachel to take his place. One morning she hears him ask the mailman to watch the kids in the kitchen so he can go get one of the girls who is climbing up on the fence and not obeying his order to stay in the yard, but the mailman refuses to step over the threshold and into the house.

Her body heals enough and at night, she and Hal crash together in a wild, bruising way, like the punches they want to throw, but restrain themselves from landing. They are using their bodies to try to make it right and each time they crash together, bruise each other against walls and floors, when they separate they are knocked further apart. And when she falls pregnant again it's this desperate bid of her body to move on, to be able to use her body to move on.

The next miscarriage happens at the school gates, the stares of the townies and teachers and kids with such gossip twitching their lips. And her kids, such worry on their faces. Then that ambulance ride, the EMTs almost afraid to touch her, it seems. The third miscarriage takes her when she's down at Chick's hardware store, buying a new laundry line and a new shovel, and he is lovely and wraps her in his long coat and drives her to the hospital himself. A clutch of lost states. Nebraska? Illinois? Missouri? Oklahoma? She's given up part of herself freely, willingly, and finds now she will have to haul it back in thinly woven nets.

Slowly this heat between them tempers down, the sand stubbornly refuses to dissipate, and Rachel sits not pregnant, unable it seems to get pregnant, and knows that Hal will never have her in the same way again; he will never have all of her again.

BREAKING THE BANKS OF
THE MISSISSIPPI

Rivers bend and twist as they get older, like an old woman bent over holding her gnarled walking stick with knobbly, arthritic hands. We know why they do this, how they do this, like we know how storm clouds form and why earthquakes pound the earth together and shake it apart. Some people die, some rivers dry up, and those left behind, carry on. These kids had touched their dead sister, felt the weight of her in her small casket, and seen her into the ground. Every night she's in the skies above them, and her maps of stars and weather and brightly colored topographies arrive in their deep sleep and they learn to use them as guides and some of the kids still make room for her in their games, like she's growing up beside them. This is what some people do.

'Let's play ghosts in the graveyard,' Tex yells. 'You all be the ghosts, I'll catch you.' The girls squeal. As the Corners run away, Naomi holds out a hand, like there's a smaller girl running beside her.

'Hide behind the sandbox,' she tells her, 'he won't see you there.'

Tex glances past the fence at his dad's hat, just visible above the top of the hill. He's sitting out there in his travel chair just where the path starts to get steep, slick if it's been raining, searching for his stupid birds. Tex turns, faces the garage and starts to count backwards from twenty, his sisters dashing to find hiding places behind him. He takes quick peeks under his arm.

Hal watches the bird-less space before him, waits for some bird, any bird, to make it worthwhile. His thermos of coffee leans against the chair, his binoculars on his lap. In front of him, all is still; behind him, the kids play in the backyard, laughing. When he got home they didn't catch his hand and ask for him to be a horse, so he came down here on his own. Hal closes his eyes and waits for birdsong.

'Dinner! Lasagna all around,' Rachel shouts out to the kids and Hal's stomach rumbles. The screen door squeaks open and bangs shut a few times. A female cardinal flies towards then past him back towards the house and her nest. No child calls out to him, nor does Rachel. No child comes and hooks their hand into his. Not even that girl who every once in a while sneaks up to him and gives him a hug. He always tries to sit stock-still hoping she'll stay a bit longer, say something. But she slips away and it's hard to believe she's been there at all.

The sound of silverware on plates rouses him and he folds the chair and carries it in the crook of his elbow. He walks lightly, with only his son's company to look forward to, closes the gate carefully, and stops on the porch to lean the chair against the wall. Voices ring out from the kitchen.

'The best, Mom, absolutely the best,' says Flo.

A chorus of yums.

'Thanks, girls. Now pass that garlic bread.'

'Me first.'

'Just one piece at a time.'

'Do you want me to cut that up for you?' Flo offers.

'Please,' says one of the girls.

'Me too,' requests another.

'Of course, Utah.'

When he steps into the room, the voices stop. His face cycles from a smile to a grimace to a stern look to a small smile again. He doesn't know how to be, it's that simple.

'Smells good,' he says and in a handful of strides he's swinging open the door to the dining room. When he's left, the kitchen comes alive again.

'How small do you want your pieces?'

'This big.'

'Wow, that's almost big girls' pieces...'

Hal sits down with his dinner and his silent, stupid son in front of him and tries to do what he can to make the meal pass more quickly.

Only six kids, five now, and only one son with time passin them by. He chews, trying to remember them: Flo, the oldest; T of course, picking his nose; then the three girls, related some parched, chaotic. Arizona, one of them is Arizona, but the others blur, make him dizzy, clouded over. Even if he can't remember them, they're easier now that they're older, but he misses having an infant around, misses how content Rachel is when she's pregnant and nursing, misses that rare kind of quiet at night when everyone is asleep and how a newborn baby cries out, like a chick, calling for its mother.

Rachel has had three miscarriages. Each time he comes home and holds her while she weeps and he has to make a dinner that no one will eat. Once he had to change the clothes of a girl who wet her pants and Hal has to stop himself from getting annoyed at his wife. He's here, making it up to her, making it right, and she's not holding up her end of the bargain. At work, all builds have their problems, inevitable glitches, no matter how he plans ahead. But if the plans are flawed, or if he has to respond to the unexpected, he simply makes the changes and gets the job done. His family is nothing like that. He's been at home, he's been attentive, he's done everything on those stupid lists and still his house and his family are a mess.

He wants to fix this and he's awake with the need to take every chance he gets to make sense of it all. Like Goldilocks trying each bed, each bowl, he moves about his territory as it sleeps looking for signs he understands, for weaknesses he can fix.

He watches Rachel, his son, the map, the yard, the kitchen and even in the early morning hours the place rushes, thrums and is blurry. He rubs his chest to calm the start of an itch, rubs his eyes as they burn, and if he breathes slowly the mirage of what is before him slows to a heartbeat but again and again, just before it comes into focus sleep arrives and he collapses wherever he might be.

First thing each morning, as the sun rises, when the first child gets out of bed, the house boots him awake and he climbs into his truck and goes to work.

MYTHOCARTOGRAPHIES

With her belly empty, Rachel wakes with the house, the world outside barely lit by a weak sun. She's been dreaming of the nights when her Uncle Walt would wake her up to share his most recent cartographic acquisition. In the middle of the night, after an excursion to a mainland library, his hand would be cold on her foot as he shook her awake.

'Wake up, Rachel. Wake up. Look at what I have for you. This one is incredible. You won't believe the detail.'

Walt's cheeks were ruddy, hair wet from the sea-haar, his hands red from the effort of rowing, from the wind. He would slide the small parchment out from the cuff of his sleeve and together they'd pore over the map. Her favorite map was of the Mississippi, a Joliet original, delicate, stolen, hers.

Here and now she could go anywhere and she considers packing up her kids and driving a direct route to the ocean, but that's not a plan, that's quitting, and even as she thinks it the house gasps for breath like an asthmatic. She places a calming hand to a wall above the bed's headboard and whispers, *you're the home I've chosen.*

She grabs bunches of maps and books lying about her on the bed and goes down to the hall and spreads them out over that floor. She's been thinking a lot about the lines we make that are meant to mean something. A map isn't inclusive, but a selective interpretation, and never exactly as you expect it to be. This is what Rachel loves about maps: how they mislead, how everything you know cannot go into a map, how even the most detailed map can lead you astray if you're not paying attention.

They're stuck in the Four Corners, where between two layers of pressed rock—the tilted Precambrian and flat-lying Paleozoic—there's the thinnest fissure of absence where the geological proof of a billion years should be. A great unconformity. Unconformity defines the geological norm: pauses and absences around which we build the big picture out of little facts. Without proof, we only make educated guesses and geologists, like cartographers and archaeologists, are storytellers.

Their map just looks lopsided. Texas and the three Corners rise proudly in the west, Colorado falls away to absence, and Florida juts like a disappointed chin of an unnatural island in the southeast. The wall bulges, the distance between these disparate states growing irreconcilable.

Standing at the edge of the desert looking at the plains, the continental divide at her back, she looks in all directions, up to the sky, and lastly her gaze turns inwards and she decides her destination. She moves in closer, runs her hands over the gulf states. The South. Humidity so thick it'll drip from her skin and gather in pools at her collarbone. Redoubtable rivers, tides and black water. Taking her time, letting herself imagine a hundred different journeys, Rachel seeks out the rivers which will take her where she's decided to go. And slowly, for there's no way to do this but travel there, on foot and by boat, mile by mile, she follows the Arkansas River through Colorado, Kansas, Oklahoma and Arkansas until she arrives at the sorrowful, powerful Mississippi and steers herself and her family down this river to the wide heart of her next daughter.

❦

THE SOUTH

HEAT

On a crisp September morning, Rachel sheds her obligations to marital fidelity and the men of the town know it. Rachel wears a fertile air like perfume at her wrists, along the smooth line that runs from her shoulder to her neck, dancing at the tips of her hair, and slung like low Levi's on her hips.

She walks down the back staircase that leads into the kitchen, the mock slave stairs the father-in-law she'd never met had built, and the doorbell rings as it does every day. She pauses and listens to the squeak of the front door swinging open. Alan the mailman stands there, his loose dusty red hair falling down over his face as he separates the Fremonts' letters from the rest of his route. He keeps his flushed face down, holds the letters low near his hips to hide the fact he wants something he's never been able to hope for before and he can't let her know it. But Rachel knows, has willed it to be so. She notes that his weak jaw, will, most likely, be the sort that skips a generation.

Rachel puts one hand round the back of Alan's neck, and the other in the curve of his lower back. Letters scatter. She leads him through the hall and into her own domain where she fucks him on the kitchen floor. All the words he has never understood make sense, wild vistas charge at him, she highlights the ridges, the valleys of his skin with her finger. Alan is not skilled, but as he realizes she will not laugh, will not pull away, he eases into his own way of making love to a beautiful woman.

He is nothing like Hal. That's what she notices. He smells sweeter, is sweeter, gentler. Her body is at peace; her mind is in battle. Hal did this with Sandra. Countless times. Gave in to a different desire. This is survival. She's moving them forward, her and Hal, the family. Maybe she'll even have another son. Love is infinite, it's this ocean and she's in the middle of it, deep water to all horizons.

Years from now she'll realize, toes tipped off the end of a pier her hand held by a child yet to be conceived much less born, that the very instant she and Alan go at it on the kitchen floor, that

ELIZABETH REEDER

unconsidered and uncontrollable disappointment, small as an atom
splitting, unnoticed as the first fleck of dust which settles after spring
cleaning (and as quiet), comes into existence and works its way into
the gears of her family. It's at this moment that their dream changes
so irrevocably that it could no longer be considered to be in the
likeness of anything or the seeking to recreate anything.

It's simply gathered, residual speed which propels her forward
from this point and out into the future. Over and over: adaptation,
failure, and hope. She is not just one thing, she is many: not just
the daughter of Roanoke, not just Rachel Fremont, or Mama, or an
incomer in this bizarre mid-American backwater; she is everything
at once, and just herself, losing things, getting lost.

All too soon she leads Alan back to the front door, and he walks
over water he'd never noticed before, brushing his hand, unwittingly,
over the place on the wall that will become the state he's just helped
to create. Rachel touches a finger to his lips in a redundant gesture.
He will keep their indiscretion to himself and deliver the mail for
years after, hoping for the same powerful touch, the salty rocking of
her body.

Together they gather the dropped letters from the hall floor and
he never again feels he has permission to approach her with more
than the day's mail.

A turning in the air beckons Hal home early. The house has become
clear and free, easy to breathe in and the hall smells of fresh cut grass
and open skies. Something expected of him is no longer demanded.
When he stands in the doorway to the kitchen, the children pull
at him and annoy him as usual. It's not them that have changed,
it's Rachel.

'Good evening honey, if you want a shower there's plenty of hot
water for you.'

She kisses him and that night she accepts him into her arms.
After, as she sleeps soundly, her face unlined, her questions answered,
e realizes she's managed to get rid of all that goddamn sand.

THE BOOK CLIFFS

Glenda, the librarian, watches the woman walk through the doors as they slide open for her and the children that surround her. The Fremont woman, it must be. She carries a girl, who looks to be about four years old and two other girls walk beside her. When she sets the girl down, the child runs for freedom, head tilted up. She takes in everything like it's the Grand Canyon at dawn, the Louvre at dusk, the Atlantic Ocean after midnight under a full moon. She walks up to the biggest shelf, reaches on tip-toes, pulls down a book, glances at the cover, and drops it to the floor, letting it fall open. A rock falling from a book cliff. She sees the exposed pages, pauses, and then she pulls another, and another, from the shelf. She gathers speed, running, books are objects to be used, bent, folded, fingered, written in, useful, used as doorstops, as pillows, everyday items of amazement, revelations, usefulness. Her mother seems taken by surprise, perhaps curious, and stands watching her daughter.

Glenda is charmed by this girl who is gleefully propelled by some inner force of curiosity and mischievousness to create havoc. Glenda has often had the urge to do exactly as this child is doing, and so she is jealous too.

Hearing the commotion, Sue, the junior librarian, comes from the sci-fi section pushing a metal cart, notices the mass destruction wrought by the Fremont girl and shouts at Rachel, 'Why don't you watch your kids? They're savages. People who can't handle the kids they have should be prevented from having more.'

'Utah, honey. Come to Mama.' Rachel encourages the girl towards her with the promise of a hug. Utah drops the books and stands with her arms straight at her side, rigid, and she cries. She cries like she's been cut open, like she's hungry.

Rachel moves forward, scoops her up. Holds her tight. Her sisters too. Glenda feels such a thirst, almost dizzy with it.

'It's okay, honey. It's okay,' says the mother.

The book girl cries. She cries and what she knows is nothing. It's a bare, stark fact.

Glenda watches on. So this is Rachel Fremont. She's never actually seen her before. Why does no one talk about her beauty, the clarity of her eyes? How even when she's on bent knees held, pulled by, completely aware of everything her kids do, she remains herself?

Sue smashes books onto the cart. 'Travesty. Travesty. There'll be a fine for this one. A fine. Do you understand the importance of these? Do you get it? Do you even have a library card?' She pushes the cart into Rachel, who leans a little with the shove, but resists. 'Get out, get out now.'

Glenda pushes the cart back with a firm hand.

'Sue, why don't you take your break?' Glenda says, bending and gathering the books. She puts a hand on Rachel's back. 'Take your time Mrs Fremont, all the time you need. These will be waiting for you at the counter.'

Glenda's palm is dry in an instant. Where is her moisturizer? Her thirst deepens. She goes to the back and makes herself a cup of tea. She splashes one towards Sue, out of habitual courtesy, and brings a mug to the counter for Rachel.

Glenda has four kids of her own, eleven grandkids, and knows that a full nest like Rachel's speeds towards empty and takes your will with it, and with that in mind, she gathers a few extra books and puts them on the counter.

The girls have calmed down, Rachel takes a sip of the tea and tells them a story. It's not one Glenda knows: 'There once was a girl, a pretty girl who looked a bit like you,' she pulls them closer. 'She'd left home too young and floated on rivers, past the world, in her handmade boat called a coracle, a round boat she made out of the trunk of a tree. She floated past islands of cedar trees, past waving prairies, all the way to rugged burning bluffs and cobalt fields of mist. She couldn't ride through the mountains so she hid her boat behind a tree, climbed the mountains, and then built a new coracle on the other side. She traveled down the Columbia River all the way to California. She was sixteen, alone, and had found her way by following a map her uncle had stolen from a library, which could have looked like the one we're in now. And although that's wrong to do, stealing, she loved that map because it reminded her of him. She kept the map wrapped in plastic and stuffed down the back pocket of her jeans. It was a wildly imaginative map, the best Meriwether could do.'

'Who is Meriwether?' one girl asks.

'Meriwether Lewis of Lewis and Clark, the best explorers this continent has seen. This girl used the map, and her own smarts to travel the rivers to the ocean. She did this because all rivers yearn, like she did, for the sea. And she made it to the Pacific Ocean, to the coast with an open view, wide as the eye could see to the west horizon.'

'Wow, all that way on her own?'

'Was she happy?' another asks.

'Maybe. Yes. But she didn't have everything she needed; she was looking for something and she'd not found it yet, the sea wasn't enough.'

'What was she looking for?'

'Scrumptious little daughters, a whole bunch of them. Just like you.' She squeezes her daughters tight, pretending to nibble their cheeks and ears, and they squeal. 'Okay girls. Let's get ourselves home. Get some lunch into you.'

Glenda has made up library cards for each of the girls and one for Rachel and is ready when the Fremonts approach the desk.

'I can order books too,' she says.

Rachel nods. 'Thank you.'

'There's no limit on those cards, none at all,' says Glenda.

Rachel puts the books into a shopping bag and slips the bag over her shoulder. The three girls hold hands and they all walk to the car.

Behind Glenda, a rustle of air announces Sue's return from her break. Air through teeth, a tire deflating, a snake on the prowl. 'Do you believe that woman? Do you believe it?'

'Yes, I do,' says Glenda. 'I believe she's got her hands full with those girls.'

'It's not right,' says Sue, 'not right at all.'

'That's where I disagree with you. It's not only right, it's perfect.' Glenda runs her hands along the counter out from her body. 'What you feel there Sue, that's jealousy.'

She could blind you, that's for sure, that kind of beauty, you either want to screw it, or screw it over. Glenda's been listening and the Fremont woman fills the local gossiping hags with jealousy, their men with desire. Some women too must feel something tender and sweet low down when Rachel passes by, no doubt. Glenda's no small-minded, small-town girl, she's got Manhattan in her blood, raised by Dan and Tim (and Donna their live-in maid and social cover-up) in the Upper East Side. Both gone now, of course, and she's ended up too far from where she came from. Maybe that'll change. But it'd be hard to leave Richard behind and he won't be going anywhere, resting six foot under as he is. Her daughters have begun pressing her to move to Vermont, and she's been tempted. But she's not ready. She's still strong, clear-headed, and she's not keen on the babysitting either. She'll wait until the grandkids are older.

She taps her pencil eraser side down on the counter. The sound is muted while her eyes are sharp. Thirty-seven years and the dirt under her nails is this place; the library started with cut-price, overstock books from city bookstores decades ago. The oxygen through her lungs holds corn and she always knows when a storm is coming long before the clouds darken. The only birds she knows are the ones she sees out the library windows, the glass doors. She knows it, this place, it's in her and she looks like a native.

Rachel though, she'll never be able to pretend to be from this place and lets everyone know it with those names. As if she and that husband of hers had to shout it: *This place is not worthy. This place is not enough! This place is not good enough! We're not from here.*

Of course they could be saying something else, like, *remember there's a whole, wild world out there and isn't it good to be home.*

This town could be named Fremont. Sure, some old-timers mumbled complaints about Hal's buildings, begrudge him his success, and then there are the things not spoken about openly but aired by dovetailing wooden boards together and staking them in the ground in backyards to serve as focal points at private picnics. Or there's the looping of ropes over branches in jest or warning. Yes, he's son to this town, whether they'll admit it or not.

Hal will never be able to leave, even if he considers it. Which she's sure he doesn't: they'd have gone by now if it was a real option. Stubborn, like his old man. Smarter and just as numb-skulled. 'He'll never be able to leave,' Glenda says it out loud, under her breath, as her and Sue watch the Fremonts pack themselves into their station wagon.

'Who?' asks Sue.

'That fool of a husband of mine. Dead and buried years before his time and why? Sheer stupidity and now he'll never be leaving this place.'

'May he rest in peace,' says Sue as she crosses herself. 'And who'd want to leave anyway?'

LOUISIANA

Louisiana is a wide, contested land, a tidal place exposed to violent and inexorable change. A place where the dead don't stay below ground without concrete coaxing; lies don't stay buried either. When things go wrong the whole world knows it.

Rachel is tired and in need of a rest, of redemption, and her arrival in Louisiana does not bode well. As the land becomes more populated, it's harder to see just the land and not the poisons, the wars, the human mistakes set upon it. It's a state so at risk that she finds herself facing the amorphous wetlands coast and walking backwards to higher ground.

What you aim for, what you hope for, is not what you get. Lines on a map do not prepare you for what really is. The wide water breaks up the land as it becomes the ocean, the oil fields break the water-horizon with their platforms, and the power plants eat through the earth, punching the sky with their stacks and curling smoke. In a field of battle that used to be a gathering of trees, the ground is burnt by the summer sun, and Rachel stands among the stumps and around her is only grief, only the stillness after battle.

Rachel glances over her shoulder towards the Corners and sees ancient people building dwellings, places of worship, and intricate and instructive roads of travel and trade. She sees a people surviving and then, when that wasn't challenging enough, they slaughtered each other in the houses they'd built, burning the evidence. They often couldn't protect their own and it's a place not much different from where she is now.

Every night Lou takes her to brooding, vibrant places. People cram in, breath on her neck, bodies press against her, hot, thick like the air she breathes, all this want, this desire. She feels sweet and low all the time. Even now color doesn't spare her, doesn't take anything away from her, she wants it all voraciously. The river doesn't satisfy like she'd hoped, nor does the coast, and the city is wild. Wide rowdy crowds fill the streets and she's twirled and swung and romanced and she lets herself go, accepts beads and catches men in the lasso of her own, her hips are liquid and solid, dark alley couplings, temporary beds drawn against walls, slow meetings as dirges pass outside seedy rooms, rude couplings in clean white mansions, intimacies among the unmarked land where bodies have fallen and are buried, and many of these meetings are more like rituals, more like grieving.

She cries out as she dreams and slides over on top of Hal, her eyes smooth with sleep and believes he's someone else.

One trimester surges into another and on towards the final date. The world is so much larger than she ever imagined. Those maps of Walt's were just a start. In one book, she finds over a hundred maps of how the land switched hands between union and confederate, so many battles and on each page a simple number in the upper right hand corner chronicles the total number of people dead in each battle— some fighting for freedom, some for slavery, some for profit.

She's full, huge. This baby brings her color. As the contractions start, Lou places her among a funeral procession. It's hard but she doesn't flinch. On one woman's face, a mother like herself, the tears are easy, a solid flow, and she walks slowly, with her back straight and shoulders easy. This is something she bears, something she carries.

This is life. The history of dying is shared; the history of hardship is shared.

Rachel's wide here, her borders are mercurial, her needs unresolved. Music, all the time song, and she watches the bodies in the fields, the black men and women mourning their dead in sparse woods behind a big house, escaping through tunnels. Creole through everything, and before that original land, original people, incomers, poverty, migrants, the birds flying south in winter, north in spring, passing through, blessing the land, blessing those who bother to look up, who listen for the calls of rare birds, not of this place, but those who call it home for moments in time, who call out and give the space above this troubled land beauty.

Hal has been spending more nights working at the office. So when Rachel calls him and says, 'Louisiana,' he picks her up and drives her to the hospital. But the next child is slow to enter the world and Rachel tells him to go home. Which he does and it's in a rushed, single flourish that he makes the next state. The coast is rough and looks like it's in a state of flux, vulnerable to acts of nature.

Gathering his growing family together, he mounts the new state on the wall, scraping an edge of it up to its nearest neighbor, Texas. As he tests the borders and name of the new state, kids buck and elbow and harangue each other behind his back. When he turns, ready to glue Louisiana to the wall, he expands his chest and the melee of voices fall quiet enough so he can be heard:

'Hey kids. This is Louis. Your new brother and you will have lots in common. This next one will be a boy. I feel it in my waters.'

But Hal's waters are shallow and murky. He waits for the babysitter and then he goes to the hospital, asks a nurse, who says, 'another girl,' and Rachel's asleep when he stops at the door. He disentangles the little football rattle from the bunch of flowers he's brought and puts them, unadorned, into the vase beside the bed. He leans over and kisses Rachel, 'You've done good.' Then he kisses the forehead of the little girl lying in the bassinet, who is cute enough, and he drives home.

In the empty hall, Hal tips the wooden chair against the opposite wall and stares at his map. Then he waves his free hand vaguely (the other holds a local amber bourbon), his voice growing ever so slightly less enthusiastic with each girl who arrives, and says to no one in particular, to no one at all in fact, 'There you go, that's you up on the wall.'

It doesn't give him the same rush it used to.

AUDUBON

'Louisiana, this is your father. Hal, meet your daughter.'

Hal winces slightly but knows that soon enough she'll take the baby away again. He holds her away from his body and she's still, warm, light in his arm. He looks down. This girl has long dark lashes that flutter, with a tint of red to her brown hair, a broad line for a nose, and a bold sweep of a birthmark on her arm, like she's ready to take to flight. She had been restless at first, but now she's asleep. He pulls his arm in closer, runs a finger along her cheek, tucks the thin blanket around her bird-like body. He walks her through the house and out the door. He takes her to the edge of the yard and she frees her arm and flaps it like a delicate wing. The sun moves across the afternoon sky. When she starts to cry, he imitates a cuckoo and she quietens. It's some time later when Rachel comes to take her back inside. 'She needs to be fed,' she says. The girl cries in Rachel's arms and when she's done feeding her, she brings the girl back to Hal and together they fall asleep in a lawn chair, under the warmth of a blanket.

In future years, amidst the clatter of the house, the clambering demands of Rachel, and the quieter pressures of his mistress Sandra, and with the other children arriving, growing ever louder, the only one who Hal will spend time with easily is Lou; she loves the birds and silence. In those early years, she will take his hand and lead him all the way down to the creek and together they'll watch the seasons change, birds migrate, passing back and forth, and he and Lou will grow into each other's company, drinking hot chocolate and eating cold cheese sandwiches placed unwrapped in an Audubon lunch box. Lou, in her silence, allows him to leave the house and its faults clear out of sight.

Sometimes they'll go for longer walks and she'll want to go out on her own, exploring, and he'll let her go. Watching over her, while pretending not to. When they turn towards home again, in the failing light, he never leaves her floundering in the muddy path. She won't always let him hold her hand, but he never, ever, leaves her without knowing how she'll get home safely.

Lou's red hair shocks the skilled gossips, but without too much fuel the rumors don't travel far or well. Startling and unavoidable different physical attributes will start with the eighth child, Missy, and will continue right up through the last, Ginny. The girls—short and tall, lean and chubby, green-eyed and brown-eyed, skin brown to less brown, athletic and curvy, in no particular order or combination— certainly do not seem to be within the normal genetic swing of a faithful two-parent family.

No one will want to say anything, but the paternity of some of the children most certainly looks to be in doubt.

ON THE ROAD TO THE GRAND CANYON

'Miss Arizona Fremont! Stop running amok in the house.'

'Amok? I'm running very neatly,' Ari replies, deadly serious, 'out that door.'

'Dragging Utah with you?' Rachel queries.

'Uh-huh.'

'Come here Ari.'

Ari drops Utah's hand, and swaggers towards her mom. Before that day Rachel would not have believed that a five-year-old could swagger. 'Bring Utah too.' Ari turns on a dime, takes her sister's hand and yanks her forward. Utah looks surprised, windblown and ecstatic.

'Look at your sister's face.'

Ari peers. She takes her hands and runs them over Utah's smooth features and gives her sister a hidden thumbs up.

Utah grins.

'You didn't see it a minute ago, in motion,' Rachel counters. 'She was terrified.'

Rachel watches Utah try to choose sides between her reliable mother and her thrilling, demonic sister. Her eyes shine and twinkle like gyroscopes catching the sun. On seeing this daring in Utah, Rachel moves on. 'And what about little Lou? If you run, you might trample her right underfoot.'

'I won't mom. I'm careful.' Ari stamps her foot to make her point and the jostled floorboard shakes Utah like Jell-O. Utah grins.

'I've watched you, you're wild.' Rachel tries to keep her face stern but she can't quite manage it; she loves her firecracker of a child. A small smile bunches her cheeks and Ari sees it, a pride of sorts. 'I mean it, Ari. Don't give me any of your cheek. Do not run in the house. Do what you like in the yard, but you will walk in my house.' Rachel turns to get the laundry from the machine.

Naomi rushes around the corner, a bag slung over her shoulder, her dark eyes stormy and wild.

'We're going to the Grand Cayman,' blurts out Utah. Rachel turns back and crouches so she's on the toddler's level.

'Canyon,' whispers Ari despite herself, then, 'shhhh.'

But Utah is on a roll, she is going where the night is a huge sheet stretched across the sky, where they can prick holes and make up their own constellations. Ari promised. 'We're running away.'

'You are, are you? Today? My little a-mazement wants to leave me?'

'Uh huh,' Utah says, less sure with the hug and kiss her mom plants on her.

Flo walks in carrying Lou and notices the hobo sacks slung over Ari and Naomi's shoulders, 'Going on a trip?'

'We're going to the,' Utah pauses, looks at Ari, 'Grand…Canyon.'

'We mean it,' Ari insists. 'We're going to the desert.'

'We're going to find Cole,' states Naomi.

'We're going to swim in the sky. Big dives, Ari promised. She promised.'

'I know you mean it,' says Rachel, kissing Ari, then Naomi, 'but you might need to wait until your thumb is big enough for passing cars to take notice.'

'What?'

'We'd miss you if you went,' says Flo, casting her mother an exasperated look. 'You need to build your strength up for a journey as long as that. You need to be able to survive in the desert for weeks at a time. You hadn't thought of that, had you?'

Ari balls her fists.

'Well, you can make yourself strong by running.'

'You could take Utah to the end of the block, in a circuit.'

'A circuit?'

'It's when you run and jump and climb in a circle. It's a form of training,' says Rachel.

'But just make sure you get back for dinner, you'll need to keep your strength up, by eating right,' adds Flo.

Utah reaches up and takes her sister's hand and they proceed out the door. Once on the driveway, and then the sidewalk, they drop hands and let their arms flail freely as they run.

'There'll be lemonade here for you when you get home,' Rachel shouts after them.

UPSETTING THE NEST

It's called a playground. Enclosed on three sides with a fence, a padlocked entrance on the southeast corner with the red-bricked building on the fourth side, all exits blocked by teachers who have no sympathy for the Fremonts who keep appearing at the school.

Three times a day the school empties its bowels of various combinations of 104 kids and then traps them there in the square like a boxing ring. At least that's how eight-year-old Tex sees it. The bell rings and they stampede out. Tex tries to climb over the fence towards freedom, but his feet get caught in the twisted metal; a sharp tear of pain as he cuts his hand on the filed metal on the top. No escape.

His face becomes a punch bag, tight and new. His baby-fat stomach gives way beneath the punches, like a loose and lumpy pillow.

The McCrae brothers, the Lowell gang (Cindy, Joe, little K), Tom Quint, Sarah Ryerson, Jake Martin… the list of people who torture Tex grows longer each year. Today it's Tom Quint in a clean challenge and fist-fight, their classmates forming a circle and cheering on the stronger of the two.

Flo watches from the window: it is all she can do, trapped in history class with the angelic-looking but mean as a dog Mrs Pearson. She's been trying to protect her brother more often, because it's clear he can't protect himself. Mrs Pearson refuses Flo's three polite requests to go to the washroom and orders Flo to sit in the corner, believing Flo's mother (that Fremont whore) to have slept with her husband, Mr Pearson—owner of Sharp's Butchers and long time Rolling Stones fan—last February. Mrs Pearson believes that taking out such adult issues on children is perfectly justifiable.

The town doctor's child sits in the other back corner with a dunce cap after his mother provided a most unfortunate misdiagnosis last week.

'Debbie,' Dr Simpson had said, 'you are a hysterical,' Dr Simpson didn't like to use that word, but it was the most concise and effective word in this instance, 'hypochondriac with a paranoid streak which you will need to watch before you outcast your whole family. This,' she continued, holding up Mrs Pearson's offending foot, 'is simply nothing more than a nail with the habit of needing to be trimmed. It does not need, nor will I provide, surgical removal because it is not ingrown, it is simply growing.'

Mrs Pearson looks out over her class of fourth graders and curses all people willing to dismiss the pain of others. Damn it if that toenail didn't ache this morning, and if gangrene wasn't waiting around the corner, and damn it if that whore's daughter didn't want special privileges with the bathroom, and what is that sound coming from the playground? And damn it all if someone isn't going to pay for her pain.

If Mrs Pearson had realized that Dr Dorothy Simpson and her own husband, Ted I'll-get-you-the-meat-you-need Pearson, had found a topic of mutual interest at a PTA subgroup meeting, in this very room of all places, and a long discussion—with subtle eye contact and brushing of hands with other hands—had followed and that they are now in the midst of a torrid affair, well, if Mrs Pearson had realized this then, really, the whole class would have been damned; there just wouldn't have been enough dunce caps and maybe luck would have been with Flo, for Mrs Pearson would have shooed them all out the door and onto the busy street outside, yelling, 'Dodge them if you can!'

Flo is distracted by her brother being beaten to a pulp outside the window. Her name floats up in Tex's barbed wire voice, and the class turns to her, or those who can lean out the window to watch the ugly piece of bullying taking place on the blacktop. Flo never does learn the finer details of the Battle of Natchez, not that Mrs Pearson is particularly forthcoming, distracted as she is by people failing to recognize the pain of those who didn't write the histories. 'And what about the women of war! What about them? Just left behind that's what. Feeding the kids, taking care of everything. Where are the books about them?'

At the final bell, Flo races out to the school gates and waits for Tex. She clenches and unclenches her fists, but the bullies walk by, having had their fill. Tex limps out, his face starting to swell, his knuckles fresh and unscathed because he never even fought back.

'Oh Tex. Just swing your arms, you're bound to hit something.'

'I can't, Flo. I want you on the playground at the same time as me!' His demand catches in his throat like a whimper.

'I can't be there. You know that. Our classes are out there at different times in this rotation. And you know Mrs Pearson.' She twirls her finger by the side of her head, rolls her eyes.

'She didn't call you the tramp's offspring did she?' Tex says, giggling despite his pain, wincing as the smile smarts his split lip.

'Not today, she had poor Kevin Simpson, "that charlatan quack's mistake of judgment", stuck in the corner. She just didn't let me out of the room.' Flo doesn't tell Tex how her stomach flipped and churned through history when she could not escape. How she'd have climbed out of the window, if there hadn't been bars on it. She takes his chin in her hand, moving it side to side, 'It's not so bad today.' She hands him a cold can of cola, bought for this purpose, and he places it gently against his cheek.

'Thanks, Flo.'

'You're welcome.' The hill stretches before them.

'Race you!' Flo says. 'Up the hill and up the tree.'

'You're on,' Tex shouts back, seeing as he'd already started to run. And knowing he needs bolstering, Flo runs, giving him a good race, arriving at the tree just before him, in order to give him the fast side of the tree, the easy oak, which he notes but doesn't question. He climbs for his life, he beats her up to the usual limb. Beats her! Whooping, whooping, swinging his legs for a minute, his hips loose and warm, his bandaged hand an asset, like a glove. He is high, higher than he's been before and, emboldened by victory, he climbs further.

'Tex, be careful.'

'I win!'

'Yes, you win. We can get down now.'

'You can, wimp. Not me.'

Small twigs and dry grass whistle and waft to the ground. A nest holds up, but just barely, under the strain of his quick assent and nervous jerkings. Tex doesn't even hesitate, just a bird's nest.

'Tex, the robin's nest. Be careful!' Flo shouts, hearing their dad's pickup in the drive.

Tex climbs to a thinner branch, just strong enough to hold his weight. His triumphant eyes survey his kingdom; his realm is grand, but tiny, from this high and he notices how small Flo looks standing at the base of the tree, her face concerned. Legs swing and hands cling. High. He is too high. Pain spikes down his legs, his hands cramp, cold creeps into his bones. The sun hits his face, but does not warm him, and the house sways from side to side or maybe it's the tree, one gust away from collapsing. So soon it'll be night, and he knows that it will fall fast, unsympathetic to his predicament.

'Flo, Flo, help me. Flo! Flo.'

'Get in the house,' Hal barks at his daughter, then he looks at his disgrace of a son. 'Help your mother with dinner.' Tex holds on tighter and looks down.

'Dad, I'll get the ladder. I'll help him down.'

'You'll do no such thing.'

'It'd be easy,' Flo persists.

'Flo! Dad!' Tex clings with one hand and waves the other. The robin's nest teeters and an egg tips out. Breaking on the big branch lower down, a small viscous bit of yolk falls onto Hal's shoulder.

Hal speaks loudly, words directed at Flo, voice directed at the top of the tree. 'He got himself up there and he'll need to find a way down.'

Hal stays outside, sitting in his chair, watching the creek and its sparse birds until dinner is ready. The birds make this house a homestead: the bullying jay, the summer hummingbird, and the reliable robin, precarious nest and all.

Tex, his gormless son, perched high in the tree, clutches at a branch above and shudders with his fear and the evening cold coming in. Surely any son of his should be able to get down under his own steam. Surely Hal won't have to help him down.

Surely.

Hal eats alone in the dining room, stoical, remembering other days, before Tex, when he'd eaten with Rachel, lovely meals of sex and sunsets augmented by the occasional feast of food.

Night falls. Metal utensils clink in the kitchen, round faces at the window watching him. Naomi's hands soothe the air in front of her and the sky remains cloudless, the wind calms.

Tex hears feet round the base of the tree. In the dusk he can't be sure who, or what, it is. Then he hears little Ari's clear whisper:

'Tex, it's easy. Use your hands, turn around and then find places to put your feet, like climbing down a ladder. You got up, you can get down.'

What is she, five or something? He can definitely do anything she can do. But when he tries to turn around, his body and the whole tree shake like it is the end of the world.

When Hal goes outside after dinner, another egg lies shattered on the ground. He knows there are two more up in the nest waiting to be knocked out by his witless son, and so it is for the birds, not for his weakling son, that he tips the ladder against the tree and holds its base.

'Get down you bird-killing fool.'

And Tex knows that even if he is prized above the others, he has still been stuck in the tree like a stupid kitten, until night fell. He understands, for the first time, that he is dispensable, and if not replaceable (even he understands that his mother will never have another son), regrettable. He can still get things wrong. He can still be punished.

THE NEXT ONE

Hal has been ignoring the state of the roof since the beginning. He loves heights, but to be honest, simply has too much work to take on a big job like that. Such a boring job, nothing like the pelican porch he is building for the Williamsons on the east side of town, or building the school annex. Rachel hounds him and, eventually, Hal sends his best roofer to sort it. Ken Ishikawa arrives first thing in the morning and gets to work, sometime, perhaps, late afternoon. For a quick worker, he sure knows when to take his time. Rachel appreciates a man who can linger on the finer points, be clear about the details.

He takes her up to the roof from which she can view her twenty acres, 'It's not very pretty is it?' he says.

'No, not very.'

'But it'll do.'

'Yes,' she says, 'it'll have to be enough.'

Their affair lasts the exact length of time it takes him to re-roof and gutter the house.

Seven months into the resulting pregnancy and it's sunrise on a school day. Rachel sees an early summer storm and goes to meet it, leaving the kids at the breakfast table under Flo's watchful eye. The storm races in and it downpours onto her hair, her shoulders, the ground; the cloud giving itself up to the earth.

Shirley used to always call her in when the rain came on, called her most strongly when she had the least likelihood of returning. 'I can never see you when you're out in the rain, you disappear out there, it makes me nervous.'

Rachel's arms run with water, her t-shirt and jeans are soaked through, and she wonders if she's invisible out here. As the cloud tries to pass her house, it lingers as if it can read her desire, but eventually clear sky pushes the rain on down the hill and Rachel cannot follow.

'Come on guys, let's start the day!'

Rachel packs Flo, Tex and Naomi in the rear-facing seat of the station wagon for easy disposal at the school. Ari and Utah, just shy of school-age, sit in the back seat and one-year-old Lou is in her car seat beside Rachel.

At the school gates Tex rolls out of the back like a storm losing its identity, blows his mother a kiss and waits, out of necessity, for his sisters. Flo climbs out and then helps Naomi. They both clasp clean hands around Rachel's neck and kiss her. Turning towards the red brick entrance, its low glass doors flanked by teachers, Flo takes Naomi's hand and Tex walks beside her. She deposits Naomi in kindergarten, squeezes her hand and puts the other out, palm up, for her sister's payment for safe passage (a rusty barrette), then drops Tex off and makes her way to her own class, eating the apple he's given her.

Rachel shoves the door shut and the car rattles. Today her children seem bright and clear. Flo's jaw has lost some of her baby-fat, her face finally growing into her attitude. Rachel pulls away from the school and when she turns the corner her boat of a car rolls into the stream of traffic.

The grocery store is busy and she has to park in the outskirts of the parking lot. Halfway to the door she finds a cart, places Lou into the seat, reminding her gently not to kick her mama's stomach. Ari and Utah hold hands and she wonders how long the peace will last. Not long, she thinks, because when she looks up she sees Sandra, childless, free and easy, husband romancer, abstract artist, occasional midwife, walking towards her with an easy earth-mother grace. Rachel braces herself.

'A beautiful morning, Rachel,' Sandra says, placing a light hand on Rachel's arm as she passes. Her skin is smooth and small light lines make her eyes bright when she smiles a smile that is easy and generous. Rachel's arm is warm with her touch.

'Yes, it is,' says Rachel. Both women have slowed and turned towards each other. Rachel steps out from behind the cart, her round belly proud and vulnerable.

'May I?' Sandra asks, holding her palms forward at waist level. Rachel should say no but instead nods, almost shy. The mistress places her hands on Rachel's belly. The veins of her strong, bony hands pulse.

'She's a quiet one. Isn't she? Bright though.'

Rachel smiles. The baby flips in her belly.

'Perhaps not quite as quiet as I first thought.' Both women laugh. Sandra's laughter is full and clear, like a tiny source of fossil water. 'And these girls? Are they peas in a pod?'

'Absolutely not. These three,' Rachel places her hand on each Corner's head in turn, 'these two dry like the desert, and this one,' Rachel reaches back over the cart to ruffle Lou's red hair, 'she's got hands dangerous as a swamp.' Each of the girls fight to be the one who reaches up and uses her arm as a trapeze. Bending her elbow, she swings each Corner in turn and then gently rubs Lou's leg.

'You're very lucky. Motherhood is not something I could do, and definitely not with the grace you've got. Good luck with the next one.'

Rachel flushes, at ease when she should be uncomfortable, pleased with attention she should shun. 'Thank you.' Sandra pulls her into a hug, presses her cheeks one then the other to Rachel's.

'You girls, look after your mom, right?' The Corners nod and gather around Rachel's legs as Sandra moves beyond the cluster of Fremonts and on towards her car.

A few more strides and Rachel pushes her cart through the entrance without ill-will. She chooses her groceries and as she places each item in the cart she leans and brushes her hand against a girl's cheek, wipes a nose, answers a question. Rachel reaches up on tiptoe—for although she is always perceived to be tall she's just average height and still has to stretch for items on the top shelves—to reach for a box of steel wool. The box is just beyond her reach and her pots will, this week, just have to be cleaned with a bit more elbow grease.

'Slut! Slut! Slut! Slut!' The words come right at Rachel, bunching up like sonar against something solid.

The woman's skinny tongue flicks through her teeth on the L as she stands there, ribs jutting out, blocking Rachel's way. Lou sits in the seat, Arizona grasps the thin metal sides of the cart, and Utah stands like a hood ornament in front. Arizona calmly replaces Lou's pacifier and then all three girls look at their mother, for there can be no doubt who the shout is aimed at.

Mrs Reverend John Boyle stands before them, posturing with her chin and chest out and calling Rachel a slut in front of her children.

'Stay away from my husband!'

People can't get past, given the bulk of children and the angry wife clogging the aisle, and don't go around because hey, who'd miss a show like this. They never hear Rachel talk much; sure they see her around, to be honest they notice the spring-like quality in the air when she walks by, the way birds chirp, the air grows lighter, and they think of sex but they never think the word: slut. Until mud-eyed Rona Boyle stands there shouting, to be honest, a little bit louder than the situation calls for, most folk of the town have never made the connection, never thought Rachel'd be capable of infidelity. With all those children and another on the way they assume she and Hal breed like rabbits, for they remember the stories of Hal Fremont bringing home his young frisky wife and the sounds they made, the scenes they created, bare legs in the backyard, hilarity coming from almost every room in the house. Sure those things hadn't been as prevalent in recent years—they've heard rumors of a drowning, miscarriages, a mistress, of howling at the full moon—but nothing that everyone hasn't experienced in marriage—except the moon bit. Now this allegation is new. Riveting.

Rachel's laugh is hearty and husky as she picks up Utah and puts her into the cart—luckily still empty enough—does the same with Ari, and wipes her eyes free of the tears of laughter. Holding her side, standing straight and breathing calmly to keep giggles at bay, she approaches red-faced Rona Boyle.

'And when I say, with all respect due the wife of a man of God, when would I have time to do anything like that? And why,' she continues, 'if I had the urge to stray from my gorgeous husband, would I choose a lazy lard ass, poxy-faced, mean-spirited man like yours?'

Rona flicks her tongue, leans in and musses Lou's hair. 'What lovely red hair, I didn't know it ran in Hal's family.'

Rachel swats her hand away from Lou. 'Actually, it's more of an auburn and it doesn't run in Hal's family, it runs in mine.'

Her girls, sensing a glorious finale, kiss and wave their hands as she pushes the cart past Rona Boyle.

Then the four Fremonts do a huge shopping and the family will feast for the next week on foods of fancy. When Rachel goes to pay at the checkout she finds a tiny pot of fuchsia paint in her purse: a gift from quick-handed Sandra. Missy kicks her ribs.

All that fuss over a bit of color to her hair. Just wait, thinks Rachel, til they clap their eyes on my next one.

MISSISSIPPI

Hal starts spending more nights sleeping at the office. It takes less time than going home at night and driving back in the morning. Plus all the play and talk and negotiations tire him out. He sets the alarm for four am, gets up without hesitation, folds and stores the campbed. His dad's old leather DOP kit, now his, sits permanently beneath the sink and it holds the basics: shaving cream, razor, extra blades, soap, comb, deodorant. He washes up in the sink, shaves in the small circular mirror that hangs above the sink. After he cleans himself up, he puts the coffee on before Kitty arrives at six am to assign the men to their jobs and the day.

Sometimes he runs a vacuum around the place, washes any dirty cups that have been left in the sink, although Kitty cleans before she leaves each evening. *Fremont Construction* stretches across the glass front door in crisp black letters. It annoys him how fingerprints mar its impact and before it's light outside, he cleans the door with vinegar and newspaper, like his mom used to. It's about professionalism, pride of place. There are one or two other construction firms in town, but none work as hard and to budget. Then he goes over the work schedules and pending contracts.

'Good morning, Mr Fremont,' Kitty says as she opens the door and the bell attached to its frame announces her arrival.

'Good morning, Miss Fraser.'

She turns the light on, places her purse and a small, white wax paper bag on her desk, beside the phone. 'Cup of joe, this morning?'

'Pot is already on.'

'I brought you a bear claw from Benson's.'

'I'm not sure about pastry this morning,' Hal says patting his barely-there belly, 'not sure if it's good for this paunch.'

'Either I'm blind or you're joking with me. What paunch, Mr Fremont?' she smiles and opens the bag.

'With you and that claw, I'd be overloading on sweetness. Why don't you take half?'

She blushes and brings him half on a plate and coffee, black. Then she sits at her desk with her own cup and a small bit of pastry for herself. When the phone rings or the door opens with the first of the men, she's ready.

Kitty refills his cup, makes a new pot, and gives him a thermos for the day, if he's going out. She doesn't do his laundry or dry cleaning and she doesn't order flowers for his mistress. She makes him coffee, answers the phones, and finds Fremont Construction more than a pleasant place to work.

Late in the afternoon Hal often shaves again, and deals with any issues that a day produces. Out on the north side of town, on a building site where the foundation has been laid with an alarming lack of skill, Hal looks at the buckling concrete and then to cloud-cottoned sun which is eye-level and about an hour from twilight. 'We have to start from scratch,' he says. 'Eyeball this, Jason. Don't tell me you don't see it. No house will sit right on this.' A light rain falls, each drop echoing within his hard hat.

'We could just even it up a bit.'

'What?'

'That's what your old man would have done,' the foreman says.

'I'm not my old man.'

'It'll take us an extra two weeks.'

'There's no other way to fix your mistakes.'

'It'll delay the start of the cinema.'

'And whose fault is that?'

Hal holds Jason's gaze, backs up for a few strides, turns on his heel and drives out of the flooded, potholed, uneven site leaving the town and all its shit behind. It's been a boon year for passage migrants. His weekends and his evenings fill with rarities. He's been leaving work to drive out to the reservoir at sunset, going back to the office after dark. Small birds in the trees, waders on the sanded 'shore' have been particularly plentiful. They're difficult to spot, and so flighty, always in movement, it's hard to get a handle on them. He's even been downstate to the forest preserve. Good watching that day. He's been ticking off the species on the list he'd found in an old box from childhood that had been stuffed into a hole in the wall he and Bill had created.

He remembers a time when the house didn't exist. It was just a hill and they'd lived in a trailer perched at an angle, graveyard-side of their plot until it was built. At first the house stood as simply a house, and that hall had just been a hall in the house.

From the start his mom made her mark on the house: she lined her plants on the windowsills, made all the curtains by hand, and then the smells of living, of her cooking and cleaning, permeated the air and sometimes, suddenly, they can be stirred up by the kids playing or a wind shifting what had settled. From within these memories she whispers to him, 'This is home. Your home,' she says. 'I like what your young wife has done with the place.' The world around this house moves as it will and he cannot change it. In her house he'd felt safe, then it was theirs, his and Rachel's, and now it's all Rachel's and it does not give him peace.

It had been his dad's fault they'd died. He was going too fast, he didn't take care of that car. 'It's a death trap, Lawrence,' his mom would say. 'We've got money in the bank, let's get a new one.'

'Until it stops dead, it's still our car,' and he'd spend the money on another small farm holding at the county line.

'All the balls in the air,' Mom used to say about Dad. 'He's carrying too much.'

And he's not doing it well, Hal'd think, not well. People will think the same thing about him. This is what he's thinking now: that he's dropping things and failing to change anything, falling to carry the burdens he's chosen.

The birds inspire him, the new cinema design is genius, it'll win him some awards. A seminal work, he's sure of it. Even the town planning committee saw it and rushed through the permits. And now this delay, Jason should be doing better.

Hal's been asking a lot of his men and there have been grumbles.

'The shifts are too long.'

'Too close together.'

'Wages are higher in Missouri,' they say.

Not much he can do. It takes risks and sacrifice to be a part of something that will change the whole look and reputation of the town. He reminds himself to say as much to Rachel. But he's not been pitching new-build family homes, his bread and butter. Maybe he'll need to take a few weeks and focus on that. Boring, but they need the money. Those girls go through so many clothes, so much food. He needs more help, he needs more peace and quiet. Every once in a while he sees Sandra in town and wonders if she misses him. When will Tex be old enough to help out? To start to take up the mantle? Maybe Frank Stelt could start selling plots and designs for the Manse development. He might be up for doing some canvassing, him off with a bad back and all. Hal could put on a small commission rate as incentive. Even a few sales would give them a cushion. He's got land to the west and to the north as well, distinctive with loads of possibilities, looking out over the fields.

This year the birds are tricky to observe for long enough to distinguish the subtleties in their plumage, their behavior. But he's persistent. Patient. He steals time. It calms him, watching, categorizing, noting identifying marks; he appreciates that what he learns from one bird can be applied to others; that there are boundaries and they're predictable once you learn them.

He's thinking of building a new house for his kids, for Rachel. It would still be on the hill, he'd salvage the best bits of the old one: the hardwood from the floors, the columns, the worn but perfectly fine stairs, the windows. The design would need flight, punch, stolidness. He'd carve details around the windows, make a bigger kitchen for Rachel, maybe a proper back porch, he'd do up the basement, make it less of a dungeon. A nest, safe and protective, but all the time perched at the edge of flight, part of the house as sky. He takes out a pad, starts to sketch. The lines plod, fail to meet. His head is heavy, he can't see straight, his brain is thick. He lets the crumpled, failed image fall to the ground.

There's a clean sheet of paper in front of him. Birds flutter in his head, the generous simplicity of the plains stretches before him, and he whips off the idea for a new town hall with a statue of a founding father facing it, in the middle of the town square. In less than twenty minutes the whole thing is there, perfect, perfect. He'll run it past Mayor Kent. He tries to ride that feeling to his new house and he starts a new page but the white of the paper blinds him even as night falls. He rolls all the plans up and starts in on the invoices. The phone rings.

'It's the hospital here, Mr Fremont. Had to look you up in the phonebook and was thinking we should have you on speed dial.'

'What is it?' he says, knowing full well.

'Your wife is here Mr Fremont, if you want to come see her and the baby, when she arrives.'

'It's a girl?' Hal asks.

'Oh, I don't know that yet. Just assuming.'

He finishes the paperwork and drives over. Rachel hands the baby to him, and she's a pretty little thing, with a unique face. He doesn't see himself there, but he sees Rachel and it's enough to tell him she's a Fremont. Still, another girl and he's forgotten to bring flowers for Rachel. 'She's beautiful,' he says and Rachel nods and accepts her daughter back into her arms.

GOSSIPING WATER

As if in a cartoon, the Fremont house up on the hill bulges out like a balloon and back again with the bellowing of voices and the unconcerned ruckus of the living.

On most days townies gather like geese on a cold winter's dawn and take off. Gossiping like the proudest gaggle, they flap by in formation: Mrs Pearson up front flanked by Jen Haley and Mrs McCann just a step behind her, other women falling into position, and when one flies smoothly into a store, a new goose steps in to fill the gap. They pick up and drop off children who on occasions like this remain incredibly, pointedly, quiet. All ears.

'Did you hear what she's done now?'

'With…'

'And…'

'That whore.'

'And an incomer at that.'

'She'll bring shame on the town.'

'Those poor kids.'

'I heard that the oldest girl is a bit of a bully.'

'And that Naomi is following in her footsteps.'

'Well someone has to protect that poor boy.'

'Sweet thing.'

'A pretty boy, really.'

'No wonder with all those girls.'

A delicious pause as they catch an updraft and ride a mini-thermal.

'I knew what she was up to with the last one you know. It was in the air.'

'Lou's red hair gave the game away.'

'Did you hear Rona Boyle in the store a few weeks back?'

'Wish I'd been there. Red hair running in that whore's family. I doubt that very much.'

'My Charlie has red hair.'

'So do Tom Latck and Joe MacKenzie.'

'She could have had them all you know.'

'Or the postman.'

Pennies drop from heaven.

'Alan!' they cry gleefully.

'And the last one?'

'A dead giveaway.'

'You think she'd be a bit more discreet.'

'But Ken was there, he re-roofed their house. I hear that it took him twice as long as usual to do the job.'

'It is a big house.'

'With lots of things to hammer in.'

They laugh again.

'Imagine, a Chinese baby.'

'He's Japanese.'

'Actually, he's American,' says Ms Jack who has been silent up until now, new to the town and more than a bit taken back by what she's hearing.

'Whatever. It's the brass neck.'

'I don't know how she does it. Having all those kids. So fast.'

'Witchcraft.'

'What?'

'It's how she heals so fast. You've seen the lights, right?'

'Always a light on somewhere in that house.'

'All hours of the night. She's up there creating potions to heal faster.'

'And to attract our men.'

The very practical sound of air through teeth.

'What are we going to do about it?'

'Hold onto them tight. I've asked my Ben not even to go to Joe's for gas. You can't be too careful,' says Mrs Haley.

'But what about her?'

'We do nothing. A woman like that, she'll bring on her own downfall. Just wait and see.'

Big Joe stands ringing up Ben Haley's gas and smokes. Both men look up the hill with longing, hoping for a glimpse of the ever elusive, beautiful Rachel Fremont.

'She's hot.'

'Amazing.'

'Bit aloof though.'

'Untouchable, despite the rumors.'

'My wife hates me even coming here for gas.'

'Wish I was Ken Ishikawa.'

Both men pause, imagining such a gift.

'I've tried to hold an umbrella for her in the rain,' offers Joe, 'to let her know I'm kind, you know.'

'She prefers to get wet; I've seen her standing on her sidewalk in the rain, just standing.'

'I've offered to carry her groceries. All those mouths, the small ones always at her feet, but she refuses, no matter how many kids she's holding on to.'

'Lucky guy that Ken.'

'What is Hal thinking?'
'Who'd cheat on a woman like her?'
'A Fremont man, that's who.'
'The fool.'

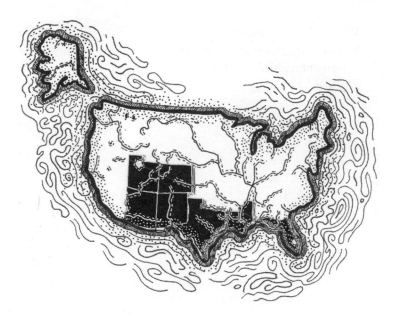

RIDE LIKE THE WIND

Chick from the five-and-dime drives up the hill, Arizona in the passenger seat and there's three bikes in the back of his truck. He stays behind the wheel while Arizona whistles Naomi and Utah over so they can help her unload them.

Even at six years old, Ari has an unerring ability to make contacts with the right people and Chick, older than a grandpa would be, has taken a shine to her. He'd get almost anything for her; he'd stop clocks for Ari, if he could, of course he would.

The girls teeter and fall over for a few hours, but get the hang of riding easily enough.

Flying downhill, Naomi knows love instantly, exhilaration beyond all the blandness of Midwestern life and when she's going full pelt she feels Cole there with her, pushing her forward. Utah follows her and then Ari.

'I'll race you to Old Simpson's farm.'

'You're on.'

Naomi wins easy. The first time she's ever beaten Ari at anything.

'You're a natural, but your butt is going to be sore tomorrow,' Ari says as they're all riding a leisurely pace back home.

By the time they get to the hill their legs are too sore to pedal. The day is bright and easy; Naomi is in a rare magnanimous mood. They buy popsicles at Big Joe's and then push their bikes the rest of the way home.

While her sisters park their bikes in the garage, Naomi stands at the top of the street contemplating the hill. Her mom comes out onto the porch carrying the new baby in one arm, 'Show me what you've got.'

Naomi hops on her bike and flies, really flies down the hill. She flings her arms out to the side for the last stretch before she grips the handlebars and screeches her brakes at the bottom, grins. She rides her bike up and her mom walks down the steps.

'I just can't imagine going that fast.'

'There's just the one hill.'

'It's enough.'

'Definitely don't try downhill skiing, mom. It would do you in.'

'I worry about you, Naomi. It's too fast. Too dangerous.'

Naomi kisses her mom on the cheek, 'Look ma, no hands.' And down the hill she goes again. The Corners don't worry at all. It's exactly the speed that captivates them, exactly the risk that keeps them going, and they go and go and go.

Utah carries a notebook with her wherever she goes. A small one for her back pocket, with a skinny little metal pen that is stored in its spine. She stashes her bigger notebooks just about anywhere you can think of in the house and always carries a pencil case with all sorts of writing utensils: pencils, pens, markers. Whatcha writing, is what her sisters ask. None of your business, she replies. And it's true. 'ords and more words and other lines that shape themselves into ~ures, sometimes, nonsense at other times. Of the bike ride she s: flying flying flying a thousand times, all different sizes. She uses a pencil and makes the letters thicker and thinner, and draws the hill and house and the road they rode all the way out there, but not far enough, not for her. She could just keep going, ditch the bike, and walk, feet to the ground. She's found a loose floorboard and when she finishes a notebook, she puts it in there beneath the floor of her bedroom. When she shoves her notebooks in, there must already be old dry paper in there for she hears it crumple and tear as it resists being shoved further in towards the supporting wall.

LIGHTNING STRIKES

Naomi observes the playground from on high, watching injustice from her perch in the tree. Second grade exhausts her.

Greg McCrae's eyes are artificial blue, an alien blue, blue like a slap. His teeth point to no good, like a vampire's grin. His brow thick as a caveman's. He breathes in the sweetness of autumn and blows out sour air.

Bubba is the chubby kid who sits against the brick wall of the building during recess, beneath the windows of the school's kitchen. The smells and sounds of cooking swirl like a protective fog. He sits reading, trying to be invisible. The whole playground bulges with kids who avoid his feet as they retrieve a kicked ball and never even notice that he's sitting against the wall.

Naomi loves to watch Bubba. His face is open and self-possessed and he always has a comic book with neat, uncrumpled pages opened like a flower across his legs. He has a sense of who he is; she can see it: something she doesn't have, something so many of her sisters have had since birth.

If Bubba has a last name he never answers to one in class and only responds when the teacher halts at Bubba; his father is simply known as Big Bubba. 'Just Bubba,' he says, quiet, respectful, Buddha-like in his refusal to be swayed.

Below Naomi's tree, Greg, the school's biggest bully, begins daily rounds.

He yanks Sissy's curls, prissy and utterly pullable, even Naomi can understand that temptation. And later, when her soothing hand touches Sissy's head, a curl wraps her finger like a ribbon.

Greg tips over a kindergarten tot, who is just getting the hang of a training-wheel-less bike, borrowed and now scratched from the fall, the push.

He steals Tommy Scott's bat just before it's his turn to hit another pop fly, a chase ensues, and Greg tips the bat, neatly, over the fence and Tommy has to walk the long way round, pulling on his t-shirt trying to divert attention from his embarrassed blush, to retrieve it.

The McCraes, like the Fremonts, are a presence in the school: the McCraes a bit slow, a bit thick, and persistently mean and overlooked; the Fremonts odd, smart and persistently, infinitely, visible.

The teachers ignore the silent physical taunts occurring around them and Greg and his bullying brother Bill go unpunished on most days.

Flo can break up a bullying session like a falcon among small birds. Tex is a punchbag, only saved when Flo is around. Naomi is neither Flo nor Tex and Greg has not yet figured out if she is a target or an enemy. Neither has she.

A push for Linda Crow; an elbow for Les Taggart; a trip for running Lisa Kline; and a rough foot down on the hula-hoop for Sarah Sanchez.

All a warm up, a cracking of the knuckles for Greg McCrae who is not only observant but persistent too, damn him. For Bubba, who has sat unnoticed for almost the entire recess, is his next target. Naomi up in the tree sees it coming.

Big Bill McCrae exits the building and meets Greg as reinforcement, and together they stride up to the quiet not quite invisible boy.

'Baby face.'

'Scabby nose.'

'Bookworm.'

'I'm gonna crush you.'

Relentless. So close, blisters of spit on his face.

'Hey there, Hubba Bubba.'

'Why don't you blow us a bubba?'

A wad of gum spit into Bubba's hair. Bubba is disturbed. Irrevocably.

'Your dad's a cripple.'

'Your mom's a whore.'

A line of pink bubblegum and saliva slobber down the right side of his face. Gaggingly sweet.

'Ugly boy. So ugly your mom left you.'

'Deserted you.'

'Orphan.'

The McCraes are not original, but they are effective. The bricks of the building burn and dig into Bubba's back. No spatula knocks on the window. No hair-netted cook comes to the rescue. Spit pools in his ear.

Bubba glances around but doesn't see Naomi slide down from her tree, but even if he had, he wouldn't have been comforted because she is an unknown entity and how is he to know that she won't join forces with the McCraes? Bubba has no choice but to pull himself away from the building and the brothers step in closer, his head hip level. Greg first rubs in the gum and then yanks Bubba's head along with it. His face swells, turns red and Bubba catapults himself onto his feet and, keeping his head down like a butting ram, breaks apart the brothers (they let him, what an opportunity…a Bubba out in the open).

The McCraes circle Bubba as he walks, a pair of hawks hunting a rabbit, hyenas attacking the weakest of a flock. Ready to eat him alive. Pick at his bones.

Bubba wants to shout. MS. He has MS! He's the best dad, he wants to yell. All of which is true. I don't need a mom; I don't need her, he wants to yell this too, but would only ever, even to someone he trusted, be able to whisper it, untrue as it is. A few years ago she ran away with some cowboy who lives in Miami. 'He's a cowbo his dad says, 'just a cowboy. What did she see in him?' Later Bu finds out that his mom's new man is simply an electrician, a cowboy of an electrician.

She left them before the MS. As her figure receded down the front path, his dad pulled Bubba towards him in a deep hug, roughing his hair with a knuckle, 'Hey Bubba, it's you and me against the world.' And for a while it was. But recently it has just been him, little Bubba alone against the world.

Naomi starts her rounds, keeping a quiet eye on Bubba like you keep an eye on the weather when a storm is brewing in the gulf in September. She follows in Greg's footsteps whispering, *It's just words. Don't you worry they'll get theirs one day. Don't you believe a word.*

Bubba runs into a football game, but instead of getting support from other kids, the players disperse to other parts of the playground. He is alone, kids watching his demise. The brothers circle circle. Tossing out words: cripple, unloved, orphan, she left you, what did you do to make your mom leave, she doesn't love you. Circling. Hulking over, hovering in ever decreasing circumferences, and then they dive. Bill grabs Bubba by the neck and shoves him towards Greg who tosses him back to Bill and so it goes on. Bubba flops back and forth like a rag doll, a twist of skin with each catch and shove, his face falls inward and his eyes flip up towards the sky like he might find help there.

Naomi starts circling too, but in a broader orbit. When she stops walking to watch, to decide what to do, she is pulled inextricably toward the scene of the crime. Behind her clouds amass, dark billowing things, folding and expanding, engulfing everything blue and peaceful and predictable.

Naomi steps forward. 'Stop it,' she says, not all that loudly and definitely not that convincingly.

Greg makes as if to swat away a fly. 'Bzzzz, a wimpy Fremont. Shoo fly.'

'Mind your own business,' adds Bill, twisting skin and shoving Bubba.

'Stop it!' Naomi says again, louder, a fury turning her ears red. Lightning sheets the sky in warning.

'And what are you going to do about it?' Greg holds Bubba this time and looks at her. He sees a timid girl who he can take on with one hand tied behind his back. 'You're just a Fremont. Shove off. Now!'

'Let him go.'

She grows bigger. The sky curls down over the school, obscuring even the brick of the building, eating up the playground behind her. Kids run for cover. The hairs on Greg and Bill's head stand at attention, their arms too. A buzz, not unlike the heroin buzz they'll like so much later, hums through their bodies. Not only do they not stop, they don't even pause.

A push with arms outstretched and Bubba hangs suspended between the brothers. 'Remember, I asked you nicely,' Naomi says as she takes a step back and becomes cloud.

From the shelter of the school Utah has been watching her sister grow a conscience. When a thick storm enfolds the playground, Utah waits for two lightning strikes. She is not disappointed.

ALABAMA

Something dances in on the air, a sudden ripple of a tide on the change, a lost seagull making a racket in the skies. Rachel leaves the dishes in the sink and goes to stand on the front porch. She skims her eyes over the cracked pavement of the road, glances at the graveyard beyond, and then gazes down the street at the long row of disparate houses. Her dead father-in-law's absent-minded fetish with architecture doesn't distract her because, despite the vast difference in designs and grandeur and lines, all the houses manage to look the same.

Her head pounds, in a good way, with the strong beating of her heart. She knows exactly what she is doing out here, apron round her waist, kids safely asleep or at school. She is looking for the next one, and down at the bottom of the street, taking long sure stri the sound of each step loud on the quiet street, he is running to

Or so she thinks. She's become cocky again, searching, finding, getting. And this man, wearing short shorts despite an October frost in the air, and flashy running shoes, fits her bill exactly. He is a hulk of a man, big for a runner, more like a football player, and he arrives out of season, bringing sea air with him. He runs up the hill, gazing over the houses and dismissing them as some people do. Mounting the top of the dead-end street, he does a neat turn, right foot, left, right again, like a line dancer, and runs back down the hill. He's dismissed her too. Rachel wishes she'd kept her dishtowel in her hand, it's a better image, her standing drying her hands like nothing has happened. Like she hasn't lost her touch.

Her eyelashes weigh down and she closes her eyes. There's nothing out there. Then, faintly, she hears a shift. The crunch of running shoes on frozen grass. When she opens her eyes he stands only an inch from her. The street has to turn away: it's like a bad romance film, all chiseled jaws and heaving bosoms.

This running man isn't just good looking, he speaks too. 'Couldn't let you think I'd be that easy.'

'Ah, but you were.'

He picks her up with his right arm, pulls her body tight along his own sweaty frame and carries her inside, kicking the front door shut with his foot. He shoots his arms out against the doorframe and keeps them in the hall, one hand on nameless land, the other on the Atlantic.

The house crashes when their bodies meet. They bang against the wall, the floor, the staircase. Despite the fierceness they take their time and the babies sleep on.

When the deed is done, he pulls up his shorts, plants a quick kiss on her lips, and runs down the hill and out of town, riding away on whatever strange wind had carried him to Rachel.

's pregnancy is quiet for Rachel. It's a small coast, pretty for what /orth, and the land is sturdy, like a body built for action. Make use of what you have, Alabama tells her, no need to wander too far. This is it: home, family, resources. Conserve, conserve.

All the Corners are now in school; Ari loves recess, Utah reading and writing, Naomi stays silent about the whole experience and the house is peaceful, less parched with them gone for six hours a day. It's a relief. Lou fills the house with color, so much color, paintings and drawings and herself and out in the garden she plants flowers in dramatic designs that change with the time of day and the season, and she and Missy play together like a dream, so different, somehow temporary, but Rachel can't guess at why she thinks that. This coast has been the rest she's needed and she allows herself to believe it'll last.

Full term, nine peaceful months, and Rachel is at the front door when the first contraction grips. Her stomach curves beyond the threshold and then back towards the house. Her feet will not take her any further today: this girl wants to be born at home. She closes her eyes and behind her the kids run through the house, a game of hide and seek which has devolved into a chase. Whooping and pounding, they knock knick-knacks off shelves as they race past. Arizona, the most daring of all, fearless as she uses the banister as a balance beam and does a flip off the end, landing in a run. Her sisters can't even keep up with her as they run in a more traditional fashion, keeping their feet more or less close to the floor, the steps, and they wish they had their sister's ability to fly. Rachel grabs the doorframe with the next contraction. Okay, Bam, you win.

'Flo, come here sweetwater,' and she arrives with Missy on her hip. 'Why don't you bake some cupcakes or spritz cookies, get all the girls involved. Alabama looks set to be born at home.'

Rachel retreats to her room. Flo will keep an eye on her sisters, gathering them more or less together in the kitchen, baking sweet things. Tex, with his bruised belly and back, which he thinks Rache doesn't notice, has taken to sewing up in his room, gathering any his sisters' clothes that need darning or hemmed or let down. The not noticed the kindness but Rachel has and she'd like to thir can hear the resistance and the give as the metal of the needle pulls a path through the cloth.

The phone only rings once before the midwife picks it up. 'Can you come to the house?' Rachel asks.

'On my way.'

'I'm not saying it'll be soon.'

'I'll bring a casserole and some fruit for the kids.'

Bam's silence deceives. Belies her ergonomics. Her intense habit of building. You can't make noise in the womb, you can only make hassle: you can bruise ribs, press down on a bladder, and Bam is no bruiser, no troublemaker, so she holds herself peaceful until she can warn everyone of the noise she's going to make.

This baby has stamina, and when she arrives her voice could bring down the house. Luckily, she and this house are fast friends from the start. Bam never just walks, she crashes, knocks things over. A brute force to be reckoned with, she'll end up with bruises on her shoulder, hips, knees. Her triple dimple legs and infant arms keep curious sibling hands from doing accidental harm. From a surprisingly early age, she'll have a knack for tripping up or otherwise bowling-over her brother.

At three, she'll sleepwalk into an unknown wall crawlspace and from the hush of night her screams will ring out, her pounding will shudder the house. Even Hal wakes up, gives a redundant nudge to an already awake Rachel, and pulls the blankets up to cover his head. By following the noise like a fault line, she finds Bam.

In years to come, Bam will drive Missy's car into Wilson's reservoir, share a fight with Texas that only she and he will know about, and, not long after, she will build and build and build until she creates something which has the potential to save them all.

THE HEART OF TEXAS

six months, Bam can sit up if you put a hammer in her hand. She tolerate the plastic pegs, and Hal has had to find and fix up the old wooden blocks of his childhood—at Rachel's insistence—and once he does, Bam sits there for hours making noise. She is the only one of the girls who will ever ask Hal if she can hang out in the basement (of course he refuses), and she bellows and bangs until he buys her a complete set of full-sized tools (but does not give her the mini-workbench he built for his sons) and, when she is older, he does move the power tools out to the garage where they can be shared.

She grows into a sturdy toddler and one Saturday a lull takes over the house. Leaves have fallen en masse and without provocation the evening before and Rachel rounds up the kids on the back porch. The Corners link arms, Naomi's elbow making a triangle at her side for Colorado to hook her arm through, twelve-year-old Tex scowls as only a boy can, and the small ones stand rosy-cheeked with future mischief. Rachel humors them with rakes of assorted sizes and encourages the younger ones to use their hands or any means possible. 'Make the biggest pile you can. Right in the center of the yard. Your father can bag them later. You too, Tex. The exercise will do you good.'

Before he can protest, Missy grabs his hand and drags him down the back stairs and into the corner of the yard most needing a good rake through. The Corners circle the sandbox like dust-devils and gather the leaves into a pile upon which others can build.

Rachel kneads the bread dough and Flo finishes making the lunch. With flour up her arms, and laughter echoing from the yard, Rachel grins.

'I'll put the cider on, they'll get cold soon,' Flo offers, wiping her hands on a dishtowel.

'You can join them you know. We're basically done here.'

'Who'll help you?'

'Flo, I can take care of things in here.'

'I'll just put this on and then go out.' She steps around Bam and says in a baby-friendly voice, 'You go Bam! What are you building? A fence? A house?' Flo pulls a big jug of cider from the pantry, pours crowd-sized glugs into a pot along with a few sticks of cinnamon and starts to heat it all on the stove.

The first frost still clings to the edges of the grass on this, the first cold day of the season; the sun only makes it glisten rather than disappear.

'Dance,' commands pretty Missy, holding up her hands to Tex, and he lifts her onto his feet. Together they twirl, the weight of her tugging on his hip, each time they swing around. Tex whoops loudly, being stood on and danced with, and the sky opens and the frost crisps beneath their feet. Tex occasionally picks her up with one cool hand, lifts her by the waist and places her back on his feet. After a few twirling minutes, Missy leaps unexpectedly from his grip and pulls him into the pile of leaves. He twirls around and tickles her lightly. Her generous squeaks alert her sisters and within minutes all are tumbling and tickling and catching their breath before diving back in. And Tex is right in the heart of things, tickling, being tickled, his baby fat protecting him, making a soft cushion for his sisters, laughing, his lungs so full and free he can't imagine how he'd breathed before. He stretches at the bottom of the pile thinking, this, this is what I've been missing.

Rachel glances out the window at her kids enjoying themselves and sees Hal come up the hill. His forays away have been creeping back into his routine, she's not always quite sure where he is and the house and the kids are once again showing signs of his inattention. But it's been quieter and more peaceful and when Hal doesn't come home for dinner, Tex eats in the kitchen with all of them. When she asks him to do the dishes, he does, without complaint and once or twice he's helped her cook. He has a real knack for flipping the hamburgers and making potato salad.

Hal stands just inside the gate, waiting to be asked to join in. Just scoop one of them up, it'd be easy, Rachel thinks. But there is Tex, so clearly dancing like a girl, among the girls, giggling and tickling. Hal's shoulders shove back. 'Damn it, Hal,' she murmurs and disappears into the hall, placing her hand on the heart of Texas. 'Remember this feeling, Tex,' Rachel whispers at the map.

A burning in Tex's chest, *this is what I have been missing.*

'Tex!'

The gust of his father's shout scatters the leaves but even Hal cannot separate the pile of children.

Inside, Flo whispers, 'Stand up Tex. Tell him. Tell him what you need.'

Tex disentangles himself gently from the girls. When he stands and faces his father, maple and oak leaves cling to his curls and Missy, not quite realizing the seriousness of the situation—for her father never evokes the same hesitancy in her as he does the other kids—continues to tug on his leg.

'Missy, let go.' When she doesn't, Tex jerks his leg forward, shakes his foot sharply and, with a small yelp, she's flung out to the ground. Something rips in his hip and it fails to click back into place. Naomi rushes over and swoops Missy up in her arms, cooing, absorbing her salty tears. Ari and Utah tut at Tex and continue to sit and pick leaves and desert flowers out of their hair.

Tex doesn't know where to look and his heart is making too much noise for him to hear what it's saying. He stands not knowing how to do the right thing. What the heck is the right thing? He's ready to speak. For the first time in his life he believes the words will come. Maybe he'll talk about love and family and the pure pleasure of letting his hair down once in awhile, and how they all need each other, and how his heart burns and his legs like the weight of dancing and how... But Hal has already turned his back. Flo lets out a quiet gasp of disbelief.

Hal stomps past them all and through the kitchen barking, 'When's lunch?' Without waiting for an answer, he proceeds back down to the basement where he strides back and forth, and having no state to work on, turns on the local radio.

Tex helps to gather all the girls together but eats in the dining room with his dad, who says nothing. That night in bed he listens to his sisters whispering, laughing, and keeping each other company on the other side of the walls. Big double beds hold lots of bodies and shenanigans. Bam in the crib, and Missy in the safety bed, and the older girls who soothe the younger ones (or harass them) when they wake up with the sound of the wind through the thin walls. Then all the girls sleep, lulled by a tide of waves and Tex sleeps, uneasily at first, and then deeply.

Rachel made Hal's dinner without seasoning, and put it on a plate improperly rinsed so it'd taste a bit like soap, and Hal said nothing. She told him that the cake didn't rise for dessert, gave him real coffee and is pleased to see him agitated, his hand trembling slightly when he slides his long bare legs into bed, the coldness of his feet seeping through to her side of the bed. She's surprised he's come to bed at all. Even with that, she'd usually take his feet between her own, one at a time and rub them to warm them up. But not tonight.

'You better do something about that attitude of yours, Mister. I don't see a hunch on your back or a wart on your nose, but people might just mistake you for an ogre.'

'Don't get me started, Mrs.'

'Started, Hal? You're joking. If you think anyone else is in the wrong here, you are completely delusional.'

The bed is warmer when he leaves and the house quiet. Rachel won't hear the bell pitched buzz of the clippers as wind-blown sleet rattles the windows and icy sounds hide the worry of the house.

When Hal gets out of bed he shuffles into his jeans and pulls a t-shirt and sweatshirt on. He takes his electric clippers from the bathroom drawer, enters his son's room and shears Tex's curls close to his head, his son sleeping through the whole thing, and then leaves the house.

Early Sunday morning and the sky should be full of birds. Hal's on the edge of town, the edge of everything, sitting in his chair, legs cramping, remnants of his son's shorn hair like cat hair on his sweater and dawn arrives suddenly, ugly even. Silent skies remain empty.

Just one bird would be enough. Hal scans the land in front of the horizon with his binoculars, then the horizon-actual with his scope, and the strip of land between, again with his bins, looking for a bigger bird, a bird of prey. Nothing: the whole world has fallen silent.

Wait. Something. He sweeps back. Leaving his car, he walks down the county road, then through a field, he's closer now and it's tall, almost two stories high. How could he have failed to see it with his naked eye? Standing at the base, the wood smells fresh-cut, roughly hewn, and it could mean anything. It could mean anything at all. But it's right next to the bundle of acres he's just bought for an exclusive housing development. It's visceral. It could mean anything, but it doesn't. He remembers watching his dad, on that rare occasion when Lawrence was furious with drink, raging at the town.

'We Fremonts,' he'd say waving the bottle, his body unsteady but his glare strangely sober, 'we will not tolerate this. We most definitely will not leave.'

Hal storms back to his car, silence hides nothing. Nothing. There's more than one way to yell. This will not happen, not on my watch, he thinks. All he needed today was one damn bird, that was it, just a single bird to distract him from his ridiculous son. Instead he got a newly cut cross, beveled in warning.

Which line had he violated? Or had they moved the boundaries?

He throws his backpack in the trunk, hears a nasty crack. Damn it, damn it. He'd left that pick axe in there. He'll need to replace at least one lens of his binoculars. Cutting Tex's hair will not be enough, the boy needs to learn order, needs to learn restraint.

Flo is washing up from breakfast when Tex walks in. He looks like someone tried, but just failed to actually scalp him.

'Tex, your beautiful curls. Oh Tex.'

He hands her the razor.

'Cut it close, all around. Dad's right, they never suited me anyway.'

But they had suited him, they both know it, and the space that stretches between Flo and Tex, for the first time, seems insurmountable. Flo gasps with the distance she feels from her brother and puts her hand on Tex's shoulder, but he shrugs her off.

Rachel sits feeding Bam, watching Flo cut Tex's hair and knows that her boy with the curls and luscious plump face will soon b gone. It's clear. His soft borders will sharpen to edges with all he goes through at school and in this prison of a house; his teeth will tear meat; his heart will harden and be shaped like a mallet. She catches glimpses of his battered body as he bathes or reaches to an upper shelf for a book—the kids at school are showing him no mercy and he's not learned how to fight back. His eyes plead with Rachel not to mention the bruises, not to draw attention to his failures. And she doesn't. She encourages his smile and congratulates him on the homework he brings home with average marks. But she never mentions the sewing he does for the family or how his beautiful stitches move in and out of skirt hems that float and twirl as his sisters play.

When Flo is finished she wipes away the stray fine hairs as well as she can and Tex scratches the back of his neck. With his pale underarms and childlike actions he's still just a boy and Rachel leans over and kisses him on both cheeks, rubs a few circles on his back.

'Stop it, Mom,' he says, 'I'm not a baby.' His lips are a newly drawn artificial line across his face with his hair cut so close to his skull. His eyes snap, snap to a blue which is crisp and distant.

Hal goes down to Dale's hardware, an outdated store selling cut-price, usually damaged stock. Dale is behind the counter and he sells him the padlocks wholesale, doesn't ask what they're for.

'I'm going to lock up the food from my pudgy-faced son,' Hal offers up as an explanation.

Looking at Hal the whole time, Dale spits chew-juice into an empty pop can. It's a sound Hal hates. 'Them boys, they're the ones who're hard to raise. Girls make the noise, boys make the trouble.'

'Damn right. Too damn right.'

He goes home and padlocks each and every cabinet in the kitchen, and the fridge, and the door to the cellar, and even the extra freezer out in the garage that holds frozen beef patties, hotdogs and buns. His voice booms:

'Tex is not to be indulged.'

By which Hal means fed.

'Surround yourself with strength and sensibility,' Hal tells Tex at dinner. Tex, shorn head and already hungry, nods. 'Do not bend to the will of others. Do not believe what they say. Do you hear me? You are not to abandon this town, Tex. You are not to sell this house. Us Fremonts, we're not adventurers anymore. We're builders. Damn fine builders, Tex. You remember that. This is who you are. And this stupid town needs us. They fight it, but we've made this town. Without us there'd be a couple of barns, a general store with three half-empty shelves, and a rundown caved-in single pump gas station.'

And a shit load of bigots, cheeks thick with chew, spinning tales on uneven porches, thinks Hal.

Tex is starting to understand what being a Fremont demands of him. On his way to bed, out in the hall, the lines of his landscapes cohere and darken and when he notices them, they are not as he expects, but they look muscular, sure of themselves and that is enough.

When his dad rattles him awake at two am, Tex gets dressed without protest. Maybe this is some sort of coming of age hazing. 'Don't say a word to your sisters or to your mother about this, Tex. Not a word.'

They drive, the axes in the back are so heavy they stay still despite the off-roading his dad does. The air outside is the perfect temperature for a crime. His dad drives without his headlights and Tex adjusts to the half-moon dark soon enough. He doesn't see the cross until his dad stops. He can't imagine how he missed it. Once he notices it, he can see nothing else.

His dad holds his fury so tightly that he remains calm. His swing is sure, swift, smooth. Tex learns this: even as your heart races, keep your hands steady. His dad is beautiful in rage, in movement. They don't need both axes to bring the cross down. The corn cushions its fall. Tex moves in beside his dad and they hack at the arms, at its axis, until no carpenter could put the thing back together.

Morning breaks clear and the youngest girls jump up on the 'Mama, time to get up. Mama, we're hungry.'

Rachel's skin is translucent where it's pulled at, her cheeks still soft from their kisses, and she picks up a girl. Motherhood educates her and will have to be her rest. She's her own company and a few days back she'd spotted the cross on one of her drives out of town. Her dangerous drives, the ones she always has to force herself to turn around from. Sometimes she's gone a hundred miles before she turns back home, each arc of her three point turn another opportunity for escape. The cross wasn't natural on the landscape, she saw it right away as the imposition it was. She wasn't upset, just surprised some folk hadn't made some sort of gesture well before this. She's handing out buttered toast and pouring juice and when she glances out the window she notices it's gone.

THE KEYS

Antagonism is a key. Flo knows this. So when Hal gives her the keys to the padlocks, she isn't fooled.

The lockdown makes cooking a real pain and when Hal is not at home, the cabinets and all the secrets and nutrients they hold, are aired.

Flo, with Rachel's help, has sets of keys made for each of the kids, which the girls keep hanging around their necks. Tex, who refuses his set of keys, receives regular offers of sustenance, especially from Missy. At first he shakes his head and looks away, but as the weeks pass his 'no' becomes stronger and louder and the offers of help decrease and then stop altogether. Flo never offers and an unsteady truce continues.

A cold wind blows across the empty streets and the shabbily built podium lists with the gusts. Hal sways right along with the rest of the attendees and award winners. At least the podium moves when it needs to, Hal thinks. His family, on the other hand, has stagnated and if you stay still in this world it'll stomp on your head as it passes by. If he'd had any sense, he'd have torn the house down when parents died and started anew. Of course. That's the answer. Sure it has history but it also has those damn crooked walls. This morning he saw it in the rear view mirror: the slanted porch holding up the perfectly confederate columns. But this is what we do. We procreate. We promise we won't be as bad as our fathers, as our mothers. We carry their names forward, but believe we'll do a better job.

When we use an old name for a place we're settling in, we live our inheritance; we proclaim a place what we need it to be: Sweet Home; Homestead; Nova Scotia; New England; New York. Of course this is what we all do. Name our kids after the places they've been conceived or after things they represent for us like Hope.

That's what Fremonts do: we see new things and name them. We name them after something familiar. What a stupid idea. What had he been thinking?

He's never considered himself a political man and he's not. In fact, he shuns wheeling and dealing and does just enough handshaking to get the new contracts, the awards. Today's award is for the gym and cafeteria annex to the school. A relatively small, pedestrian project. Hal had convinced them to put windows in the cafeteria, so the kids could look out at the playground, the river beyond. A lot of the kids appreciated this, in particular one very vocal boy named Matthew Kent, heir apparent to the Mayor.

The Mayor catapults his skinny and drawn frame out of his car and walks up to Hal. He wears his high school football ring on his middle finger, and slides it up and down unconsciously as he stands. He slaps Hal on the back. 'Great work son. Great work.'

I'm not your son, Hal thinks. Even if you are Mayor. Not your son. I'm building your town for you and you don't even see it.

John Kent's hand is sweaty when Hal shakes it, and he avoids meeting Hal's eyes. The plaque, fake-gold plated, is hollow where it punches out from the wooden mount.

Not much of a lunchtime crowd. The head gardener gets an award too, for the plants he landscaped down the middle of the main street and a town planner for his sewer design. Hal holds his plaque above his head like he's an Olympian. No one shouts his name out in victory and the ceremony is over in under ten minutes.

'I hear that Frank Kovach is doing some great work in Akron,' starts the Mayor. 'His museum of agricultural machines draws people from all fifty states. Just for the building.'

'I hear he's good but has quite an ego on him. And that one of the walls has a crack in it already.' Why is the Mayor talking about some plonker from Ohio?

'I was thinking of getting him to town, to design my new house. Well, mansion really. Any chance your plot is going? That you're planning to bring your house down?'

This is your last award, that's what he's saying to Hal. You're on your way out Fremont, my son.

Sandra had arrived halfway through and watched the proceedings, leaning against her car. 'You're doing great,' she says when Hal goes over to her. She buys him a drink and the bar is empty and quiet. She's independent, sure of herself, and when she takes his hand and leads him back to her new apartment he does not resist. He remembers now, this is his place of rest. He'll keep it quiet this time. He'll make it work: being with Sandra makes him a better man, and he'll still be there for his family.

TAUK TAUK

The keys of the calculator click far too fast as Rachel types in their outgoings, the paper unfurling to the floor. Lou, Missy and Bam chatter in and out of the kitchen, pull on her and want a snack, want her to read to them. They play, whine and talk the whole time. Taxes due and she does what she can with the household outgoings and income but this year the difference crushes her. What has he been doing at work if it's not making some money to feed and clothe his kids? She knows what he's been doing: he's been obsessing over those damn grand designs, and now his town hall is going before the committee next week and the family never sees him and even when he's here he's not present, and those big projects always run at s, because he won't scrimp on quality and the town won't turn out their pockets. This town doesn't deserve the attention he gives it. They've asked him to redraft this design and he has. With that guy from Ohio throwing his hat into the ring, Hals been pacing the halls and agitating the girls. She notices the paint under his nails, on the soles of his boots and finds she doesn't mind like she used to. She just wishes he'd bring home more money. And he still has those two lots of land lying empty for over a year, and hasn't even got the signatures for new houses, much less been able to break ground. Her girls tumble in.

'Mama, play tag with us.' Lou's eyes smile, her hand pulls at Rachel's and in reply Rachel pulls her close. Color and risk and she knows why she chooses family. 'I can't today. Why don't you three play hide and seek?'

If they're disappointed as they run into the hall, Rachel doesn't see it.

'Close your eyes,' five-year-old Lou directs. She'll be the captor leading her young prisoners to the lost place, into the maze from which they cannot emerge without calling for help, and if they're lucky someone will take pity on them. 'Missy, close both eyes! You too Bam,' Lou says. 'Trust me.'

When she puts her hands over their eyes, Bam and Missy see rainbows, fireworks, a deep dusk sky black-blue with a receding storm.

'I'm not going to get lost this time. No way,' says Missy.

'Sure thing,' says Lou, 'I believe you, really I do. Keep 'em shut. The house doesn't like cheaters. Remember that the last girl who cheated,' she nudges Missy with her elbow, 'ended up with a black eye from the edge of a jutted railing.'

'Whatever,' says Missy, knowing that her right eye still holds a faint yellow crescent beneath it.

Lou leads them up the stairs, through hallways and doorways, helps them to step over doorstops, and the air around turns cool and hot in turns.

'Not this time,' Missy says again. She's been in and out of every room in the house, trying to memorize them.

Lou puts the two girls shoulder to shoulder against the wall like they're facing a firing squad. 'Today we'll play hide and seek. You need to find me, and when you find me, you'll have found the hall.'

'Easy peasy,' says Missy, focusing on the map in her mind's eye, it's there, calling to her.

'What she said,' says Bam.

'Count to twenty,' Lou's voice retreats and just like that the colors behind their eyes dissipate. 'Go.'

'She's gone.'

'We can open our eyes.'

'No Bam. We gotta count.'

They count, using the one-one-thousand method. With each number they call out the hall moves further away, the map grows quieter until they reach twenty and they open their eyes and are truly alone.

'Which way?' asks Bam.

'Hmmm.' Missy thinks, she looks at the walls, the floor, the way the light from the doorways is slanting. She goes to the hallway, walks a few steps in each direction. Touches the wall. Bam follows, finger to lip, mimicking Missy's gaze.

'Well?'

'I don't know. Okay? I don't know.'

'Hey girls,' shouts Lou and Missy and Bam turn quickly enough to see her disappear around a corner. Sound of feet pounding up stairs.

Stairs running up? Both girls thought they were at the top of the house.

They run after Lou. The hall narrows at the end and does a sharp turn and becomes stairs, which go up for six steps, flatten out into a landing, at a right angle and then turn into fifteen or so stairs going down. They run. At the bottom they can go left or right.

'Right,' says Missy.

Bam races right; sees Lou's red hair just disappearing at the end of the hall.

'Aieeeee,' she says.

Running, running. Knocking their knuckles off the wall as they go. The hall dead-ends. Missy nearly crashes into Bam when she stops.

From behind them there's a laugh.

'Here,' says Missy, noticing a crawlspace above them as they walk back down the hall. 'She went up, and then back.'

'No way.'

The girls walk back to and beyond the stairs that had brought them here. Further on there's a bedroom which looks familiar, Tex's? But it's not on the corner, so it's a trick. There's a big light up ahead, like it's from a skylight. 'That's it, that's it,' shouts Bam. 'We did it.'

They start to run and the light disappears like a switch has been flipped, leaving only a thin strip of cold light, like you get through a slit of a prison window. They keep running towards this light. 'Whoah!' shouts Missy. Her voice echoes, the light is two or three stories above them. It's like a cave. Cold too.

'Brrrrr.'

A metal door clanks shut, the last chink of light disappears.

'I don't like this,' says Bam.

'Shhh. Listen.'

There's dripping water. A sound of splashing. 'Rats?' says Missy. And that's enough.

'LOU! LOU! Let us out!'

There's no reply.

Lou hears girls cry.

'LOU! LOU! Let us out!'

'What's the magic word?'

'Please Lou. Please Lou.'

'Close your eyes,' she says. They do. They feel a hand take each of their hands. Behind their eyes it is bright, sunlight, a breeze. 'Keep them closed,' says Lou. There's heat on their cheeks from above and they let themselves be led.

Rachel hears the girls but can't quite tell where they are. Sometimes they sound close by, almost at her shoulder, other times their voices echo as if they're in a cave. They're running, laughing, that's for sure.

Through the open front door a dark sky portends high winds, rain, hail, a tornado. Thunder perhaps, or a flood. Tears are a definite possibility. They haven't come: not today, not for a long time. Her body is not right. It's dammed up. Despite this, she gets it all done. Of course she does, how can she not? Her family depends on her. The tender nature of raising kids to know themselves, when you yourself fail every day to see them for themselves, worries her.

Even when they're not here she listens to them, their needs, their demands, their stories. This unspoken need is deafening. She's been through rivers, mountains, walked for miles over sea-polished stone. Discovered things, found treasures, and yet mistakes define her direction and she's increasingly aware that she's being a witness when she should be a guide.

Lou leads Missy and Bam, who are squeezing their eyes shut, into the hall. 'Okay, open them.'

The hall, the map. Their mom.

'Wow.'

'How did you?'

'Not telling.'

Each girl falls to the map, hands running over the places she can reach. They laugh, Lou loudest of all. Bright bright bright. They spread their hands in a row over their states, wrists kissed by water. And each girl makes sure she brushes the little place of brightness on the water off the east coast that has a beating heart, and they look up at the sky through the skylight as if it'd explain this trick of light.

'Tauk tauk,' they say, the auk clucks where their tongues meet with the roofs of their mouths. Lou and Missy run to Rachel, hug her, and take her cheeks in their chubby hands. Bam stays at the map and from northwest to southeast she draws her hand over the shape of states her family makes, turns to her mother and grins, her mouth and the map both curve into perfectly lopsided smiles.

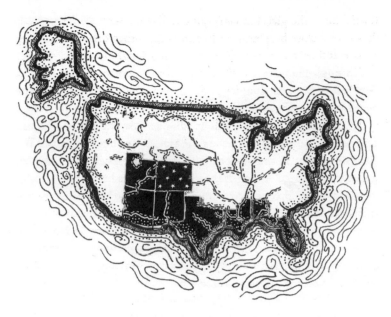

INHERITANCE

Tex's leg drags awkwardly and, like his inheritance, holds him back. Flo is freer having neither: she doesn't have a limp and she sure won't be coming into any money.

On this hot August day Tex's heart races faster than his legs can carry him, faster than Flo lets him go, and no one seems to care that his face will be, in a matter of a quarter of an hour, if he doesn't get to school, pulped. Unwilling to be rushed, Flo tempers her brother's pace with a steady footfall and a firm hand on his skinny arm and Tex knows better than to fight her.

At the bottom of the long hill, Flo glances back at the hordes of girls tailing her like inexperienced undercover cops, and her protective instincts kick in. She might be in high school now but she needs to make sure the rest of them are okay. Her sisters trip along but nonetheless work together and Flo knows they'll be able to take care of themselves.

Tex, on the other hand, truly needs her help. In fact, at the moment, he's demanding it. 'Flo, can I have my lunch box back?'

Flo looks at him, then behind him to the trail of girls snaking their way to school. She stops abruptly and the line halts, crashes. Flo turns around. 'Come on, pull yourselves together!' And with the wave of a hand she encourages them to pass.

Pushing the other hand out at what approximates chin level, she accepts the tolls they pay: a cookie (chocolate chip, half eaten), a penny, a pebble, a chewed pencil, a fluffy backed sticker of a race car, a used wet piece of gum (she doesn't flinch), and a shoelace. Four-year-old Missy hobbles onto preschool with one laceless sneaker in one hand, Arizona holding her other hand and her holed sock finding each puddle with Biloxi Naval accuracy. Naomi steps on his foot as she passes; Utah pretends to trip and has an open marker in her hand and it sweeps across his clean shirt. 'Ooops,' she says.

Shoving the stash into the pocket of her jeans, Flo takes long draws on her cigarette and sighs deeply. She lingers over every action. Rolling her eyes heavenwards then towards hell, and then back to the sky, she makes Tex wait. His limp (psychosomatic according to Dr Pearson) has hampered him for a year or so and he watches as his sisters become circus-colored dots at the end of the block, elbowing and tripping each other. He knows he has to get to school to catch that window of non-bullied arrival. Flo knows this too.

'Flo. Give me my lunch box.'

'Wait a second, Psycho-so-matic.'

'Flo!'

Smoke escapes her lips slowly. 'That would be a no, my dear Tex.' Flo pushes her face close in to his, zigzagging her chin back and forth for effect. 'N. O.'

'Yeah,' he says, 'I got it the first time.'

Flo performs a small agile dance of victory in front of her limping brother and then sprints down the block towards the high school. He will have to suffer his fate alone and Flo does not seem all that upset by this fact. Oddly, neither is Tex, for all the Fremont kids know that nothing Flo does outside the walls of the house—making Tex late, giving protection from bullies, giving him her old tests to study from, taunting him, or keeping the extra sandwich and apple for herself—will make a difference in the big picture. The big picture being what happens at home, back in the shadow of that damn map.

Flo deposits all of her siblings safely within the grade school fence and, with her free hand, she divvies up their tolls: she tosses the half-eaten chocolate chip cookie and the used piece of gum into a hedge and deposits the penny, pebble, chewed pencil, fluffy backed sticker of a race car, and the shoelace to keep for the birds in their backyard (who build their nests from almost anything, and Missy will like that, finding her lace woven into a strong structure next summer), into her patchwork schoolbag, wipes her hand on her jeans, and saunters to high school. At the corner she pauses, searching the solid red brick building for signs of weakness. She spots the smooth sliding windows, the way the big evergreen hides any escapee from the watchful eye of the principal. An open campus, fenceless: perfect for her purpose of free movement and self-realization. She'd accepted the cigarette from a sweet looking brown-eyed boy, just yesterday outside Big Joe's. Now she holds it like a secret turned in towards her palm, flicks it in front of her and grinds it out with her heel.

Flo arrives late and has a note from her mom in her pocket (which won't be used). The vacant halls stretch in a yawn. The homeroom class turns towards her as she enters. Her name reverberates on Mr Bentley's lips.

'Flor-i-da Fremont.'

'That's me.'

'Please be on time in the future.'

'Oh that. I had six siblings to drop off at the dive round the corner.'

'Was that an apology?'

'No, sir. An explanation. I will most likely be late every day.'

'And where did you learn your manners?'

'From my mother, in what most of the town calls "that whore-house." I just call it home. If I'd learned them from Hal, he's my dad, I'd just have scowled.'

'Please sit down, Miss Fremont.'

'Thank you sir. Nice tie.' Flo smiles and winks and then plonks herself in her seat. Seven hours, every day, just to herself.

There are things Flo needs from her freshman year, and there are things she doesn't need. She doesn't need to be popular or 'educated' or taught how the world works. She doesn't need friends or a boyfriend or anything social. She needs time to think so she can plan the next twenty years. She needs to figure out what college she'll escape to.

She likes the shape of her state, the curve of her shores, the tender foray of islands out into the expanse of water and the very independence of her borders. But as she sits there waiting for the first bell to ring, a mockingbird sings its pretty little stolen song, and despite her bravado and her plans of escape, Flo misses her siblings.

Tex arrives at school just before the bell.

The gates looming ahead will soon be slammed shut. Home lies behind him; the school building and safety, stand fifty yards ahead of him. Blacktop against his heels, hands tightly balled in his pocket, Tex rushes, nearly runs. This time he'll make it.

Greg McCrae, who has had to repeat eighth grade, holds a kid aloft by the collar. The kid's face is red, an unhealthy red.

This time I'll fight back, Tex thinks.

'Can't breathe, can't breathe,' the other boy rasps. 'Let me go. Please.' He's begging. It's pathetic.

Bill, the other McCrae, waits until Tex attempts a dash and swerve past him and then he's grabbed Tex too, without taking a single step. His hands sharp like claws. They'd been waiting for him. Bill holds him by the belt loop and the collar, which chokes him as he's lifted. 'Pansy Fremont. You wuss, you faggot.'

'You fat losers have never been kissed. It's a shame, wouldn't want you to be left out.' The other kid's face is red and shiny, like bubblegum.

The other boy doesn't even squirm as Greg shoves him against the gate, a deep rattle.

The bell, the bell, Tex hopes.

'Ms Jack!' The other boy looks around, pleads for an adult when none is within spitting distance. 'Dad. Dad! Please save me.'

'Here's the Fremont fat boy.' Bill holds him close and at the same time away from himself like he smells. 'Ripe, sweaty pansy.'

'Fremont, meet…'

Greg elbows his captive. 'What's your name, kid?'

'Bubba.'

'Hubbabubba?'

'Fremont meet Hubba Bubba.'

'Hubba Bubba meet Fremont.'

They hold the boys aloft facing each other. The brothers have a hundred pounds of muscles on the other kids, easy. And their meanness makes them tough as tires, sharp as stakes. Tex thinks, I'm not going to whimper, not going to.

'Kiss him,' Bill orders, 'kiss him.'

A crunch of onlookers surrounds the boys. The bell finally rings and is ignored.

'Kiss kiss kiss kiss kiss kiss kiss.'

Sweaty and gross and crying. Tex is not really standing but lifted and pushed at him. The other brother shoves Bubba in Tex's direction.

No, no, no, thinks Tex. Not him.

Sweaty and crying, bubblegum cheeks Bubba blubbers. Bubba right there. Not him, Tex thinks. And they're smooshed together. Smooshed, mashed. A brother at each of their backs. Push, push and they collide. Headbutt, their noses bleed, crack of teeth, and the brothers push and push and move the two boys around simulating kissing whether they want it or not.

'Fat boy and fat boy sitting in a tree, K I S S I N G.'

Let me die, thinks Tex.

'Open your mouths!' And there's blood and salty tears. Taunts. Kiss kiss kiss.

Let them die, let them die, thinks Tex.

A chorus of voices, 'K I S S I ...'

Tex and Bubba sitting in a tree. Tex thinks he can hear the voices of some of his sisters a bit louder, more insistent than the rest of the crowd.

The second and final bell rings and kids pass on both sides racing to get into the building, glancing but not wanting to get caught up in the fast grasping McCrae hands.

'What you looking at Goldilocks?' Bill scowls at a girl passing by. 'And you, want a bit of this,' he adds, grabbing his crotch with his free hand.

The brothers release the boys with a shove. Bubba lands and catapults himself up in a flash, running past the brothers, giving them a wide berth and never giving Tex a single glance.

Tex has been trimming down. Skinnier than he's ever been. After tying his jeans with rope for weeks, a gap at his crotch, long t-shirts to hide his shame, this morning he'd finally been able to button the new skinny jeans. One of the Corners had cut holes in the knees but that wasn't the point: that morning his jeans had buttoned but he was still an easy target. Damn Flo, she's gonna pay.

At lunch thunder booms and pandemonium reigns in the lunch hall. Flo finds a far corner of a far corner table, and the quiet chocolate-eyed boy finds her, and they eat in silence while a food fight rages around them. In the afternoon, she continues on as before, interacting, being witty, asking and answering questions, and all the time holding herself deep in her head, safe, plotting.

Flo finishes school later than the younger Fremonts and she envisions them walking home under the auspices of Tex, who has stepped up to the plate and shouldered his new responsibilities. She dawdles, listening out for birdsong, and spots Tex walking ahead. He's alone and lingering with privilege. She bets he delegated his responsibilities to Naomi, damn him, and Flo's sure her sister's scuffed knuckles will prove it. An edge starts across his face, a new hardness, and Flo feels a sting in her gut and the mockingbird sings out, like a scratched record, hiccupping through the same song again and again.

Tex justifies his slow pace on this journey home by blaming his limp, that ache Dr Sampson calls 'phantom', but there's nothing phantom about it. The hip clicks and grinds and sharp-shoots pain like there's the tip of an arrow lodged there. No way is it phantom. He walks slowly past Big Joe's and the huge block stretches up, eight houses on either side of the street, the graveyard and their house at the top.

Bubba was weird, ugly, and yet he'd tasted sweet, like apple and cinnamon. He must have had oatmeal for breakfast. Bubba's mouth had been hot, but his lips were cool and his sweat, it felt real. Tex imagines that's what it would be like to wrestle with him. His teeth were sharp, his hands left burn marks where he tried to push Tex away. These points of contact remained full of heat for Tex. His own arms had been flung open and he hadn't known what to do with them. Their bellies touching, and lower, and Tex hopes Bubba hadn't felt it. Thank god the McCraes hadn't seen it. He'd have been dead. Dead. Tex counts out the steps beneath his breath.

118, 117. He picks up his pace, burping with the carbonation of the bubbles from his can of pop. His arms flung out, he'd been given, taken, accepted.

Flo races up to him.

'Tex!' He doesn't even turn around but instead picks up his pace again, 98, 97, 96

'Tex!'

86, 85, 84, 83

'Please!' Flo yells.

That halts him as abruptly as if she'd pinched him. Then he starts to race on again, thinking it's a trick.

65, 64, 63

'Please,' Flo says again, quieter.

52, 51

Tex stops, she draws up beside him and he starts walking again.

50, 49, 48

'You didn't have to do that this morning. It was mean.'

'No it wasn't. You were fine.'

'No, Flo, I wasn't.'

'You're standing here aren't you?'

He can't tell her about the smooshing and the name-calling, about the sweetness and terror. He can't tell her about Bubba.

20, 19, 18

A hand on his arm, and she steps in front of him, but off to the side so that the house dominates his view.

'What do you see?' Flo asks.

He takes a step to the side. His movements are determined, shut down; his wide stance is iron-jointed. 'The house, I see home.'

'Is that enough?'

'Yes.'

Flo turns and they both look at the house. In this light, it looks okay from the outside.

'It'll fall down one day unless you and Dad take care of it, you know.'

17, 16, 15

Tex walks on. 'The house?' he tosses back to her. 'It takes care of itself.'

3, 2, 1 and the screen door bangs shut behind him.

Flo remains outside, assessing it all. Hal is in the process of putting in new insulation, and the roof was replaced awhile back, and he has grand plans to paint it in the spring, but Flo looks down where the earth buckles ever so slightly near the cement base and thinks, no one is paying attention to the foundations.

She walks to the back door, the unhappy sound of keys jangling in her pockets, and she swears she hears the house creak and sigh.

HOMEOSTASIS

The Corners ride their bikes out past the town, out to the fields and creeks. They stir up mini dust bowls and Arizona doesn't talk much, she doesn't need to. She's skimming by in school and doesn't care. Years are passing and Naomi will be going to high school in the autumn, Arizona the year after. The blue bluffs dull to grey and the girls turn around, legs burning. Sweat drenches their backs. When they hit town, Naomi and Utah take the basketball off the back of Naomi's bike and start to shoot some hoops. Arizona stretches her calves and starts her run.

As if the Fremonts needed it, Ari has the habit of bringing all attention to herself as she runs through the town. Compact, built to survive extreme conditions, with a long enough arm-span to be a natural climber, she doesn't stop at running but moves to extreme running, free running. A few years ago, she'd started with a two-mile run and at the half-way point where she'd pivot to run back home she'd leap-frog back and forth over Peterson's fence, jump the fence, run ten paces, jump the fence, run ten paces, along the length and back. Every few weeks she'd add moments of suspension and climbing and leaping and more distance.

She eventually built to a quick, daily four-mile circuit; the town section includes roof-running and jumping, a flag pole, and one particularly sturdy awning at Bausbaugh's five and dime. Ol' Chick B always tips his hat to her.

'Hiya, Ari. Looking good.' Or 'You're looking a bit tired, want a lemonade?' Today it's: 'Not as much clearance, are you doing your push-ups?'

And she responds, as she always does, 'Looking dashing, my Chickadee.'

The other shopkeepers gossip and chew and shout out their thoughts without censor.

'Keep your hands off my awning!'

'Run around this!'

And once she's past they mumble to each other.

'They shouldn't let her run wild, not like that.'

'Heading for a fall that one is.'

'Fast rust has a way with Fremonts, that's for sure.'
'You just never know.'
'You never know.'

After her free runs, Arizona often falls asleep on the couch as her siblings play wildly all around her. She's all or nothing. Her body makes small supple movements as if she's flying and able to control the world with the smallest movement of her hand. When she sleeps water gurgles beneath the house, a protective force of water that runs through, trickles over, gathers in the house. It morphs, slows, and speeds up again, but often takes the shape of water held in the palm of land as creeks, cricks, hidden and bidden, and always there to follow. Ari will never die of thirst for she takes this water with her.

SOUTHERN CROSS

Across the river from the school, in Olson's field, three crosses go up. Rachel sees them as she drops the younger kids off at school in the morning. She'd planned to head out of town for a few hours but once she parks and spots them a hundred yards across a dying thread of water she's frozen to the spot. She wants to think it's neutral, that they don't mean anything, but her whole body knows it: they're a warning. They're warning her and she sits in the car, her kids with her. She lets out a small gasp. A small resolve.

'Pretty,' says Bam.

'God signs,' says Missy.

Arizona touches Rachel's shoulder and it's not thirst Rachel feels, but power. 'Mom, do they mean what I think they mean?'

'Yes, they do.'

Everyone sees them across the blacktop, there's an open strip of undeveloped land that leads right to the main drag around the cement town-square. It's not like the Fremonts are the only mixed-race family in town, it's not like they're the only ones targeted, only that's how it feels. They're the ones making noise, they're the ones who refuse to be invisible. If only Rachel hadn't been so very noticeable in her infidelity; if only Hal didn't fight so hard for the high-profile projects; if only their kids had the ability at all to blend in, even the smallest bit.

Instead of escaping out of town, Rachel goes to the store and gets stares from the same old-timers, but nothing more. A few of the women even soften towards Rachel, like they wish they hadn't run off at the mouth like they did to their men, husbands, brothers or sons, who are far more likely to act rashly. Other than the newly constructed symbols of love and charity and sacrifice, nothing really changes on this morning.

At recess the crossed shadows ripple on the still winter-narrowed creek. It could fall to anyone to get outraged. After school the Corners ride home, break the locks off the cellar door to the basement, off the garage side-door, and they strap the axes they can find onto the back of their bikes, ride to the edge of the playground, unbind their tools, ford the river, which barely reaches their thighs this time of year, and chop the things down. They don't wait for the cover of night.

'No way,' says Arizona, 'we're not hiding.'

Kids run wild on the playground, roughhousing, having football practice, running the track; parents and teachers chat on sidelines but no one is willing to take responsibility for something as big as this.

Across the river the girls chop things down with ease and speed. This town, this town thinks too much of itself. This town thinks that the past is the only future. This town is theirs. This town is their home. You fight for home. You fight for family.

Rachel leaves Flo at the house with the younger girls; Hal is still at work, and Tex has been lost in his room for some time.

The Corners build a bonfire that can be seen from the next town. People watch from a distance as Rachel Fremont screeches to a stop in the school parking lot and walks right through the water towards her daughters. Rachel and the Corners watch the fire as the dark around them grows darker, safer. Myth will have it that they strip off their clothes and dance naked around, and then through, the flames. That their eyes turn red and they rise into the sky and curse the town, that they call to their sides the will of evil spirits. Truth is that the three girls and their outsider mother sit and wait for a hostile crowd to appear. When nothing transpires and the fire has burned to embers, they ford the river again and go home. Flo meets them at the door, a hug for each. 'Dinner's on the table.'

Later Flo and her mom sit and drink cups of tea. Flo reaches out and touches her mom's hand. 'Lou, Missy and Bam watched the whole thing from the window. "Pretty lights in town," they said. Then Lou said, "Sparks, sparks in the sky." And then she cried and I couldn't get her to stop.'

With the Corners gone way into the evening, Tex makes good use of the time. He creates a slow puncture in the front tire of Naomi's bike—maybe she'll take a wee tumble. He melts the soles of Ari's favorite pair of running shoes and he glues all the pages of Utah's journal together so it's like a rock when he's finished. If he could find her stash of old notebooks, he'd take them and stick them to walls of the house or maybe even school. Utah always looks at him in this way, like she knows something he doesn't and he doesn't come out well in the scenario. 'Watch it Tex,' she often says, 'I've seen it and you'd better be careful.'

She's as crazy as Naomi if she thinks she can see the future. He mocks Naomi for her habit of still making space for Cole, and speaking of her as if she were still alive.

'She's dead,' he says, 'and you're crazy.'

Ari has to be held back from punching him and Flo says, 'Really Tex, really. Couldn't you be more inventive, or more sensitive? Maybe you could just behave yourself?'

'Tell them to stop being duds, and I'll stop pulling them up for their stupidity.' Naomi can't really take the criticism and he's starting to see there isn't so much fun in that. His wars with Flo are subtle and all about the long view. They both know it. In twenty years time they'll take the final tally and he'll win.

His sisters always retaliate. Sometimes by breaking the chair he sits on in the dining room or short-sheeting his bed. They're quite good with bugs but he has developed a tolerance and so his reactions are faked and they've not really found anything that can get to the heart of anything.

A week later, a Friday late afternoon, and Arizona stretches her calves and starts to run. For some people, logic and learning create pathways. For others, it's instinct and experience that gets them where they're going. Both require knowledge, people just acquire it in different ways. How Ari thinks isn't how anyone else thinks. She doesn't have words for what she feels when she runs. She runs along lines only she can see: broken-in paths, young rivers, intersecting and connected by infinite or nearly infinite paths to the same point. Each route has its own danger, its own excitement. Maybe what she knows—her instincts—are a kind of topography only she can see and it's in constant flux. She trusts not only herself but the ground, the objects built up from the ground, and she trusts her hands to grip, her arms to swing, her legs to bend and spring and absorb the shock of the landing. Her body is inexhaustible and it has never let her down.

When she free runs her timing is breath and she breathes steadily towards the time when she can leave this place at her back. She has a few different routes she runs. First time around any route she tests and practices each and every element, checking each distance and learning the momentum she'll need, the push from her legs or arms. Today she starts slowly on a well-known route. Jogging out to the edge of the field, she places a firm hand on the cross-plank, jumps the low wooden fence, three strides, and back over, she does this until she's passed nine posts. She jumps up onto the solid end-post, pushes off, does a somersault in the air and lands lightly. Lifts her head. It's quiet, no one out at all. It's like the grey sky has brought a warning and people have chosen to stay in for the evening. Now she starts to hit her stride.

Up to the school, across the blacktop, giving a wave to Utah and Naomi who shout hello back and stand at the edges of the court to give her room. She climbs the basketball pole, swings off the ring, lands, does the other pole. Across the grass towards town and up the pile of broken tiles to the top of Pearson's roof, and from that roof to the roof of Cuttey's the locksmith's. Leap across to the long, angled storage for the brick factory and down to the street. Jump every other sidewalk square and leap to catch Chick's awning for a single swung loop and it's wrong, all wrong. Although the pole is her hand it's no longer attached to anything solid and she's still flying forward towards the building's brick corner, the top of Chick's head just visible at the edge of her sight, as he's come out to meet her. She doesn't want him to see this, it's going to be ugly.

But Chick sees it all. 'Ari!' And it's his yell that brings Utah and Naomi running. His beautiful girl is a pile on the ground, unconscious, bones through the skin of her arm, her face cracked open with a fissure from her forehead to her jaw.

'Don't move her.'

The girls kneel around, their skin, the edges of what they know, ache. The ground parches out from where Ari lies. In an instant it browns, cracks, and this drought spreads into branches and limbs of parched earth. By the time the ambulance arrives, the creek has evaporated and the ground has taken the water from the pipes.

Utah stands outside Chick's store, waiting with Arizona. A window meets itself at a right angle. That's what her teacher said and Flo confirmed it. Utah puts her fingertips together, stretches her flattened palms like planks, and her hands make half of a square. A doorframe meets at right angles and a door makes a right angle at all its corners. When you close a door, there's a space between them, ninety degrees, and they're separate, can be separated. A cross intersects and creates four corners, pointed inwards and proves that not all corners are generous, not all corners have integrity.

In space, and in the ground, Utah and her sisters exist because two planes stretch, intersect, and continue to stretch. We're right angles extended, she thinks, the surface of our borders shared.

A corner of a building is a right angle jutting out into space. This is another corner that is not safe.

Rachel gets the call and tries to keep Flo at home with the girls.

'No way, Mom. I'm coming with you. We all are.' Flo puts on Bam's coat, Missy's hat. She calls up to Tex, and when she gets no response she runs up to his room, opens the door.

'Manners! You should knock!'

'Arizona is in the hospital, come on.'

He's sitting, reading magazines and doesn't look up. 'You all will do just fine without me.'

'She's your sister, Tex. Come on.'

'I'm staying,' he says, 'Ari wouldn't want my help.' Flo turns and runs down the hall and then the stairs, scooping up her youngest sisters.

'Hey, close the door,' Tex shouts but she is long gone.

The Fremonts know the ER, they've had plenty of mishaps, accidents, broken bones, a few stitches, many fights between the kids, but nothing like this. Ari is unconscious and her wrist broken, her elbow cracked, her ankle and ribs sprained. Rachel stays at the foot of her bed, Missy and Bam sitting on her lap. Lou with Flo sit on the side by the door and the Corners are rooted to the window-side of the bed.

'Flo, can you go call your father? Tell him what's happened.'

Coins in hand, Flo walks down the hall. Beige tiled floor, white walls scuffed at waist level from gurneys. She holds the receiver of the payphone slightly away from her cheek, punches the numbers in quick succession.

'Hal. Pick up the phone, you screw-up,' she says to his answer phone at work. 'Your daughter might be dying. Get your butt to the hospital.'

Hal's at his desk at the office, the volume of his phone turned all the way down. The planning meeting is in two days and he has to get this job. The town hall is his, he's been dreaming about it since before he met Rachel. This building, the town square, the name Fremont, chiseled into the corner stone.

Rachel and the other kids all stay with Ari and a purple sky kaleidoscopes with fast moving black clouds, and no one but the Fremonts and a few hardy nurses can find Ari's room with ease. Cassiopeia glows so brightly she can be seen in the afternoon sky, through the clouds.

Hours later, Rachel tries to stay at the hospital, but the nurse won't hear of it. Neither will her supervisor. He points to a sign, the visiting hours long since over.

'But I'm her mother.'

'And I'm the boss. We've already been too lenient, the kids shouldn't be in here at all.'

Around her, her kids are restless, hungry and anxious. Naomi and Utah look unwell, she should get them home. If Hal were here, she could give him the kids and win the fight to stay. But he's not here. 'Come on, we have to go home. We'll be back first thing tomorrow.'

Each of the girls, in turn, kiss Arizona. Rachel last. 'I'll be at the map, Ari. Meet me there.' Flo and Rachel gather the girls together, stuff them all into the car and take them home. They walk them in the door and to bed. No one protests. Flo falls into bed beside Lou, with her shoes still on.

Rachel's alone and continuing her vigil at the map. A physical pain fills her chest, she cannot lose another girl. The island off the east coast pulses and her children crackle, asleep, but barely, they're rested on the edge of waking. She hums and it soothes them.

Walt's singing had calmed her too, a long time ago. She doesn't remember it except as a story. So she tells it as a story in the hall, to the map, and her children dream it.

'Just here,' she points, 'in this bright water, there's an island shaped like a heart and its shore varies with the tide. It has sandy beaches and cliffs and pebbled inlets where small smooth stones clatter together with the tide's force.'

On this island lived a girl, a pretty girl who was an orphan but still much loved. When she was only a week old her mom had died, and her Uncle Walt and Aunt Shirley took her in and raised her among their sons when her father said he couldn't raise a girl. Walt, a big man with a rumbling laugh and a quick temper, had only known boys and yet this tender girl stole his heart, right from that first day.

'You're a wifey for her,' teased Shirley.

'I sure am,' he said. 'We're going to raise her right. No amount of love is too much for her.'

Walt never slept deeply when this girl was a baby. He always listened for a sigh, whimper, or cry and he'd be up in a flash taking care of the girl's every need, singing her songs as she slept, woke, slept again. 'With so much loss she shouldn't have to ask more than once, not at this age,' he'd say to Shirley when he returned to bed.

It was winter and sound travels clear and fast in cold air. The girl gave a single cough and Walt heard it. It sounded like something had broken loose and made her cry out. Up in a flash and he was beside her crib without having to turn on a single light. He knew the way barefoot, with closed eyes. The girl lay choking. He turned on the light. He picked her up, supporting her head, her wracked body, coughing, coughing, choking and her body felt limp but for the power of each hack. He checked her mouth and nose and saw nothing obstructing her breath. Blood appeared at the corner of her mouth and small tears of blood escaped from her right eye. Like a shot deer, something stalked and lost. He used the edge of his shirt, wiped the blood. Kissed her cheek. 'Shhhhh.'

'Shirley!' his voice boomed tender and loud at the same time. 'Shirley. Get the boat.'

He would not let go of his girl. Shirley rowed the three of them to shore. She rowed swiftly across the half-frozen, dark, winter water and the ice knocked the boat but Shirley was strong and Walt's resolve would have bust up an iceberg if it had gotten in their way. Once on shore, Shirley led Walt by the arm to the ER.

'She'll be fine. She'll be fine. We got her fast. This is not her time. Not her time, Walt.'

An aneurism, they said, and the doctors whipped up some magic, and said she'd have died without Walt and Shirley's quick thinking.

'She'd have been dead by morning,' a young woman doctor said.

The girl's eye worked fine after, almost as good as the other, and it looked normal enough, slightly lighter actually, like a twinkle.

Rachel pauses. Hours have passed toward morning, but it's still night, and Rachel's heart aches for the parents she'd left behind, for her daughter lying alone at the hospital, and for her husband who has not bothered to come home. She continues the story.

Now I didn't tell you about her dad. I've said she was an orphan, and the facts of the situation bear that out, even if her dad was still living and breathing. Before she was born her dad, Trevor, had been charming and generous and was head of the Island's ruling Council. The youngest ever, but turns out he had a tight mean soul. He made a bad decision when she was born and it poisoned his soul. You see the girl was the first girl ever to be born on the Island. There'd been no law against it because it had just simply never happened before. Trevor could have made the choice to love her and to love her mother. Instead, he banished the girl's mother and she died in the midnight riptide. He disowned the girl, the only child he'd ever have. Walt and Shirley believed the girl belonged to the Island, that she signaled a much-needed change, and they took her in even though it meant that some people on the Island shunned them. Within the year, they'd risked their lives to save her.

The girl's father didn't falter or soften his heart. Walter saw Trevor all the time, walking the path between other houses, but not to Walt's and Shirley's. If he glanced over towards his daughter and her guardians, Walt did not see it, did not want to see it. The girl was his now, his and Shirley's. His boys loved her and she lived smack dab in the middle of it all, holding her own. Prettier of course, than his boys, but that task wasn't a tough one. Walt was never a looker, Shirley either, but both were strong—pull-a-cart-with-one-arm sort of strong—and together they were a force to be reckoned with. Shirley's face gave away her soul's intentions: feminine, undoubted, thin, strong cheekbones and jaw, well apportioned lips, dark eyes, and just a flash of red to her hair when the evening sun caught it. It's her hair he'd seen first all those years ago. But he'd not kidnapped her, he could tell by her walk she'd never go for that. A slow-courting. Months. They met in the library where she worked and talked books over in the corner, until the mistress of the house fired her for failure to comply with the regulations of the system. If only she'd known what skills Walt acquired during the courting. One day Shirley followed him home to the Island, in her own boat that would be the boat she rowed to shore to save Rachel. A boat that to this day knocks against the Island women's pier when the tide is high with a storm. Although Trevor disowned his daughter, he didn't let go of her. Instead he held onto her like resentment and he held his own soul in his hands and twisted it tighter. When she was sixteen he called an Island-wide meeting and decided she no longer had a right to live there.

Walt and Shirley stood behind her in that meeting, ready to fight for her. Shirley with a knife strapped to her leg beneath her skirts, Walt with a brass knuckle hidden beneath his folded arms, and both willing to be fueled by an anger the girl had never seen but somehow knew was there, in protection. Walt would die for her. Actions make the man. He was her father, Shirley her mother. The girl wished for this family with all her heart and found it already to be true. Sometimes truth has a different name than you've been taught and sometimes family is found, family is made. And unmade.

The girl held her dad's gaze. He thought both of her eyes were the same, for you had to look closely to see gleam of survival in her, and he never saw her, not really. She stood across from him and she knew that he'd have never have taken her to the mainland's hospital, he'd never have heard her cough in the first place. Never have pressed her to his chest while Shirley rowed. Risking everything. This man, stupid and proud, bullheaded and mean, did not have the ability to save her. She wondered about fate, about whether her mom died in order that Walt and Shirley could save her later. It didn't matter. It didn't matter who'd fathered her, who had raised her, the Island was her home, and she had a right to live there.

'Mom was true to you,' she said to her dad. 'So was I. If you do this, you're alone.'

His jaw pulsed, his eyes glassed-over and then his face lost all emotion as he banished her in a booming voice, his arm flung out as if to strike her. But she'd stepped away out of range and taken the first stride of a fast run.

'Go!' shouted Shirley.

'Run!' yelled Walt waving his arm. 'We love you. We'll find you!'

Already on her way, already desperately sad, she heard a cry and glanced back to see Shirley knocked down. She made to turn and run to Shirley but Walt looked to her, everything in him beamed love and protection and he shouted, 'Go. Don't stop. Go!'

Survival is survival.

Walt made sure she was running a clear path to the cove and then he bent down to his wife. 'She's safe,' he whispered. 'Our girl is safe. I've spoken to the water and it knows its charge.'

Rachel presses her hand to Arizona. 'And the girl ran clear of all that might hold her back.'

The morning remains dark but the birds start to get restless and she speaks to her children once more. 'Kids, know this. Sometimes family is chosen. Sometimes blood isn't right. Sometimes family is made. Walt and Shirley blessed the girl as their daughter and the water carried her to safety.'

Hal's never seen a sky this color, pitched black and blue, no moon at all. A single constellation flickers through clouds. As he climbs out of his truck, the storm takes swipes at the ground with parched fingers and marks his cheeks with flying dirt and pebbles. He has to push both the car door and then the back door to the house closed with both hands, and he's thankful when the latter stays shut. The house moans with the wind.

When he walks through the hall, the map aches with a slow dull light and Rachel sits on the chair, forehead resting against the gulf.

'Rachel?'

'Go to bed, Hal.' Her dulled voice does not negotiate.

The map looks warped, off-color.

'It's too late, Hal. You can't do anything now. You're too late. They kicked us out of the hospital at eleven. I'd have fought harder but I didn't want to leave Flo to take care of all the girls. If you'd been there it'd have been different. Now she'll be alone all night.'

'What are you talking about?'

'Don't even pretend Hal. I'm beat. I'm beaten. Go to bed. Sleep soundly. Go to work in the morning. It's what you do.'

'Rachel, what are you talking about?'

'Your daughter, Hal. Arizona. Someone sabotaged Chick's awning and sent her flying. She's a mess. We're lucky she's alive and we'll be luckier if she walks again.'

'That girl never walked anywhere. I see her race past the office almost every day.' She flies past his window, at dusk when he's watching birds and flips him the finger, but he doesn't say it to Rachel.

'Don't you answer your phone anymore, Hal?'

'Not with a deadline like this coming up. That guy from Ohio arrives tomorrow, he's staying at the Mayor's house.'

She puts a hand up, interrupts. 'Hal, stop it.'

'Akron's going to steal…'

'Did you hear me?'

'I can't lose this…'

'Stop.' She's out of the chair and gripping his arms. 'I get it. More than that, I tolerate it. It's destroying us, but I tolerate it. You need this work. I get it. But stop excusing yourself. Our daughter nearly died today because some fool in this town doesn't like the way we look, or act, or something. This wasn't a general warning. This wasn't Miss West frowning in our direction. This is their attempt to scare us away.'

'They won't run us out of town.'

'Are you sure about that?'

'I've got land, Rachel. Lots of land.'

'But there's nothing on it and we're close to defaulting on the second mortgage. You're not building anything that supports us. How am I supposed to raise this family? It's your business. Do what you think best but you can't spend all your time dreaming, you can't go so big that you can't pull it back. We've got all these kids, Hal. We've decided to have all these kids. That matters. Step up for us. Another of our girls nearly died today, this one because she's a Fremont in this ass-backward town. Because she doesn't belong here. None of us do.'

'That's wrong thinking. We all belong here. This is our home. We've built this town. That means something.'

'People obviously don't think so. There were three crosses erected. Three, Hal. One the first time, then three; how many next time? A baker's dozen? Next time will it be in our backyard? Will they stop there?'

'You knew about the first one?'

'Of course. You could see it from the kitchen window.'

'How long was it up?'

'Long enough.'

'I mean it. How long?'

'Two days at most.'

'What do you want me to do now?'

'Fight for us. Go see your daughter.'

'You said they kicked you out.'

'They did. But I had all the kids with me. I'm here and you can go to her. You're her dad, fight for her.'

The last thing he wants to do is go out into that weather and drive to the hospital. It gives him the creeps, those sterile walls, the soulless halls. He pulls Rachel into his arms.

'Forgive me. Please.'

Her back stays straight but she does not push away. 'Go be with Arizona, then come back home and be with us.'

Outside the wind whips branches and large objects fly across the road, but Hal drives with speed and determination to the hospital.

Dark, and shadows in the dark. Ari's not afraid but she is alone. No one and then someone. Holding her hand. Smells like her dad. He smells like hard work. Dirt and sweat and something metallic. He cries and the bed shakes just a bit. He doesn't fit in the hospital, but she's pleased he's here. She can sleep now knowing she's safe. 'I'll take care of this,' he says. 'I'll take care of you. We won't lose you too.' She knows his hand will be dry, crackling dry, because when she's sick she takes everything she can get. But he holds on. He lays his head down on the bed to get some sleep and the weight of his head pushes the bed down and rests against her ribs. When she wakes he's sitting again still holding her hand. 'You've done a good thing, Ari. A very good thing.'

His palm will have a permanent mark, two lines intersecting in space like a base beneath a weathervane or a conjecture of where she and her sisters meet in space. If you were to stretch the right material around this shape, you'd create a globe, a whole world.

'The bolt of Chick's awning rusted away,' Buck Harrison, the new Sheriff and too big for his boots, says to Rachel and Chick the next morning, as they all stand looking up at the place on the building where the awning used to be connected. 'You can see it here, right at the joint.'

'Impossible,' says Chick. 'I check it every Saturday morning. There's no way I want that girl hurt. No way at all.' He looks at Rachel. 'I love that girl like she's my own.'

'Are you sure she's not yours?' Buck says under his breath, both Rachel and Chick hear him. It's a hilarious proposition, fifty years between them, and at any other time they'd give it the hearty laugh that comment deserved. Today is not a day for laughing.

Rachel squares up to the Sheriff. 'Serve and protect, Buck. The whole town.'

This man of the law clears his throat. 'I hear what you're saying, Chick, but the facts say something elsc. I'm sure you'll want to press charges, Mrs Fremont. Isn't that right? Someone will have to pay for what's happened to your daughter.'

'I'd never hurt that girl. Never,' Chick says, hat in hand.

Rachel touches his arm. 'I know that, Chick. You have nothing to worry about.' She turns to Buck. 'No, we don't want to press charges. This has nothing to do with Chick. This is linked to those crosses that came down. They were the warning, this is the follow-through.'

'They didn't mean anything, ma'am. We live in a Christian town, sometimes pleasure in the Lord makes a fellow want to rejoice and make grand gestures of praise and thanks.'

'So the fact that one cross came down and they put up three more, that doesn't make you suspicious?'

'I've no idea what that means.'

'That's strange Sheriff, because I know exactly what it means.'

Buck faces Chick. 'Mr Bausbaugh, do you want to press charges against the girl, trespassing an' all? Destruction of your property.'

'Are you high, Buck? Really? Have you lost your marbles?'

'Well, I know a few other people who want to instigate an investigation for individuals who have destroyed some private property recently. I've been reluctant to do it, but you never know.'

'That'd be an interesting case for you Sheriff, for the whole town. Acrimonious. I'm thinking. Might split this town's vote next time you're up for election.'

Buck's hand runs smooth rings around his hat, he doesn't blink. 'Are you both sure, we're square on this thing? No charges on either side?'

'We're sure.'

'Then I'm done here,' Buck says as he climbs into his car, turns on his siren and lights and throws up dust as he peels away.

'I don't know how this happened,' Chick says, fingering the rusted joint, 'I watch after that girl.'

'Of course. We know that. Don't you worry, she'll be fine. I think she'll like the scar—she was too pretty before.' Rachel smiles at him.

'You're just saying that.'

'Come on, I'm needing a few things for home. Show me what

you've got.' The snapped awning lies alley-side against the building and Rachel points to it. 'I'll go halvers with you for a new one?'

'Nah, I was just going to leave it down; why risk it?'

'Because that's what life is, risk. That's why Ari does what she does. She'll be out here the day after they release her and there's nothing you or me or anyone can do to stop her.'

Rachel takes his arm. 'Do you have any gold leaf in? And a small tin of cobalt? I could use a new brush too.'

'I have everything you need, Mrs Fremont.' As they walk into his store, they both avoid looking at the dried trail of Ari's blood.

Hal spends that day at the hospital and then goes home and barbeques a dinner for the kids while Rachel stays with Naomi, Utah and Ari at the hospital. The whole family sits outside, wrapped up warm, joking and enjoying the break in routine that a crisis creates. The next day Hal goes to the Committee.

'Let him build it,' he says, flicking a wrist towards the guy from Akron who doesn't deserve what he's going to get. 'Me and my dad, we've given everything to this town. We've had vision and shared it with you. Listened to your views and desires, and together this town has grown, it's growing into a beauty. But now ugliness is taking hold. Small mindedness. It's bitter and full of rancor and I'm not going to fight it. If you insist on this path, if you insist on choosing an outsider rather than one of your own, if you choose his inferior plans to my proven track record, that's your choice, I'm not going to fight the low road you've chosen.'

Hal hands out a map of the town. 'It's color coded: my holdings are in blue, the mineral rights I hold are green, the water rights are red.'

Men shift in the chairs, there's a held breath only realized when an exhale stales the air of the room. No one knew Hal owned this much.

'All I have to do is do nothing and you all are screwed. But I'm not going to do nothing. I'm going to sell my holdings to people who will strip this place bare, who will leave behind poison and drought and I guarantee it, in twenty years, you and your children will be gone and this place will be a ghost town.'

'You'd be shooting yourself in the foot, destroying what you've built.'

'No guys, I'll build somewhere else. That's the thing. If you've got talent, you take it with you.'

'Now Hal,' says the Mayor, standing up, taking a step towards him, he all but pushes Akron aside. 'Don't be hasty. Don't make any rash decisions.'

'I'm willing to be convinced, John.' Hal gives him an even, neutral stare. 'But I'm promising you now, if any of my children is hurt ever again, I will not hesitate. There will be no negotiations and it will be personal.' He tips his hat to the Mayor and to Ted Pearson from the hardware store, knowing full well that rust doesn't move that fast without a bit of trade-strength acidic help.

Hal's personal assistant, Kitty, drives the contract and the budget—far more than he'd asked for—up to the house. When the family isn't there, she leaves it between the doors.

On Saturday morning, Hal takes the Corners and Lou to the hospital to bring Ari home. The nurses, true of heart and always able to find her, bend down and kiss her forehead. 'That'll be a beauty Ari,' they say, touching the bandage over the scar. 'You'll be a beauty.'

Arizona flexes her toes. What she knows, what matters, is that she'll be running again in no time. Cleanly broken bones, a hard-earned scar, and she's got plans.

THE FLOOD

Mountain, southern blackwater always has reason. Even in its purest state, even as it's better to drink than the clearer stuff, it always carries a warning.

The rain starts on a Sunday early in November and lasts ten full days. Cold blasts of spray lash at the windows while thunder rattles the roof tiles. It's a rain that takes people back to the very wetness of the stuff. Skin grows soft with the richness of the air that warms unseasonably by the hour. The gutters overflow and if this continues long enough, the house will become an awkward ark floating across flooded plains.

Nothing can take the grin from Rachel's face. When the garage roof caves in and floods the car, Rachel throws her head back and laughs. She clutches her side, holds onto the garage for support, and lets the rain wash her clean. Rachel's dark hair hangs wet and smooth, well past her shoulders. Her skin emphasizes the clearness of her eyes. Even Hal looks good in the rain.

The girls dance and splash, unconsciously remembering a world where they were safe and cherished and surrounded by their mother. Up in his room Tex hears the rain, does push-ups and sit-ups, and every so often stands just to the side of the window and watches his sisters play. His mom invites him out into the rain, Flo and Missy too, and Tex feels the hint of freedom in the air, this joy, but his hip aches, sharp and fresh, and he doesn't answer them through his closed door.

The rain inconveniences Hal: he can't work at the sites; he can't go see Sandra; he can't escape this house which pushes him upstairs as the basement fills with water, water which keeps coming and laughter buoys up the house with wet footprints trailing in and out of rooms. His wet girls splash and ask nothing of him. Rachel releases the house from all routines and chores and lets time run wild, slow and fast through the rooms of the house. She seeks Hal out, presses him against something solid, kisses him and then runs through his fingers.

After days of rain the river crumbles its banks and torrential outbursts crash uphill. Hal remembers his birds: the small clutch of this year's nests in precarious river trees. He dresses in all his rain gear, tells Lou it's not safe for her in this weather, and goes down to the river.

'I'm going to go see to your father,' Rachel says to Flo. 'Look after your sisters.'

Hal finishes transporting the nests to a box and carries the box further up the hill where he wedges it into a tight space betwee boulders. Rachel joins him, pulls him back down the hill, where the debris-thick flood rushes at their feet and she strips him down. Hal can barely hold onto her and she cradles him safe above sharp fins of rock. Every day for a week they meet on that hill, where the brow of the hill obscures their rude acts of love from their children and curious neighbors. With rain still falling, barefoot and muddy, they pick their way uphill, holding hands like teenagers.

The rain lightens, the air grows clearer, and they can see three houses rather than just the one next door; then the gas station appears and in one big gust of wind, the whole town lies exposed before them. A freezing wind comes behind this freak wet front and they know the rain has stopped and everything will be as it was before.

A LINE RUNNING HIGH TO GIRLS

The young Fremonts crash through days, weeks, birthdays and holidays. Rachel and her kids have been alone more and more and the house settles into a hectic balance. 'Work,' Hal says, 'is overwhelming. I'm doing it for you and the kids.' And their bank balance is healthier and she knows it's true even if other things are keeping him away as well. Her daughters' dolls are pilots and Missy and BamBam know the names of every piece of construction machinery going. They play hard. Rough. Fighting for themselves, and their place in the mass of bodies. She worries that it's easy to get lost; it's easy to think you're no one when your dad never calls you by name.

Outside the flood washed away much of the topsoil and stripped the hill of its quiet green growth; there's rock underneath and the roots of trees cling to what is left and although Rachel hopes that some bright brisk wind will come and drop earth and seeds, to protect this fragile place, she doesn't wait. She hauls new dirt up the hill in the station wagon and enlists kids to help her spread it, build up new vegetable beds, buoy up the maple in the corner by the fence. This will e the year for fecundity.

Lou gardens quietly beside Rachel for the first few weeks of the season and then she branches out, dragging dirt and carrying tools to small patches that she makes fit for growing. Lou plants seeds in a circle around the house. She's secretive, drawing birds to her as she works. The seedlings break the earth, and later, flowers appear.

The garden, the flowers, bring the birds closer to the house. Blackbirds sing at dawn, attracted by the water and brush. Hummingbirds feed at seven, filling ears with a buzzed frenzy of wings and Flo helps Lou change the sugar water every week. Lou plants Jerusalem roses to bring them to her and works magic at dawn, coming to breakfast with dirt under her nails. The flowers she plants bloom and close in succession, a clock, sundial, flowerdial.

Sometimes Utah joins them and for her each seed she plants is an idea or a memory. When they flower, they're stories she tells to Lou and to her mom. Today she's out with her desert sisters and Lou and Rachel are alone.

Rachel weeds the beans and carrots, the tender spinach and hardy cabbage, thins out the potatoes. She doesn't look up as Hal arrives home, her eyes go to Lou, the bright one, standing with her arms open, face lit by the sun, birds dashing and swooping around her.

Hal knocks one foot and then the other against the stairs, freeing dried clumps of mud but he keeps his boots on, his head someplace between work and wherever he's going next, and trails filth into her house.

Rachel pulls at weeds, plows through tight earth with her fingers to loosen it up, and hums a song inspired by a bird that has been hanging around the garden all day. The tune helps Lou to settle back to work.

Time passes, they sing and work and by the time Rachel realizes that the sound she hears is the screen door slamming, Hal is already at the car. 'It'll be a late one,' he says to Rachel. 'I may not be back until tomorrow night.' He runs his hand over his chin-stubble.

'But Dad look,' shouts Lou, running to him, 'see, a vermillion flycatcher. She's been here all day, she stayed just for you.'

Hal's eyes follow the rarity as she leaves her perch and flies out over the house towards the graveyard. 'A beauty,' he says, 'but she's gone now. Good eyes, Lou. You're getting good,' he says.

Hug her you fool, Rachel thinks, hug her. Give your daughter a kiss.

One foot and then another into the car which he starts and moves off before he's even closed the door. Rachel stops watching and scoops Lou up into an embrace. Her daughter now has a center of onyx, the start of the hardening of her heart. She kisses her cheeks until they're rosy, until she feels her daughter hug her back.

'Her song too,' says Rachel. 'Did you hear that?'

'She's gone now. What good is her song if it's gone?'

Lou tramples a few beans on her way into the house and Rachel stands and listens. The house rocks with laughter and fighting and from her place at the center of the family Rachel can see just about the whole world change before her eyes; it's one of those subtle things that happens suddenly. Time holds no sway over Rachel; it is simply the bedrock she crashes against. With each passing minute her children move away from her and out into themselves, but before they break free she has years of diapers and hungry mouths, dirty hands, snotty noses, heavy tempers, high pitched cries, in-fighting, gulps for air, fevering foreheads, worrying coughs, bodies needing to be held, healed, picked up, let down, washed, dried, kissed, and the house is full of homework and questioning minds, selfish niggling habits, naughty hands, picky mouths, oscillating moods, late nights, early mornings, attention-seeking behavior, and growing pains. Like all big families, their home-life is a semi-orchestrated, semi-inspired chaos—it is a grand mixture of exuberance and disappointment.

GEORGIA

The carnival, all the rides and the small accompanying circus, comes to town. The circus is not big, perhaps cousins rather than brothers, but the kids love it.

Elephants circle with women teetering on their backs and popcorn vendors pass over-filled, half-warm containers of popcorn down long rows of rowdy kids. Rachel, two weeks overdue with Georgia, gets her kids settled into seats. Tex snags the aisle seat and pretends he doesn't know who these loud girls are. Tall waxed paper cups of cola come along the aisles slopping and splashing against plastic tops, sticky brown sugar-caffeine syrup creeping from under the lids, dripping drops on all assortments of clothes. The Fremont girls reach, grab and share and eat their fill.

Tex's feet stick to the floor, his shoes are stepped on and scuffed. His belly full up with soda. The girls laugh and point and crawl and reach and shout over each other and back to friends from school and cheer on the lion tamer and the trapeze artists. His sisters are insignificant as he watches the calm grace of the tight-rope walkers and the swooping of the men on the trapezes and he imagines the wild rush of letting go and catching, letting go and catching, such bodies and sweat and sweet daring.

When the show finishes, Rachel guides them towards the long promised rides but most of them need a pee and they swerve toward the Porta-potties. Tex can't bring himself to open the door, much less make himself go in there. Who knows what'd gone on in there before him. He'd fall down that hole, he knows it, his little butt wouldn't be enough to stop him, or his new shirt would flit across a surface and pick up a fleck of poo, or worse, something invisible and deadly. He gives up his turn and waits for his sisters. They take forever but when everyone has gone but Tex, Flo threatens to take them all on the tilt-o-whirl, slapping him on the stomach and back in a clap, and he nearly pees himself. He's so over this family and despite his mother calling after him, he heads back to the house.

Rachel gives a quick wave to Tex, which is unreturned, and shakes her head as she leads her girls to the mini-train. They almost fill two cars and it's here that Rachel makes a guttural gasp and her waters lift the train as if on a wave. 'Hold on kids,' and her impeccable Fremonts grip the train confidently, unshocked by any water their mom can produce. 'Georgia is coming.'

They sail forward and come to a rest nearly where they'd started the ride. 'Mom, are you okay?' Flo climbs over a few seats to get beside her.

Her fingers grip at her belly. 'Take the girls. Call your father. Get him here as quick as you can. Call the midwife.'

'I'll phone,' says a woman Rachel does not recognize but who has taken both Bam and Missy by the hand. Missy goes easily. The woman smiles at Rachel. 'I'm Angela Jack, the math teacher at the high school, and my daughter Joanne is in Missy's class.'

Rachel yells again and everyone steps away. There's no medic, no midwife. Rachel's breath comes short and fast and her brow furls. She grips the side of the train with one hand, her belly with the other.

Out of the gathered crowd, who are all keeping their distance from the Fremont woman, steps Sandra. A small boy holds on to her belt-loop.

'Can I help you, Rachel?'

Rachel looks at her, breathes fast through her mouth. She nods and then shakes her head, unsure.

'You're Flo, right?' Sandra asks.

'Yes.'

'I'm Sandra. Your mom and I have met a few times in town, I've got training as a midwife. Can you take Johnnie here? He's my neighbor's son but if you take him with you, I'll pick him up later. I'm going to help your mom.'

'O…okay.'

Sandra takes off her thin sweater, wipes Rachel's brow and shouts out at the gathering crowd. 'I need towels, a blanket, something. Give us room. Now!' And to Rachel, 'Breathe Rachel. You'll be fine.'

Rachel closes her eyes, nods and then yells once more and this unstoppable contraction means that here, on an early evening train stranded by a flood that skews its electrics, the tenth Fremont enters the wide world.

Sandra rides with her in the ambulance and when the hospital discharges Rachel after only a few hours, she comes up to the house in the taxi too.

With the drama and the lights of the carnival and Sandra and all her help and this sweet red-faced bundle in her arms, Rachel feels… she doesn't know what she feels.

Sandra gets out of the taxi first and goes around to open Rachel's door. Rachel hands her Georgia as she pushes herself out. 'She's pretty,' says Sandra.

'Yes, she looks like…I don't know who she looks like.' A face to grow into, she supposes. She accepts the baby back into one arm and with her free hand she rubs her temple, which aches, as does her sternum, and her body pulls away from her.

'Thank you Sandra, I don't know what I would have done.'

'You're a survivor, you'd have survived.'

'Please do come up for some lemonade, or something harder.'

'No, I'll make my way home. I just wanted to make sure you got home safely. And I need to get Johnnie.'

'I'll have Hal drive you both home.'

'No, definitely not. The walk will do us good.'

'I insist.' She walks slowly up the stairs and opens the front door and shouts in. 'Hal!' They hear his feet pounding up steps and through the hall and out onto the porch and the look on his face just about says it all. He looks between one woman and the other. He's got marker on his hands and sawdust on his clothes.

Hal stands for a second as if remembering something he should have known like instinct. He leans over and kisses his wife and the small infant in her arms. 'Another beaut, she is. Was just making her state. Figured you had it covered at the hospital, you usually do.' His lips smile but his tight jaw limits their curve.

'Thanks to Sandra, it all went well.'

'She did all the hard work,' says Sandra. 'I'll just get Johnnie and we'll walk home.'

'The skinny kid? His dad came and got him about an hour ago.'

'Hal, I'd like you to give Sandra a ride home.'

He looks at Rachel and she nods, her face smooth, the baby at peace held in the crook of her arm.

'Sure thing,' he says, 'I'll get my keys.'

He drives quickly and they both sit for a minute in silence. He gets out of the car and opens her door and offers his hand. Sandra takes it and they kiss, briefly, while their hug is longer. Nothing has changed, and something has and he drives back home.

It's the middle of November and Rachel's days are busy: she takes care of the kids, gardens, and baby Georgia calms when her mother is on the move. Beneath Rachel's eyes dark circles deepen, her cheeks thin, and the sight of herself in the mirror always surprises her.

Hal has been working all the time. Rachel doesn't know what deal he made with the Mayor, what part of his soul he relinquished, but the townies' intimidation has stopped and Hal has become uglier somehow; he's brought home more money and less, she'd like to call it kindness, but maybe it's happiness. More money and less happiness.

She has Georgia in a sling and they're walking through the yard and along the creek and through the fields. Then she retraces her steps, goes inside and gathers the lists she's posted for her husband and throws them in the trash. He'll do what he can, when he can. That decision settles in her, not exactly easily, but it's a decision.

There's a roster of chores for the kids too, which she keeps stuck to the fridge, although a quick glance reveals that they seem to fall unfairly on Flo and the Corners. Tex promises to pay some of the younger girls who are duped into doing his share. Well, Missy anyway. Missy believes he will honor the careful tally she keeps.

Tex has found a stride in high school, has fallen in with the popular crowd and seems to have taken up partying. He's rude to his sisters and has taken to eating alone in the dining room again, by choice. On Friday nights a big teenage boy picks him up and they often don't see him until midday on Saturday, or even Sunday.

'Tommy, this is my mom. Mom, Tommy.'

Tommy steps forward and shakes her hand, like he's already a man and then he and her son climb into his car. He pulls away from the curb slowly but she hears him burn rubber as he hits the main road. When Tex comes back she tries to pull him into a stiff hug but he resists and she has to settle for ruffling his hair. 'Where have you been? We've missed you.'

'Out,' he says. Sometimes, 'We went to the city.'

'Where'd you stay?'

'With friends.'

She calls Hal at the office and tells him, 'He's too young to be away like that.'

'He's a boy, Rachel. You said his friend has a car?'

'Yes.'

'Then they'll be fine.'

'I seriously doubt it. Our son is becoming a waster.'

She hangs up and rubs her temples. Stands, paces. Since Cole died, Rachel often walks through the days and the nights; she moves slowly, running her hands over walls that might buckle, fences that need mending, the trunks of trees with rings which have grown so thin they can no longer support the larger branches in brisk winds. But this is different. She's distant, her kids are over there, her husband too, and she's here, detached, heavy and weighted and her head hurts, all the time, behind her eyes. She puts her ear to the ground to see if clearwater has turned thick; she lifts her eyes to the sky to see if any star or system burns too brightly; and listens for the bird who'll sound an alarm. She's restless and struggling. And so, awake and in sleep, Rachel seeks anything concrete to give proof to the feeling of dread, but she can't find it.

BORDER FAULT

Even though Tex has never particularly liked food he still misses it, the junk of it: SpaghettiOs, Doritos, grill-bubbled cheddar cheese, his mom's hot chocolate, Flo's buckwheat pancakes. But he abides by his dad's hard-knuckled lock down. His body slims, his face narrows, a jawline emerges. He's helped along by the Corners' habit of putting finely chopped chilies in his dinner. The harsh lines of the haircut and his newly acquired leanness definitely make him more rugged—but can never completely rid his face of the violent urge it seems to inspire in other people.

He manages to grow too despite the limited food, and now stands as tall as Flo, if not as strong. He's only a sophomore but soon he'll be a senior, king of the school. He's been hanging out with Tommy Newton, who is wild, much more wild than Tex, and every time they make it back from the city in one piece, Tex feels he's grown an inch, really toughened himself up.

He got home about three this morning and it's only five on a Saturday when the light in his room goes on, the overhead. 'Get up, Tex. You're coming to work with me.'

This time of day is time for no one but truckers and farmers and his dad.

'Coffee's on. Be outside at the truck in five or I'll double the hours you're working for the week.'

'Can I drive?'

'No.'

'I'm old enough to work but not…'

His dad doesn't bother to respond. Tex puts on jeans, a t-shirt and saunters down to the truck and climbs into the passenger seat. He lifts a plate filled with his mom's cookies and puts it on his lap.

'What are you wearing?' Hal asks, irate.

'I don't know. Stuff I can get dirty.'

'What do you think we do, roll in the mud? I'm not stupid, you're not getting anywhere near any machinery. I'm starting you in the office. Go make yourself decent. You're the boss's son, get that into your head. Might not matter to you, but it matters to others. One day you'll be telling them what to do. If you don't garner respect, no one will listen.'

He puts the plate on the dashboard and goes back to his room. There's light on the horizon and this is bound to make his dad mad. They're late.

When he returns to the car Tex is wearing khakis and a polo shirt.

'Better,' says Hal, 'here's a thermos.'

'I don't drink coffee.'

'With the hours you'll be keeping that'll change.'

'Can I have a cookie?'

'What are you, three?'

'Why'd you bring them then?'

'Best to bring Kitty a gift on a Saturday. Remember it. Keep whoever looks after the admin sweet.'

Hal shows Tex the office. Fake wood paneling, fake lino with gold squares and flowered centers. The windows have blinds but no curtains and the desks are utilitarian, the metal chairs sit on rollers, with ripped cushions, and are held together by vast lengths of duct tape. 'Have you thought about redecorating the place?' Tex asks.

'Why would I do that?'

'People will trust you more if your place looks like somewhere they'd want to work or live in themselves.'

'No one comes here but my men.'

'It's depressing,' says Tex. 'No style at all.'

'I don't want flash, I want productivity. You're raising a good point though about your conduct. Keep your eyes down, Tex. Get the work done. Leave everything else to me.'

Kitty comes in, her face freshly made up, her skirt pressed.

'Coffee, Mr Fremont?'

'No thanks, Kitty. We got ourselves some at home.'

'Ah, so this is Tex. Good to meet you.' She holds out her hand.

Tex takes it and kisses it.

'Ah, charming like your dad.'

Hal interrupts, 'I've got plans to talk over with John. Why don't you show Tex the phones, Kitty.'

'Sure thing, Mr Fremont.' Kitty turns to Tex, flicks her head to get him to come to her desk. 'It will be great if you can do the phones. I'm usually chained to this desk. Now, there's two ways to answer calls. You'll start with: "Fremont Construction, how may I direct your call?" We've only got two lines, so you just press the button that's lit-up, ask your question, hit hold, press your dad's internal line, tell him who's on the phone and then let him pick up that line. Don't answer any questions, because you won't know the right answer. One day, on your dad's nod, you'll be able to ask, "Fremont Construction, how can I help you?" You got that?'

Tex wants to kill himself. Working for his dad will be torturous but for the first time in his life he'll have plenty of pocket money.

At six they drive home together. His sisters are already eating. He and his dad walk past them with the slimmest of greetings. 'Give Tex an extra helping tonight,' Hal says. Tex follows him through to the dining room, looking back over his shoulder and grinning at his sisters.

After dinner Utah sits at the kitchen table and writes it how she wants it to be. She finds herself drawing each member of her family.

When she draws Tex she keeps to hardwired words like place names and body parts. Near Tex's heart she pulls out a red pen and writes LOVE. Almost immediately she picks a wide marker and Tex is left with a black smudge of a heart. She rushes to finish, his feet mere sweeping scribbles of unreadable words, and then she shoves him into her folder that's full to bursting.

This sheet wakes her up in the middle of the night, pressed together with all her other drawings, and she knows she'll only be able to get to sleep again if she gets rid of it. She slides it free and the paper flaps in front of her as she runs in her bare feet down the hall and the back stairs. In the kitchen she pulls out the trashcan and rips the sheet of paper into the tiniest pieces she can manage.

Rachel sits on Hal's rickety old chair, the heat of remembered sex pressing the back of her thighs, and she observes the map. It's beginning to look like it holds up the wall, not the other way around. Utah walks past with a glass of water and kisses the top of her forehead, 'There's a bed upstairs Ma.' But Rachel doesn't move and when Utah is gone it's only a short while before the house sleeps and she gets up and stands close to the wall.

'How are you, old friend?' she whispers to the map.

Rachel runs her hand over each state, closing her eyes, whispering, reminding, encouraging. Her kids sleep deeply, rocked, while the softest of hands push aside their hair and kiss their foreheads.

After hours at the map, hours she couldn't track if she tried, her belly tumbles, her legs anxious for movement and the sea and Rachel falls into a light sleep. Her island is brighter than it's ever been, and there's a song she hears, a mournful tune one sings beside a sickbed and when she wakes she's humming it, her thoughts, for reasons she couldn't follow to a source, thinking of Walt, sweet Walt, and her body aches for her family, her first family and for an island. She has an urge, such an urge she can hardly think clearly.

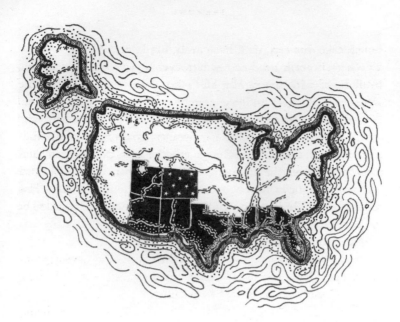

WEFT & WRECK

Rachel is agitated. Her Island flickers in distress and throughout the day the kids press their dolls to its surface in cloth-kisses. The roof is fixed and holding up just fine, but the internal plumbing clanks every time someone so much as gets themselves a glass of water; the paint peels around the windows; and the porch seems to be separating itself from the main house. Her belly is empty but ache prickles her feet and cramp winds its way down her legs. Walking helps, but only a little; Rachel paces the house, the block, the fields; she slides beyond the borders of the house and town; she searches through the fields and down by the quarrelling creek and into space with her mind racing and her heart beating; Hal still does not know the names of his own daughters and is, at this moment, still refusing to take the kids away for the day and give her some peace.

'We don't all fit into the car. What'sherface will be a nightmare,' he states.

After a minor scuffle, Ari, who still fails to take due care in the house, take due care with her family, has knocked over Georgia, who herself needs no excuse whatsoever to have instant and loud intolerance with the family, and who will not be consoled and squirms on Rachel's hip hiccupping her dismay. Thirteen-year-old Naomi has packed her panniers and loaded up her bike (again) and is still too young to leave on her own, and Bam has found a full-sized hammer and loose floorboard nails that need pounding in some room upstairs and the house shakes, bam bam bam bam. Rachel has had enough. Above Georgia's caught gulps for air she answers Hal, sarcastically, 'Which one would that be, the one you can't stand to be in the car with?'

'You know, the one who yells all the time.'

'Because she's moody, because she's banging things, because she has images in her head her hands won't draw quite yet, or because she's an infant and doesn't know any better?'

'They're all the same. I don't want to be stuck with any of them.'

'They're your children, Hal.'

'Really Rachel, what's wrong with you? I'm doing everything I can to raise them right, and they still refuse to give me peace.'

'What's wrong with me? They're just kids, your kids, and they want you to notice them or acknowledge they exist. They see how you favor Tex. They see that Hal, and…' Rachel flounders, tries to calm herself. 'They know it's not fair. Do you understand? I know they'll be stronger for it, living without your attentions, having each other, having me, and being able to be themselves because you can't bother your ass to tell them apart, but I worry that they'll waste their time trying to get you to care, to impress you, when, obviously, you are impervious.'

Hal picks at his fingernails and cuticles. Which one is banging? She has a solid swing that ends with what sounds like clean hits to the nails, but damn that noise. His head hurts. He doesn't understand what the big deal is, they have a house, a roof, food on the tables, and they grow up whether or not he can remember their names.

Rachel moves Georgia to her other hip, her back aching, her whole body heavy and tired and frustrated and when Georgia's voice erupts that one decibel louder, Rachel simply raises the volume of her still-calm voice above her daughter's whimpering.

'You're being an asshole, Hal.'

'Now, Rachel,' he says moving in, his hands opening in a placating drawl of familiarity towards her, 'that's awfully strong for someone who forgets things occasionally. If it's so important can you write me a list?'

'You're kidding, right? Lists have worked so well for you in the past. What would you want a list of anyway?'

'Our kids.'

'You're joking.' Rachel gives him a blubbering Georgia.

Hal nearly fumbles the hand-off. Tries to avoid the toddler's dripping snot. 'No, I'm not. You know: their names, birthdays, physical and other attributes. They all look the same to me.' His daughter stops yelling but her face stays an uncomfortable red, the tears plentiful on her cheeks—the simple shock of having no idea who is holding her.

'This one is Georgia, product of the flood. She's yours. I'm leaving. For the rest of them, look at your damn map, Hal. They are all up there if you cared enough to see them.'

Rachel strides to Hal's truck and never even glances up when Flo shouts, 'Mom!' Land creaks as plates shift, and bordering water builds towards a seiche. All the windows of her house light up like an alarm, the doors are flung open. Flo yells hoarsely, 'What the hell have you done now, Hal?'

The toddler dangles from his big hands, crying. 'Don't you speak to me...'

'What the hell have you done?'

'Take her,' Hal requests, holding Georgia out to Flo.

'No way. I'm taking the station wagon, I'm going after Mom.' She picks his wallet up from the hall table and leaves through the front door.

The girls look at their dad, then at Flo's trail of swirling rage, and there is no decision to be made. Girls follow Flo. Tex watches his dad, waits. He'll run after his wife, show her he loves her, he'll be here, he'll do this. Tex waits.

'Do not talk to me like that!' Hal yells after Flo.

Flo guns the car. Tex shakes his head. 'Really Dad, that's the best you can do?' and he runs down the driveway. He bangs on the car window with his open palm, Naomi grimaces but opens the door, and he jumps in. Lou stands in the hall, tears streaming, lips tight and says quietly, but not all that friendly;

'I'll stay and help you with Georgia. There's no more room in the car.'

A knot of blue hope offered, linked to his wrist. He holds out the baby.

'Help. Not do it for you.' Lou walks to the front porch and yells. 'Bring her back! You better bring her back!'

Rachel's hands flow over the steering wheel. Her window down, her hair flies to freedom, a small vein of a cramp sticks in her calf, and her feet itch for movement. She drives for hours, for days, her Island is calling out to her, waiting for her.

The family bulges out the rusting bulwarks of the station wagon, making it ride low, sweeping the pavement as they cross miles and rivers and states; lemon drops are sucked and Cheetos scoffed. Flo follows a car, a feeling, the clear line on a map, a wide destiny leading out to a disappearing sea.

The saltwater sharpens in Rachel's nose miles before she reaches the sea. At the shore, she stops the car and stays sitting, gripping the steering wheel, afraid that if she lets go, if her feet touch the shoreline, she'll take to the sea at a run and not look back. These are familiar waters and her body knows these currents, knows its own course.

She chooses the long rickety pier and as she walks its length it sways lightly beneath her with the high tide. Her dress ripples, flimsy against the cooling breeze, and she looks out to sea. Faint houses edge against the water in the mist riding the tide. Rachel sways with the pier, grasping the brief, fleeting moment of solitude, her first meeting with the sea in so long. She could just take off her clothes, jump in and swim, her arms are strong as ever. Stronger even.

When the kids arrive, their mom's car sits abandoned before them. Missy races down the pier before the others have even gathered courage. The other kids stand by the car for a few minutes and watch the figure of their mother grow smaller. And then they run.

Fingers lattice through Rachel's. Missy squeezes her mom's hand.

'I can feel it move,' Missy says quietly, meaning the pier, the water, the life rushing through her, and she looks up at her mom and sees her as she is: exactly there and far, far away out of reach.

'Me too,' Rachel says, the only difference between the life within her and the movement of the sea… one burning, one cool.

Missy spreads her fingers wide and then grasps more tightly.

'Exactly as I remember it,' says Rachel.

Gulls swoon over the water, waves crest and break like mini-urges for freedom, and the occasional pelican flies by on the way to the islands hidden by the haze, awkward and oddly majestic.

In the air, all familiar. Rachel remembers. She tries to let go of the hand binding her to land, but the fingers refuse to release her. Rachel leans to see the floor of the sea. Blue, endless.

Flo grabs her mom's other hand, Tex wraps his arms around her waist. The three kids lean their weight back from the edge and hold her tight, disallowing her jump. At her back, determined deserts, deltas, mountains, canyons, rivers, cities, valleys approach her.

'Different than I thought it'd be,' Missy whispers, holding tight.

Back at the Fremont house Georgia cries and cries. The sound she loves has stopped. A seashell no longer held close against her ear. Georgia cries louder. Hal figures out how to feed her and how to rock her until she falls asleep. Georgia finally sleeps. When she wakes up, she doesn't cry so much. She even smiles and plays with Lou.

'Mom gives her a bath sometimes,' Lou offers.

He finds everything he needs by the tub. 'You have to watch her all the time, or she might drown.' And he does watch her, and Lou too. Georgia splashes an inordinate amount for such a small thing—like chickadee in a birdbath—but otherwise seems to adjust to Hal's unpracticed and awkward ways.

Her skin smells great when he holds her close. Lou eats a yogurt and banana for breakfast and then Hal takes them both for a walk. Georgia doesn't really like the outdoors, not like Lou does, but she stays quiet, a hand on her dad's beating heart.

Hal doesn't have a chance to watch many birds; Georgia is heavy after only a short distance and he helps Lou over rocks and muddy bits. His bird-watching daughter spots the birds with skill.

'Look, Dad, a cardinal.'

'Can you tell me what color red it is?'

'Red like a brick.' Lou pauses, scours the trees and air, she knows this game, 'There's the male.'

'Why is he more brightly colored?'

'Because he lures predators away from the nest. She blends in and keep the eggs safe and sound.'

Dad and two daughters sit on big rocks about halfway down the hill and look out over the creek and the field beyond. Georgia sleeps easily. Lou and Hal sit attentive, looking for other birds. A movement catches their eyes, a big slightly awkward looking bird. Its big bill carves the air as it flies. The bird flies almost soundlessly, a languid beating of wings as it follows the curve where there should be water, where no bird like this should be seen in the wild, heading south to the ocean.

'Dad?' Lou asks, guessing, wanting affirmation.

'A pelican, sweetheart. A brown one I think, but I'll have to check with Mr Audubon when we get back to the house.'

'And where is it flying?'

'To the sea, it follows the Mississippi. Like your mother, it's at home by the sea.'

'I want her to come back, Dad.'

'Me too, Lou.'

Hal knows that somewhere decisions are being made and he desperately wants Rachel and their kids back.

'Will you help me?'

'Sure, Dad.' She takes his hand and leads him up the hill and into the hall. 'This is Florida,' she says. 'She's the oldest and the smartest and most reliable.' She places his hand on Florida, his palm stretches and meets a land he never really sees, and for a second, he feels the slate black of his daughter, the light and strength of her borders, and he knows her. 'These three are mockingbirds,' she says, pointing to Flo, Tex, and Missy. 'Naomi is a roadrunner; Ari a wren; Utah a California gull, Cole was a lark bunting, and Bam is a yellowhammer.'

Lou leads him through each state, giving him a bird, traits, hints, skipping over her own, whispering only, 'My heart is a river. I'm a state of passage migrants.'

The tide turns and leaves brief treasure maps etched in the sand. She knows this feeling now, Walt is at risk, he's dying. She won't be able to save him, like she failed to save Cole. Sadness takes to the wing and swoops like bats in the night. Behind them evening approaches, the cool of early autumn moves in, and the Fremonts sit on the pier, dangling their legs over the edge. The desert, for the moment, is at their backs and they all wait until their mother is ready to leave. Night falls and they no longer keep company with fear.

Some places exist as more than one thing, the space between high tide and low tide, for instance. Water that is always water, even at the lowest tide, is ocean. Land that is always land, even in the highest tide, is land. The space between, which becomes land and ocean in turn, exists as the littoral. Areas in flux exist as something indefinable, elusive, and have been named many things: littoral, liminal, penumbra, no man's land, ecotone, twilight.

Rachel believes these places keep their ambiguity even as they are named. Stars puncture the dark, the water pushes at the earth and their hearts beat through it all. Slowly the kids will realize they have access to infinite maps. If they're smart, they'll learn they don't represent a single place, rather they're moments and places of transition and sometimes even the space where nothing is certain, where nothing is as it is expected to be.

The Fremonts sleep in two cars and, in the morning, they drive a short way and fill up at a diner, blueberry syrup the agreed on favorite. By the end of the drive home they almost forget why they went to the shore; all they can remember is the way they sat and forgot all about time, about food, about anything but that feeling.

Hal greets all his children by name and asks about their trip to the sea. He doesn't even need the elaborate system of birdcall prompts he and Lou had devised. He helps them out of the car and realizes how different all the kids are, how they look so varied. The air changes around him depending on which child passes by him. The Corners emerge and he understands why he's been so parched for years.

'How was the ocean?' he asks them all as they sit drinking hot chocolate in the family room.

'It was huge,' says Bam gesturing with outstretched arms.

'And familiar,' adds Missy. 'You'd have loved it, Lou. There were all these bats, crazy flying bats, just shadows in the dark.'

'No one jumped into the sea,' Flo adds. 'And that was great.'

'I'm glad you're back,' Hal says.

'Did you learn anything Dad, aside from a few names?' Tex asks, with a smirk.

Lou puts a hand on his shoulder. 'Well done, Dad.'

As the children fall asleep, he takes the youngest kids up to bed. He carries Missy and Bam like sacks of gold-dust, one on each arm, the warmth of their sleeping breath almost familiar. 'Build me something to be proud of,' he whispers. And to Lou, who he carries next, her eyelashes flapping like wings against his cheek. 'Don't fly away too soon.'

Hal puts Georgia to sleep, kissing her hot cheek and inhaling the baby smell that floats from the top of her head. He stands and listens to his kids sleep and already they're retreating from him. He pulls out the list, goes through their names making notes and trying to etch his memory with his children. He can recall six with ease, but struggles with the other four and he's disappointed in his own efforts.

In their huge bed Hal stretches out behind Rachel. 'You came back.'

Rachel says nothing, breathes in, holds her breath.

'You were free to go.' Hal closes the space between them, curving to meet her. 'They're not all mine,' he whispers.

'No, Hal.'

'That's right,' he says, slowly. 'I've not been here for you, not really.'

She wraps him to her and promises nothing. Bats fluttering in the eaves, taking to roost in the attic. Still they help each other to breathe: Hal underwater, Rachel on dry land; and they sleep. Hesitantly, peacefully, eventually.

Morning comes and everything is settled and still unsure. The girls hug and kiss her throughout the day, just to make sure she's not going to leave again. They check in on her as she cooks; follow her around the house as she vacuums. When the mail arrives there's a map tube addressed to Rachel Roanoke and there's a map inside, a gift from Walt. The tube has been traveling for some time and has stamps from around the world. Inside, at the bottom, there's a small bag filled with a handful of dirt and another envelope of seeds.

CLEAR AND BLUE AND DEAD

Naomi starts track during her first week of high school, on a dare from Flo.

'You'll be great at it. I just know it.'

So Naomi stands out on the field, in shorts and a t-shirt, not at all sure of what she's doing. High school requires adjustment, a different tack. Flo is a junior, Tex a sophomore and when she arrives the legacy of the Fremonts precedes her. She finds it hard to live up to.

Vultures strike during that first day of practice, before the time trials have even begun.

'What kind of name is that, New Mexico?' His face is smooth with his bullying, his eyes ice-blue and familiar.

'It's Naomi.'

'New Mexico, I hear that your mom likes men, loads and loads of men.' His friend joins in, both of them hulking out. 'Do you like men too, New Mexico?'

'I'm a real man,' the familiar boy postures, moving closer to her, in particular, with his groin. In the background footballers laugh.

'You're a real asshole,' Naomi says as she stands her ground.

'Yeah, you Fremonts are half-breeds. Especially that little Chinese girl. I'm sure your mom just went exotic and regretted it.'

Japanese, she thinks, half Japanese. 'That's my sister you're talking about.'

'Half-sister.' He starts to circle her. His breath smells like a sewer and she remembers him.

'Oh, so you can actually do the math now, Greg. Impressive.'

He's much changed from all those years ago when he bullied Bubba, and lightning strikes had sent him and his brother to the hospital. But she'd know him anywhere. By her side her hand hardens to a fist. 'You going to argue with a Fremont?'

'That's exactly what I'm doing. You slow as well as ugly?'

Her punch does not have warning. He stumbles but stays standing. Naomi moves in. With her standing so close, his hair stands on end. A strange blue light gathers at the top of the flagpole. 'They say lightning never strikes twice. Are you a gambler?'

Greg McCrae scrambles away. Across the football field, storm clouds gather and a thunder-clap knocks his baseball cap off his head. Naomi wants to feel that rush of sky connected to land through a bolt and she lets one rip. It strikes the pole and shoots to the earth in one glorious flash. She laughs. 'We showed them, Cole,' she shouts. 'We showed them!'

Tex is beneath the bleachers with Rob from his homeroom when the lightning strikes. They don't stop what they're doing. A hard sudden downpour follows and wet feet pound the track. He doesn't know exactly how he's ended up here. A dare about drinking, a challenge that ended up with them wrestling and then stopping. They hear the runners on the track, a rumble of thunder. Their own sweet breath, edgy and foreign. And then the lightning strike. Tex gasps, quietly, but the boy who doesn't smell nearly as good as Bubba slaps a hand across his mouth. He tastes all right, but he's not yet discovered deodorant. Rob doesn't know what he's doing, despite his bragging. Neither of them do.

'Don't say a word, Fremont.'

'You think I'm stupid?'

Rob leaves and Tex neatens himself up, smoothes back his hair that's grown a bit longer and is in need of a cut. Whistles blow out on the track, some races are just starting, others are coming to an end and when Tex emerges he has new eyes. Is he? He wonders. Yes. That one? No. That one? Definitely.

Naomi comes home from track practice soaked through with sweat. Flo had expected her to be grinning but her face is hardened. Flo takes plates off the drainer and stacks them in the cabinet.

'How was it?' Flo asks.

'I'm on the team. Fastest time. 1000 meters. Coach thinks I'm a marathoner, or I might be good in the triathlon, since I like biking.'

'The swimming might be an issue.'

'I suppose.'

'What's up?'

'I just don't know how you do it. Standing up to people. Being violent. I don't like it.'

'But it was just track tryouts. No violence involved.'

'Unless you're a Fremont. I punched Greg McCrae, and then made him run away.'

'Run?'

'Yeah. Like a baby.' Her voice sharpens with a hint of a pride, a smile.

Flo grins. 'Why is that a problem?'

'Well. I got detention. But really, I just wanted to be left alone. To put my head down and run around the track. And this stupid family made me, made me…'

'Stand up for yourself?'

'No. Made me punch some guy. It's like I had to protect not just myself but Missy too.'

Flo hands Naomi some water and a sweatshirt so she doesn't get a chill as she cools down. 'That's part of being a family. You did the right thing. Missy is worth standing up for.' Flo says it slowly, 'That's what you do for family.'

'Don't you get tired of it?'

Flo doesn't hesitate as long as she should. 'Yes. Of course, sometimes I just want to be me.'

'That's it. I don't want to be a Corner or a sister or a fighter. I don't want part of me to be hanging on the wall for the world to see.'

'We can't get away from that. What goes on in your head is your own. Trust that. Be that.' Naomi taps her head, shakes it too, 'It's wild in here, sometimes. I think sometimes I'm trying not to think, not to…'

Nodding, Flo goes to the fridge and considers what she can make for dinner. 'You'll figure it out. It's never simple.'

Naomi goes upstairs to shower and Flo starts to make dinner. When Tex comes in from school he's flushed and disheveled. 'Naomi is crazy,' he says circling his finger near his ear. 'People hear her talking to no one in the hall and today she punched some guy and got detention. In the principal's office she shouted, "But we didn't do anything." She's a total nutcase.' He shrugs his shoulders and Flo looks at him, stops what she's doing to just look for a minute. He shifts. Not out of weakness, but like it has nothing to do with him. His eyelids are slightly heavy, narrowing.

Turning away from him, Flo shakes her head and gets back to work. Her mantle of responsibility is thick and heavier than she'd expected. It weighs down her shoulders and it pools too, like oil or mercury in her gut. She never used to cry but now she often feels on the verge of a real sob, but doesn't give into it. She blinks back the tears and stands up straighter. It gets harder to hold them back when her sisters are taunted or running against an unfair world; harder every time Tex fails. His gaze used to have a fire in it with that whorl of an eyebrow giving him a hint of welcome humor. That fire that was love and hate and better than what she sees now, which is clear and blue and dead.

The next day Tex makes a big show of asking Christie Marley out on a date and then they start to go steady. They're the couple to watch, the couple to beat. He cheats on her with Jessica Delt, at a dance, a bottle of bourbon between them. Tex is a great campaigner, could make a fortune in advertising. If he drinks to the point of foolishness he likes girls well enough; they're soft and they take his needs into consideration. When he kisses them he has to think about other things, trees, diggers, anything. He thinks about Rob or the sweet taste of Bubba and he wants it all to be simpler. Listening to girls' jabber exhausts him. He can only imagine what marriage would be like.

His dad persists in calling him a wimp and Tex asks Brad, some guy from the rugby team, to help him with the free weights, to bulk up. Brad obliges. Tex starts to realize how good people can be at keeping secrets. Their sessions together lengthen and yet somehow Tex's strength plateaus.

His dad was right about the coffee; Tex also learns to wear layers in the under-heated winter office and lots of deodorant in the absurd unairconditioned summer days. Kitty is an imbecile, hankering after his dad and it makes him sick. Honestly though, without her, his dad would have succumbed to squalor long before. The office is disgusting in a deeply disturbing way that could only be fixed by a complete renovation.

By the time he's worked in the office for a few months, he understands the significance of those papers his dad slipped out from behind the map. His words have a resonance that had been lost to him when he was six. He has sisters, loads of sisters, and who knows how many more to follow: that's a lot of competition for scant resources. Even Tex now sees his situation resembles the Yankees playing a little league team but still, he has to stay ahead of the game.

Tex tries to build things with his hands on the sites, for a short time. But he's useless. 'It's good to know your limits,' his dad finally says as he sits with another injury, next to another half-completed job that will have to be redone by a real laborer. Tex, somewhat reluctantly, agrees. But keeps his hard-hat, visits the builds often. He learns something about the brilliance of big buildings, of safety and risk, and the beauty of men and machines in motion.

So Tex takes some business classes at the local college and becomes proficient at knowing the types of buildings, extensions, and repairs Fremont Construction is best known for. He's very interested in total project renovation.

'Fremont Construction and Interior Design,' he says as he answers the phone.

'Just Fremont Construction,' corrects Hal.

'Fremont Construction and Interior Renovation,' Tex says as he answers the phone, thinking himself alone.

'Just Fremont Construction,' corrects Hal from the other room.

'Fremont Construction and Design,' Tex says a few days later. Hal doesn't bother with words, he just slaps his only son's head.

'Don't be a fool. We design and build the damn things, let the fools put stuff in them.' Later, when Hal leaves to negotiate a good deal on a new digger and dumptruck, Tex slips into his dad's office.

'You shouldn't, Tex,' Kitty warns. 'He'll be mad when he comes back.'

'What will he do if he finds out?'

'Have your head on a stick.'

'Yeah right.' Tex runs a hand over his thinly covered skull. He rifles through Hal's inbox, skims his to-do list, breaks into the locked drawer only to find a few drawings and boring ones at that.

'It's the Mayor on the phone,' says Kitty.

'I'll take it.'

'Mr Fremont isn't back yet, Mayor.' Kitty giggles. 'Alright, John then. Can I have him give you a call?'

Hal's truck pulls up and Kitty ends the call. He doesn't like to be pressured first thing in the door.

'Skedaddle Tex. Get out of there.'

Tex has shuffled the papers, a few have fallen to the floor, he's left fresh coffee rings on the desk, broken the lock on one of the drawers, left a trail of powdered sugar crumbs at the corner.

'Tex, have you been snacking on junk food?'

'No way, Pops.'

Of course Hal knows that not only he has been eating donuts, but doing it in his office. It's like a kid having sex in his parents' bed, to prove he can. Didn't know Tex had it in him to make a stand. He's honored by Tex's interest. He'll have spotted the plans for the concert hall, maybe they can talk about that at dinner. The Mayor had courted him hard today. It's a big job but the payment offered has come down again. It'll make this year's budget run to a deficit.

'It's been a tight year all around, Hal.' The Mayor patted his skinny belly, acted like he's tightening his belt.

'I've got kids to feed,' Hal said.

'And whose fault is that?'

Hal couldn't help but think he had a point but that it was beside the point.

'And my oldest wants to go to college in the fall.'

'All hands on deck. That's what I say around my house. You should put her to work instead.'

Again, he couldn't fault John's thinking. She could work in a diner, or the library, or something.

'Oh yeah, before I forget. My wife, Midge, Ridgeway was her maiden name, you might remember her from school, you were a year below her, she said. Well, she saw this article and she remembered you had a brother Duncan.' He hands Hal the magazine, tapping his finger on the cover with a grin Hal can't decipher until he sees the photo.

'I did, but he died,' Hal says.

'Oh, well, keep the magazine anyway. It tailfins into your line of business, in a way.'

Hal forgoes his visit to Sandra and drives home. It's cold as he parks in the driveway and he gathers up his thermos. Rachel moves through the playing kids on the lawn, her arms full of beans and tiny new potatoes, and follows him inside. 'Cup of tea?'

'A beer.'

'Sounds good.'

Dropping the vegetables in the sink, she takes out two beers. Hal sits at the table, puts his arm around her waist as she gets close enough. He takes a swig of beer, coughs, 'I've been thinking that Flo should get a job. We're going to be short in the coming year. Tex has been helping out, We need Flo to do the same.'

'She'd work with you at the office?'

He laughs. 'No. She could work in a diner or something.'

Rachel doesn't let him know that Flo already has a job and a savings account. She starts shucking the beans. 'I think she should work with you. Sell houses to incomers. She'd be good at selling.'

'Who'd trust such a young girl with their life's savings?'

'You said she was nearly an adult.'

'You know what I mean.'

'They trusted you. You were only a year older than her when we got married, and as handsome as Flo is pretty.'

'No. It's not her place. Let her go out into the real world. Prove herself.'

'Like Tex has to prove himself.'

'Every day, Rachel. He has to prove himself every day.'

'How's that working out?'

Hal slams a hand down on the table. 'I can't employ the whole family. Really Rachel, be serious.'

Rachel continues to lean a hip against the sink as she works her way deftly through the beans. 'You're wrong, Hal. She's smart and can always get the kids to eat anything put in front of them. She'd be able to sell a run-down working farm to a Manhattanite. She'd make a lot of money for you. Strengthen the business. But if you don't think so, she'll get herself a good job over the summer.'

'I'm not saying she should get a job for the summer, but for good.'

'Hal, she wants to go to school. She's earned that, she's worked hard, without complaining. Without her help I wouldn't have survived this all.'

'So you're saying you can't afford to lose her either.'

Rachel halts her work, wipes her hands on her apron and then puts them on her hips. 'Don't put this on me. She's just a kid, she deserves to be able to get out of the house, live a bit.'

'Let her live a bit on the job. She can't go to school. We can't afford it and the family needs her here. It's that simple.'

'Then you tell her.'

'I will. Of course I will. When it comes up.'

Dinner over, decaf coffee drunk, Hal holds up the brand new *Architecture and Interiors Today*.

Tex watches, bored, until he sees the magazine: the nightly lecture is finally getting interesting. On the cover, behind two men standing with arms around each others' waists, is a gloriously stark minimalist room. So simple, of course, simple. Maybe his dad has thought about it, maybe they can start to offer a design service. Tex could run it, he could become an architect, he could go to school in New York. These old boys on the cover have immaculate taste. Tex looks at the fabric of the couch, hand-tanned leather, he thinks, impressive. And the men wearing well-tailored, well-cut trousers, casual. He wonders where they shop.

With a single, pointed jerk of his wrist, Hal rips the cover from the binding, and the flame of the candle catches and engulfs the corner. Tex blinks, Hal swears as the burn moves in an instant to his fingers and he drops the smoldering detritus onto his dessert plate next to the crumbs of a rich chocolate cake which, of course, Tex has been denied.

'Tex, this is the sort of thing some people think is okay.'

And Tex thinks, what do people think is okay? Minimalism? High quality leather? The Versace shirt?

'And I'm telling you that it's not.'

Hal leans over, looks at his son who has slimmed down and bulked out, nearly a man, handsome, garnering respect on the sites. He's told Hal he's planning to run for class president in the fall, which promises to be a heated battle with the Mayor's son. 'This sort of thing could ruin a business or lose an election.'

Hal pushes his chair back and exits the room slowly, with the sobriety an occasion like this merits. Tex remains sitting with his hands folded politely in his lap, with due deference, staring at the left behind coverless magazine. When he hears the basement door fall shut, and smells the soapy smell of pipe smoke, a new habit his dad's taken to at moments of stress, he secretes the magazine under his shirt, and escapes up to his room.

And there, belly-flopped onto his bed, Tex inhales. The index tells him who has gone up in flames: Mr Jorge Williams and Mr Duncan Fremont open their inspired and immaculate NY penthouse to *A&I Today*, words by Colin Fraser, photographs by Isabel Schwartz.

His dad's warnings make some sense and he's already been practicing survival and success. Being a Fremont is good practice: be one thing in your heart and head; be another thing out in the world. He thinks about rooms he can design, maybe houses too. He wants to live in a city and he plans to make enough money to set up a Fremont Design there. The pages of the magazine flip and flip and flip back and when he's had his fill, he flexes his feet and goes to sleep.

When Tex shuts his eyes his sleep is pure dark and heavy. He doesn't dream but rather falls into a state of oblivion. Tex loves sleep. It's this retreat in his head that's always true even as it's one thing then another. Black, safe and hollow or loud and bright and full of abandon. His sisters seem bound together by sleep, and he hears them talking about the places they visit; they talk about the colors, an island, and maps. They talk about the stories they hear. Tex only has the vaguest sense of what they're talking about: every once in a while this hollow of black felt becomes liquid and smooth swirls of color sweep through like fingertips circling on his temple.

UNINTENTIONAL NEPOTISM

Flo's exhausted. Her life is truly hard work. Every day, after she's helped with dinner and the dishes, bathed the younger girls and put them to bed, and gathered the older ones into some sort of semblance of nighttime repose, she works on her homework, long into the night, often pacing the halls working to memorize historical dates and battles or chemical compounds so she can properly balance equations. She has a 3.98 grade point average and applies to Brown University.

Flo has held this dream, this secret close, but now her mom knows something is up and is standing there watching as Flo opens the letter. It arrived with the morning mail and Flo imagines how her mom's fingers must have itched to open it. But she didn't. It's pristine. Her mom will be so proud of her.

Flo picks the letter off the table in the hall and slides the opener along the top of the envelope. Freedom. Outta here. She reads the first page and then the next: a full scholarship. Her heart has no limits. Free, she thinks, for four years. It's all she'll need. She'll come back, she'll have to come back, she knows that. She looks up towards the kitchen where her mom stands in the doorway and her mom's eyes lock on a spot on the wall just beyond Flo's right shoulder and she sees it there, in the hard dry red spot at the corner of each of her mom's eyes, in the drawn exhaustion of her mom's face.

Flo stops. 'Not this. Not this too.'

'We need you here, Flo. Your dad was supposed to talk to you. You'll have to get a job, bring some money in.'

'I got a scholarship. He won't have to pay a penny.'

'Flo, we need you here to help out.'

Her mom's hands are boneless. Her shoulders defeated. And

Flo doesn't care. Damn her and her insistence that they stay in this shithole. Damn her fertile fucking habits that leave her with the burdens of all these kids, and Flo too, by default. And fuck Hal, for everything. And this hope, this unquenchable, unquashable hope they all seem to have, that something they do will actually make a difference to this stranglehold the universe has them in. Shaking shaking, ah-ha it says, this is what you get for being nice. For believing it matters.

Flo roars. She doesn't open the back door at first. Instead she smashes it with violent kicks from her boots. The wood of the bottom splinters and she pushes it aside. From the garage she grabs an axe. Trusty, effective, focuser of rage.

She goes over to the wedding maple, now nearly 30ft tall with a thickening trunk. It's grown well and Hal often brags about it. 'It's youthful and strong like our family.' And Flo swings. A satisfying sliver of tree chips out. She hits it again and again. The whole thing shakes. And fuck you and fuck you and fuck fuck fuck until the word loses its meaning. Flo loves this tree, but so does Hal; him and his precious birds. There's a nest of baby birds in the maple for the first time this year and she doesn't care. Not one bit. Her arm aches. She swings; the tree gives in and falls away from the yard and onto the fence. Flo drops the axe and sits on the fence beside it.

In the house a steady stream of girls kiss her state. Rachel, who has not moved from the kitchen table, has her head in her hands.

At dinner time, Arizona and Utah start to make some burgers, and Rachel goes and sits beside Flo.

The sick feeling in her stomach is still there, and she knows it will always be there. She's weak and obligated. She and her mom sit and do not talk. Her mother is getting older, has had enough. Shit, she's only eighteen and she's had enough.

Her mom rubs circles on her back, touches her face and hair. Such color and suddenly Flo feels it again, this damn tenacious hope.

'I've just killed a tree and three birds,' she says.

'The neighbor's cat got one chick this morning, so you only killed two.'

'Gee, that helps.' But they both smile, because, damn it, it does actually help.

'I'm sorry Flo.'

'I know you are, Mom. I just had this dream. It was only four years.'

Rachel hugs Flo again, kissing her on her cheek, her forehead, her hair.

'I've got to go make sure that Ari and Utah don't burn the place down.'

Flo doesn't move, she sits and Naomi comes back carrying two bottles of root beer. 'This place sucks.'

Flo nods. 'Get out. Get out as soon as you can.'

Hal comes home in the early hours of the morning and walks straight upstairs to bed. It's once he gets up in the morning and is out on the porch with his coffee that he notices the tree. He calls back into the kitchen towards Rachel.

'What happened to our maple?'

'It was the damnest thing,' says Rachel. 'A freak wind blew it over, in one clean crack. The girls were beside themselves.'

Hal looks across the yard and then at his wife. 'I can see the axe marks. That tree did not just fall down.'

'Think what you want, but that's what happened.'

Hal bangs and shouts and swears all day. When he sits in his chair with his binoculars at sunset, Lou sits beside him.

'Someone is going to pay.' His eyes seem full up, but Lou is not swayed.

'Leave it Hal, just leave it,' Lou says.

Fabian Veracruz sits next to Flo in algebra, two rows in front during biology, across from her at lunch, and keeps a quiet vigil of all things Flo Fremont.

As a freshman, at school, Flo had been at ease, walking free, laughing, swinging her bag. A world unto herself. But whenever Fabian sees her in town or at school once her siblings arrive, she always looks different: surrounded, pulled on. So whenever he can, he places his body like a force field just outside Flo's space and, in his mind, keeps her safe. In her mind too, he's sure of it.

Not that she really needs it. Cross her or any of the Fremont brood and Flo moves with a swift and unforgiving defiance. When logic and intelligence don't do the trick quickly enough, she sorts problems with brute force. Her sister Naomi has means that are just as effective, and even more fun. Fabian grins. He likes the very adaptability of the Fremonts.

It's April of their senior year and for the first time in four years Fabian puts himself into her path.

Flo, who has kept a quiet vigil of her own, sees his cocoa-dark eyes and his thick long lashes like a girl's. He has perfect eyes, Flo sees that.

'Would you like to go on a date?' Fabian asks.

Tex has come up behind Flo and he stands close, his breath on her neck. Flo stands straighter, pushes Tex back with a hand. Mercury in her veins. She clears her throat.

'I can't,' Flo says.

Fabian should have known that she wasn't free in that way. She stands tall and she says no. She smiles though, blushes. A no, but not final. He'll just have to wait until she's free.

'That's cool. You have to babysit,' Fabian says, pointedly looking at Tex. 'Tell you what, it's an open offer.' And this boy steps forward, puts a hand on Flo's arm, and plants a kiss on her lips.

Kids have already started to pair up for the junior prom and Tex is planning to ask Jessica Delt, who he's been dating for a month or so. He's been spending some time with Brad too, who last week let it slip that perhaps maybe he's had a thing going with someone else for a while and could they just keep this thing between them to themselves. That suits Tex just fine. At school he's all about the girls and makes a big show each day of taking Jessica down to the ice cream parlor when the day's done, holding her hand and kissing her when folk walk by. It's bright and sunny and the town is crowded with kids and adults and the day is one of those days pitched on the cusp of summer. The line for ice cream is out the door and Tex and Jessica stand close together, kissing and then turning to talk to other friends in the line.

Matt Kent, mayor apparent, slaps Tex's shoulder. 'You certainly have bulked up recently. Who you trying to impress? This little lady?'

'What business is it of yours?'

'Feels like you could put these pecks to better use.' Matt stretches his hands over Tex's chest. 'You think that's going to make you powerful enough to beat me next year?'

Tex drops Jessica's hand and steps forward, slapping Matt's hands away. 'I'll beat you no matter what I do.'

Matt laughs. 'You will not take what's mine.'

Tex hastens a stance. Being stronger in theory is not the same as being able to fight a mean boy. Matt makes the first move and Tex doubles over with the punch. Matt knees him in the chin. Pain. More pain than before. A tooth is crushed on the ground. The cheers are overwhelming for Matt as the boys tumble through the crowd of students and townies and out into the street. The traffic stops. Somewhere out there Tex hears a lone, loud cheer, 'Don't let him beat you, Tex.' It's Brad. Lightbulb. Tex knows who Brad's been dating and also knows that he won't intervene in this fight. Tex feigns a drop, rolls, punches Matt's kidneys. The boy arches, drops to his knees. Tex moves around the front and gives him a square right hook. His head snaps back but his arm shoots forward to punch Tex's groin. Tex reacts, hopping back so the jab hits his thigh. Matt recovers and tackles Tex. The boys wrestle and punch. Matt knuckles Tex's hip again and again. It's a bloody fight and when they're hauled off each other there's a few chipped teeth, a broken jaw, and no respect gained between the boys. Jessica cleans his wounds and doesn't complain about how he ruins her bright new sundress.

It will take a few weeks to patch up his teeth, for the black eye to recede, for his limp to get back to normal. His first day back at work, which is the day after school ends, his dad slaps him on the back, obviously displeased he's been fighting the Mayor's boy, but pleased that it was a good clean fight where Tex held his own.

'I'm proud of you, son,' Hal says. Tex is still tender but doesn't show it. Tex has learned a few things in the years he's been working for his dad. He's learned to keep his mouth shut about what he really wants or thinks. He's learned to ask one obvious question during any of his dad's lectures so it appears he cares. 'What does this do?' for instance. He's learned he likes spending time at the sites and he's learned he can get away with almost anything if he puts in two solid hours of work before he takes off for the day.

In the summer between junior and senior year Tex puts in as many hours at the office as he can manage. He and Brad work out nearly every day, until Tex tells him that what they're doing isn't really for him. Brad doesn't believe him, taunts him, but Tex doesn't back down and at the end of July he kisses June Prior very publically in the town square and his breakups with Jessica Delt, and with Brad, are assured.

FLICKER

The small ball bounces and Joanne Quest's hand sweeps across the ground picking up the final two jacks. 'I remember you arriving at kindergarten with only one shoe on,' says Joanne, making another toss.

'You do?' asks Missy.

'Yeah.' Bounce three, bounce three, bounce three, bounce one.

'I remember,' Missy says.

Joanne stops for a second, 'You took the other one off and walked around barefoot. Mrs Logan demanded you put on your shoes and when you refused she had you standing in the corner, all day.' They both giggle. 'After school one of your sisters carried you home.'

'Ari.'

'She's cool. Your sisters look after you.' Joanne scatters the jacks again and misses the second four. She hands the lot to Missy.

'It was my oldest sister who took my shoelace,' Missy says, starting her turn.

'Really?'

'Yup.'

'Why would she do that?'

'To make me strong.'

Joanne and Missy have been timid playground pals for a few months and have both been hesitant to invite the other home. Missy concentrates on her turn, bounce pick up, bounce pick up and asks, 'Do you want to come meet them?'

Joanne smiles. 'Totally.'

After a Saturday trip down to Big Joe's to buy some jawbreakers, Joanne meets the sisters and Tex, and pretty Mrs Fremont but not Missy's dad. 'Where's your dad?'

'You mean Hal?'

'I suppose.'

'He's always at work.'

Everyone knows what Hal Fremont does, he builds houses that look like birds in flight.

'And what about the map?'

'Where'd you hear about that?'

Joanne blushes. 'It's the talk of the town really, but no one's ever seen it.'

'You're welcome to have a look if you can find it.'

'Find it?'

'Yeah. It can be hard to track down.'

'You're kidding.'

'No, I've been trying all morning. Georgia's been annoying me and I wanted to give her state a good whack. I'll show you.'

And the girls go off, hand in hand. They find her mom's turret but don't go up to her neat eight-sided cupboard; Tex's room has shelves filled with magazines and walls covered in images ripped out of design magazines.

'He's going to be a great designer, he'll do the inside of the houses I design and Bam builds,' says Missy.

They stumble across a small room with a round window and a desk, with a drafting board and various pencils all lined up. A room for Missy to remember. They can hear Bam hitting her hammer off something, the whole time, but they never find the hall. Three hours later, parched and hungry, the girls stumble into the kitchen.

'Not today, eh?' asks Mrs Fremont.

'Nope, not today.'

'Maybe next time you'll get to see it,' she says, ruffling Joanne's hair.

Joanne doubts it, but she smiles because somehow it doesn't matter as much now.

In the school halls words follow Missy.

'Chink.'

'Bastard.'

'Nice roof on that house of yours.'

'Has your mom had the roofer in lately?'

Missy's old enough to know that bullying is just a stance people take. She refuses to curl her shoulders in, although that is what she has the urge to do, and she demands that her feet walk, not run. Sometimes bodies are felled behind her by her sisters: Flo, Naomi or Bam. But she doesn't need rescued, not really. She needs for the words to drop like feathers but they don't, not quite. They are small magnets pressed to her heart and they might do some damage in time, but not just yet.

And Bam. And Bam. And BamBamBam. Bam and Bam and BamBamBam.

Beneath everything, during waking hours, is the sound of Bam. Outside the ground absorbs the noise of her, inside she walks like an elephant. There's absolute certitude in the way she moves, a steadfast resolve and the girls grow so fast. Georgia nearly two, Bam already six.

Her mom often plants kisses on her head mid-swing. 'My beautiful Bam,' she says. Bam's hands produce the best sounds with the help of a hammer. It reverberates through her bones when she hits things. Metal on metal and she only hits things that can take it. Never one of her sisters. Right from the start her mom told her that was bad. But she already knew it. She only ever, really, has the urge to hit Tex, and only when he stands in her shadow and pretends to be doing chores.

She doesn't like the sound of things falling down: gun shots, explosions, wrecking balls, bullies (but of course she protects Missy when she needs to). She likes the sound of things coming together: the click of Legos, the scrape of the erector set tightening. Later she'll love the sound of a hammer on nails, of roof slates jammed into place, of wooden fence posts taking purchase in the earth.

Even now she monitors the house, walking around its perimeter like a surveyor. She keeps an eye on the lean of its walls, the sunken earth around the basement windows. If sound had substance, Bam would be what holds this place together.

WITNESS

Flo walks into town and imagines herself dressed in a suit, buttons open to expose just enough cleavage to imply she'd lived a bit, and then she would lead them through the houses, selling them. But her dad doesn't want her to earn any money from him or make any money for him. She'll just have to do that for someone else. Priscilla Colt is the best realtor in town and that's where Flo begins and ends her job search.

When Bam could barely walk, she was able to kick Tex. And even now when he passes by, Bam bares her teeth and growls like a bear and although anyone with eyes can see she'll grow into a well built, wide shouldered girl, Tex doesn't see it somehow or he'd have been nicer to her in preparation for the day when she'll kick his butt.

Animosity is instinct and can be triggered by anything at all: the freckles on his arms or his weak smooth hands, unmarred by real work. Animosity, sure, but it could as easily have been adoration.

And Georgia screams and kicks and punches. For no reason. Flo has been guiding her through the Saturday morning, often holding her firmly, but warily, like you'd hold a bomb with a feather trigger. She's been given grace, compassion and a light touch and still the little nightmare yells and head butts when Flo hands her the underpants Georgia had chosen herself, and she claws Flo's face as she tries to slide the gaudy pink barrette into her too thin hair. Georgia throws the cereal she's chosen across the kitchen and finally Flo throws up her hands and Bam, who can think of at least twenty other adventurous things that she wants to do and the tools she'll use to do them, is given the task of painting Georgia's toes hot shiny sparkling pink instead.

'Please,' her mom says. 'Just while I clean the house.'

'Please,' says Flo. 'Just so I can get stuff from the garden and catch up with some work.'

So Bam paints Georgia's toes the color the loud two-year-old chooses and still she screams and smears the polish across the sofa. The smell, the uselessness of painted nails, the squirming, the screaming, the tears, the theatrics.

'No! No! No!' Bam shouts as she runs outside. Missy follows her quietly, her pad of paper under her arm and her pencils bulking out her pockets. 'Outta here,' she says as she closes the door quietly behind them both.

'Where's Tex?' asks Rachel. Georgia pulls at her legs, howling, streaking nail polish on Rachel's clean jeans.

'Upstairs in his room,' Flo offers.

'Take her up to him.'

Flo picks up Georgia, who punches her legs in all directions, screams. Flo holds on tight and carries her upstairs. 'Your turn,' she says to Tex.

'You all are useless. She's easy.'

He holds up *Vogue*. 'Georgia, come here. Look at the pretty pictures.'

Rachel sits in the rocker on the porch watching Arizona and Bam taking apart the sandbox. About time someone had. Six-year-old

Bam, who already seems as tall and wide as a teen, watches how thirteen-year-old Arizona handles the claw of the hammer and Ari's a good teacher, slowing down to show her younger sister how to work it. Then Bam goes at the nails with the claw of her hammer, knee on the wood as leverage, and although it takes her longer than it will in the future, she manages to work each nail free before too long. She works steadily and her technique improves with each slide beneath the nail and the rocking pull back. Together they work hard and look beautiful side-by-side, working away. They disassemble it from the top down, and Missy arrives and stacks each newly freed board neatly beneath the lee of the garage roof, and by the time they reach the floor of the sandbox, all the sand has disappeared.

In this life Rachel is witness and conjurer, a mother, and she is restless. She wants this. She has sought this out, traveled by water to the boundaries between land and water that are always in flux. Creating a family is a crazy grand gesture, an act of conjecture and composite, and at the heart of this way of life is a brave leap of faith so powerfully sweet and sharp it's blinding.

A DESERT MAN IN SEARCH OF WATER

Rachel works through a knot of hair at the back of her head and as she smoothes her fingers over her skull they linger at a strange amorphous soft spot, the size of a penny, behind her ear. She stops, feels the skull go from hard to not so hard, and realizes that despite her efforts her brain has, after ten children, begun to turn to mush.

'Take some night classes. See what you can do.' That's what Glenda says when Rachel tells her what she's found.

'I think it might be too much to handle.'

'You can always drop them if you're not happy.'

Despite having a soft spot, Rachel is Yale smart and it only takes her about thirty seconds of sitting in Dr Jonathon DuPre's geomorphology class to realize there is absolutely nothing wrong with her head.

Jonathon DuPre has never paid much attention to women. They're not nearly as daring or scary, and therefore as satisfying, as spending months living off a wild land, facing death in any number of ways, any number of times a day. At least that's what he thinks until Rachel Fremont walks into his class. He tries not to stare; he leans against the desk, looks down to his notes. Sure he's heard the gossip about the Fremonts but why does no one talk about how beautiful she is? He cannot keep his eyes from her as he stumbles through the day's introduction. He's trundling through like a runaway train, ignoring raised hands and pleas for him to slow down.

'Professor,' Rachel says, clearly, plainly. 'Professor. But Professor...'

He stops, he has to stop. She's talking to him and he pushes himself away from the desk, clears his throat and looks at her.

'Please call me Jon.'

'Professor DuPre. You've been saying that the land is what sustains us.'

'In balance with other things.'

'That's confusing to me. I'd always thought it was water.'

'Biologically you're right. Without water, earth would not exist nor would any life upon it. But land, it's solid, something we can hold onto, define ourselves by. Water runs through your fingers.'

'So does dirt, sand and dust. Without water the land is dust.'

'True. And water is fascinating, defines the land, but this is a geology class, we study rocks.'

'And water cuts rocks.'

'Sometimes.'

'Even in the desert.'

'Especially in the desert. Do you have any other questions?'

'It wasn't a question.'

'Can I get back to fossils found in the Pacific Northwest?'

'You mean the ones carried by water.'

'As I was saying...'

Rachel had expected Dr DuPre to be a suited, bespectacled man who used long words in complex sentences. She'd expected to feel out of place. Instead she finds a young, rugged, wiry man leaning against a desk at the front of the room. During that first class he talks informally about each and every one of her children and takes her through rising fissures and receding water and for a hike along the edges of tectonic plates.

This professor tries to pretend he's talking about land, but through and beneath all his rocks and landscapes run rivers, water tables, and ancient basins of waters. Finally, near the end of the class, he talks about rain and dust storms; about how stars look above a desert floor; about how mankind has taken a backhanded, uncalled for slap at the earth and how one day he'll pay.

He stops her as she leaves the classroom. 'You're the one who wrote the entrance essay on the aquifers.'

'Yes.'

'I wondered how you knew so much about these places and then after I'd lived here for about, oh I don't know, a minute, I found out.' His hands rest on the desk, as they're forcing him to stay where he is. 'Your entry piece was impressive. You know your water particularly well.'

'I'm from an island, it's in my blood.'

'And your children's?'

'Absolutely.'

'And yet you live here. Why?'

'I could ask the same of you.'

'Temporary post, bum knee that needs an operation.'

'You walked a mile too far?'

'A flash flood took me for a ride.'

'Ah, so water's given you a rough deal in the past. That explains some things.'

'Not really. I'm a desert man.'

'I don't think that's strictly true. I think you're a desert man in search of water.'

And he is. He walks her to the car, trying to keep the distance open between them. She, so obviously a married woman, so obviously taken, so obviously the most astute woman he's ever met. He thinks she used to be thin as a rake but now she's child-curved and soft and strong, and it takes every ounce of Jonathon's will not to embrace her. He wants things he can't name, he sees in her, god what does he see in her? She blinds him, before revealing exactly how far the world can take you towards perfection.

It's Rachel who presses her body against his. He does not diminish her, or give her thirst, and he does not have a lesson to teach her.

They take fieldtrips and spread blankets on the ground exposed beneath the sky. They hide nothing from each other, not her family, not his restless nature, and Jon travels a lot to remote and wild places and they talk on the phone, make plans for when he comes back. They fall in love, he still with the desert at his back calling him, she with Hal and a family a mile away, pulling her back home.

She is thirty-five and he is thirty-two when they first meet. It's hard to remember their youth given the lives they've already lived. It's easy to imagine that they'll die, forty, fifty years having passed… out on a fast, thin boat and she'll vanish without a trace, a wave rushing back to the sea, and he will be found, a small face of sedimentary rock growing out of the deck, the kind found worn down to sand by the caresses of the ocean.

Jonathon DuPre is a patient man who understands the nature of water and knows that one day he will be level with the sea. The Carolinas and Ginny, Rachel's last three children, will emerge dark and intelligent and blessed.

SUMMER

One year and then another and the hot July nights make the early mornings crowded. Flo catches Hal just before he gets into his car; Lou, Missy and Bam stand beside her. She's been working at Priscilla's solidly for two years, barely taking a day off, but now Priscilla has made her take a full week. 'Go get a tan,' she'd said.

She stands between Hal and his car while Tex is already in the passenger seat. 'Can we go to work with you, Hal?'

'How many times have I told you? Show me respect, call me Dad.'

'Dad, then. Can we go? I'd love to see where you work, Hal. What you're working on.'

'No, it's not a place for all of you.'

'Why not?'

'Because I say so.'

'Please *Dad*, I just want to see what you do.' Lou, the sweetest thing, cherry red, stands beside Flo and puts in her own request.

'I build things.'

'I want to wear a hard-hat,' says Lou. 'Just like you.'

Rachel stands at the back door and lets a whistle rip. Hal looks at his wife, who looks a bit haughty standing there. She crosses her arms over her expanding belly. When did they...?

'Sure,' he says. 'Pack a lunch girls, we're going to work.'

'Does this mean I can stay at home today?' asks Tex, his hand already on the truck door, one leg stretching to the ground.

'No, sir. You're coming too. Maybe you'll learn something when I give them the tour.'

Hal will take them to a pet project of his, a new house on its own private lot by the forest preserve, then to the office. Missy climbs between Tex and Hal in the cab and Flo, Bam and Lou hold on for dear life in the flatbed of the pickup, laughing.

Georgia had tried to climb up but Rachel rescued her. 'We're going to bake some pies with our berries,' says Rachel as they wave the truck goodbye. Georgia claps her hands, her big cheeks rosy and shiny. 'Right after you take a little nap.' Rachel picks up the phone, dials Jon.

Compacted earth beneath his boots, Hal walks backwards, palms up, arms open, and directs the kids' attention to the skeleton of the Jones's house. The girders exposed, each room clearly marked off. 'The hall will be here, glass doors here, recessed alcove here.'

'What's this?' Missy asks. 'And this? How does this work? How did you figure out the height of the rooms? The depth of the window? Can you show me the drawings?'

'What pictures?'

'Of this house. The plans you drew of this house?'

'We can do that at the office.'

'Thanks Dad,' and she loops her hand through his, for a few steps, until he extricates himself from this girl.

Back at the office Kitty has disappeared. 'I asked her to get you guys some snacks.' He looks out the window. Her car is gone.

'Here girls. I'll let you take a look at some of the things your dad's going to build.' He quickly twirls the new number-combo lock on his flat file. The drawer pulls out slowly, dozens of plans laid flat. Missy's by his right elbow.

'Cool. What is this?' She points to the top drawing and Hal slides it out and puts it on the top of the plan chest.

'This is the Mayor's new house.'

'Fancy,' says Flo.

'Ugly,' says Lou.

'It's what he asked for, girls. That's what business running a business entails—pleasing the customer.' Still the thought of building that house makes Hal tired and he's been stalling.

Tex leans over. It has a pool out back, a hot tub on the sundeck. A billiards room. Two living rooms. A dining room. A dining kitchen. He starts to count: eight bedrooms. Two family dens. Seven bathrooms. Three-car garage.

'Where does he get the money?' Tex asks.

'By skimming off the building budgets,' Hal says, then backtracks. 'I mean. I have no idea.'

Eight-year-old Bam stands next to Tex and pretends to be enthralled. Instead, with a penknife she's sharpened she cuts Tex's belt loops one by one until by the end of his enthrallment with the mayor's wealth, he's holding up his jeans with one hand, swatting out at Bam with the other. She dodges him.

ELIZABETH REEDER

He persists and slaps her head as he walks out of the office. 'Watch it bruiser. You're in my crosshairs.'

With Flo working so many hours out of the house, Missy has taken over serving Hal and Tex dinner. When she goes to clear their plates, Tex offers his to her. She reaches for it and he lets go. The plate smashes on the floor. Tex smiles but doesn't move, not even when Hal tries to stare him into action. Hal pushes his chair back and with his napkin helps Missy clean it up.

The next morning on the front seat of the car, Hal finds a competent sketch of a house on a hill. *Thanks for the tour Dad. Love, Missy. PS It's of our house!* But it didn't look like their house. The columns are gone and balconies circle the house on each floor and look to be connected to each other by outside stairs. The roof slants in front, and in back a large, enclosed space holds a long table and benches. It's not quite as big as this house, but it feels like something Fremont. Beyond the house, which may or may not be built on a hill (now that he looks closely), he sees a horizon, shimmering in heat. Such fine lines, now this is a house he'd like to build.

Tex sets the alarm to get up early. At four he climbs out of bed, does a few push-ups before getting dressed. They wind him. He'll do more push-ups after his run. He puts on shorts and a t-shirt. He lifts each knee in turn, hugging them to his chest. He stretches his arms above his head. Ari usually catapults herself down the hill and Tex considers it. He starts but it's steeper than you'd think and his stride goes comical, out of control, so he slows to a fast walk. It'll do. At the bottom he does a sprint, gets winded. Starts to walk again. Soon the day is cut in two, light and dark, with light ascending. Tex walks behind Joe's to find the narrow river path and follows that around to below the house. Nestled in the curve of the creek the surface of a tent ripples in the breeze. Birdsong at dawn and voices too. His mother appears and Tex steps behind a tree. When he looks again her nightgown flies in the wind and she looks like an angel. A man joins her and he's dark against the white of her dress, which whips, whips. She rests her head on his shoulder and he puts a gentle, protective hand across her back and pulls her in tight.

Tex backs up to where the bank hides him from their view. When he's clear, he starts to run. In Joe's parking lot he does push-ups. Then he runs out on the country road until his ankles ache. He does more push-ups. When he gets home, his mother is dressed, the coffee is on, and she smiles like she's honest.

Work. Rachel. The House. Sandra. Birds. Work. The House. Tex. Work. Kids. Birds. Tex. Sandra. Work. Work. The House. The House. Work Rachel Work Rachel Work. Another State. Water. Girls. Desert Girls. Tex. Work. Birds. Sandra. Work Work Work. Tex Tex Tex. Work. Work. Work. Rachel. Kids. Work.

Hal's feet hurt and itch, bunions from his boots, athletes' foot. His rough calloused hands do not respond to Rachel's or Sandra's remedies; his hangnails rip back without teasing, leaving his hands blood-streaked. His back twitches with little electric claws. And his lungs ache.

His house still has the best views in the county and lately one of the girls—the one who makes all the noise with the hammer—has kept up with a lot the repairs the house needs and it looks better than it has in a while. Sometimes, from certain angles at certain times of day, it looks like a lighthouse and Hal comes to realize that lighthouses don't call you home, they're simply there to warn you of hidden rocks.

GHOST CANYON

Seventeen and still a year shy of graduation, Naomi sneaks out of the house, in the middle of a new moon night. It's just her and her bike's thin lines of metal intersected beneath her, and together they speed forward. Her panniers are full and before bed Flo had slipped her over a thousand dollars saying, 'At least one of us can get out of here.'

She's fast. Exuberant. Naomi lifts up her arms above her head, sweeps them in a circle, and she's lifted off the seat of the bike and finds herself surrounded by sky. A pitch of dark space before her, she's half-herself and half-wind.

Back on her bike she flies, flies, flies, beneath Cole's sky she flies.

Utah only knows Naomi is gone because she hears the faintest sound of her sneakers on the driveway. Her gears are well oiled and have their own sound. And she'll ride out of sight, until she knows she can slow and not be pulled back by Mom or by Utah or by all of them who feel as if the earth might just stop turning without her here. The bats with their manic wings beating in the night above are shadow on shadow and that's what Naomi is too as she moves from one boundary into another, from one dark into a different dark, and she'll go west and south and west following the directions she reads in the sky. In her way, she's trying to find Colorado. She's trying to make her way home. This is what Utah has to believe. She's heading home.

The Fremont house is woken up before dawn by a weather system putting pressure on the very frame of the house. The earth beneath its cellar aches, contracts, bulges. Inside girls' stomachs churn and rebel; a line for each bathroom forms; blood drains from faces and hands; and cool compresses stretch across foreheads as bodies lie on beds. Rain slices at the windows, the wind whips the trees against the paint, and the outside of the house will look ravaged when daylight arrives. Rachel can't walk for the pitching of the house. The Carolinas rebel in her belly and an old pain slices across her forehead and deep into the socket of her eye.

Hal falls out of bed. 'Do something, Rachel. Do something!'

Rachel makes her way out into the hall, but does not make it to the bathroom. Hal's chest hurts, his eyes ache. Lou whispers hints in his ear and they mean nothing. 'Stop!' He careens to his car. Typical; this is exactly the disaster his family seems to produce. Exactly what he'd be avoiding. At the office, although the weather has lost its mind, Hal can stand without falling. On the hill, his house looks possessed.

Tex sticks his head out of his room. 'Can't a boy get any peace!' And slams his door. He emerges a short time later, neatly dressed. Even though his face is drained, he staggers down the hill to work.

The girls acclimatize, drink water and wait for things to calm. Naomi is missing. Rachel tries again and again to get out of town and follow her daughter. She's seventeen and that's not old enough to be out there alone. By mid-morning the river has burst its banks and cut off the town. Rachel and Flo drive to Hal's office and Rachel pounds on the office door.

'Open up, Hal. I need your help!'

The lights are on but he does not come to the door. She waits but there's no movement. So this is how he wants to play it.

She considers taking the car and driving right through the door and when she gets in she puts the car into drive.

'Stop, Mom.' Flo puts a hand on her mom's hand on the steering wheel. 'You can't do that. Let's go home and make a plan.'

Rachel reverses the car.

'Don't worry so much,' says Flo. 'She'll be fine, she knows what she's doing.'

'What is she doing?'

'Getting out of this hell hole.'

Rachel isn't sure. She worries about Naomi. She's so quiet, holds so much to herself and often, it seems like she's talking to the dead. All these years on and she's not sure her daughter is right in her head.

All day and night the sky churns itself into a frenzy and Rachel imagines the weather front stretching from this place to wherever her daughter is. She doesn't imagine that the storm exists to give Naomi time for a clean escape.

By late afternoon the next day she's decided. Her car isn't sturdy enough and Rachel drives Jon's truck and takes Utah and Arizona with her. The sky has cleared and they all feel the relief in it.

'Just head west,' says Utah. 'She'll keep to the county roads.'

'We got a late start. I'm sticking to the main ones, until we get closer.'

Her girls talk about places they think she might be. She's talked about a few canyons, and other places… They look at maps, they can't decide if she'll go to New Mexico or Colorado. Rachel doesn't know either. As they approach this land she camped on during her desert pregnancies, fear leaves her. Her Uncle Walt travels with them, has been with her strongly since he died. He places a warm hand on her shoulder, there's nothing to be forgiven for. Naomi, he suggests, might not want to be saved.

You can map anything, Utah thinks, write anything. A map can reflect and represent as well as direct. It can clarify, it can confuse. Naomi is out there, riding along cliffs, which are just like the edges of jutting corners if you think about it, this defined edge pushing out into space and existing between one thing and another and another. Earth, sky, water. Family, place, self. Naomi thinks she's not alone, she thinks she can talk to Cole, but it's just foolishness, missing someone isn't the same thing as being able to talk to them. Being lost isn't the same thing as having nowhere to turn. They should have said something before now, should have got her some help. What does that mean? It means she shouldn't be out there alone, she should be here.

In the Fremont house one of the taps in the kitchen won't stop dripping. Bam takes a walk down to Pearson's to get a new washer. The square sign hanging on the door says closed. She goes to Chick's but it's not the sort of thing he carries. She buys a reloadable box-cutter just because it looks weighty and efficient.

'Bam, is that thing in the paper this morning true? Last year did your brother fight the Mayor's son over a boy? Is he gay?'

Bam looks at Chick. This is news to her. This is great news. A gift. 'If it's in the paper, sure thing.'

She holds the Stanley knife by her side. Flicks the blade forward and back. Forward and back.

His dad drinks his morning coffee out on the back porch, having made it up to the house after four days away. One of the girls is missing. Tex is out on the porch too, reading the *Chronicle*. He sees it in the upper left-hand corner, shakes the paper to give him a clearer line of sight. It's basically two questions placed in the personals: only a tiny box of innuendo at the back of the paper. A year after the event.

> Last year two prominent sons fought. There was no winner. We all assumed they both wanted to be President. What if, instead, they both wanted to be Queen? What if they didn't fight over an office, but a boy?

He's going to kill Brad for this. Tex pushes back his chair and tucks the paper under his arm, quietly. 'Leave that son, I want to read through it.' Tex puts the paper on the table. Maybe his dad won't notice it. Maybe he won't say a word. He goes into the kitchen.

'Fairy,' Flo says. 'Butt fucker.'

'Virgin bitch.'

'Oh, that hurts so bad. I'll shout your secret, if you shout mine. I'm sure Dad will be very interested in this. Very interested.'

'I don't know what you're talking about.'

'I'm sure you do. And they call our sister Bam. Do you take it or do you give it?'

'It's bullshit. I've got a girlfriend.'

'You've got yourself a beard.'

Tex pushes himself close to her. If they were to fight, he's not sure who would win now; she's a whole lot tougher than he is, but he'd be able to land a few punches, that's for sure. 'Leave it, Flo. You don't want to know what I'll do if you say this to Dad. You don't want to know.'

'I don't care who you screw. Not one bit. But Dad does. Start pulling your weight around here, and I'll keep it buttoned up.'

The phone rings. 'Dad, it's for you.' Missy shouts.

There's a bellow that's loud and a silence that's deafening. All ears to the door.

'I see, Mayor,' Hal says. 'I see. Yes, I understand. I don't agree, John. It seems to me that it's just a rumor. There's no harm in it. It won't come to anything. No, I don't. I don't want to contradict you, but he's been a lad around town this last year with the girls. There can't be any substance to it. Yes, I agree about when he was younger. But now, this feels like hot air. No mayor, John, I don't recommend that course of action. I don't think you should give credence to this. No, I've not talked to him. Yes, I know you're up for re-election in November. I wasn't really sure you could run for a third term, but I guess anything is possible. Seems to me you'll be fine. Now, hold on there. Do what you feel you have to John. It doesn't sound smart to me. Not smart at all.'

Tex waits for his dad to call him in. He doesn't. He doesn't talk about it at dinner.

'We're going to have to work some long hours Tex, are you up to it?'

'Yes.'

'Good.'

During the next week, the Mayor fires Hal from the job of building his house. The council members question Hal's skills, and send him a letter saying they will not accept any bids from him for new projects. Pictures of the Mayor's son leaning in towards another boy with an implied sexual intimacy circulate. The image of the other boy remains hazy, while Matt is very clear. The Mayor publishes a rebuttal and requests that the anonymous source come forward. In November, Kent loses the re-election to Ted Pearson. His son had already gone to college and no one can remember seeing him after, not at the holidays, not over the summer, not even at his dad's funeral many years later.

Rachel and the girls spend a week out west and they find nothing, no clues about Naomi at all. Back at home they file a missing person's report with Sheriff Buck.

'So you lost another one?'

'Yes, Buck, yes I did. Another big bad Fremont has been let loose upon the world. Lock up your children, lock your windows and doors. Beware the full moon!'

They drive up the hill, the twins turning in Rachel's belly, swimming like it's their whole world and that world is good and Rachel feels a surprising peace. In the hall, the map is robust and healthy, New Mexico included. Naomi is a year older than she herself was when she left home. She'll be fine, she tells herself, her daughter will be just fine.

THE CAROLINAS

Fall held some wild rumors, but they didn't seem too dangerous. Tex has made a mess and he'll have to sort it. None of it surprises Rachel, and his new girlfriend is garish but he doesn't bring her around often, which is a relief. His face is tight and she can't hear his heart, even when she sits on his bed at night and watches him sleep.

New Year turns over in a mild winter. Her pregnancy with the Carolinas has passed from something unsure into something sought out. As the days lead to the birth, Rachel walks along the coast through shallow water and inlets. A long journey, but peaceful. Her Island, Menatauk, watches her and she puts a hand up in greeting. It looks benign but she knows what's waiting for her and she's going to have to work herself up to setting foot upon its shores.

On the fourth of January, a day so warm the creek runs with rainwater, Carolina comes out first, open hands, strong lungs. Carley arrives second, fighting fists and open eyes.

In the hospital the perfume of the Carolinas' breath, the broad stretch of their smiles (it is only gas, Rachel knows that), and the coy brashness of their eyelashes, reminiscent of dark-eyed juncos, all remind Rachel of a fast clear running mountain stream which, as it loses altitude, stretches low and slow and wide. Rachel holds the newborn twins and knows she has ridden the Carolinas, like inevitability itself, to the sea.

Hal holds them, one at a time. 'They're so fragile,' he says.

'They're beautiful Jon. They look just like you.'

The payphone is so cold it nearly freezes to his ear, like a tongue to ice. Alaska stretches behind him. Twins. His. Rachel never asks him to come home. He hangs up the phone with a grin and a pang: she never asked him to come back.

Jonathon DuPre walks on. When he does hold his daughters, weeks later, his knees buckle. This man, who can survive years in the desert, the rigors of the toughest mountains, the worst weather, is reduced to tears by the beauty of his girls.

'They're so strong,' he says, 'already.'

These girls have so much coast in them and together they face Menatauk. She can't grasp it yet. They look a helluva a lot like Walt must have looked as a baby. The space on the wall remains newly painted but without any states fixed there.

She dials the office number, Kitty puts her through. 'Hal, where are the Carolinas?'

'How should I know? Wait, you've lost more kids? Really, what sort of mother are you?'

'Their states, Hal. Where are the states?'

'Oh, that. I'll do that this weekend. I've started them, they just need the finishing touches.'

'Could Flo or Lou or Bam get them and complete the job?'

'No!'

'Soon, Hal. It's sort of like naming a baby, or taking down your holiday decorations, if too long a time passes it becomes indecent.'

The weeks pass into months. Winter turns to spring and the paint gets scuffed by the rough play of the Gulf states.

'Okay girls,' Rachel says to Missy and Bam. 'Do what you have to do. I don't want to know how you get it done, but let's get those girls up there.'

Bam picks the lock to the basement. It's amazing down there. The main room just at the bottom of the stairs is big, the size of the hall and has a concrete floor while the rest of the basement has dirt floors and walls. She's got a flashlight and walks around. Missy is at the top of the stairs yelling, 'Hurry, we don't know when he might come home.'

There's a huge workbench and a tiny one beside it, with fist-sized tools. Who built that? There's a picture of Hal's mom and dad, her grandma and grandpa, above his workbench and a gingham tablecloth draped over a wobbly drop-leafed table that has a dirty mug set on top. At the edge of the workbench is a Bunsen burner with an enamel coffee pot. Beneath is a mini-fridge. She opens it: beer, beer, out of date milk. There's an old chair in the corner, with a pipe resting on its arm. She didn't know her dad smoked and when she lifts it up there's barely a scent from it, the tobacco is black and old. Maybe he doesn't smoke, maybe it's someone else's. There's a maze of rooms and she starts down one side of the basement and notices the walls giving up some of their constitution into small piles of dirt.

'Bam, get the sketches for the Carolinas and get out of there.' There's a creak on the stairs.

Bam goes back to the workbench, opens the file drawer. Sees the Carolinas. She grabs some of the tools they'll need and heads back up. She shoves the lock shut and together she and Missy go down to Chick's for the rest of the stuff they'll need. They slide up the garage door and work. It's April by the time they finish.

Rachel blows the cork off a bottle of champagne and she and Jon stand at the back and toast to the twins now secured to the map. The girls drink apple juice and clink glasses.

'To the Carolinas,' says Rachel. 'The prettiest craftsmanship yet.'

'Hear, hear,' says Jon.

'What's for dinner?' Tex asks as he comes down the stairs, spots Jon and stops dead. 'What's he doing in here?'

Even in a period of relative stability there are thousands of small quakes a day. The faultlines snake around the earth, below ground and below oceans. Even the Midwest shudders occasionally. This is the movement they talk about, why she thinks of the earth as stubborn— its solidness forces impact and fracture and thrust. And yet fault-lines allow for adaptability, elasticity, for rebound and transfer. A strike-slip, a sideways jerk. Friction, fracture, growth. All the signs of disruption and yet we can never tell when the big ones will hit.

We build on unsafe ground and then stare in wonder when it bucks us off or drowns us. But that's the thing, there's really no blame to the inevitability of asperities. The weather being the weather. The land being the land. Quakes cluster and storm and flourish along our faults. We survive the main event and have to survive the aftershocks. The hurricane hits and then the storm surge follows. Rachel thinks of moments of transition as places of deeply undefinable altercation: neither dark nor light, neither in trauma or in peace but in a state of constant agitation.

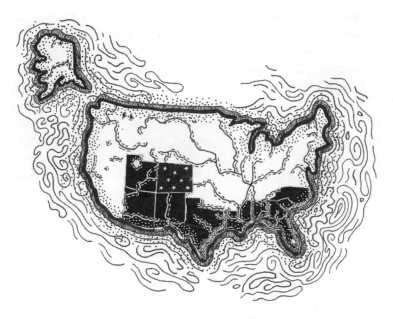

ONE FLEW OVER

Work Work Work Work Tex Rumor Tex Non-payment Work Rachel The House Sandra Work The House Bills Debt Tex Work Work Work. Work.

It's a long winter, and the spring and summer are no different. Failure chases him and he can't quite sprint himself free. 'It's a fast mover this time,' Hal shakes his head. 'A fast mover.' His head slowly falls onto the desk and he sleeps.

He wants his kids to stand in the order of their birth, and have them bark out their name, age, coordinates, borders, state birds and flowers. To do it every time they speak to an elder, to him. Actually, nametags would be helpful. Only Tex and Lou stand out. And that oldest one, he feels he should remember her—south, he thinks, she's south. She has to work hard but it's no reason for her to be so rude, and to call him Hal. Most of the girls call him Hal now. As if that is going to win them favors.

Some of them seem so capable, but they open their mouths and these noises come out, high-pitched, weak, too loud, wrens, chicks needing cared for. He's tried, he really has. He memorized their names for a whole day. But who could expect him to hold onto all that information in the midst of the chaos of that house. It's impossible.

His birds are deserting him: a roadrunner limps by and then is gone; the cactus wren grows muffled and then disappears altogether; the bird of prey flies in ever higher, widening circles looking down, giving a disappointed shake of its head from side to side before flying west on powerful long wing beats.

Something catches in his throat and moves lower down into his chest. It is dry and persistent. An irritating itch. He misses that roadrunner, the California gull, the cactus wren. Lou. Sand sticks in his lungs, wet with the tide. Impossible to clear.

But he keeps trying.

The damn itch in his throat travels down his neck, and he clears it, coughs, and the effort just to breathe makes him tired and Tex has grown up into a tall boy, stronger but still clumsy. Tex makes the effort though, working at Fremont Construction. He has an eye for detail, but tends to get distracted.

'We're builders, not renovators,' Hal had to say, often, at the beginning. But since the newspaper fiasco Tex has focused. He has definite management potential.

'I think you should run for Mayor,' Tex said the week before. 'That would solve these problems you're having.'

He'd laughed him off. An absurd idea, but very interesting. Very interesting.

Twelve-year-old Missy thinks that one strike will kill her but it doesn't. Tex stopped dancing with her and still her heart beats. He refuses all her offers of food, he won't look at her blueprints and yet still she breathes. He doesn't thank her for the gifts she gives, or the work she does for him when he lets her in the back door of the office and she does filing for him. Or when she answers the phone on

Kitty's days off (pretending to be Kitty) so he can go into the city and do whatever he does. And when she asks him to try to get her some legit work at the office, Tex refuses to speak to Hal on her behalf. One night at dinner when she's serving she asks her dad outright if she can work at the office. Hal bellows a no. But Tex doesn't stay silent, he starts to speak. Her heart fills. And then, he agrees with Hal. 'It's not really something she'd be good at.'

Still her heart beats.

The sisters watch the drama unfolding between Missy and Tex. She's in for a crash, they think. Don't try to love a narcissist. It's a good lesson. Do take risks in love, they think, but make them smart ones. When history weights the future too far in one direction, protect yourself.

Bam is not willing to play the waiting game. It didn't take much pressure on that guy Rob for him to cough up the proof he has. Bam puts copies of the photographs under Tex's pillow with a ransom note. 'Pay Missy what you owe her, with interest. Get Hal to give us some legit weekend work at FC.'

The twins aren't good sleepers in those first few months and Tex suffers, the pitch of their cries wakes him. Tex doesn't answer Bam's threat and she doesn't follow up. Some bluff, he thinks. He's still dating June, which is easy now that she's away at art college. Jon is often hanging around the house, he even sometimes eats dinner with Rachel and the girls in the kitchen and Tex doesn't understand why his dad tolerates it. Although his dad hasn't been home that often and he might not even know Jon exists, for all Tex knows. Still, his dad has got to get some balls. He has to take control. At spring break, June talks about how lovely Bam is. 'What a nice girl,' she says. 'She's into photography. We're meeting next week and she's going to show me her photos.'

'Okay,' Tex says to Bam the next day. 'This summer. I promise. This summer.'

In June, Tex shows up at a site with two of his sisters. Hal agrees to let them try their hands at a few minor activities. The strapping girl walks the beams with ease. How much has she grown in the past year? Only ten? She nearly looks like she could lift a car, maybe with one arm.

Hal swells with pride.

A girl. Not even his.

It quells.

And Tex. He stands beside him in a suit too nice and neat for a building site, his curls gone but that face, and Hal can admit this to himself, is still, always, utterly punchable.

'The county has all but strangled the life out of us,' Hal says.

'What's your plan?'

'To survive, Tex. To survive.'

Hal collapses onto the bed after dinner. Another boring dinner with his son. In bed Rachel holds him. Together they breathe. The room spins and in the center she keeps him calm. Not hot, not fertile, but familiar, comforting. The dark of her kisses feel like resignation.

On Saturday mornings Lou gets up first. She makes careful lunches with unwrapped sandwiches placed in lunch boxes. She prepares unbreakable flasks: one filled with hot chocolate and one with black coffee. They used to mix them together in the bright-handled plastic mugs. Recently, at thirteen, she's started to drink the black coffee straight.

More often than not Lou sits at the kitchen table, waiting for her dad to show up long after it's clear he's never even come home. Usually, as her sisters wake up, eat breakfast and go to their days, Lou sits there, still waiting.

'I'm going out to garden,' Utah says as Ari, dressed in shorts and a t-shirt ready for her first run of the day, passes by them both, 'do you want to come with me?'

'Or you could join me,' Arizona offers.

'No, I'll wait for Dad.'

Now it's Bam, axe in hand, 'Gonna chop some wood, wanna join me? Two birds, one stone.'

Lou drops her jaw, aghast.

'Ooops,' says Bam. 'You know what I mean, you can watch the birds, while I chop.'

Lou ignores the obvious flaw in that plan. 'Nah, he'll be home soon. Don't want to miss him.'

Eventually she moves to the porch, then out to the yard watching Utah work the earth, and then she goes up to the bedroom. Dark shadows swoop through and the house falls quiet and nothing can shift her.

Sometimes she simply goes bird watching on her own. Each day she leaves lists (mainly fictitious) for Hal on the dining room table. Birds she's seen without him: probable, probable, impossible, possible, probable. Birds with messages in their songs.

It's often dark when he comes home and grabs a change of clothes.

'Twat twat twat,' Lou sounds out as Hal walks by.

'You used to be such a nice girl,' he says.

It's a routine she knows and sometimes she follows him on a bike to where he ends up. Sometimes it's the office, other nights he goes to his mistress.

Lou sometimes goes to Sandra's studio and stands outside, looking up at the window, in all kinds of weather, looking at the yucca on the sill, two figures moving in and out of sight in the mysterious, unseen space of the rooms.

Sandra has always thought about her relationship with Hal as a private agreement made between consenting adults. With Rachel in the know, no one would get hurt. The affair has given Hal somewhere to go where nothing is demanded of him. She has always believed it made him more present at home, a better father, a better husband. She doesn't idealize their relationship, which is defined by things it's not, by things they don't do. They don't talk, they aren't soul mates, they don't solve each other's problems, in fact they rarely even know them.

Hal gives her simple pleasures. She enjoys the musky smell of him, crushed pine and lemongrass, wild garlic and sawdust, metal shavings and piecrust. Hal never puts up a front with her, rare in a man. Her ex-husband had hundreds of faces but none of them had eyes that actually worked. His ears must have been broken too, for him to be unaware all the town-chatter about his wife and his boss.

The rain batters against the window and Sandra goes to watch. One of Hal's daughters stands beneath her window looking up and they see each other.

'Hal!'

'What?'

'Your daughter, Hal, standing out there in the rain.'

He comes to the window and peers out. 'There's no one there.'

But she had been there, an arc of light bursting out of her in quiet fury. Orange at the far edges but a crisp white light guarding the girl against the dark of the night. With the girl gone, the light disappears too. Sandra can't forget it. There are no victimless crimes. She has a responsibility and she'll take that on. She promises herself.

Over the next year people stop paying the money they owe to Fremont Construction. Instead they buy up any land that's going. Hal gets lots of lowball offers to sell what he owns. He stands firm. He works all the time, finishing the projects they've started, going small again, towards the family builds.

Tex bribes Missy to do not only his chores, but to catch up on some of his paperwork at the office on the weekends, when Hal's out bird watching or wherever he goes.

Hal's internal clock is shot. Like someone took a sledgehammer to it. It's not that he sleeps at odd times, it's that he can't seem to wake and his dreams are so vivid. If he's been running in his dreams, he wakes and his legs are sore and his lungs ache.

In his dreams Rachel puts cold compresses on his forehead and presses against him and they are man and wife like the old days. Their kids are all boys, sturdy boys with names like Chuck and Lance and Butch and they love him unconditionally.

He wakes to the dull grey walls of his office, weak light through the closed blinds, and the rusting file cabinet opening, sliding back, light footsteps retreating, the door closing. He sleeps again. The sun is bright, Lou and him and Sandra, out of state in a park. The girl and the woman move in bold streaks of color against the blue sky. Birds bestow blessings of shadows onto their faces before passing on.

The phone rings, is answered by Kitty out at her desk, and the room quietens. He can't move, there's a rock on top of him. It's fallen from a cliff but it's loose and made of packed dirt. The scrape of a shovel. Has he been digging? A weight, a pressure. It's comforting, settles a worry he has. What is the worry? Rustle and movement and Rachel is here. She's had her hair done and she smells of a thin perfume. He's never known her to wear perfume. She's skinny too, almost skin and bones. He's been worried about her, hadn't realized how skinny she'd become. Hadn't he been paying enough attention? What about the baby? Did she lose another one?

She undoes his belt and lifts her skirt. Hidden sex. Rachel doesn't do this often. She likes them to strip down to skin. This is secretive, sexy sex. His breath comes up short, a pain, and he moves through it.

'Yes. Yes. Give it to me.' Her voice is ethereal, maybe she's only half on earth. Maybe.

Hal pushes deeper. He will take all of her. He loves his wife.

'Ah, Mr Fremont. You're a bad boy.'

He didn't ask for this. Kitty's hair is stiff and smells of hairspray. Her hip-bones dig into his stomach. His nostrils flare with the earth of her. His hands fall to the mattress, his head too, and sleep takes him.

His lungs heave him awake. Pressing. He rubs his chest. The irritation is deep accompanied by such cramp. Work has been torture, he got into bed with the devil and boy if he doesn't know it. So much still to do. It's a shame he stayed, wasted himself on this town. But his dad would be proud, he didn't give up. The concert hall is almost complete. His design. The payment doesn't matter. His girl drew a house which was magnificent, it was a child's drawing of a house, but he could tell. She'd nailed it. He flies around the town, familiar with almost every beam, every nail. He looks for Rachel. He wants to show her the opera house he's going to build. He's rented a helicopter so she can see what he's planning next. It's extravagant. Where is she? This is his town, he shouldn't just build it, he should run it. She should be here sharing this with him. He realizes he hasn't seen her in ages. Where is she?

He wakes. Sits straight up. The blinds have been pulled back. A girl runs by and flips him the bird. She smiles nicely but her gesture is crudeness itself. He doesn't care for her, never will. Some kids are just wasters.

He puts his boots on, they keep his legs straight from the hip. He'll go out and stretch his legs. Find Rachel. Tell her his plans. Where they're going. She'll appreciate that. His crotch itches. He scratches it. Swears. He screwed Kitty. That's so not part of the agreement.

Tex spits as he gets out of his car, his three-day bender in the city thick in his mouth.

Jon's playing HORSE with the Corners at the basketball net he'd bought, his well-used pack tossed onto the grass. Rachel sits on the porch with her feet up fanning herself. It's August and Jon is going to be gone for nearly three months. The twins sit by Rachel, propped up by pillows.

'Do you want to play?' Jon asks Tex.

'Are there no lines! No lines at all!' Tex yells.

Of course there are lines and they're pushed at all the time, sometimes they stretch, sometimes they break, and sometimes they are simply crossed.

It's just after eleven pm when Lou pushes her mom's car into neutral and lets it roll down the drive and the hill and then she turns the key in the ignition and burns rubber on the road out of town. She swings by Tom Harrison's house. He's leaving in a few weeks to join the army, so he's a safe bet. She wolf-whistles from beneath his window. She'd been letting him court her but playing hard to get. For various reasons he thinks she's sixteen, her driving to meet him being the main proof he has. Her foot taps on the pedals, her ring knocks against the gear shift. She hums a song and he kisses her when he gets in the car. His hand like fire on her thigh.

'Shhh,' she says. 'I want to take you someplace. Behave yourself.'

She cuts the engine a few houses from Sandra's and they coast with the lights off.

'I like your style,' he says.

'Quiet.'

The light is on in Sandra's apartment. Shadows move inside. Raised voices fall down through the open window.

'Just a few more nights a week. I could bring a few changes of clothing here.'

'Where would I keep those?'

'With your own.'

'It's crammed in here, Hal. You've got a home. And an office. Find another place to put your crap.'

Tom leans over and starts to kiss Lou. She lets him. Pulls him closer, looks up, all in line of sight of the window. The streetlight making the interior of the car bright. Tom puts his hand up her shirt and Lou accidentally leans on the horn, rests her elbow there for five or ten seconds. Tom starts to pull away but she holds him where she wants him and slides herself off the horn.

She looks up. Sandra comes to the window first. Her dad's face joins her. Tom gets excited, starts to push up her skirt. She looks up and waits for her dad to yell down, to protect his daughter. But he doesn't. His face retreats from the window. Sandra stays and then she disappears. Lou shoves Tom off. 'Get out.'

'No way. You started this.' He lunges.

She aims an elbow in his direction, makes contact with something that gives just a little before she hits bone, and gets out of the car.

'BITCH!' he yells after her as she runs. He slides into the driver's seat and takes off after her.

Sandra has rushed to the bottom of the stairs and watches Lou as she cuts up between houses and the car screeches to a halt and she hears a boy shout, 'Slut!'

EXUBERANT FAULTS

Georgia's clothes have been worn before. By tomboys, especially that outrageous BamBam. The knees are threadbare, as are the elbows, the colors faded to ugly, and the cuffs of the shirts have dirt so deeply embedded that even Rachel's tricks can't clean them. The repairs are always immaculate and she doesn't know where her mom finds the time but some pretty stitching can't make the clothes bearable. Georgia despairs and begs her mom for a few dresses, a pair of patent leather shoes but Rachel won't budge: hand-me-downs were good enough for all the other girls, Georgia will not be an exception. The rough denim makes Georgia's skin crawl, and the cuffs of the plaid shirts are too long and often hide her hands, her lovely hands.

Despite the fact that she dresses in hand-me-downs, Georgia tries to make friends at school. She knows that friends equal survival and eventual escape. But Georgia is foul tempered, impossible to please, too good for this nowhere smalltown hicksville flatland place, and the smart townies keep their distance.

Georgia watches her sisters bring home occasional friends and so she decides to try it too. With a candy bribe, she gets a girl named Tara to accompany her home one day after school. No sooner are they through the door than Tara asks, with the subtlety of an axe, 'Where's the map?'

Georgia leads Tara into the house through the thriving kitchen. Not less than half a dozen girls are in there at various ages, various stages of growing up, doing homework, finger painting, eating snacks. Pictures, odd ones, all black with small pinpricks or asterisks of white, some with faint trails of light, fill the walls and they look like places you'd see in a dream.

And Tara realizes that she's been brought here by a rather pale, dull offspring in what is an extraordinary family.

'What's your mom like?'

'When she's around you feel like you're drowning.'

Missy pipes up, 'That's unfair Georgia. It's like floating.'

Georgia rolls her eyes, turns to Tara again, belligerent. 'I hate swimming. And Mom makes me feel like I'm being held under the water.'

And with that Georgia leads Tara around the house. Bumping into and being introduced to sisters and more sisters, Tara realizes that they are scrupulously avoiding the central corridor of the hall, the front door, and the front rooms. It's like the girls live on one side of the mountainous house, the sunny side, and she guesses that they leave the other side well alone.

The girls play card games, fight over seats in the kitchen, hands in each other's hair, braiding or entangling, as an observer Tara can't tell. Sometimes each girl stands out, distinct, unique and nameable. Other times they unite into a single entity without borders or differentiation. Given their vast differences in appearances Tara thinks these moments have something to do with tricks of light and she blinks hard to refocus. Sometimes it helps, sometimes it doesn't.

It's easy to be surprised by it all. The noise and constant movement. Strangest names for kids ever. Maybe if Tara had been better at geography she'd understand it all, but as it is, she only has the vaguest understanding about how it all fits together. If only she could see the much gossiped about map, it would all make sense.

'How about a game of hide and seek?' Tara suggests.

'If you can't think of anything better.'

'I'll give you home court advantage. I'll be it.' And Tara turns her back, covers her eyes and starts to count. Georgia walks calmly to the one place she knows Tara wants to see, the one place she'll never find. She sits down and stares at that stupid map. That huge, that mis-shapen, that unfair, stupid map. And she waits.

When it grows dark Georgia makes her way to the kitchen. Tara sits there, mouth full of cookies she's helped Flo make. Giggling with Georgia's sisters.

Georgia raises her arm and points her finger out the door. 'I want you to leave, now. You were crap at hide-and-seek.'

'I tried for forever and couldn't find you. Lou found me up in the attic somewhere and brought me down here. Sorry Georgia.'

'I want you to leave.'

Tara leaves and is never invited back to the Fremont house.

'She seemed like a nice girl,' says Flo.

'You would think that, wouldn't you,' cuts Georgia.

Utah has been waiting at school for over an hour. There's been a long cloud burst and water races down the gutters of the streets, in sheets off the roof of the building. And it doesn't pass like a thunderstorm, it hovers there over the school and she's stuck under the awning with heavy bags of books and even the janitor comes and locks the front door and slips happily into his car. It's nearly dark and it isn't her mom who comes in the end anyway. It's Flo, all the girls in tow.

'Sorry I'm so late. I had to feed them dinner or I'd have never got them all in the car,' Flo says, 'hop in.'

Utah puts Carolina on her lap. 'Where's Mom?'

'She's stuck at class. She should be back when we get there. How were your exams?'

'Good, long. If I do well, and take some classes this summer, I could graduate in January.'

'Arizona will be happy, then you both can move out west. Congrats.' Flo hands her a folded over napkin, with a piece of cake in it. 'I've been working for Priscilla for four years, she brought me a famous Rennie Bakery cake from the city to celebrate.'

'Thanks Flo,' and Utah takes a bite and gives each of the twins a small bit. Carley plays with a hole in Utah's jeans. It tickles. She hugs Carley. Smells the baby smell of her hair.

At home she helps Rachel and Flo with the girls as they clamber inside and up to bed. As they eat dinner they hear Arizona outside. The rain has stopped and she's back from her long run. She's graduating this year, just barely passing her classes, and she's working at Chick's and volunteering at the soup kitchen. She's promised Utah they'd leave together, when Utah graduates next year but she's itching to be gone, and grumpy, so very grumpy.

Arizona doesn't come inside. Instead she is outside running at the building, running up, flipping over—throwing herself against the building again and again. Boom boom boom. Ground ground wallwallwall ground. Left right leftrightleft together.

Her thoughts, the sound of her movement, the same.

Go gogogogo GO.

The door doesn't even creak its hinges when Hal opens it. Nor do the floorboards protest. A rare thing, the house with its defenses down. Hal walks through the kitchen, brushing his hand along the counter, a puff of flour appearing and disappearing in the space of a single breath. He moves in and out of rooms he hasn't seen for years; he takes off his shoes and creeps like a thief casing the joint.

The plaster cracks running in the corners of the rooms are fresh, the paint which has failed to resist them, old. The furniture has been bashed by kids' rough play and the clutter seems to be trying to give the sagging walls a bit of support.

Hal counts back. Twenty-three years ago, that's when he brought Rachel back here. It's a long time and the map's surfaces are dull and disappointing and he moves quickly beyond it. Hal makes his way through the house, spiraling up and around the rooms. When the door to Rachel's room swings open and a few paint pots tumble off the stairs, he's breathless and stops to rest.

Outside the big windows of the turret there's the pale light of the waning moon; his houses blanket the ground with graceful roofs upturned, ready for flight. The whole town ready to flee. Even the fields seem to be lying in wait for something. Hal realizes that it has been years since he and Rachel have tried to move onto the next state.

Paints cover every surface, some are cracked dry from having been left opened and others have glistening splashes on their tops and sides. The white of the windows and sills is pristine. Books and pages and pages of notes cover Rachel's desk. Hal shifts some pages and sees her sketches of what look to be scars around continents, pictures of eclipsing moons, and one photograph that has all the oceans shown as thermodynamic swirls of colors. Tornadic swirls sweep over huge sheets of paper layered with notes and questions in Rachel's neat hand. He flips pages, there's Russia, there's India, the Northern Territories, the Antarctic. These aren't maps, they're travel plans. She's not going to stay here with him, she's not staying.

He leans heavily on the desk as he heads for the stairs and then lets the banister take his weight. It creaks and halfway down it gives way. Hal lands awkwardly at the bottom.

'Rachel,' he whispers. 'Rachel.'

She comes out of the bedroom in a house-dress, and he sees that she's pregnant again and he knows it's not his.

'Here, Hal.' She leans down, places his arm around her shoulder. He can't take any weight on his left ankle.

'A sprain or a break?'

'A sprain, I think. The ankle's twisted, I think I caught the shin on the door.'

She supports him to the bed. 'This is where you should have come when you got home. Not messing with my things.'

The ice she brings is cold to the point of pain.

'I'm out of arnica,' she says. 'I can get some tomorrow and that should help with any bruising.'

She leans over and kisses him. He counts six grey hairs swept back amidst all that black. 'You're so beautiful,' he says.

'Stop it, Hal, we're past that now.'

His hand reaches out, plays with the waist of her dress. 'I'll never forget that first day. Maybe…'

'Maybe we should have gone on a date first?'

'Yes,' says Hal. 'A naked one.'

He tugs on her hand, she is careful of his ankle. 'I will never understand you, Hal. Never.'

'I'm a simple creature. Painfully simple.'

PASSAGE MIGRANTS

Lou and Hal still share a rare outing. They walk side by side: Hal's strides growing shorter, Lou's larger. They sit in silence.

'Dad,' Lou starts.

'Shhhh,' Hal says.

Hal clears his throat, trying to fix the dry tickle that seems ever present these days. It gets in the way of the birdwatching and it grates on Lou and so she goes in search of other things. Creatures she can rely on.

Hal is getting old before his time. Lou is restless now when they sit watching the still air and unoccupied branches. Abandoning him. The birds leave him and flock to her.

'Dad,' Lou says, 'it's so quiet today.'

'Shhhh,' he silences her, binoculars raised high seeking birds that have already fled, his breath growing raspy. 'How I like it.'

'A yellowhammer,' she says. 'Same as a northern flicker, right?' Lou adds.

He nods and they watch it drill holes with its perfectly designed head. 'Its brain is cushioned to absorb the shock of the blows,' says Hal.

Sort of like my heart, thinks Lou.

Her dad's had choices, he's made them badly. They're looking out over a barren river and trees freed of birds, she sees him clearly, a forty-two-year-old man clinging to ideals that have failed him. He clears his throat again.

So she leaves him sitting there, on the edge of a cough. She leaves him as he is going to leave her: unsupported on the long walk home, and she goes off to find a boy to play with.

The school walls are filled with graffiti. New paint, same old, same old.

Lou Fremont is a slut.

Fremont meat is cheap.

For a good time call Lou Fremont.

Utah spray paints over the graffiti in the girls' bathrooms and then goes into the boys', past the guys pissing in the urinals, past the guys making out in the cubicles, well after the final bell has rung, and she spray paints over those phrases as well, and under the bleachers, and at the bus stop. She tries to get it all.

Kitty shakes Hal awake. He's sleeping near all the time now when he's not trying to get up her skirt and calling her by his wife's name.

'Mr Fremont. Mr Fremont. It's Lou on the phone.'

'I'll call her back.'

'She says it's urgent.'

'Tell her I'm out.'

'I already…'

'Tell her you were wrong.'

'I can't. She's crying.'

'Then tell her you're fired.'

'Mr Fremont…'

'Get out. My family is my own business.'

'You'll be sorry,' says Kitty as she picks up her purse, opens it, takes out the office keys and places them on her desk, which although neat, is full to bursting with papers and files and mail and regular tasks she gets done efficiently. She snaps the clasp shut. 'So very sorry.'

Rachel walks into the police station and Lou sits on a bench waiting to be processed. Lou stares beyond Rachel towards the door, to the place where Hal should be. Rachel can't fill that space but she'll do what she can to protect her daughter.

'Hi there, Mrs Fremont,' Sheriff Buck Harrison says. 'Looks like your little heart-breaker has been breaking some laws too.'

Rachel goes to Lou. 'How are you honey?' Lou's shoulders are tough and fine, her hair wild and belonging to no one in the family but her. For a space between seconds she's just a kid and then she becomes a teen with attitude.

'I'm fine, Mom. Fine. He's just pissed because I dumped his son.'

'You've been dating someone?'

'Apparently,' says Sheriff Buck. It seems that Buck's son, Tom, had been sending home letters from Army training saying that little Lou Fremont had his heart, saying that when she goes to college next year, he's going to go AWOL and be with her. 'Your thirteen-year-old has been occupying herself with the shenanigans of much older and still foolish girls.'

'Like?'

Buck's face has aged, sun-chiseled crags instead of laugh-lines and crow's feet. Rachel sees something familiar in the dark circles under his eyes. 'Telling people she's sixteen.'

'I haven't told anyone I'm sixteen.' Lou stands up, hands on hips. Her voice and face calm, because it's the truth. She'd testify to that.

'Driving a car is the same as flashing an ID.'

'You've been driving my car?' Rachel turns to Lou, her outrage not quite hiding a pride in her daughter, for her attitude with this horrid man.

'Only after dark.'

'After curfew,' adds the Sheriff.

'She doesn't have a curfew,' Rachel says.

'The town does, on school nights.'

'What proof do you have of any wrongdoings?'

'I caught her speeding, for one thing, and I have a list of boys who say she's been selling sex in the back seat of her car.'

'Mom, I've never…'

'What boys?'

'My boy, for one.'

'Show me the list.'

Connor Maltor, Tommy Smith, Jason Sewall, Kurt Neill.

'Pretty impressive huh?'

'It's not true, Mom.'

'She's never going to admit it, Mrs Fremont. But this list doesn't lie. I can get sworn statements by the end of the night, if that's what you want.'

'I hate to play this game with you again Buck, I really do, especially considering your son has gone off and joined the army the first day he could sign his name to the papers and get out of the house you run.'

'He's a patriot.'

'Maybe.' She looks to Lou. Holds her tongue, stays on topic. 'And I don't mean to tell you how to do your job, or that you should know the law a bit better, but I do believe that each and every one of these boys should be arrested.'

'On what charge?'

'Statutory rape, of course. If they had sex with my daughter, they are guilty of having sex with a minor. Thirteen isn't even a negotiable age, no jury will find them innocent.'

'She offered it.'

'I did not.' Lou takes a step towards the sheriff. Fire sparks from her eyes. Rachel steps between them.

'How does the Army feel about convicted rapists?'

'She…'

'Doesn't matter. Release my daughter.'

'She's still been driving underage.'

'Give her a citation, a court date, whatever. But on this other charge, you'll be hearing from our lawyer.'

Glenda's son in-law calls the Sheriff the next day, acting as their lawyer, and the Sheriff says, 'What list? What charges?'

Sandra is on the phone with her sister who is sounding better and they've been talking for over an hour. Hal knocks at the same time he opens her door. He takes a hold of her hand, the one that's not holding the phone and pulls her to standing. Gives a little cough. Smiles. Pats her arms. She shakes herself free and puts her hand over the phone, 'I'm busy, Hal.'

'Do you want to get hitched?' he asks.

Sandra drops her arms and the phone and laughs. Laughs until her ribs hurt.

She picks up the phone, stands up, rubbing her ribs and talks into the phone, 'You still there Hannah? I'm going to have to call you back.'

She takes a step back and puts her hands on her hips.

'You're still married, Hal.'

'That'd be easy enough to take care of.'

Sandra ignores this obviously false bravado. 'Hal, this is me you're asking. It's an absurd proposition.'

'It'd be great. Just you and me. Here. Or somewhere else. We could pack up and go.'

'This is crazy talk.' She's no idea where he's getting this. 'What about your family?'

'They don't need me.'

She remembers Lou standing outside her window. She thinks of Rachel alone with all those kids. She's already alone too much. 'You're blind, Hal. No, I won't marry you.'

'Or I could just move in.'

'Hal, don't push it. No. Never.'

He tucks a stray hair behind her ear. 'You don't mean that Sandi, not really.'

But she does. She really does. Not only for now, but any time. He's looking drawn and smaller. 'Come here, Hal.'

She makes him leave before midnight and tells him to go home but knows he'll drive east, towards his office. The damn fool.

She calls Rachel the next morning. 'Rachel, I was wondering if I could borrow one of your daughters.'

'Which one?'

'Lou.'

'She's not really in a good way at the minute.'

'Tell her it's me and that she'd be doing me a favor. I'll pay. She knows the way.'

Lou laughs when her mom asks. 'She wants me to do her a favor.'

Rachel lets it slide. 'For cash, Lou.'

'Why didn't you start with that?'

Sandra and Lou first load all her paints into Sandra's truck and then they drive to the old Kelly brick factory. The town is full of the bricks the Kelly family made. The south wall is the size of a basketball court and teenagers often have raves out here, in the summer.

'I didn't just want to throw it away,' says Sandra. 'I wanted to do something with it.'

Lou doesn't ask why she's getting rid of the colors, what she's going to do now. She doesn't care.

'I saw you in that car with that boy,' Sandra says.

Lou has never seen so many colors. Although some of them look familiar, her mom's used them for the map, many appear secretive and timid in the tins.

'I should have protected you.'

'No,' says Lou.

'Yes. Any adult who saw that should have stepped in.'

'But he didn't.'

'No, he didn't.' Sandra shakes her head. 'At least you protected yourself. Which is more than I could do at your age. More than I did.' They pull out the tins from the back of the truck. 'I want there to be no confusion at all, I owe you and I will not fail you again.'

If you take the top off of the paint before you pitch it at the wall, the explosion satisfies more than if you leave it capped. Making the extra effort to twist off a cap hardened with paint, or to wrench off the circle which seals the tin, pays off. Sometimes the glass jars holding rarer pigments break on impact, but the plastic ones or tin cans bounce and hit the ground, which also becomes covered in paint. Sandra had told Lou to dress in clothes she could ruin and now Lou appreciates the warning. The sound isn't as good as smashing glass against a wall or onto concrete, but the colors, they're better and overall more satisfying.

They throw like artists, like major league pitchers. They pitch the containers fast, moving past each other to find good places for the lime green, the candy red, the helio yellow. This process satisfies Lou in a way she can't describe.

Hal holds the nest aloft, cupped in his upturned palm. He's been working on it for months. He protects its copper weave from the rain with his other hand as he runs towards the house, towards Rachel. This is his creation. It's his life's work. This will bring him summer on a winter's night, a world in his palm, the perfect idea made real in all of its simple proportions, nature's template. Fremont Construction will build housing developments full of these, but they'll call them forests, streets will be branches. Homes will be nests.

Through the window Hal sees Rachel in the kitchen. Her belly is big, her eyes dark, and she's happy, singing to herself. He has no idea where the kids are. He puts the nest on the window sill, protected by the eaves: it will make a bigger impact in situ. He opens the back door and she's surprised to see him but her smile is genuine. Beautiful. She's still his wife. She'll always be his wife. He spins her, his hand above her head, stepping towards her to catch her close and they turn together, apart, together, the curtain billows in, a breath of cold wind full of night with kisses of stars bringing punches of light. There's bread cooking in the hot oven and with the heat of it, despite the season turning from fall to winter, she's wearing a summer dress with an apron over, her belly pushing at the fabric. And they're turning, turning.

Hal is in his bare feet, jeans licking the tops of his feet and a t-shirt, not old or new but one he's been wearing for a few days which smells just a bit too strongly of him. There's a new thinness to his frame that should have worried her but instead she finds it attractive. He's not rasping or coughing, he's dancing with her, his wife.

She doesn't have to look hard to see the real man he is, to know why she married him. She doesn't have to even think why she stays. This man is alive in her arms. In sleep they move together and apart, the night and the heat and their bodies know which breath to follow, tributaries and causeways, cricks and creeks and hollows, ebbs and flows, and sleep takes them together and later they make love and yet neither could tell you for sure whether it had ever happened. At some point Rachel wakes up and walks out of the room and out into the night on another excursion fueled by worry she won't remember and Hal wakes to an empty bed, wakes up his son, and drives them both to work.

Lou comes home in the early hours of morning and on the window sits a nest woven out of copper thread. It's a gift from her dad to her, an apology. She looks up, the house is quiet and dark and at peace. She palms the nest and takes herself to bed.

NIGHT CREEK

The land is brown and hard and dry under the full moon. The wind has no personality. Dirt, dry as drought, gets caught in her back teeth simply from running, from climbing. Ari is always trying to get this place out from underneath her fingernails. She is eighteen, and she is still here. Stuck like Flo. Even the running does nothing to dissipate the restlessness that has built up: not running, not even by kicking doors or chopping wood with BamBam. Sweet, tenacious, tough-as-nails Bam.

Her family drives her mad. Her mom worst of all. So quietly complacent. She runs harder. She flies over a fence, climbs up onto the roof of the school, jumps off and rolls. Runs again, flat out, pumping her arms. How she gets through life. She made it through the chore that is school, barely, and tries to follow the trails that Flo and Naomi cut, but it just isn't worth the effort. She's started to call homeless shelters out west, to see if anyone matches Naomi's description. They never do. The Fremont name is on many lists at organizations who help runaways, listed with Ari's number, so they can call her if Naomi shows up.

Ari sprints up the hill past shadowed houses, with a quick neutral glance at each, and then towards the last dark house, her house; she looks at it with the same disdain. The damn thing. So wilted and unchanging. Sweat gleams on her skin, and she takes the back steps two at a time, avoiding the well-known creaks. She presses the light on her watch: 3:30 am.

In the dark of the kitchen the door cuts a swathe and a black shadow arcs across the floor. Ari is practiced at stealth and can make it through the entire house without a sound, without knocking furniture or knick-knacks and definitely without brushing that map—there's no surer way to wake up the whole family. Ari creeps through the kitchen, avoiding the chairs and the counters, but on this occasion she runs into her mother's hand as it gently grasps her wrist. A small noise of surprise.

She breathes calmly while her eyes adjust to the inside dark.

'Shhh,' whispers her mom. Upstairs, girls stir as plates shift beneath them all, grinding and realigning. 'Can we talk?' Rachel breathes shallowly and there's a glass of water on the table.

'I'm going to bed,' says Ari.

'You've seemed upset recently. Do you want to talk about it?'

'Since when do you care?' Ari's voice is haughty. She tries to keep it under wraps with other people, but lets it rip with her mom.

'Since always.' Rachel takes a gulp of water.

Ari grimaces, her mom so cool, so prepared to protect herself. 'Always? You've got to be kidding. You're either at a class, or at that damn map looking after his handiwork or screwing around with that new man of yours or out for one of your impossibly long walks or watching the younger ones.'

'You mean the girls that can't yet look after themselves?'

'So you're saying I can look after myself? Then why bother even asking? It's been going on for ages and you only ask now.'

'Because now seems like the time I need to watch out for you.'

'Like you watched out for Cole or Naomi? Good job there, Mom.'

'You were going to leave with Naomi, if I remember correctly.'

'To look after her, Mom, that's the difference. You just let her go.'

'You Corners, you're so defiant, so private. I didn't see it coming.'

'It'll be your fault if something happens to her.'

'Nothing will happen to her.'

'How do you know?'

'I just do. So do you.'

Ari thinks of the maze of water she tracks daily in her head. How clear Naomi is, how present and alive, still stubborn, and just fine. But she's doesn't trust that, not completely, and she's certainly not going to give her mom any ground.

Her mom continues, 'Plus you were there that night too. You could have stopped her.'

'You're the mother. She's your responsibility.'

'We all have the responsibility to look after each other.'

Ari exhales, exasperated. 'That's not going to work on me Mom. You can't just opt yourself out; opt me in. Don't kid yourself. You barely do what you need to do to keep this joke of a family going.'

'We are a family. A good one at that.'

'No Mom, we're a zoo. An orphanage with absent parents and five different fathers.'

'Stop right there.'

'Why? I don't get it. Why didn't you just leave Dad, rather than put us all through this?'

'Through what exactly?'

'The embarrassment of being part of this family. It's obvious that your marriage is a sham. You're the talk of the town.'

'I haven't been listening.'

'Well your kids don't have a choice. We have to hear it. Every day at school. Everywhere we go in town. You should hear what people say as they pass Chick's since I've been working there. It's a nightmare.'

Rachel stays silent and Arizona laughs.

'Listen. I've done what I've had to do. I've adapted to the situation. Survived. Are you saying that Lou or Missy or Bam are any less a part of this family?'

Slip sliding, '…No.'

'Then what are you saying?'

'I'm saying that you could have left him.' Ari sets her jaw, thins her lips, her low eyes desperately seeking a mother. 'You should have left. And taken us all with you.'

'Do you think that you'd have been happier? You would have still been a Fremont stuck in a place you don't belong. You're not upset because of me, Ari. Don't get confused. This isn't about me, or being a Fremont, this is about you. Where you should be. Place you can leave behind. Family stays with you. And you'll want to take us with you when you go.'

Ari thinks, go. She can leave. She said she'd wait for Utah to graduate but she didn't know it would be this hard.

She looks at her mom, who continues, 'I don't want you to go. I'm worried you'll die of thirst out there.'

'Mom, there's plenty of water if you know where to look.'

'When I was pregnant with you girls, I could never find enough water.' Her mom rubs her chest, in memory.

'You never looked in the right places. And Mom, I'm not you.' For the first time Ari knows she's capable of thriving in the desert, without her mom, without her sisters. 'Even though you and I are looking for the same things, we'll find them in different places. That's why you could let Naomi go, you knew she'd follow the roads, stay in civilization. You believe she'll never die of thirst.'

'Exactly.'

'But Mom, isn't there other stuff you need? Not girls, not family? Doesn't living here hold you back?'

'I can't afford to think like that. I couldn't afford to leave. It'd be admitting defeat. And I am not defeated, just adapting.'

'Did you know that most people who die in the desert don't need to? They are within easy distances of water, if they knew where to look. But they panic, trust their eyes rather than gathering other knowledge and they die. I know where to look.'

Rachel takes her daughter's hands. 'I know you do.' Rachel kisses her daughter on each cheek. She stands back, places a finger to her parched lips. 'I won't stop you when you decide to go.'

OF SOUND MIND

The campbed's mattress presses into Hal's spine and back like a bed of nails rather than a thin mattress hung over air. Hal's not sleeping but staring at the ceiling. Heart racing, he's having trouble getting a deep breath. He calls Sandra who says that it sounds like he's having a panic attack. It's possible. So much to do, he could use more hands around the place. Better hands. A girl sat at Kitty's desk today, one of his daughters. She's one of the mockingbirds, a clever girl and she's been here more than Tex recently. What is she, twelve? Is it even legal that she's working? Her drawings are good, she puts them up on the walls. They're good, she captures something in her drawings.

The other day, in town, he saw his oldest daughter working at Priscilla's, the best realtor in town. She had her own desk and everything. Word getting back to him that Fremont builds are being sold on for profit. He remembers her, she used to serve them dinner, listen, hug him.

Another girl comes to mind too, that tall one? Built like a football player and she's been doing work around the house, some painting, repairing the fence, strengthening the banister on the stairs. She does a good job, but she won't meet his eyes, not that he'd praise her or anything. She's angry that one. What does she have to be angry about? She's been hanging out at the sites and the guys find her useful. She always wears her hard-hat, doesn't ask to do more than she's able, and he allows it and hopes nothing goes wrong. His girls are smart. They could make a difference here. What has he been doing?

He gets out of bed, turns on the desklamp and gets a pen and some paper. He's going to change things. He's going to make some changes. What century is he living in? How did he ever think it'd be a good idea to be so strict, to be so aloof, just because his dad did it? Especially when he saw how well it had worked for him. All his brothers scattered the instant they could.

His girls.

He starts to write. *I, Hal Fremont, of sound mind and body do hereby declare my possessions to be equally divided among my children.*

He chuckles, what sort of language is that? Sure Ralph drew up his original will, on long paper that unfolds like something special, a thick blue paper on the outside. Something so fancy for someone like him. He'll call him tomorrow. He'll call his doctor too. Hal rubs his chest. His lungs hurt. He puts the pencil down, puts the paper in the drawer with his house designs and lays back down on the bed. He has so many tasks to complete and it seems to him he's having trouble doing the things that most need to be done.

His heart races too fast for him to sleep. He goes home and sits out back. He's been thinking. He's been watching. Tired, his binoculars heave on his chest. They're so heavy and his chest is so tight, itches all the time. Deep inside and he wants to put his hand down his throat and scratch his lungs. 'Can you scratch my back?' he asks the small one, the dark one, who looks nothing like his grandmother, or him, Missy, that's her name and she's got sharp nails and she scratches. She's been sitting quietly beside him for a little while.

'Here?'

'Yes.'

She keeps it light and sharp and it helps. She rests her palm down on his back and there's a heat and then it's cool, his coughing calms a bit. He can't catch his breath.

Missy goes inside to the kitchen and gets some lemonade for herself. 'He doesn't look so good.'

'Who cares?' says Flo.

'That's your dad you're talking about.' Rachel walks into the room and takes pastry dough out of the fridge.

'Where's Lou?' Missy asks.

'I don't know,' replies Flo.

Rachel presses a crust into a pie plate and looks out the window. Hal sits in the yard facing the fence beyond which the hill slopes down. He won't be able to see anything from there. It worries her, he'd only sit there if he didn't think he'd be able to make it back up the hill. His shoulders shake. Rachel puts a hand on her belly where

Ginny is quiet. Her own ankles are swollen with pregnancy and she's slow too.

'Flo, why don't you go down and keep him company.'

'I'll make the pie, you go.'

'Flo. I mean it.'

Flo lets the door slam. Hal jumps at the sound. She sits on the fence.

'I miss the pretty maple.' He grabs at his chest, rasps.

'Should we go to the hospital, Dad?'

'No. I'm just tired. A lot on my plate. Just tired.' Her dad lets his head relax forward and he tries to get his breath. His breathing grows steady.

'Let's get you to bed,' she says, 'so you can sleep.' He leans on her. She holds him up and maneuvers them smoothly into the house. They pause at the bottom of the stairs, look up. They look steep and together, wordlessly, they decide against attempting the climb. As they turn the map shows itself powerfully today, all aglow with health. The irony of it. They walk past and he squeezes her arm.

'I know,' she says, 'it's all Tex's. Isn't he a genius, to deserve so much.'

'You,' Hal starts but coughs instead. He lies on the couch and Flo covers him with a blanket, brushes her hand over his forehead and when she's sure he's asleep and won't remember the kindness, she kisses his cheek.

During the night, what starts as a soft hopeful clearing of his throat transforms into a hatchet cough and a sharp pain in his chest. He bruises his lungs against his ribs and, eventually, has to choose between coughing and breathing. He chooses coughing and then coughing up blood. He ignores it, stuffs the blood-stained handkerchief in his pocket and gets up for work. A girl gets into the car beside him holding two thermoses of coffee.

'Where's Tex?'

'He's in bed.'

Hal's too tired to argue and shifts into neutral and coasts down the hill. Today's an important day, the groundbreaking ceremony. The sun is barely up, but he'll get there early. He parks in the middle of the flattened ground where the new city hall will be built.

No one is here, Hal thinks. Rachel isn't at the ceremony. She's never around anymore. She's not there and he knows they've failed. It's a cornerstone, he wants to yell. A cornerstone with my name on it. Our name. She's not here and he's abandoned. They've failed.

No one's here. Has he got the day wrong? There's no cornerstone yet. It's barely been cleared of the old building. At his back runs the main street, with its historic storefronts and rattling porches, ambling its way towards the other end of town. Hal turns to take a look and his feet get caught up in each other, he's off balance, starts to hack and falls hard, the hand he puts down to take his weight crushed awkward beneath his body.

Hal imagines they'll put up a plaque in his honor, in this gathering place. 'For a great man who built this town.' And visitors will look up to the swoop of the ceiling, and think of the man who had a vision and then built it.

Missy watches her dad stagger to this patch of dirt; they don't even have permission to build here any more, work stopped when Pearson got into office and yet Hal looks crestfallen that there's no building. When he falls she gets out of the truck and checks on him. 'Dad, wake up. Dad,' Missy says. She's tempted to slap him, but refrains. She sees Ari as she's running past, calls her over. Ari runs full speed until she's upon them and she jumps to a stop, kicking up dirt.

'Get your ass up, Hal. Hal!' Ari shouts in his ear.

'Thanks, Ari. That's really going to motivate him.'

'He loves that stuff, it's his own style so yeah, I thought it might.' But when rudeness doesn't wake him, they're pretty sure they have to take him to the hospital.

The doctor's initial diagnosis is a heart attack, but the EKG comes back normal. None of the expected bloods are elevated. She rubs her chin. 'Maybe. It's something else. Any ideas Mrs Fremont?'

'He's been tired,' says Rachel.

'And he coughs a lot?'

'Yes.'

'Is he out of breath?'
'Last night, yes.'
'Has he ever worked in a dusty atmosphere?'
'Of course, he's a builder.'
'Does he work with asbestos?'

Rachel sits beside Hal's bed. Her feet are swollen and her head aches. She feels heavy and Hal doesn't wake, not really, his breath is labored and the nurses say he's having trouble getting oxygen, which makes him sleepy. Sometimes his breathing sounds painful and his forehead is wrinkled, his cheek crushed against the pillow and his eyes are dark and sunken. She wants to lie beside him but she's too big. She stands up and runs her hand along his arm, it's cold and dry. She presses her cheek to his, kisses him. He coughs and recovers.

'Sure are beautiful,' he says. 'Aren't they Rachel, our sons, they're beautiful.'

He doesn't know what he's saying, it's clear and she should just let him be but the words slip out, the correction. 'Our children, Hal, our children are beautiful.'

He rasps and coughs, grips her hand and she cries out. Such pressure, deep and low near her spine, and it's sharp. It's a contraction, she thinks, it's just a contraction.

'Mom, are you okay?' Flo asks. Rachel breathes through it.

'I'm fine,' and she's still leaning over and her knees are giving way and her elbow digs into Hal's ribs despite her efforts to hold herself up. Flo takes her arm and helps her sit again. Her legs are wet, her waters have broken. She looks down and there's blood too. She still grasps Hal's hand. She can't let go, she can't do this alone. She can't raise this family alone. He'll get better if she stays, his breath is smoother, she can correct his wrong-thinking.

'Mom, is that normal?' Missy asks, looking at the liquid staining the floor.

Flo stands again, reaches over Hal and presses the button for the nurse.

'I'm fine, Flo, I'm fine.' But her face tightens and there's such pain, such pain and the world goes to black.

The girls sit with their mom and she's distraught, calling out, trying to get out of bed, to go back to Hal. She's collapsed twice already trying. The doctors say not to worry but have her hooked up to all kinds of monitors. Out in the hall Sandra arrives, hesitates by the door, looking down towards the wing where Hal is, takes a step towards him, and then back, like an aborted line dancing step. Smoothes her hands over her skirt and walks without further hesitation towards Rachel.

'I'm the midwife on call,' she says, 'I hope that's okay.'

'Hal, I should be with Hal.'

'It's just a bit of indigestion, he'll be just fine. Or maybe man flu,' says Sandra.

'We'll go,' says Flo, pulling Missy up. 'You're in safe hands here, we'll go make Hal buck up and get better. We'll bring him in to see you soon.'

'Great,' says Sandra. 'Rachel, I think Virginia is about ready to meet her family, don't you?'

There'd been an alarm, a brouhaha and then the women's voices fade. His leg doesn't hurt as much anymore, the pain is focused only in his lungs. The bed is hard and the angle is all wrong.

Hal doesn't remember a single thing anyone has done to make him proud. Not a single thing. They could have tried harder. He doesn't remember how he got these blisters on his fingers, the cut on his arm, or the ink under his nails. He doesn't remember what shoes he was wearing this morning. His feet are bare now, beneath a sheet. He doesn't remember what it was that taught him he had no control over his own life.

Two of his daughters sit beside his bed and there's a weight at his feet. The rude one who flips him the bird has left already. Good kids stay. Flo's here. The oldest. The one who walked him inside last night. She'll look after him even though she's a bird killer. He'd seen her smile after that maple came down. Of course he knew. Tex, it's all yours, Hal thinks. No one else deserves it. No, that's not right. Tex, you're fired. You're spoiled. His lungs hurt. Don't work with asbestos, he wants to say. Or mercury. Or flirtatious women. Watch yourself, Tex. Diversify. Don't get caught. So much to tell him. Try harder. Try harder. His son, his only son, lies heavy at his feet. He tries to move his toes, there are girls in the room, they're looking at him, expectant. They want him to be something he's not. He wants to be this thing. He'll get better and he'll make it right. That's the oldest, she's familiar. She's looking at him, almost like she loves him. And the smaller one, so young, so dark. Both with his dark eyes. Big eyes. Rachel's eyes. Where is his wife? He loves Rachel. Too much. This impossible love. Not made for this earth, this overcrowding, this place. He should have taken her to the sea. There are birds singing. Birds. His girls. His girls are singing for him, outside the windows. The ones here, they're here to pick at his bones. His sons, his most beautiful sons. Their song is familiar, on his cheeks are Rachel's kisses. 'I know you did the best you could, Hal. You had all of me, Hal.' It's a whisper, an impossible whisper since he's lost her already. Years ago to other men. But someone holds his hand with a light cold touch. Light. 'I love you Dad. I love you,' says the small girl who isn't really his, but is here and that's something.

'Fight, Dad.' Flo orders, 'come back and make this right, Hal.'

'That damn map, it'll never get finished now,' says Hal. 'But we have a fine son don't we Rachel? Rachel? Rachel?'

But she isn't there. Hal coughs. Tries to sit up but can't. Coughs more.

'And it's all yours, Tex.' Cough. 'Everything.' Cough. 'Let me tell you a few things to help you along…' Hack hack hack.

But Tex has fallen asleep along the bottom of the bed. It's Flo and Missy sitting doubled up in a tight fit of a hospital chair, watching evening fall, who hear every word their father says.

Missy's mouth drops. It shocks her to hear that this is the way the world works. To Missy it doesn't matter that Hal is not her biological father, or that she is a girl and doesn't deserve much of anything.

These facts never even occur to her. With no history behind her, no birthright at all, she gathers her forces together and whispers into her brother's ear.

'It's ours too, Tex. Don't you forget it.'

There is something free in the way the girls leave the room, they aren't jubilant, but disappointment has released them from hope.

VIRGINIA

January stills outside, bitterly cold. A small wind of snow blows a whisper across the façade of the hospital. Whines. Hal's asleep, his breath thin and labored and then impossible.

Hal comes to a little while later and Rachel is not here and he knows that's wrong. She'll be at home with the kids and she needs him to help out more. The room is empty aside from a lump at the end of the bed, he kicks it and it rolls away, briefly, and then falls back like a big coat.

Hal pulls the IV out of his arm and busts himself out of the hospital. His gown flaps a bit in the wind. He doesn't know how he has the strength but he's stronger than he's felt in months, in years. And awake. The world is bright and full of frost. The pain is gone and his chest is clear. He could run for miles. He won't though. He'll take the car. It's not in the hospital lot, since none of his family is here to witness his miraculous recovery, but he sees a truck with its door wide open and he takes that. Sparks the wires under the dash; he hasn't done this since he was fourteen and his dad whipped him good, but he saw Sheriff Bob laugh through his beer-browned teeth and knew it was a normal thing for a teen to do. The truck moves fast, faster than his heap of junk would.

Rachel's out there somewhere and there are lots of things he wants to do. Lots of things. Things he hasn't even had time to figure out. He wants bigger things. He doesn't want this town, not really. This backwards, backass town that never really wanted him or his family anyway. He and his brothers could have taken on the town, but they'd run away with their tails between their legs and left him alone. Hal had stayed to show this town he was good enough. And if he'd earned some grain of respect, his kids certainly had not. Good kids. Flo still helps racist Miss West next door, brings her milk, butter, eggs and cigarettes. He bets she doesn't even hope the old witch will die soon. Even though Rachel told them all never to speak to her again, after Arizona's birth. Flo had been here for him, but she's gone now. Why didn't she stay? They certainly haven't raised reliable kids. She could have given him a lift. He'd made Rachel tell Flo she had to stay at home, not go to college. He and Rachel argued long and hard about that one and Flo was disappointed, told him he was being unfair but Rachel wasn't paying her own way, much less the way of any of the kids, but who was he kidding? All those girls at her skirts and all those maps pulling her towards different topographies, to alcoves and rift-valleys. Rachel could have gone somewhere else, but she's stayed. She'll stay until nature takes her away.

The whole town appears to be in flight. He couldn't have planned it better. The streets live not so much as borders but as rivers and conduits; it's familiar, this shape. They could have limited their kids to here. This layout, this plan. But they did not. They did not limit them to something small-minded, something without potential for interpretation. His house dazzles on the hill.

The lines between the states dissolve. No corners to the corners, an uplift, something shared, a place to meet in this world or the next. Their kids shimmer, oxbow and silt, spring floods and winter buildings, everything in flux. Except Tex who remains iron clad, immutable and completely unviable.

Hal has been away from home and he knows that now, too far from home as he drives recklessly, tailfinning, skidding, turning turning on black-iced streets. Tex should be here, for his mother. He swings back to the hospital and yells up at his hospital room. 'Tex, you asshole. Get down here you ingrate.'

How the hell did he raise a son like this? One who didn't respect his mother. He's clean-shaven with haughty eyes. Who does he look like? Not like me, Hal thinks. Certainly not like his mother. When he doesn't come down, Hal turns around and starts to drive.

I've been stupid. Stupid as hell. Unfaithful. Stupid as hell. And the pokes with Kitty. That's something I'll have to make right.

Hal hits the accelerator and the truck speeds so fast up the hill that at the top the tires lift and it flies off from the road and then the truck disappears altogether and Hal is alone, just himself, surrounded by a cobalt evening blue sky so rich, so thick, it's a gift to have it lick his arms and face and his body takes form, shape-shifts and he flies towards his wife, the love of his life, who needs him.

The pain is immense, there are complications. The persistent alarms fade as they give her gas and she's freezing cold because someone has left a window open and she's out in the middle of a frozen field, the ground beneath her, a dark frozen sky above. She is graceful like a leaf bounded about by the wind. Her tears freeze on her cheeks as jewels. In her chest she only has half a heart and it's dying, losing its will.

'You're not alone,' Hal whispers and it sounds like a song, a calling.

'We've failed,' Rachel cries.

His girls are there and they'll surround their mother. They're a family, they know how to love. Good people draw good people to them. Will he be considered a good person when he's gone?

Hal becomes a bird and he circles, ascending. He's waiting, hoping. Rachel looks up, he soars, soars, and then he flies hard and fast to a place he's never been before.

She hears a strange bird cry and at first she thinks it's her daughter, but her cry is different, she hears Ginny too, giving an infant cry, short and gulping. This other call is high and full and circles and circles, spirals higher and higher. She looks up. He's a beautiful bird, a rarity. Those who don't know anything about birds won't realize what they're missing. But Rachel does, she knows exactly.

The nurses rush in and wake Tex up. His dad's monitor bums out a monotone. His white face now looks cold too. Dead. His father is dead.

'She's an idiot,' the nurse says. 'Asbestosis or emphysema, sure, maybe contributing factors, but not the reason. Did you see the bruise on his leg?'

'A pulmonary embolism.'

'Of course.'

Tex stands and looks at his dad. Waiting for a twitch, a twinge, something.

Nothing.

Tex leaves the room and a nurse catches up with him near the elevator.

'Mr Fremont, what do you want us to do about your dad?'

Tex looks at her nametag. Sarah. Sarah scrupulously avoids using the word 'body'. He skims over Sarah and taps his foot impatiently for the elevator. 'Call my sister Flo. She'll take care of it all.'

Tex goes home. He has choices to make. The door is open, broad fields have nothing upon them; he could wipe the slate clean, plant and harvest as he sees fit. He could fly the coop, he could go to New York City, he could knock on Duncan Fremont's door and offer to get him on the cover of *A&I* again.

He's alone. The map sits on the wall, determined in all its unfinished glory. All his. He touches his head: his shorn curls and his distinctive skull. Tex feels his hip stiff and hesitant, and yet finds that his hands know exactly what to do. When he hits his hand flat across his state the envelope slides down smoothly, like he's tripped a switch.

He snaps the Will open with a flick of his wrist. He reads it, but it isn't necessary, he knows exactly what he is entitled to.

Everything. All of it, his. The world is his. His capable, clambering sisters disappear from his sight. He stuffs the envelope back into place, they need to know it too.

His.

That night at the Fremont house Missy and Flo gather the girls around. Tex has taken his car and disappeared into the city. Rachel insisted on being released from the hospital, saying that her husband had just died, pointing to her girls, saying she'd have plenty of help. She stands in the doorway between the kitchen and the hall holding Ginny, not needing to see the papers to know.

Behind the biggest state, stuffed between wood and the wall and big globs of dried glue, they'll find Hal's wishes. Flo reaches her hand up behind Texas. A bit of plaster falls but the envelope stays firm. She makes a fist and gives Texas a swift, clean hit and down slides the envelope.

'Tex,' she says, 'everything to Tex.' Flo and Rachel's eyes meet. The binoculars and bird books, the business, the house and their miserable savings.

'Mom.'

Rachel sighs, slams a fist on the doorframe, and Ginny cries. Rachel soothes her. The bastard. Twenty-four years for this. Not a single penny for her or for their girls. Not a single one.

The girls argue.

'Bastards. Both of them.'

'Tex isn't going to share it.' Utah runs her flattened hand over the map.

Bam gives his state small jabs.

'You never know what he might do. He might come around,' Missy says with a nod to Flo who adds, 'He deserves a chance to prove himself.'

'I wouldn't be surprised if he kicked us all out,' says Lou. The map gives off a heat, glows orange and red.

'He won't do that.' Flo puts her hand on Lou's shoulder. The room cools. 'He needs us. I think we should give him time. I think we should play the game, be nice, and give him a chance to realize his mistake.'

'Just let him get away with it?' asks Arizona.

'For now, yes. He's weak just now, when he gets stronger, he'll look out for us, we're his sisters.'

'Yeah, right.' Bam says.

Flo slides the envelope back up behind the rich state of Texas, and Missy and Bam run down to Joe's store and then in the kitchen the girls lift big spoons, not silver ones, and eat their way through three huge tubs of double chocolate fudge swirl ice-cream, and a small pint of peppermint for Lou.

The girls disperse. Having palmed Bam's lockpick, Missy disappears off into the night. She lets herself into the Fremont Construction office and works with the lights off. She remembers the code Hal had used on the desk-lock, turns the dial and takes each and every drawing her dad had made out of the drawer.

Hal had saved almost everything, which isn't something Missy expected. She always thought of him as having one foot out the door, a light bag with only a few necessities slung over his shoulder. Turns out he'd photographed all of his builds (including old black and whites of his dad building their house), documentation of problems (old oil tanks buried where a house's foundation was to go, buried electrical wires), even uncovered archeological remains. On two occasions geologists came to look at uplift oddities. Then Hal had photographed his men going in with bulldozers and cleaning the place out. Hal's snapshots, what did they attest to exactly? Pages of notes: *5/6 7:22 am the first breaking of ground.* A file for each building he'd ever built. His documentation was more detailed in the early days, like how a baby book of the first born is thicker than for those who follow.

On the top of the pile is a crumpled, well-read sheet of paper. It's a list of his daughters, in Lou's hand, a bird beside each, and notes he'd added later. Next to Missy's name: talented, great eye for detail. It isn't until a few months later she finds another single sheet of paper amidst this stash, in Hal's own hand, unsigned but definitely Hal's, and it could change the whole family. *I, Hal Fremont, of sound mind...* She carries that note everywhere, usually in the small pocket on the right side of her jeans, but doesn't share it. She often pulls it out and reads it over and over again and she never once, not once, doubts her rightful place as his daughter.

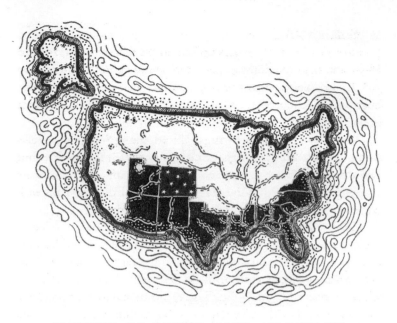

IN THE GROUND AND ABOVE IT

Four days after he dies, they put Hal in the frozen ground with minimal fuss. Flo thinks, it's just another day, just something you do when someone dies. Hal was complicated in life and also just too damn simple. And now?

It's quiet in the house, and to and from the cemetery, and they all notice Tex's new Armani suit and no one says anything. Flo watches her brother as he stands with his hands crossed in front of him. He appears blank of any emotion other than arrogance but she wants to believe it's a cover for how confused he is. The days of him crying in the face of bullies are over but she's not sure what strength he carries now.

Some people from the town are here; Sandra stands at the back during the burial, but comes up to Rachel after and the women embrace through a few breaths, whisper to each other. Rachel touches Sandra's face and Sandra kisses Rachel's cheek. They nod and turn to other funeral goers. What the people of the town know is that death brings change. It's a tossing up of cards into the air and wondering how they'll fall. They leave food neatly wrapped in cling-film on the porch, return to their houses, and look up to see how future history will unfold. They gift trademark dishes: meatloaf, buffalo wings, potato salad, lemon bars, and pans of brownies. The Fremonts aren't an all or nothing family, this isn't an earthquake or tornado, the house will not burst into flames of grief or altercation or revolutionary acts of generosity and selflessness. This is erosion, a weathering, a logical unfurling of what has come before.

They heat up the dishes that need heating, and touch up the map with delicate brushes while they wait. The air in the house is cold and still and Hal gives no sign as to how he should appear on the map. Tex disappears after the funeral and by the time he arrives home the girls have made their own plates and sit eating in the kitchen.

'I'm home,' shouts Tex, lingering in the hall.

A few of the girls shout *Hi, Tex*, but there's no pause in conversation, no forks held suspended, no direct invitation, it's just dinner and everyone is welcome. They don't pause but the girls and Rachel are waiting for Tex to put his head around the door and pick up the plate which has been left on the counter for him. After a minute or two they hear his feet on the stairs and they, like the townies, continue to wait for change.

The girls eat. It's a normal meal, not fast, not slow. Girls push their chairs back, clear the table, run the tap, wash and dry the dishes. The leftover food is put into containers and stored in the fridge. They clean storage containers to be returned to their owners with a thank you note. Utah and Arizona go upstairs to start to pack; Flo takes the twins to bed; and the other girls disperse, mostly hanging out and helping the Corners with their things. All told it's been more than two hours.

Rachel sits in the kitchen feeding Ginny by an open window, an act a bit too daring for this cold snap, but it's the only way to bring the outside in. Ginny's new eyes watch her mom. Rachel's never seen a newborn this alert. Right amongst her girls, watching the house return to normal, Rachel looks for a sign, listens for a song to tell her something she needs, like a mockingbird singing a litany of places, names which tell her that Hal used to say his children's names under his breath. But the birdsong is no different than any other day. There's no flocking of starlings or crows or children who gather to mourn the death of their father. There's no son who will undo what has been done.

Tex pushes the swing door in its full arc, the past pinning the future to the wall. 'Where is everyone?'

'I don't know.'

'And my dinner?'

'It's in the fridge.'

Utah has received her exam results and is so done with high school. She and Arizona get ready to leave; there'd have been no point really in making a fuss. Their dad had never remembered their names in life, and they can't bring him back from the dead to make him learn them now. There's nothing more they can do to help their mother survive this place or to make their brother any less of an asshole.

'Come out and visit,' Ari tells her mom and her sisters.

'Sooner rather than later,' Utah adds. She's got a small compass in her hand, which she hands to Lou. 'If the stars don't come out, you always have this.' The compass has a broken needle that always points in her direction, following her like a magnetic north.

'I'll be sure to use it, when I need it.'

Rachel holds Ginny close and says to her desert girls, 'Come home, any time. You know where we are.'

Lou ties a bright red bandana around Utah's neck. 'Always keep the sky above you and the ground below. If in doubt, climb to safety and keep this place at your back.'

'Thanks Lou, I will.'

To the younger girls, Arizona is just another dry sister, the strange one with the lean body and flare of a temper; the one who rarely sleeps in the house, the one who carried Missy home from her first day of kindergarten, shoe in hand; the strong one who twirls them and makes them laugh and push themselves that bit harder. The one who runs and jumps and swings her way through the most bizarre obstacle courses and always encourages them when they tag along. She's the one with the scar.

Bam sits on the roof of the garage looking at the house and yard wondering what she'll be able to save now that Ari is leaving, she's the only other one around this place that has any ability with tools.

Ari climbs up to her. 'Wow, from up here you can really tell how much work this place needs done to it.'

Bam doesn't know if she can take it. All this leaving. It weakens everything. 'You don't have to go.' She pouts in a way that doesn't become a ten-year-old who knows better. 'You could stay.'

'We can't, we've waited long enough. But we'll come back to visit. And you can come out west too.'

Bam starts to hammer, futilely. Light tears falling. Arizona hugs her and kisses her cheek. 'You're the one,' she says, 'who will keep this place standing. You and Missy.' Then Arizona climbs back down and she and Utah leave, with one rucksack each (and a few boxes mailed to the Flagstaff PO) and the house sags, becomes more ordinary.

'Dibs on their room,' shouts Bam as she bolts up the stairs, cutting off smelly little Georgia from getting there before her. 'Just try, just pretend to even try to be able to take me on.'

For a few weeks the house feels a bit like a rattle. Bam and Missy and Lou move into the Corners' room, and it's brighter and more at ease and the girls often talk late into the night. Flo is gracious and moves in with Georgia and the twins. The house shivers itself into some semblance of new balance. Slowly moisture comes back into the air, and loss too.

Tex stands by Kitty's desk and has fists full of bills. It's been three months since Hal fired her, only a week since he died, and there's a knee-high pile of mail. The door to his dad's office is closed and he doesn't even want to know what mess is waiting there for him. The letter opener shaped like a bird's wing is sharp and he starts to open the letters, invoices mostly, one at a time and makes piles. He's determined to succeed. But it's a big backlog and his hand aches from holding the opener for so long, from gripping it to make it slice an even line. There must be systems for this. He needs help and doesn't have time to train anyone new. He digs out the phone and calls Kitty at home. When there's no answer, he leaves a message. 'Kitty, please come back. Please help me make it right.' Four days and he's already prostrating himself to a whore. His heart flutters, how do you do this? How do you take over for someone? Make that life your own?

Kitty shows up the next day with a list of demands. Unreasonable demands but Tex agrees and she sets her purse down, gives a smile, and starts to work her way through it all. She has a smile that's hard to read.

He's at the office and then he's driving to the city. He finds a party, achieves a plateau of wastedness and uninhibition, falls into the arms of a stranger who lives a block from the club, up three flights of stairs, and it's in this bed he sleeps.

Rachel takes every single item of Hal's she can find and makes a pile in the backyard. With Ginny strapped to her chest she moves quickly. Jon's out in Nepal and she'll phone him when she wants to talk. She separates what is salvageable and of quality enough to give away, from what the world will be better off without.

Bam tackles the basement and Missy asks her to keep any papers she finds. She works her way through drawers and surfaces, looking at each scrap and photo. In one of the drawers, Hal has a picture of a beautiful woman with five boys at her feet. His mother, Cecilia, if the note on the back is anything to go by. Her dad had brothers? Where are they? Behind that photo there's another one of a black woman with five more boys at her feet, Hal's grandmother. Bam doesn't know her name and there's no note on the back but behind this woman and these boys there's the Kansas house she and Missy had seen during their game of hide and seek all those years ago.

Hal had boarded up the windows of the basement and she takes those off and lets the light in. The building presses down and a bit of plaster crumbles, but the walls support the house after a bit of settling. She finds some racetrack tickets, a couple empty bottles of bourbon, a few half-filled. Thirty years of the *Audubon* magazine carefully boxed and ordered. The last year is missing, and she wonders if he let the subscription lapse or if he kept it somewhere else. Hal had hardly been down for ages. Bam sets aside the big map sketch and will create Ginny this week. Bam carries the photos upstairs.

'Lou, you might want to go have a look on the shelves down there.'

Rachel and the girls work steadily through the night, clearing out the house, and make blueberry pancakes and bacon in the morning. With OJ they toast to the Corners and their travels.

They clean the house as they go and the place straightens, lightens and sparkles. Midmorning they wrap up warm and go outside. They pack up the car with everything they can donate and put everything else into the truck. Rachel takes the donations to the Salvation Army. Flo takes the truck and dumps everything else.

Tex hasn't slept, not really, he rarely does when he's in the city. He has the rest between sweat and release and more sweat and release. His hands shake and he holds his eyes closed, he will imagine this scene differently later today. He doesn't leave his phone number or any indication of who he is and slips out the door. It's nearly noon and a full winter sun melts the ice on the streets but not the grass on the side of the road.

He has work to do if he's going to make this place profitable. Then he'll sell it and move to the city. At the office he puts on a pot of coffee, sees the number 26 blinking on the answering machine and he's just about to listen to the messages when he thinks, I'm the boss now, I should sit at the big desk. He goes into his dad's office and the drawer to his dad's desk is wide open. It's open and empty and Tex realizes that what he won't give, those girls will take.

Ginny cries, hungry for life, for truth, for her inheritance.

Rachel wakes up suddenly a month later. Hal is dead and her anger is a fist shoved up under her ribs, like a baby's foot. It catches her breath, brings in the walls. It's the love she can't bear, this house, her kids. Tex walks like he owns the place, looks at her as if to say, 'Who are you again?'

How would the conversation she wants to have with Tex go, exactly?

Tex, as your mother I order you…

Tex, don't you think it would be best if you shared your toys like a good boy?

I'm taking you to court to contest the will.

They're all laughable. He knows what is right and he will come to it on his own. He will. But here and now he stubbornly refuses to look at her, or his sisters because he'll crumble if he does. Even believing this true doesn't change the fact that he doesn't look, doesn't eat with them, that he's changed nothing since Hal died. She walks or reads through the night and in the mornings her girls often find her slumped over the kitchen table, sleeping on her arms. As they get ready for their days they sweep their hands over her shoulders, lifting and letting a few hairs fall, and they press kisses into her cheeks.

It's only been a few weeks but she's alone, restless and drowning. It's unacceptable. She's done with the unacceptable. Her last child, a tiny bird, chirps in her arms and Rachel calls the hospital.

'Yes, that's right,' Rachel says into the phone. 'My tubes tied.'

Spring turns into summer. Flo is twenty-three years old when she makes a late application to Brown and is accepted, with a partial scholarship. Priscilla lets her go part-time, down to holidays and summers.

Flo has already started to study for her realtor's exams and it's on this ground she'll build her career.

Out on the court the girls play basketball. Jon, Bam, Missy and Lou play while the two-year-old Carolinas roll the ball around the court with a surprising agility.

'Wait until they're a bit taller and they'll shame us all.' Bam is all out of breath, her hands on her knees, eyes still on the Carolinas.

The house watches carefully, cautious, eyebrow raised like a skeptic, waiting. There's much to be wary of. Tex keeps the corner room. And the money. And the deeds to the house. And the business, which isn't going that well.

Tex comes up with a plan. He organizes a BBQ out back.

'It's been nearly seven months since Dad died.' Tex lowers his head out of respect, lifts his eyes to see if his sisters show the same deference. They don't. Somehow this makes his decision even more right. 'I think that we should all pay a share of the house bills. I'll pay the mortgage and house taxes, but we can share the utilities and food bills.'

'How do you suggest we split them up?' asks Flo, beans suspended mid-pass. The possibility of college speeding away on wheels made of crumpled utility bills, waving with a nasty little grin.

Tex taps a finger on the edge of his plate, 'Each Fremont for themselves.'

Bam kicks Missy under the table and mouths *I told you so*.

'Ouch,' she says.

'What about the girls who are still in school?' asks Rachel.

'Next you'll be asking us for rent,' Bam says.

The thought had crossed his mind.

'Split among eight of us, it won't be much. It'll be good life experience.'

'Like you had,' Missy says. 'All those jobs you had through your childhood to pay for your own keep.'

Bam turns in her chair to get a good look at Tex. 'Yep, punchable,' she says under her breath.

'What was that?' Tex asks.

'We'll do what we're able,' she says.

'We can try it out. Get us past a rough patch,' says Tex, balancing peas on his spoon.

'Sure thing, Tex.' Flo picks up her barely touched plate of food, the thick sick feeling in her stomach dropping, bouncing, dropping.

In a slow line the girls follow her to the sink, where they pile their unwashed dishes before dispersing themselves through the house. Eventually, Tex gets up and adds his plate to the clutter. He grabs a cup of coffee. Rachel places her hand on his shoulder. He flinches at the touch then forces himself to relax.

'I'm watching you, Tex.'

He stirs his coffee and his back gives away no emotion.

'This won't continue forever. You can make other choices.'

'It's mine,' he says under his breath. 'He gave it to me.'

'You're not wrong about that, Tex. Hal most certainly did give you a lot you'll get to keep.'

Rachel stands and runs a hand beneath her collar and lets the breeze cool her skin. We need time and peace. Please please give us some peace, she asks no one or no thing in particular, and she walks to the hall. She glances at the map, for all that, it looks pretty good. Flo comes and stands beside her, Ginny on her hip.

'I can stay Mom. Help you through this.'

'No, Sweetwater. You go. This is nothing. We've been through worse.'

Rachel plays with the twins and puts them to bed. She picks up some clutter, runs a vacuum through a few rooms, waits for the washing machine to be free, and then sits out on the back porch for a long while after the sun goes down.

UNCONFORMITIES

AN UNSPECTACULAR RIFT

Five years on and Hal's death still rests on Rachel's shoulders, a burden she doesn't want to carry, but will, with as much grace as she can muster. She's not sure how to define what she feels. Missing? Maybe. Anger. That's closer.

Temporal gaps, geological gaps, oversights of knowledge, intent and expectations. It's a mess and shot full of missing pieces. Unconformities exist everywhere, these vast jumps between events in time. 'Sometimes they call the explanations they create for unconformities, narratives,' Jon says. 'But that's geologists wanting to be storytellers.'

'I can see how that could be.'

Jon kisses her, picks up his bag, and goes on another trip. After the elevated strain of being married to Hal, Jon's easy comings and goings suit Rachel. When he's in town he eats in the kitchen with her and the girls and sleeps in her bed. Tex makes his displeasure known and Rachel ignores his posturing.

Ginny won't hold Rachel's hand when they go into town, and she certainly won't in a week's time when Rachel drops her off at first grade. She's a big girl now. When asked, she'll hold up a wide-open hand, 'I'm this old.' A big girl who has been begging to go to school non-stop since she could talk. 'Wanna go like 'linas.' She'd been reading since she was still in diapers and Rachel can think of no reason to keep her at home. For her first day of school she has picked out a neat, new pair of knee-highs, a flowery skirt and a pink sweater. She pulls her black hair, curled tight, back into a plain ponytail holder. When Rachel takes her to the Salvation Army she picks out the cheapest, sturdiest backpack and stuffs it full with her siblings' books and trails herself around the house in this get up all summer. Rachel is not worried about Ginny's first day of school.

The Carolinas are seven and have to be coerced to go to school and Rachel bribes them with candy and basketballs and week-long visits to see Utah and Arizona out west.

Since a week after Hal died, she took over from Arizona and has been helping Chick in his store (he's had a series of small strokes) and working at the library, because Glenda's arthritis had made lifting and carrying and shelving harder with each passing cold wet weather scarp. Rachel starts as a volunteer, until Sue complains, which Glenda pays no attention to until Sue turns in her notice saying, 'I will not work with that woman.'

'And she won't work with a bigot.' And then Rachel takes over Sue's job. Every few weeks Sandra stops by for coffee with Glenda and Rachel, and sometimes she runs pajama story-time for the younger kids who show up in their PJ's and cling to teddy bears and stuffed rabbits.

Flo lasts a semester at Brown and then transfers to the state school, which is only an hour from home.

At Brown she did well, but locally she gets straight A's. She works part-time, flexible hours with Priscilla and starts showing houses. In her senior year, when she's twenty-eight, she sits and passes her real estate exams as well as her academic exams, and basically settles herself into a nice, profitable career. She shares her wages with her family but never divulges quite how good she is at her job. 'What is possible, is all in here,' she thinks as she files her bank statement and is more than happy with the success she's had before even turning thirty.

On cool mornings she puts on the heat and the radiators clank into life as she puts a blanket around her mother's shoulders. On warm mornings she opens the windows to let the house breathe, and brushes her mom's hair back from her neck to cool her.

Over the years her Fremont blood comes handy. 'See the curve of the roof there,' she says to the young couple with unscuffed shoes and perfectly ironed his 'n' her suits. 'It's like a eagle in flight, the stretch of its fingers.'

If the couple looks patriotic, she makes it a bald eagle.

When she's seventeen, Missy buys her first car, a clapped out old VW bug. It costs her two hundred bucks and it barely makes it out of old Tom Burns' lot.

'A song,' he'd said, 'I'm giving it to you for a song.'

'Yeah, a swan song,' Missy says as she and Bam push the car home, doors open, hands on the frame and praying that neither of them slip or lose their footing or slide beneath the wheels. The car makes it up the hill that once but will not make it out on the road without some serious attention.

Lou helps them fix it up. She's done metalwork at school, shop class too and she has started to make replacement parts to almost any machine. More than one of the boys seeks her out after seeing her at work on an engine. For a feminine girl she has a taut back, arms like a boxer, and a confidence using tools that's rare in almost anyone.

'It's a heap of junk, Missy.' Lou reaches down into the engine. 'Hand me a monkey wrench.' She hums and her foot taps the ground. She unscrews some part or other, holds it up to Missy. 'This won't do at all,' and chucks it into the corner of the garage.

'Hey!' Missy shouts.

'You're better off without it.' She closes the hood. 'You're good to go, if you don't travel too far. Or too fast. Give me a few more days with it and we should be able to make it last a week.' She laughs; Missy and Bam laugh too. She clasps her hands on their backs. 'You should have told me, and I'd have gotten you a deal on a car a hell of a lot better than this.'

'This is the car I wanted.'

'I look forward to receiving your call of distress.' Lou wipes greasy hands on her jeans. 'See you all later. Enjoy your short ride.'

Missy drives until they're out of town and then Bam takes over the driving, foot to the floor, not that it goes faster, but she takes the Beetle in an over-optimistic fashion along unnamed county roads among the corn. Fast. Fast. Their own undisputable country. They drink beer Lou gives them, supplemented by a flask filled with Tex's hidden bourbon. Missy had tried making eyes at Mick at the liquor store and he'd made eyes back but still wouldn't buy her booze and they laugh because this shows how long he'll be a virgin.

They often speed on, with the hipflask shared between them until they're full up with unguarded, unfounded, unreasonable hope and together they'll drive Veronica their VW, and she'll never let them down, until one day only a year later, out by the reservoir, the brakes slip and Bam and Missy are lucky she's never picked up too much speed so they don't get hurt when they fling themselves out of the doors and the car doesn't fly but continues on without them stuttering and splaying itself along no path, stalks bending beneath it, and while the car slows it doesn't stop but crashes into the water of the reservoir, sliding beneath the surface, its borders mercurial until it disappears entirely.

Georgia's nail clippings drive Bam mad. Little Miss Priss and she has no respect for the rest of the family. They get everywhere, those foul disgusting half crescents which start to yellow as soon as they are clipped: down the inside of the couch, on the floor, clogging the bathroom sink, entangled in the folds of towels. You wouldn't think that one girl could produce so much bodily detritus. She's got the normal number of fingers and toes and associated nails, but they're supported by such useless hands—that completely fail to do her household chores, or offer any support to any of her sisters. A waste of space. It's only on closer inspections that Bam notices all the eyebrow and hair in the drains, curdles of lipstick wiped on the underside of the sink, dusting of eye-shadow creating a paste in the grouting of the tiles. And all the dead skin: Georgia's ablutions crowd out so much that's good in the house. They get in the way of the free-flowing plumbing.

It's as if Georgia feels that at twelve she already smells like a teenage boy and that her body is decaying while still living. She masks it by showering herself with perfume. Bam sneezes with the smell of it: it burns the inside of her nostrils, makes her skin itch, her eyes water. Doing anything inside becomes near impossible when Georgia's around. On bad nights, when Georgia is, for some reason, at home with what she always pronounces to be her loser family, Bam escapes out to the garage with Missy.

One night Flo stops them as they sneak out. 'She has a right to find her own way too.' Out in the garage, Missy and Bam put their heads together, talking about encouraging Georgia to find her own way, right out the front door.

It's from out there that Bam first observes how the house moves further and further away from the other houses, an uplift or a downslide, she can't be sure. It's obvious to her that it needs to be protected, strengthened. In daylight, and sometimes even at night under the watchful glare of harsh light, she moves around the outside of the house fixing everything she can; preparing for this nameless, timeless threat that only she seems aware of.

It's an ongoing, ever-changing job. You have to keep on top of repairs. Right before her dad died, she'd mended the fence where the maple had damaged it. You can only work with what's before you and the rest of the fence remained roughshod, kid-harangued. A few winters later Bam fixed the kitchen cabinets which had grimaced beneath the imposed padlocks while Hal was alive and which had pulled at the hinges until most of them didn't shut properly. Missy followed behind Bam with paint and the effect was middling. Better than before, but not as good as pulling the whole thing out and starting afresh.

Once she finished, Bam's not sure about the fix-up job; and thinks she preferred the old-fashioned kitchen, with its tough lino floor and hardwearing white paint. The broken cabinets reminded her of something she doesn't want to forget.

This year, just before her senior year of high school, she pulls the whole fence out and starts again. Using some of the old wood, recut, she weaves the fence along their property line, respecting the borders of Lou's gardens, and the veggies and herbs Rachel plants. The stakes are as big as Bam herself and she swings, loving the sensation of making contact, of creating a force that moves objects. Her shirt sticks to her back with sweat. 'What d'you think?' Bam asks.

Missy scans the fence. Runs a hand along the top, kicks a post and it doesn't waver. 'It looks good.'

Lou dates boys. It's a habit and a talent. For the first few years after her dad died, she often sits in her dad's chair and watches the birds that neither flock to her or ignore her, they seem to have returned to normal. She misses the cactus wren and the brown pelicans that would sometimes curve a path along the creek. She watches birds only when she can find enough peace to sit still. Stillness, like normal, feels dull and she doesn't seek out dull often.

Her dad is dead but he'd abandoned her long before he'd died. He was there for Ari at the hospital. A daughter he didn't even like. But didn't bother to come when she'd been arrested for joy riding. Never punched the guys who wrote all those things about her on the walls. He'd sit and demand silence of her, so he could forget her when they stood up and walked their separate ways.Not long after he'd died, her mom cajoled her to work in the garden one afternoon but she couldn't settle her heart enough to kneel and give the earth that time. She'd tried and failed and was leaving and her mom caught her hand, 'He was beautiful up there, wasn't he.'

'He sure was.'

And yet it's not a memory that gives her peace.

Tex is working hard, making tough decisions and has just starting to pitch new developments (Mayor Pearson got caught up in rumors of embezzlement and bribes and the entire town hall lineup had changed) after building up their bread and butter business. Yet, according to the books, they're barely breaking even. After a few years he notices problems on some of the sites when orders Kitty insists she's placed 'go missing' but the checks are cashed anyway and then equipment safety checks she assures him she's arranged don't happen, but the certificates show up anyway and Tex suspects they might be fakes. Tex doesn't get it, but his suspicions appear to be proved when Kitty buys one of their houses in cash, from Flo, who gets a hefty commission.

When Kitty comes in with a new hairdo and Choo shoes, Tex knows she'll ruin them all unless he takes action. In the city, Tex meets a lawyer who used to be a CPA and asks him look at FC's accounts, as well as at a copy of Kitty's contract.

The lawyer takes a few days and Tex meets him in the city. He has a corner office, on the top floor of a skyscraper. He can change the visibility of the glass with a button, which he does when Tex arrives. It shifts from clear, to dark.

'These books are a mess, decades back.'

'Can it be salvaged?'

'Maybe, if you get some better help.'

'What about the contract. Can I get out of it?'

'You're screwed,' the lawyer says. 'You can extricate yourself, but you'll have to pay. You'll be liable for her indiscretions.'

'And my own.'

'Yes, sir. You are definitely liable for those,' the lawyer says, loosening his tie, placing his hand on Tex's knee.

At the Fremont house he keeps business matters mostly to himself, but still he's made it clear that they all have to pull in their belts. The girls get small jobs, paper routes, babysitting, and Flo takes up any slack the younger ones create. Rachel continues to work at the library and Chick sells her the five and dime (with money she and Flo pull together) when it's clear he can't look after it any longer. The store is now open after school and at weekends, and her girls help her out with everything and Chick still works behind the counter and remains the expert in all things.

The girls never lower their voices in the kitchen and Tex often puts down whatever he's reading and listens. It's plain, everyday things they discuss. Sometimes they veer to politics or philosophy. Sometimes their voices deepen and a girl will be crying and comforted about a run-of-the-mill disappointment. He's been known to creep to the door and try to hear. A team tryout missed, a friend who's moving away. He listens for his name, in compliment or complaint but he never hears it. At some point they stop making him a plate or even a serving he can heat up, and he eats at the Sam's out on Route 37 or brings pizza home from Travoli's. Rifts deepen, rivers widen. This protects him. If he can't cross, neither can they.

Hal left a mess at work and Tex grows older trying to fix it. He's got more political savvy and a few people have even suggested he run for Mayor. Or Sheriff. The second suggestion makes for some hilarity in the city when he tells them stories of the Hicksville town where he lives. That town seems to have forgotten his rumored indiscretions and he starts to date Kate Fullerton, a sweet bank teller. They date rather publically and when they break it off, neither of them will reveal why. Although in future years, in confidence, she'll allude to 'problems down there.' She'd been the first person to tell him that maybe he was trusting the wrong people at work. 'That Kitty,' she said, 'with her eyes only on her own bank balance, I'm amazed she can get any real work done at all.'

At home, Tex starts to do his own laundry. The girls have been tossing his clothes into any old load, no attention to whether they're colors or whites, in need of drying or not. How many outfits ruined? And one girl who does laundry has an affinity for sharing grease splatters. He'd stopped mending their clothes years ago, no one had noticed one way or the other.

In the early hours of the morning, the only time the washing machine seems to be free, his mom catches him meticulously removing each item of clothing from the washer and hanging them from the clothes-pulley Bam and Lou had rigged up in the laundry room. A rather old-fashioned contraption that both he and Rachel love.

'If I can't hang them outside, this is a close second.' Rachel says running her hands over the sanded and sealed wood which slots into the crafted and utilitarian metal holders at each end. The whole thing suspended by rope and pulleys. 'Bam and Lou did a great job with this.'

When she laughs crow's feet stomp from her eyes and she carries the years on her hips. Life looks good on her. Tex wonders how many of her genes he has. His recessive eyes, a shock of blue in a brown and green-eyed family, are points of pride. There's something in his carriage that speaks of his mom, a strength which he sees occasionally beneath his shirt, but when he strips down and bares his chest, it disappears.

'I hear you need some administrative help,' Rachel says. 'That Kitty Saprono will have left a mess in her wake.'

Tex thinks it's his dad's mess that he has to clean up but when he looks at his mom it's a look that neither confirms or denies what she says.

'I'd like you to hire Missy and Bam. Missy to work in the office, officially before she goes off to college in the fall, and Bam to get some experience on the sites, year round.'

He opens the washing machine, reaches in and grabs a shirt. 'It's not something I'm inclined to do.'

'That's obvious. It's something I'd like you to do.'

Tex gives the shirt a light shake, to smooth what wrinkles he can before draping it over one of the pulley's planks. 'They'd have to start at the bottom. Minimum wages. They get no favors being relatives.'

'They'd agree to that. None of my kids has an aversion to hard work, as it turns out.' She touches a hand to his face and then kisses his cheek.

A light touch, that's something he most certainly didn't inherit from his mother.

Bobby Burke, Lou's most recent passage migrant, is beautiful. He holds onto her waist as she steers her motorbike and both its passengers out of town and into long, green foothills and into another small hotel and she leaves him there, so he can continue forward, while she travels back to her home for the season. He's fleeting, just passing through, and that's enough for her.

She knows birds and their beautiful independence, the patterns of their migration. She's a steady, reliable state to pass through, without being a doormat, without being their settling place.

Welcome to Louisiana, the sign welcomes at her border.

Hope you enjoyed your stay, the sign says as they leave her state.

Lou holds herself high, for someone riding so low. She tries for a while to keep what she feels at bay, the pressure of water against the land, biting and dissolving its fabric. Her memories are fixed and bound to the skeleton of her moods and this infectious energy, no matter how seemingly boundless, can't quell the lows, slung so very low, that no action will right. She takes out the compass Utah gave her and it says *you are here*, she spins it and it lands at another place, *you are here*. There's nothing helpful there as passage migrants kettle and flock and she's the troubled, thrumming land they pass through, swamplands and coast, the blur between, and through her runs a mighty river that often breaks its banks.

AT THE EDGE OF THE ATLANTIC

Tex has the corner room and Georgia prefers it at twilight. The walls seem stronger, made dark and more irrefutable by shadows. Tex's drawers are always neatly closed and the room has an attended to feeling which Georgia loves. It orders her mind to be able to see the floor and have a rug that has been laid carefully and follows the lines of the floorboards.

Georgia shakes the nail polish bottle as she takes off her socks by hooking the big toe of the opposite foot into the top of the sock and rolling the sock off her foot. She stretches her legs as she continues to shake the bottle. Her hands stretch forward and she gets down to business.

She paints her toes first, in case she needs to make a quick getaway. Then she takes her time with her hands, making sure she leaves the door open a crack for an easy, handless, escape.

Tex notices the light coming from his room as he comes home from work, a hot takeaway from Chen's on the passenger seat. Georgia thinks that by closing the blinds she'll escape notice but she's about as subtle as a searchlight at midnight. Tex lingers downstairs, eating his dinner in the dining room and learning that it takes Georgia forty minutes to do two coats to her toes and fingers. He sits quietly drinking bourbon and reading magazines. Then eventually, impatiently, he shouts or laughs loudly and Georgia scurries from his room.

Once upstairs he closes his door behind him and breathes in. He puts his face to the comforter to catch the sharp familiar odor of nail polish, better in winter when the cold air holds it thick and close.

Missy answers the phone at Fremont Construction the summer before college, and soon enough Tex lets her respond to enquiries. The paperwork is a mess and he hires some guy to sort their finances. He and Tex have noisy meetings in his office, the balance sheets are something to laugh over, obviously. Once she tried the door but it was locked.

When they have long lunches she lets the machine catch the calls and works away on her first real project—a plan she has for an extension to the Fremont house, a sun porch that will run the length of the back of their house. They can knock down the wall between the kitchen and the yard, flood the room with light, and put in new cabinets and shelves and a broad counter and really smarten the place up. She puts the plans on Tex's desk and waits for his comments. She waits for over a week.

At lunch sometimes Missy and Tex go for an ice cream. The accountant has been AWOL for a few days. 'He finished the books,' Tex says.

Sitting on the wall outside the shop they people-watch and shoot the breeze.

'Did you look at the plans, Tex?'

'Yup. Me and Max.'

'And.'

'And. Well. Missy. Look, they're good. Really good. But I don't think it's something we can do any time soon.'

Missy stops swinging her legs. 'What do you mean, any time soon?'

'In the foreseeable future. Max wasn't confident of their architectural merit.'

'Excuse me? What did he say?'

'That the addition was untenable.'

'It's got its own support structure, it'll outlast the house.'

'That's not what he said. He said it unbalances the lines of the house and will cause problems down the road.'

'That's absurd. But you fought for me right? For Max and me to come up with something which would work. Right?'

'I'm not an architect.'

Missy moves in closer, her dark eyes unaccepting. Her face softens as she touches his collar, and then hugs him with her cheek to his cheek. He relaxes into her hug, exhales. She releases him. 'They're good plans, Tex.'

'They also don't fit into our business model.'

'What model?'

'The one where we build things for other people.'

'And the decorating you did in the office?'

'Necessary.'

'You gave Kitty a car and a settlement that's big enough to let her put a pool in her backyard.'

'That's between her and me. Butt out.'

'And your own car? A bit flash don't you think.'

'What people see matters. Creates trust.' Tex kicks himself off the wall. 'I'm doing a good job.'

Missy grabs his shoulder. 'You're holding down a fort that's not yours.'

'Don't go there, Missy.'

Tex looks at the historic fronts of the buildings on the main street. FC has been responsible for some of those renovations since he's been at the helm. They look good. 'It's about what Dad left. It's still a mess and he deserves for someone to do his legacy justice.'

'Me, Flo and Bam could run it, give you a cut.'

He tightens his jaw. Enough humoring, his voice slices the hot air. 'You're too young.'

'Pick another refrain, Tex. This one has a limited shelf life.'

Missy starts to walk and he keeps pace. 'It's a difficult thing you were landed with. Stressful. Sure, money, a business, a house. But a lot of responsibility. You've had a lot to learn and fast too. You know, if you shared the responsibilities, you could share the burden too.'

Tex's head moves slowly to the left, distracted by a nice set of pecs on JK Smith. He pulls himself back. 'It's not an option.'

'Why not?' Missy follows his eyes, rolls hers, and drags Tex a few feet until they can see their house. His leg still slows him down, aches, throbs, the hill is a killer when his hip goes, and his hip goes into overdrive when it rains, like he's an old man.

'It's mine, Missy. I've earned it. All those years sitting in the dining room with the old man, having nothing to say, hearing him ramble on about those stupid damn birds. Shit, I've earned it.'

'We've earned it too.'

'Watch it.'

Missy halts. Tex stops too. She speaks calmly, quietly. 'You have eleven sisters, don't we deserve our inheritance too?'

'I gave you a job.'

She stands with her hands on her hips. Shrugs her shoulders.

'And you will all always be welcome in the house.'

'How generous.'

Missy glares. Bam's right: their only brother is stubborn and stupid, a killer combination.

'He wasn't even your dad,' Tex adds, superfluously.

And mean.

Missy looks out over the town that sags in the summer heat just waiting for a dust-raising rainstorm to come and pound it all down into mud which will be ground into workaday interiors. Her heart turns hard. She grabs his chin, 'Tex Fremont, you're the bastard.' And she takes her fist and knuckle jabs his bad hip. Hard. Twice.

The hill doesn't wind her and the Carolinas play basketball in the drive. They're rough with each other and fair. 'A few hoops, Miss?'

Missy says yes and as they start to play she realizes they're taking it easy on her, giving her room to make her shots.

'Don't,' she says. 'Play full-out you two. Don't ever give that inch. Beat me fair and square. Make me work for everything I get.'

When Flo sells a house, any house, she pins notes on Tex's door. 'Another one bites the dust.'

He takes ads out in the local paper shouting FC's successes and touting for business at the same time.

When she becomes a partner with Priscilla she corners him saying, 'Call me Sir.'

When he builds the town's first gymnasium and gets a lifelong free membership and personal trainer services for a month he says, 'Wait until you see my abs. Who's the bomb now?'

When she and Priscilla expand their sales market to Watertown and Lewis and then Prairie Home, 'Eat my dirt, local boy.'

And on it goes. No one winning, no one losing, but this constant back and forth, erosion and uplift, re-forging and shaping of borders.

Lou rides a spiral up to an All Color Party (all colors of pills) over at the Brick Factory, a keg party over at Thompson's farm after planting's finished, a bong bash at the Taylors'. She believes she can control the speed of the motorbike, the obsessive details of riding, reacting, escaping; she can do anything. The forging of arches, the building and fixing of bikes and cars, the tools she creates just for a specific job.

She cuts a familiar figure on the local roads on her bike. Boys seek her out, a few girls too and Lou isn't, when she's in this mood, one to say no to anybody. While she forgoes her helmet in exuberance, which drives both Rachel and Flo mad, she always has a spare helmet for any passenger who might want to hop on.

A creeper moves up the tree, a nuthatch down. Anything that takes you so high, but not so far as to be free of this world's atmosphere, comes under gravity's pull. The spiral reverses and she falls, arms flung, head back, crying out, her ribs sore, her eyes burning with salt, the air cuts tears into the skin of her cheeks. The familiar. Days into weeks and she trades one intensity, one risk, for another.

Lou comes home smelling of day old beer or fresh whiskey. Her clothes hang off her and her cheeks are pulled taut, gone sallow. Her mom comes into the room Lou shares with Missy and Bam, her hand on Lou's forehead. She feels Lou's waters clear, but only for a second until they muddy again.

'Shhhh,' says Rachel, holding her daughter as she falls asleep, as she herself falls asleep. Together they walk through the wide wild familiar streets and low coasts they traveled through together all those years ago, those wild places of give and take and moments of extreme colors that lift and burst brightly in defiance of compacted humidity-laden worry.

In the morning Rachel meets Sandra for coffee and talks it through. 'My sister Hannah is like Lou. I'll ask her for advice about it.' The next afternoon she calls with the name of a doctor in the city. 'Hopefully she'll be able to help.'

EVAPORATING BEFORE IT HITS THE GROUND

In the mornings out on the plateau, Ari goes for a quick run, to the furthest point she can find from where she's camped, from where she's left her tour group. Then she sits cross-legged and rests by herself, in this quiet. Ari works any job she can that keeps her outdoors in the canyons, and she directs her mail to Utah's apartment in Moab. She repairs trails at the Parks, counts birds up on Mount Trumball, and in the passage migrant season, out on Bright Angel Point, she counts hawks and other birds of prey. She's willing to travel anywhere for the right job. When she witnesses her first flash flood, from the safety she's scrambled to, she falls to her knees on the narrow ledge and finds a faith, an awe of how nature works.

Her reputation for hardy resourcefulness precedes her and she starts to act as a consultant on the new wave of nature documentaries and cowboy films and she takes film crews to a barely known canyon or hidden stream. Sometimes she'll be a stunt double and they'll put make up over the scar on her cheek.

She sends her family pictures of her with dust-covered jeans, rimmed hat held in her hands, bandana tied around her head holding back her hair. A film crew caught as a still-life in the background. She makes sound recordings of the places she visits, about finding a scorpion in her bed or getting stuck on a ledge in a storm, and she sends these to her family too. Rachel has Flo listen to them first, to vet the recordings for news that might be too much for a mother to bear.

'It's fine, Mom,' Flo says, handing her the CD. 'She survived it, so no worries.'

At college, Utah studied the ecology of the Colorado Plateau and worked as a tour guide during the long summer season in the remotest parts of the Canyonlands, and it was out there in the middle of nowhere she met a boy named Joseph Lowell. He was a geomorphologist—sturdy and fearless—and totally at ease with women who knew their minds. He came from a long matriarchal line of pioneers, survivors, and he carried his mother's name, by choice.

Utah graduated top of her class from Northern Arizona University, including winning a prize for her thesis on choosing a direction when lost. Now they live in Moab and her turf is The Maze. She takes small groups, no more than three, deep into the canyons and sells articles she writes to various magazines and journals. It's not that the maze is unmappable, clearly not, but it's that once you're in the middle, the landscape itself is harsh, difficult to distinguish and you need to keep your head, take clear full note of the signs around you, and having a strong internal compass definitely helps.

When Utah and Joe exchange vows, in the summer when she's twenty-three, the white of Utah's dress blows in the cool breeze. There's nothing to fear here and everything to look forward to. They concoct plans to build a small house outside of Flagstaff with solar panels and a clever desert garden out back.

Both Utah and Ari travel a lot. They have jobs, destinations, people they are responsible for and yet out there they're always looking for something else, they're always looking for Naomi.

For Utah it's clear. She knows where Cole is—she's dead. She saw her mom come up the hill with her sister in her arms, Utah kissed her cold cheeks, pressed stars onto her coffin and helped carry it through town. That's how she remembers it, the finality of it. She can visit Cole anytime back at home, in the cemetery. When she looks up at the stars she feels closer to her, sure, but she barely knew her, she was so young, and she's always silent.

Naomi is different. Her absence is sweet and bitter and full of anger. Such power in this absence. Every storm, every girl she sees on a bicycle, every news story of a body being found—they knock Utah right off balance and she's usually so surefooted, she sees things so clearly.

Ari goes to the big cities out here and looks where the runaways gather, where people who are lost can be found. She shows an out of date picture and gets the response she expects, which is not a single bit of useful information. Together the two sisters often hike out into the desert, where the night is darkest. Those are challenging hikes and the sisters don't talk about it, going further and further out, their hikes lengthening, growing more dangerous and desperate and sometimes even Ari has trouble finding water and Utah sometimes doesn't get them back by the clearest, safest route.

It's getting old and tired, the searching, and long weeks and months pass when they haven't followed up on a lead or when no lead has come in. The sky has been dull and when they sleep New Mexico is scuffed and worn out and weary too. The whole time they're looking for signs that Naomi has been here, that she wants to come back home, and the whole time she's fading.

Out there, in many places, all places, Naomi rides. When she stops, she works in restaurants or bars and Cole is often with her and they go everywhere and clouds gather but rain rarely falls when Naomi is around and her sister shows her everything. How to be free, how to be invisible. She's promised to show her how to fly. *A fast car is what you need, and a strong and heavy foot, and that steep canyon, you know the one, with the thin line of the river far below, that's waiting for you.* Naomi knows the one and has taken herself to the other side of the world to avoid it. She stays in foreign, lush valleys and above her the sky is blue, deep blue, and sometimes Naomi conjures storms, as if by accident, and the nights are long and her sister is with her and sometimes she's kind and vast and sometimes her voice has an edge and Naomi keeps moving, she keeps moving.

There's a bridge over a familiar river. Far below the water is but a thread. The sides of the canyon walls are steep and made of sharp rocks. This time they were sure, sure it was Naomi, the cops too. Rachel stands here with Utah and Ari, and the two young women are so much a part of the desert that sometimes they disappear from sight. There's a break in the weak metal fence, where a car crashed through and then out over the edge. The driver was drunk, in a stolen car, without a license. But forensics have come back just this morning and it was a boy, not their girl. Naomi is still out there.

Sand falls with gravity into the river; their tears are caught and swept up into the sky and become clouds. Dust devils and rain that evaporates before it hits the ground. They think it's approaching, that a pelting rain will pound down on them from laden clouds. Instead it sits still, over there, in the distance. It's about waiting, Naomi has been and will continue to be all about the waiting.

The next day Utah and Ari drive to a high altitude plateau where 400 steel poles with needle sharp tips stand pointing to the sky. Along the way they see signs of Naomi everywhere, in the washes, the burnt stumps of a tree on the canyon ledge; in the monsoon summer storms she hears everywhere. When they walk among these poles which graft the earth into angles it's just these young women and an ache for a lost girl. The surrounding hills attract moisture that builds into billowing clouds. As the afternoon passes, they loosen their grasp and it grows darker overhead. The earth and sky rumble.

The tops of a few of the poles pulse blue. It's not a threat. It is just the way things are.

Awake, Rachel feels like she's drowning on dry land; when she sleeps, she dreams of going to places she's never been and one place she can't seem to get herself to return to.

Back at home, the Fremont house empties each day and Rachel runs her fingers over the map, looking for an escape route. Her kids shiver and reach for the glasses of water they always keep near to hand.

'Can't you do something, Flo?' Flo swings ideas like a cowboy slings guns. She spins the barrel of her options, smooth turning ideas, fast draws, the inevitable high noon.

Way back when, Rachel had offered Flo partial responsibility for this family, and she'd accepted. She lives here and yet the future is anything but set; at night Flo roams the halls of the house, closing her eyes and searching for other places where she can put her skills to use. They've lost Colorado, and Naomi too, at least for now. Flo goes over and over what she knew to see if there's something she could have done to protect her sisters. So far she's not been able to come up with anything concrete. Sometimes at the map Flo watches Texas flutter or recede but he's still there and she holds onto that, even as she trusts her brother less and less to do the right thing. The map changes all the time and the shifts are subtle, sometimes about color, sometimes terrain or what is built, and you only notice it if you're familiar with whatever was there before. It's a map and a wall, a landscape. She could lose herself in it, but resists; it's not the world, just one idea of what part of the world might be. Her mom has trouble sleeping and they often meet up on the couch for a late movie and a pound bag of peanut M&Ms. Nice as it is, Flo knows that it's a waste of energy to have them both worrying about the family all the time.

TALISMAN

At ten, Ginny knows she's not in line to get anything from anyone. From year nought she and the Carolinas run the only profitable lemonade stand in town; they pander to the community college students and sell it down outside Big Joe's, half-frozen in half-size paper cups with just enough room for a good shot of vodka. With the profits from the hot months, and after a year of having her own paper route, she earns enough to buy a second-hand printing press.

Ginny increases her paper route and soon patrons find a *Fremont Free Press* inserted into each paper she tosses onto porches and steps. By the next year she has independent subscriptions for her insert and a distribution of over seventy-five houses and she has just written her first book, a sort of inspiring rant on inequality: *You Don't Have To Take It*, and she sells all fifty-five copies in a week. Ginny sends all her writing to Utah who is out in the Canyonlands leading deep canyon tours and writing articles about cartographic shifts in remote places. She returns Ginny's writings with things like 'Fab!' 'Great image.' 'Do you need this?' written in the margins.

She's fighting a specific battle at home, behind the scenes, at any opportunity. 'Texas,' she says, with some regularity, anytime she finds him taking a nap or sometimes even sneaking into his too-big, too solitary room to whisper in his ear as he sleeps, 'it's not all yours.'

After Hal's death the town has diversified just enough so the Fremonts don't feel quite the same pressures. Right around the ten-year anniversary of Hal's death, Jon takes Rachel to Banff skiing. He asks her to marry him for the fifth and last time.

'I really believe that's where Hal and I went wrong,' Rachel says.

'And knowing each other for less than twenty-four hours didn't have anything to do with it?'

'Yes, something to do with it but that wasn't the fatal flaw.'

Tex lets his curls grow back but he stays lean and trim. He works at his company and the whole family lives together without killing each other. Flo cooks, Rachel cleans, and her and all girls take care of the house and garden, and the youngest girls help their mom touch up the paint on the wall. It is a gesture of something, but no one knows exactly what.

When the girls get dressed for a night out, Tex sometimes help them to color-co-ordinate their outfits and apply their blusher. Not all the girls are appreciative. Tex puts his chin on Lou's shoulder and their faces sit side by side in the mirror.

'The vixen-red is perfect for you Lou...'

She jerks her shoulder to knock him away, she wipes the lipstick off on the hand towel draped over the sink, and goes out for the night fresh-lipped.

Lou runs Chick's five and dime for her mom and spends a lot of time on the back of motorbikes, until she buys a second hand jeep into which her refurbished Triumph fits perfectly. She grieved the loss of her dad years before he actually died, but the pain of it still has a way of rising to the surface. She tries to weigh it down with trinkets: body piercings, tattoos, talismans of teeth and semi-precious rocks. She wears a silver amulet of an owl hanging from a leather thong that settles into the well at the base of her throat. The world swirls in bright colors and dauntingly clear sounds. Lovers come and go, and Lou parties with the heartiest of them. Her wide heart breaks its own banks, forging new paths every season and, in the end, she has only herself and the metal and her birds and that is all she needs or wants.

When she gets her jeep she packs her bike, her lithium pills, and her metallurgy gear into the back. Lou takes the binoculars, her dad's twitcher list, and the vixen-red lipstick. Despite his bad heart, Tex has a good eye for color.

She moves out to Portland, where she starts working in a garage but then finds herself working in a gardening center soon enough. She starts to craft gardening tools and earns a reputation for quality and beauty. Her own garden flourishes. The compass she carries in her pocket helps keep her right, as do regular meetings with her shrink. She often rides to the coast and watches the whales as they migrate, the ospreys as they fish, and this place will do for now.

Georgia's hands have always struck her as perfect. She splays her fingers like peacock feathers when she talks, their bright colors drawing attention away from what she feels to be her too-small teeth, her too-straight black hair, and her not-tall-enough physique. For the last seventeen years she's blamed her damn genes. And yet she sees some of her siblings transcend their inheritance: Ari with her athletic grace, Lou with her pale beauty, and Tex is one beautiful man. As she patiently paints her nails another flamboyant color, she curses her flat butt, her too big feet, and the embarrassing flip of a tooth that pushes her lips out.

Georgia hates the hard graft of working: the dirty water, the wrinkles, the dry line of dead skin that forms under her nails even with her persistent nail and hand care routines; The All You Can Eat Barn has aged her hands by years, maybe even a decade.

That little witch Ginny never seems to mind working. She's a little capitalist that one: with her lemonade stands, her trashy little books, and their puny print runs she's so proud of. A geek who's too stupid to recognize that there is more to life than being productive.

Flo disappears every day but she could be doing just about anything to bring enough money in; who knows, who cares? She's thirty-three and still a virgin by the looks of it and what sort of life is that? Not a life Georgia will have, that's for sure. The Corners are far away and Georgia can't even remember their faces. The Carolinas play basketball and don't have a penny to show for it. Flo pays their way, with Ginny sometimes chipping in a bit too. What makes them so special?

Georgia picks up work at the local hairdressers washing hair and then sweeping up the brashly colored, newly cut locks. It frees her from the All You Can Eat Barn. She's the salon's dogsbody and, occasionally, if she's lucky, she gets to do a pedicure.

At home Georgia practices manicures incessantly. She corners her sisters, Flo being the only one who will submit to the treatment with any regularity. Today Georgia counts her own fingers beneath her breath, almost a song as she preens and paints.

'Mmmmm, painting toenails, that's a career,' says Ginny as Bam nudges her approvingly.

'Ooooo, I'm so offended,' Georgia mocks and flicks polish into Ginny's hair. Ginny bends down, dripping nail polish onto Georgia's nice white shirt.

'Push yourself Georgia, you could make it up to ten, you know, that's the number that comes after nine.'

And then one day a stylist doesn't arrive at Mitzy's Hair Salon, and Georgia aims a bit higher, takes up scissors without asking, and gives mean, newly divorced, Mrs Smitty the worst haircut of her life. She snips a bit off her ear.

Georgia gets fired just two weeks before Mitzy's own tragic demise—when a hairdryer she's holding falls and meets a puddle of water on the floor she's standing in. The salon shuts down the day of her funeral and the space goes up for sale.

Georgia has to grovel to get her old job back at The Barn on the weekends and in the evenings, and soon she's up to her armpits in industrial strength dishwashing suds again. Poor thing, the lovely skin of her hands turns a chemical red.

The salon stands empty all spring. Georgia goes out of her way to pass the shop front, yearning for perms, hennaed highlights, and a dazzling manicure to heal her work-tortured hands. And it's not just her; the women of the town are beginning to look downright shabby. If she'd been a go-getter like Ginny, Georgia could have gone door to door selling her skills with true entrepreneurial spirit. She could have built a reputation from scratch. But she isn't Ginny or anything like Ginny.

Then one day, just before school frees them for the summer season, Georgia walks by the salon to find that the for sale sign has been replaced by a sturdy plastic sign stretching across the awning. Huge fuchsia letters proclaim: 'Norma Rae's Nails and Beauty.' Georgia loves that the nails come first.

She stakes out the joint and at the first sign of life inside she raps on the door with her hands looking just about as good as she can get them. She wears a yellow sundress borrowed from Flo. A redhead opens the door and Georgia resists the urge to whistle: her hair is swirled up into a retro beehive, she flutters her thick false lashes, and shifts her hips flirtatiously in her slim-waisted skirt.

'Are you looking for a manicurist?' asks Georgia.

'Well, I…'

'I'll be the best manicurist you've ever seen. I'm good with makeup too. But don't let me near the scissors.'

Norma Rae gives Georgia a once over, lingering on her hands.

Georgia fans her fingers. 'They look this good after working double shifts washing dishes at The Barn. I'm truly dedicated to the art of feminine beauty.'

'Nice shape,' says Norma Rae holding Georgia's hand, turning it over. 'Your face could do with a bit more color but I sure like your style. Okay, I'll give you a chance.'

'When can I start?'

Norma Rae opens the door and waves Georgia in. Georgia is so pleased that she helps Norma Rae set up the beauty stations, even paints the walls (two coats) and grouts around the shampooing sinks.

Once the salon opens, business is swift and she spends nearly every waking hour at the salon helping out with facials and makeovers. No detail passes her by and she learns fast.

'You did a great job on Grace's nails,' Norma Rae says one Saturday at closing time. It is the first compliment Georgia has ever received. 'Why don't you do Cynthia Miller's facial and bridal makeup? She hinted she wanted you to do it.'

Georgia creates a bit of romantic makeup magic and after the bridal make-over, Norma Rae gives Georgia a raise and promises that her hair washing, hair sweeping days are over. She becomes the salon's beautician and she's much in demand. With the raise and the tips, she can pay her share of the household kitty and also save money like she never thought possible. And with money, comes plans for escape.

College behind her, postgraduate degree in architecture ahead of her, Missy carries certain things with her everywhere: the sketch of the house she drew when she was nine, which her dad had kept; the original survey of the house as it stands now; the note he made when he was of sound mind; and the thank you card Tex had written to her in a boyish hand that he'd once put under her pillow: *I hope it's not our last dance.*

Missy analyses the Fremont house and tries to imagine her grandfather Lawrence imagining this house. At first she wonders how long he'd dreamt of building a house as grand as this, but as she makes her way through the house again and again, she comes to believe that he designed this house in a single flourish. The walls hold a touch of anger, a boasting, and turn a haughty face towards the town.

Sure the antebellum history isn't a pretty one but everything about this house is in balance, meant to be lived in. Even where the space is at its most undemocratic it holds potential for the walls to come down. Hal had had almost enough architectural know-how to rebuild this but she can imagine that emotionally he didn't know how to fix what his father had started. She leans against the building, her feet held up by the front porch, the graveyard in front of her, the town beyond that, and she's not sure she'd know how to rebuild it either.

In fact, she'd build a new house, set it on a few acres, on a hill where a good wind blows. It'd be by the coast but far enough inland, or high enough, so that it'd survive generations of change. She'd slide solar panels onto the roof and have a small wind turbine in the back. It'd hold its heat in the winter and close its face off in the summer. She designs a small cottage for her mom, close to the water. From the window her mom would see only blue: water and sky, and when she turned around, she would see her family.

Sorry old friend, Missy says to these four walls, we need to keep our options open. A tremor ripples through the house, up from the fluid earth, like it's ridden a wave.

None of us like it, Missy thinks.

Bam will be twenty-two in the fall, and Missy will start MIT's Architecture Degree Program. Workers swarm over dead Miss West's yard, the new owners want to keep the shell, buck up the foundations, and build a modern extension out back. The crew knocks out walls, carry materials, bare their chests; Bam's toolbelt swings back and forth as she walks, her swagger is a testament to how happy she is to be giving her dead neighbor's house some much needed structural attention. She wishes she could give it to their own.

Bam's arms gleam with sweat. She's as tall as most of the men, and as strong. Early on in the build the usual male posturing leads to an old fashioned log chopping competition, and her 'surprise' victory comes as a surprise only to those who don't know her.

'Miss Alabama Fremont,' a voice rises out of the crowd, 'I do believe that you are as tenacious as your namesake state.' One of the workers stands with a toothpick twirling at the side of his mouth, and Bam near trips over herself at the sight of this man, nearly as broad as he is tall, wide as a tractor.

She grins. 'And then some.'

'Bud,' he says, fingers tipping the edge of his cowboy hat. 'Bud Marshall.'

'Like the beer.'

'Yes ma'am, only with more of a kick.'

They work side by side for most of the build. Swings equal. At the end of the project, when he arrives at the Fremont house in a clean shirt and brushed off boots, she offers her arm and they go out walking. He invites her to the town's fourth of July BBQ and it's only a matter of time before they shack up together.

Nearly five years ago, after he'd fired Kitty, Tex had scraped the lettering from the door. Then he'd cleaned the glass with Windex and reapplied the new lettering: *Fremont Design and Renovation*.

He'd hired a new assistant as well: Suzanne Nabon. Suzanne had been the best person who applied for the job, actually she was the only person who applied. Missy had been furious because he'd hired someone new and because he hadn't consulted her about the change. Suzanne clipped her way through the office, had a quiet drawl which seemed to work wonders with the workers who called to complain, and so far she'd kept it professional with everyone. He wanted her to keep it professional.

They'd adjusted but Missy was suspicious and often furious at him. He tolerated her, and Bam too, because they were hard workers, and he had a feeling there'd be a revolt if he tried to oust them.

It's spring and they've just broken ground on a big housing

development. Bam stomps in and slams a fist down on his desk. 'You are unbelievable! How dare you. You're pushing it too far Tex. The one thing we asked you not to do.'

Tex has no idea what she's talking about.

'You promised Missy and Lou.'

Ah, they'd asked him not to build on this one parcel of land near the marshes and he'd said he wouldn't. Something about some birds. 'I bought it, I can build on it.'

'Lou says there's a colony of cranes who breed down there each year. You build there, you kill them. A whole community.'

'They'll find someplace else to live. We've done the surveys we need to do.'

'You mean your assistant paid some guy off to give you the papers you need.'

'Watch it Bam, fucking watch it.'

Tex stands and takes a few steps towards Bam. She laughs. 'You think? You think you could take me on?'

'I think you can't stop me.'

The land has already been cleared and Tex had taken photos of it this morning. If he'd remembered his promise to his sisters he would have tried to rejig the plans. Arguing with Bam wasn't a disaster, but he'd never seek out her rage.

Natural rust moves slowly. With ease and patience and if you meet it with the same amount of resistance rust will never cause you harm. He tries, he really does, to keep the issues small, by catching them early, but on one of his mid-sized developments, small niggling things keep going wrong. Things you can plan for, preventable things, and he can't understand why there are so many.

'Your brother isn't doing routine maintenance or paying attention to health and safety like he should be,' says Bill the foreman to Bam at a coffee break one day.

'Have you told him about it?'

'Many times. I keep leaving a message with his secretary too.'

'Not so much up here, that one,' Bam says tapping her head.

'I'd be more worried about what she's missing in here,' Bill says pointing to his chest. 'That apple won't fall from the tree.'

'What tree?'

'The Nabon man-eating tree.'

'What?'

'Kitty's mom is a Nabon, who got married and changed her name. Suzanne's mom never married, kept her maiden name.'

'They're cousins? He's totally screwed.'

'Absolutely.'

Tex had cleaned up the paperwork trail at work years before and had managed not to get audited. Luckily for him, because he'd have been doomed if they got a hold of some of his dad's creative accounting and Kitty's siphoning off of profits. Five years of freedom from her embezzlements and they're doing slightly better than breaking even. He's behind on some of the equipment checks and as bad luck would have it, a backhoe loses its claw mid-lift. Bam and a few men have to scramble out of the way. He drives down to the site.

'You imbecile!' Bam screams at him in front of the men. 'Missy warned you about this last summer. You were supposed to follow up.'

'It's on my list.'

'Is the lawsuit on your list?' Bam is still trying to calm her pulse after the hoe pushed her off her feet.

'Calm down, Bam. No one was hurt.'

'Idiot,' she says as she turns to leave, making no effort to lower her voice in front of the other workers.

Tex has no choice but to fire her.

It takes four workers to hold her back from killing Tex. She doesn't even get to land a single blow. Tex turns and taunts. 'Bring it on. You've got nothing I want or need.'

Tex always enters the house through the front door, so the neighbors can see him walk into his own house. Today Missy, who has flown in from school, stands at the top of the front-porch stairs and yells to him as he approaches.

'This has gone on for long enough.'

'Calm down,' Tex says going up the stairs. She blocks his way. He restrains himself from patting her arm.

'Don't tell me to do anything.'

'Missy.' His voice dropping at the end, in parental-like disapproval.

'Tex,' she replies, mimicking.

'Let's go inside and talk this through.'

She stands her ground and raises her voice. 'You screw it up and you fire Bam? That's not the way this is going to happen.'

'Who says?'

'I do.'

'Ooooo. I'm so scared.'

'Listen, asshole. Some people in this family believe in you. They think that somehow one of these days you're just going to become a human being.' Missy feels the house behind her hold its breath. 'I've believed in you.'

'I'm doing my job, Missy. You know it. You see how I work.'

'Tex, you work hard. No one argues with that. But you're missing things. You screwed this up. Big time. Bam had every right to be mad.'

'She showed disrespect and I had to treat her like any other employee.'

'You are not in the position to fire Bam because you're not her boss. She's your equal.'

'I don't know what drugs you've been doing up there with those engineer geeks but this business is mine and Bam was way out of line.'

'You can't even take responsibility for your mistakes. That's disgusting.'

'That machine was just checked. I've got the papers to prove it.'

'Sure you do.'

'Come down to the office and I'll show you.'

'Just re-hire Bam.' Missy stares at Tex. 'You owe me, Tex. You've owed me my whole life. And you and I both know it.'

'I don't owe you anything. But I'll do this because I'm generous. Because you've asked nicely. Now let me into my own damn house.'

'It's our house,' Missy says as she lets him pass.

That night, with her other sisters long gone to bed and sleep, Flo walks through the house and thinks that home is not this collection of cement and wood and steel. It is not these walls. It is not, in fact, this place.

She runs her fingers over the re-plastered plaster, the embossed wallpaper, and when she puts her hand to her nose, it smells musty. Like old cheese. This, for all the years she's lived there, is not her home. This is the building in which she lives. This building sways and rocks and protects her and yet in these quiet, still rooms, these dark hallways, she has started to fear everything: the rasping of mice in the walls, the breathing of her family, the future in which this house that is not her home will fall down. This house has a heart that is splintered. A thwarted, broken heart. It breeds restlessness. And when it falls down it will be like shooting a horse, or breaking an injured bird's neck, or chopping down a tree.

Briefly she hopes that with the annihilation of one hope, another, freer, lighter, will be born.

ALASKA AND WYOMING

Each summer Utah enters the Maze and each journey folds and unfolds into knowing and unknowing, towards the frustrating process of becoming found. Her writing is concrete and elusive; what she seeks is not always what she finds, but what she finds is almost always what she needs. In the middle of her heart a space aches for her sisters who are lost, who she has not been able to save.

During the rest of the year Utah is at home, where she's just landed a part-time teaching job at the Uni and she finds herself pregnant. Her sister Ari is out there, feral, in the desert; it's tough to get her to even eat meals inside when she visits Utah and Joe in Flagstaff.

The cowboys love Ari, some might argue too much, and her lovers' quarrels and the rather loud making up sessions are legendary in the small guide community. When Ari discovers she's pregnant by which cowboy she can only guess, she disappears deeper into the badlands that border Mexico. She could stay lost, sure, she'd probably survive, but with the way she's feeling she could also 'do a Naomi' and that's not her style.

It's a bright breezy day when Utah opens the door in a new maternity dress and sees Ari's jeans tied together with rope. 'When's your due date?' she asks.

'I have no idea.'

'You look about as far along as me. Come on in.'

'I'll stay but I stay out back.' Ari pitches her tent and she sleeps out there until sciatica hits in her eighth month and she accepts the offer of the spare bedroom. Alaska Fremont is born in August and Rachel, Jon, the Carolinas and Ginny drive out to meet the first grandchild. Wyoming Fremont Lowell joins the family only a week later.

Utah and Joe's house is tiny, in the hills south of Flagstaff, but their land is big. Family and friends tent it out back, among the pine trees. Deep in the night Ari walks out to the tent. 'Mom, can you hold her just for a few minutes? I've fed her but she won't sleep.'

Rachel who has been sleeping beside Jon, gets up and makes her way outside. The ground is rocky and cool beneath her feet. She accepts the newborn and walks back inside the house. Ari goes back to bed.

'Just five minutes, Mom.'

'Sure, Ari.'

The baby is swaddled but still restless. Rachel loosens her binding and rocks Alaska. She doesn't settle quickly, but gurns. 'You shouldn't be hungry sweetie. Your mom's done good by you. She'll be like your great grandmother Shirley, she could make a feast out of almost anything. She could even get me to eat dandelion soup, and if you've ever tasted dandelions you'd understand what a feat that was. Your mother was lucky, I never inflicted anything like that on her. Who knows what Arizona will make you eat, out there in the wilds, how thirsty you might be, but she'll take care of you. I know of no one better. She'll put me to shame, yes she will Alaska. Just like Walt did. I was never as good with the infants as he was. You'd be asleep right now if he was holding you. He had a way with babies. He'd have loved you. Loved you.'

Finally, Alaska sleeps and Rachel can't quite get herself to put her down so she walks and rocks until dawn breaks and Jon comes and takes the infant from her arms. 'Pace yourself Grandma, you're going to need your stamina.'

The end of summer meanders towards fall and the days are hot and the nights cool enough, especially at this altitude. Both mothers are protective of their infants, new to this role of caring for another being who is so small. Completely different from watching the backs of your sisters.

Jon takes the twins and Ginny to the North Rim of the Grand Canyon and then snorkeling in Lake Powell. 'It's not right, flooding a canyon and using it as a playground. Not right at all,' Jon says. But the sandstone fascinates the twins and they love the water, and dive so deep, for so long, Jon worries over and over again that he's lost them. But they always emerge with grins and the four of them change plans, stay in a motel in Page and the next day Jon arranges for them to go on a proper dive. Jon and Ginny stay on the deck of the boat while the Carolinas flip over the side of the boat, their instructor beside them, and have to be coaxed from the water hours later with the promise of chocolate milk shakes.

Rachel stays in Utah's house, cooking and cleaning and looking after her daughters and their daughters.

The babies couldn't be more different. The Lowells are a tall breed, blond hair and brown eyes and Wyoming looks almost Nordic despite her mixed Fremont blood. From the first day she sleeps solidly.

Alaska looks like Hal, Rachel hates to say it, it's not something you'd want to wish on a baby, but truth isn't something to be masked.

'She looks like an old man,' says Ari.

'A particular old man.'

Their eyes flick up and then back to the baby. 'Maybe she'll outgrow it.' Alaska kicks at her covers.

Out in the tent in the high altitude air Rachel's sleep is thick and dark and clear. She gets up anytime a girl wakes her to take a turn with an unsettled infant. But they always have to wake her.

After ten days, Jon drives the girls back home to start school, and Rachel stays in the tent. As the new mothers become more confident, they take the babies further afield. Utah and Rachel push the stroller through town and drink coffee in the café across the way from the Monte Vista Hotel.

'You could have stayed there instead of in a tent,' says Utah. 'Famous people stay there. Or used to when it had a bit more shine to its surface.'

Rachel looks up. In the heat of the day, the windows are open, curtains billow. The paint on the sills is cracked with the extremes of weather but people mill in and out of the hotel looking comfortable in this building so settled into its own skin.

The day before she leaves, Rachel and Ari go for a long walk in the painted desert. Once they get started Rachel feels as if she could walk forever, just keep going. Ari walks with Alaska strapped to her chest. Rachel would have been scared to take the baby someplace so wild but Ari says, rightly, 'I'm all she needs and I'm not going anyplace.'

To be so daring as a mother.

'I've got to enjoy it. I'm back on location in three weeks.'

After walking in the desert, Rachel's dreams are vivid, she remembers that, but little of the details. Maybe she's dreamt of a map of rivers, bright bright blue against deep earth, and everything in fine contoured movement. The rivers lead to the sea, to each other, and stretch through oceans and run beneath vast continents. They seduce her, choose me, or me, or me. Choose us all. Her feet itch. Her restlessness is clear, it's not about a child or an impending disaster, but simply her body wanting to get going.

When she wakes her feet look normal but she taps her foot, rubs the palm of her hand. It shoots color behind her eyes and she's thirsty. Lemonade, water, coffee, Ari's fantastic margaritas. More water. She travels back home, goes to work and she still has such thirst.

Some homebuyers want a picture perfect home, desiring not only the house, but to be the family they picture living there. Others like the challenge of a fixer-upper; a bit of do-it-yourself, aren't you proud of yourself achievement sort of house. They buy it cheap and then invest all of themselves into it. These people don't mind the years and years of living amidst rubble and plaster dust and disasters that call the whole project into doubt.

Flo is starting to mind the persistent, growing doubts.

There's a creaking in her ears that follows her into her dreams, and a universe of weight takes up residence in her body. In her dreams she no longer sits in the trees or flies up high: she's been grounded by this fear, by this settling, which makes her dizzy and sick. She's gripping onto a state that should be let go.

The changes at home never impact her ability to sell houses and Flo has amassed a small fortune, which she keeps very much a secret. She mocks Tex with some of her sales but keeps the extent of her success murky.

Rachel comes home from Flagstaff and during a long winter the girls struggle with their mom's moodiness. The young ones have never known their mom to be like this. Flo hasn't either, not like this, it's a different drama, different feel. She thinks herself almost immune to the mom-is-at-the-map-again-thirst, so when one hits her so hard she faints at work, Flo is a bit concerned. Priscilla doesn't waste time fanning Flo, but simply throws ice water over her. It's this no nonsense attitude that Flo likes so much.

'Thanks Cilla,' says Flo as she comes to standing, making small pools at her feet, and goes to her desk.

'You're just lucky it wasn't coffee.'

'Too right.'

Priscilla puts in her two cents worth, 'What's up?'

'I've got no idea.'

'Really?'

Flo downs four cups of water from the water cooler. 'A lot of things are going on. I think I'm going to have to prioritize and get organized.' Flo refills her glass and starts making calls.

By Friday, Flo holds deeds in her hand. She has bought a large plot of land with the sea at its front door and a long, wide plateau at its back. She's also rented a boat for her mom. It's time to give her mom permission to go.

Flo comes home and joins Rachel and Jon on the back porch. She hands Rachel a large envelope. When Rachel reads the deeds she can barely breathe.

'Are you sure, Flo?'

'Don't make me say it.'

Rachel nods and pulls her eldest close. 'Thank you.' Such a risk as a mother, to return to a land that doesn't want you. Such a daughter to let her go.

Rachel carries all her paints down the three flights of stairs. It takes four trips and then she tends to the map. She pays special attention to the outline of her and Hal's country, and the borders her kids share. She looks for a place to paint a mockingbird. She knows Hal's theory about their songs; he'd had his own song, of sorts. Unfortunately, his daughters hadn't been in it. Neither had she, ultimately. Not in the end anyway, and there is no forgiving that.

She spends sixteen hours at the map. The kids pulling on each other, rehydrating the whole time. Finally they can take no more. 'Mom!' cries Ginny. 'Enough!'

The rest of the girls agree with her. Except Flo, who no one can find. She's down by the water, trying not to plead with her mom to stay. All her fears bubble to the surface and the creek flows gently near her feet. When she returns to the house, hope and resolution have mixed to become the very marrow of her spine.

By morning Rachel's left Flo in charge, packed her bag and is heading to Menatauk.

The Fremont house always rocks at night, a boat on the ocean, waves against the side. The night Rachel leaves, the sound stops. Even the seashell Flo keeps on her bedside table has nothing in it when she places it to her ear. It'll take over a week before she, or the other girls, can sleep at ease in the house.

Toast in the toaster, cereal and milk and juice being passed around, the girls talk with dark circles curving beneath their eyes.

'It's never felt like this before.'

'It's a nightmare.'

'I'm so tired.'

'It'll get better. Has to.'

Tex walks in.

'How'd you sleep, Tex?' Flo asks.

'Like a baby,' he says. His was a dark sleep, solitary and void of color.

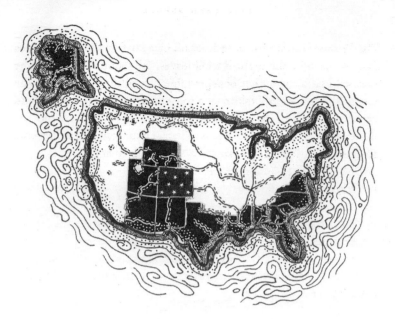

RIPTIDE

Forgiveness is overrated and some acts do not deserve forgiveness. Rachel reads about them all the time: the Holocaust, rape camps, acts of aggression, all the ways individuals become necessary collateral. You can open your heart, you can let go, move on, but you do not have to forgive. There are other options.

Before taking the boat out, Rachel goes for a swim at the beach three miles down the road from the marina. Eye level to the water, the waves long and low against the shore, Rachel floats, the water cold on her skin, goosebumps flaring there. The water magnifies the invitation of the Island, an invitation she thinks has always been here, if she had come close enough to listen.

It's a fast boat and when the guy at the dock offers her maps, Rachel declines. The engine hums and powers the boat, although it's a current that directs its course. On the Island, Rachel docks the boat next to Shirley's, which looks well maintained. The same houses, some more worn than others, sit on either side of the path she takes up the main square. Before she gets there, she heads off into the tall grass and goes behind the houses, so her approach is not complicated by people she doesn't want to meet.

Shirley sits in the kitchen, coffee percolating on the stove. Her black hair has streaked silver, her face sun-aged, but time has not muted the strong lines of her jaw, or the red of her lips. She sees Rachel through the window and meets her at the door. Flings her arms wide open.

'My girl!' She hugs her then stands back, appraises. 'You're getting old.'

'Hey!' Rachel lifts her hands in mock horror. Touches the grey of Shirley's hair, the lines of her cheek. 'I've missed you too.'

Shirley takes her hand and guides her to the table. They both pour cream and extra sugar in their coffees.

'This place feels quiet.'

'The Island has been fickle. Didn't let anyone leave, for a few years, while the first girls were born. Then the Island became inconsistent, impossible to predict, so when people see the tides change, they throw everything in any boat they can find and get the hell off. Some folk find it hard to come back. Walt, he stopped wanting to take the risk. Although he continued to have some romantic ideas about tides and what they'd carry where.'

Shirley hands Rachel an old bourbon bottle stuffed tight with a cork. The cork takes some coaxing but when it does allow itself to be freed a letter and a palmful of earth follow. Rachel funnels the dirt back into the bottle.

'I'll sprinkle this in my new garden when I move. Believe it or not, I did get the maps and seeds you sent. They took ages to arrive, but I did get it.'

The delicate paper holds its form and Walt's neat handwriting.

I spent all morning doing boring maintenance around the house, with what supplies we have. I napped in the afternoon. Shirley made whitefish and greens for dinner. The boys didn't come by but Angie's wee boy had the flu and William's wife was fit to burst with the next child, so it's understandable. My bones are a bit sore but that's what a decade lived fast will do to you. We're hoping you got safely to the mainland. One day, maybe, you'll come find us again. Forgive us, those who need forgiving. Love us, those of us who deserve loving. Every day we miss you.

The plainness of his words. He knew this might be the only message she'd receive from him and this is what he writes. He must have been quite sick then, already. His words though, hold no panic, no request for her to come and save him. She hands the letter to Shirley, who reads it and cries. 'I remember that winter, it's the winter he died.'

'I knew Walt was sick. I should have come.'

'He hoped you would.' She touches the bottle.

'I know.'

They both cry but it doesn't stop them or slow them down. 'But he understood,' Shirley says, nodding her head to confirm it.

Rachel nods. 'Do you?'

'A lot of things have died, Rachel. More than nature allots to one place in this space of time. On bad days I think he could have been saved.' Shirley inhales deeply. 'I'm a lonely old fool. Walt stood firm. He loved you until the end and didn't want you to come until you could leave again safely. Stronger. Even when our son Callum died trying to get medicine from the mainland, on one of the days when the tides were against him and he got caught, his boat went down, and still Walt never wavered.'

'I'm sorry Shirley. Callum was a gem of a boy. And Walt was an amazing man. I've missed him every day, you too.' The Island sinks beneath her, only a micromeasure of a part of an inch but Rachel feels it, holds the table. 'I've lost a girl too.'

She wants Shirley to take her in her arms and hold her like a mother but they both have such loss, they both want to be the one comforted, rather than the one comforting.

'Marriages have all but stopped. We're lucky that three out of our four boys already had wives when you left. Good women, bearing daughters and sons just as you'd expect.'

'The Roanoke line running high to daughters, imagine that. Mine certainly has.' Rachel names her children, with their proper names.

'You're kidding,' says Shirley.

'Nope.'

'Walt would have liked those names.' Shirley clears their cups, ties on her apron. 'What are you going to do about this place?'

'What I should have done a long time ago.'

'I'm not sure it's forgiveness this Island or Trevor needs.'

'I'm not sure I'll give it.'

Rachel kisses Shirley on the cheek. 'I'll be back.' Shirley is not surprised when Rachel turns away from the gathering of houses and walks towards The Dare. She walks slowly, steadily to the top; she bends to rub the leaves of aloe, to watch as the lines of the shore change, as sun on the water makes the sea mercurial, curious. It is not her job to forgive, the Island will heal on its own. An island being an island, the sea being the sea; family.

Today is a generous day with the tides and Islanders mill around on the docks, throwing things into boats, securing things within the cabins. Rachel and Shirley stand with their arms hooked and face the docks. If anyone recognizes Rachel, they don't say.

'Would you come home with me and meet my kids?'

Shirley takes her in her arms. 'Not this time, Rachel. But I will. I'll meet your kids. And your grandkids.'

Rachel stays a few days and she'd like to say it's easy. But it's awkward. Her dad's light remains on during the week she's there but she never sees him or the shadow of him cross his threshold. He is old and will die soon, and this is the choice he makes.

On the way to the mainland she has to steer the boat. She meanders her way up the coast. When Rachel gets home she places a picture of Shirley, Walt, their boys, and a baby Rachel in Walt's arms onto the mantel.

'Who is that?' asks Carley.

'That's my family,' she says. 'The Roanokes. Walt, Shirley…'

'You're the girl!' Carolina says to her mom. 'She's the girl!' she shouts at her sisters.

If Georgia's feet had been even half decent she'd wear open toed shoes all the time. The risk of it, the daring. And flimsy dresses that hang loose and low. She wants color and flattering lines. She wants outrageous hairdos and nails. She wants to flaunt the assets she has.

She's tied herself up in knots about her poor hands. Watching her sisters, she's jealous of nearly everything: the way Naomi used to rage with the whole sky behind her; how Bam and Missy are always in some creative flap; how the Carolinas claw at each other for distance that won't even be good for them. But they're engaged, alive. Georgia understands her half-life: her drooping shoulders, low slung, too big breasts, her ugly feet, her undefined cheekbones, her perfect hands.

Finally she's going to dress not how she thinks of herself, but how she wants herself to be. Her curves are not something she should hide. She's graduated from high school and has made enough money for a proper departure. Today is her day and she decides to flaunt everything she's ever had the urge to cover up. She calls a cab. If she's going to do this right, she'll have to do it from the very moment she steps her perfectly painted toes, showed off in her slingback, spaghetti-strapped red shoes, off the last step and onto the sidewalk. And she does. Bam's on the roof, Flo's at the window, and Tex is nowhere to be seen. A small audience watches her go. Only her mom standing on the porch cries and waves, but doesn't make a single move to stop her. The others don't wave, but she sees their approval, maybe even a touch of envy, as she lowers herself into the cab and swings her short-skirted legs into the seat well.

She resists the urge to flip them the finger. The ungrateful lot of badly dressed barbarians can kiss her gorgeous ass.

Instead, she almost kisses Patrick Kurtowski for what he says as he drives her away: 'So, you've made a lucky escape. What were you visiting the freakshow Fremonts for?'

He hasn't recognized her. Paris Georgia Fremont nods her sunglassed head. 'An article I'm writing, but I abandoned it. I couldn't get away quick enough.'

'Don't blame you. They're a bunch of weirdos. Where to?'

'The airport.'

'That's an expensive ride.'

'It'll be worth it.'

'Where you going?'

'Paris.'

She sits back, resting one perfect hand on top of the other on her bare knees, and watches the flatness unfold like a runway.

While Jon stays at home with the Carolinas and Ginny, Flo, Missy and Bam drive across the country to view their land. The sea rolls into shore, blue water and white breakers, as far as the eye can see. The shore cuts up to the house and then the land evens out towards the long drive.

'Should be far enough back not to be hit by a storm surge. That's what the permits say anyway,' Flo says.

'You mean we could live here?' Bam asks.

'Yes,' Flo says. 'It'll take a few years, but we'll move here. I don't know about you, but I'm not happy we're thinking of giving up.'

'Not giving up Flo, just making alternative plans.'

Flo nods, holding onto the car for support. 'So you'll build it?'

'Absolutely.'

Flo leaves Bam and Missy walking the perimeter of the plot, reading the permits and limitations. She's thirty-five, a virgin and she has a standing invitation from Fabian Veracruz to accept.

VALLEY OF THE DAUGHTER OF THE STARS

The Carolinas glisten in the sun, thirteen and athletic. Rivulets of sweat catch the sun and bounce it back towards the house. They shoot hoops in the driveway and there's friction at their borders, fierce desire to make their own names. From the kitchen Rachel, Flo and Bam watch them play.

'Why couldn't one of them have picked tennis?'

'Or the chess team.'

'It would have been a lot easier to watch.'

Carley presses Carolina into another do or die situation. Carolina outsmarts Carley and arcs an easy three-pointer.

'It'd be easier to watch if Carley wasn't constantly getting her ass whupped,' says Rachel and then she shouts out into the yard, 'girls, dinner's ready.'

But the Carolinas play on and Rachel puts their dinners in the oven, again. Carolina calls it quits about nine, 'Come on Carley, a rematch tomorrow. I'll help you with your defense.' But Carley stays on, practicing in the too dim artificial light of the garage. It's near midnight when she sits at the kitchen table and eats her dinner, scavenging the cabinets for a second helping of something that will fill her up.

Carolina defines her body by the space around it, how other players react and move, how distance stretches and contracts and she becomes herself among it all.

At the start of her freshman year in high school Carolina wants to try out for the boys' team. Of course there's an uproar, of course her whole family supports her, and of course the team can do nothing but give her a tryout.

The boys are rough and persistent with her at the tryouts. Carolina thinks this is good, it makes her work for it. Once on the team, Carolina tends to be the target of all things rough from opposing teams; her talent doesn't decrease but rises to surpass the challenges. Like most Fremonts, she doesn't bruise easily and her raw asexuality works in her favor too; not that the teens see this, or name this, but the adults notice how she blends in because she is not yet a woman, but still a girl-boy. When her teammates see her, it's like the word 'girl' flashes in front of their eyes but they dismiss it. She's Carolina: reliable, necessary to the team. Just one of the boys. And this makes sense to everyone.

Carley loves the physicality of basketball too but has never had the natural talent Carolina has and that realization is just coming to her. Still the Carolinas practice until night falls. When the moon rises, Carley puts the ball under her arm and starts towards the side door of the garage to put the ball away.

'I don't want to tire you out before tomorrow's big game.'

'Thanks, Carley,' says Carolina, catching her arm. 'I really wish you were on the team with me. We could really shake things up.'

'I'd just hold you back, you're better on your own.'

Carolina drops her hand; she can't argue this point anymore. 'You're coming to the game, right?'

'You're going to kick the Pistons' butts. Of course I'll be there as you rub Nick McKenna's nose into the court.'

In bed, with the moon waxing to full, two teenage girls dream of heat and the presence of their covers becomes too light along the length of their bodies. Too gentle. Overnight they move from childhood into a shuddering, thrilling adolescence. For the first time, this lack of press feels painful, the lack of another body pressing against their own is an absence and a need. In the morning everything has changed.

In her dreams Rachel explores the Arctic, water that has chosen a form, and this twin spring surge of hormones jolts her awake. She smiles, remembers, knows this is nothing she'll be able to control, this surge must run its own course.

The ball floats up like a bubble and then smoothly arcs to a swish in the hoop.

'Go 'lina!'

Carolina grins at her sisters in the stands and then gives Nick McKenna, her arch competitor on the Pistons, a small nod. They're even for points again. He smiles lightly, nods, and, as soon as he's able, he shoots a three-pointer and pulls ahead again.

The fast game has spectators rubbing their necks. On the court players sprint and move as teams. As they tire, their teamwork loosens, bodies just a few inches off from where they should be; both teams neck and neck, and near the end of the second quarter one of the Pistons takes to harassing Carolina, giving her a rough shove of a tackle. Carolina goes down. A whistle blows. She has a huge scrape down the side of her leg but moves to stand up quickly. A hand reaches to help her up: Nick McKenna. Sportsmanlike. His hand presses into Carolina's. Quick. Hot. Their smiles fade and are replaced by a flash of something altogether clearer and more telling. Steady. Carolina's body leans back and then forward and up; Nick's forward and then back gently pulling her up. They drop hands. A whistle blows.

Carolina isn't sure she'll be able to hold the ball. She moves her fingers and they seem to work just fine but she doesn't understand how. It feels like she has a hot coal in her palm.

'Carolina!' Ginny's voice cuts through her haze. 'Get going!'

Play resumes, and both Carolina and Nick unconsciously rub the palms of their right hands with the tips of the fingers of their left. Trying to recall the exact feeling.

Jon, Rachel and Sandra sit on the baseline, just behind the chairs for the players, and wave to Carley and Ginny who got there a bit late and sits high on the bleachers.

The seats can be a free-for-all and, after half-time, Allison Winters just beats Mark Rowls to the punch and sits down beside Carley for the second half. Carley feels her there as the crowd presses them. Their thighs touch.

'I'm Allison,' she says holding out her hand as they're jostled together.

'I know,' Carley says. 'We have English together.'

'We do?'

'I'm Carley Fremont.'

'How come I never noticed you before?'

'An oversight,' Carley says.

All Allison can do is nod.

Carley jumps to her feet when Carolina goes down again. 'Foul!'

Allison stands up and holds Carley's hand. 'She'll be fine.'

'I know. I just hate the collisions.'

The game ends. Ginny, Carley and Allison head up to the Fremont house. Ginny rushes ahead inside to say hi to Flo because whatever is going on with Carley and that girl makes her blush and she doesn't want to get between them.

Carolina isn't surprised to see Nick leaning by the fence outside the locker room. Her teammates hang back ever so slightly, looking at Carolina not as a player but as a girl. Carolina slows down to talk to Nick and, reluctantly, the rest of her team continue on to the local diner to share burgers and cokes.

'I'll get you a burger and cheese fries,' Mike calls back.

'Thanks Mike, but I'll order myself when I get there.'

'Okay,' says Mike with a nonchalance he doesn't feel. Beaten to the score by a Piston, twice in one day.

'Great game,' says Nick.

'Right back at ya,' says Carolina.

They start to walk, falling into soundless strides. Carolina feels like she's drowning, or coming to the surface, she can't decide. But it's good; either way, it's good: the light of the sun far above her, dark water pushing against her, protecting her at depths.

Ginny's palms itch after the game and she rubs her hands together and then shakes them gently to cool the desperate heat. Flo isn't here and there's no way she's going out back so she goes to the punch bag and does what she can to punch it open. Sometimes this feels too tame and she wishes they had padded the entire basement and she could fling her body again and again against the wall. Velcro would have been fun too. Fling, wrestle herself free, fling.

'Want an ice tea, Ginny?' Bam calls down, when she gets back.

'Sure.' She wipes her face on a towel and goes upstairs. 'Is Tex around?' Ginny asks.

Bam places her cool hands on Ginny's cheeks. 'Nope, he's at the site office.'

Ginny holds up the scissors and the grater. 'Want to worry his clothes?'

Bam grins, sick of all this kindness which hasn't made a single dent into anything at all, and grabs the scissors. 'That's exactly what I'd like to do.'

The house has been waiting. Not for repairs, but for change. The cement in the basement buckles and walls try to put a respectable distance between one another, as if that will save their floundering reputation for support. The now twenty-five-year-old roof concaves down towards its internal workings, like it has a bellyache. The paint peels and the house sways like seaweed in riptides.

Stitch by stitch, week by week, Bam and Ginny take Tex's wardrobe apart. They begin with his hang-about clothes: his sweat pants, his t-shirts. Partial hems carefully breached. Then they worry the joints and edges of his good clothes; with felt-scissors Bam frays the hems of his handmade wool trousers. With a white-handled cheese grater, Ginny wears through the elbows of his favorite Arran wool jumper. They think they're giving him signs he might understand.

After dinner, just as spring heats up into summer, Flo, Ginny and Bam sit on the porch reading and Tex comes home from a night in the city. He's disheveled, glowing.

'Girls, I'm going to have to ask for a bigger contribution next month. I seem to be wearing my clothes hard and how am I supposed to sell my designs looking like this?'

His elbows are worn nearly through, his pants drag on the ground when he walks. Neither fact dents his beauty in the least.

'Your clothes look awful, Tex. We understand,' Bam says.

'Sure thing, Tex. You'll have to wait a few weeks for the extra cash, so we can build up some overtime.' And with a flourish that Tex will recall as a bit too cheerful when he looks back on it, the girls have hooked arms and gone out for an evening walk.

SCAFFOLDING

Missy wears a hard hat and walks the support beams. She's nimble, almost acrobatic, like her father before her. 'He was a beauty up there on that beam,' her mom had said once. 'The most gorgeous man I'd ever seen.'

The first heat of June burns at the horizon. She walks the skeleton like a ballerina, not a bird. She knows her strengths, she's strong for her size, and she knows her limitations: she can't fly. Not even in her dreams. She's an earth creature, dirt under her fingernails, calluses on her palms. She's never shunned hard work, not a day in her life. That's why she climbs and walks and looks at as many builds as she can from as many different angles. This is what will help her do what she was put on this earth to do. This is how you change things, hands on.

As she walks the beams near attic height, she looks down through the nearly blank second floor and into the first floor of the new librarian's house. It's a pared down plan, a nearly square room, in a boxy, skirty structure, and has minimal, classic lines, natural angles and curves and a useful movement from room to room. The core of the build is to be made with the wood from the old house they'd decided to demolish after a tree uprooted and took its south end. Two floors below, the living room opens ever so slightly towards where French doors leading to a patio will be. She imagines living in this space and it's easy, the clean-lined furniture you could choose, the glass of wine you'd drink after work as you stand at the counter, the open doors which let in the sounds of the night.

She's been apprenticing with the firm's ancient, untalented architect, Max. The ex-husband of Sandra, Max is a man who still doesn't know that his wife had banged Hal for twenty years or something. Max smells like soap and still doesn't know that he's working for a son, who like the father, is an asshole. Who is she to talk about stupidity? She knows all about them both and yet here she is, still here with this old man looking at her tits, which really are too small to merit such attention, but he isn't to be distracted and when he reaches for another set of plans, which she simply has to see, he'd have brushed against her if she'd not spilt her coffee on his shoulder first. Then he smells like soap and coffee.

She knows all about her brother but she still works at Fremont Design and Renovation and keeps watching out for the old Tex, for the boy who had danced with her. In that moment he'd been given a chance to be free, she'd been a toddler and even she'd known it. The day when he could have turned into a man, but didn't. He'd had a chance to make good on the promise of his soul, but he betrayed it. He's her boy with the curls, the one who had apologized, just the once. He'd do it again, right?

Yesterday Max flirted his finger over plans of a banal cookie-cutter house, his own design, thinking she'd have an in with Tex, and she could convince her brother to let this unimaginative monstrosity be built. She stood behind him as he sat at his drafting table. He leaned back, his hips raising slightly from the chair and he pressed his shoulder into her thigh. She wanted to bitch slap him back and forth so that his greasy comb-over flopped flipped flopped. Her lips tightened and she looked up to see Tex watching Max be a scumbag: he knew exactly what Max was like. Exactly.

It's fissure. It's plates grating against each other deep in the core of the earth, it's something that never should happen, happening, right here, right now. She's a believer and it's been a charm, a shield against the world. She's believed in the good of this boy, this sweet-hearted boy, she knew it, knew it was a good heart he had. He had to have a good heart, the world wasn't possible otherwise, none of it. This is what she believes, what she believed, until she saw him smirk. Saw him waiting for her blush. He enjoyed her discomfort. She placed her hand on Max's shoulder, gave a squeeze, tossed her hair back, long and black, softly behind her shoulder.

'These are genius,' she said. 'I hope someday I can imagine such a guarded space like you can.'

It's her right hand on his sweaty shoulder, and through this hand she felt him shudder. Premature. Poor Sandra, she thought. She didn't have much experience but she'd tested out Sam Trackton, just last week, both of them in the back of his station wagon, out by the edge of the woods, and she'd known where everything went, all knees and elbows and sweetness. They've been dating, quiet, his parents wouldn't be pleased to know he'd hooked up with a Fremont but she likes him and thinks it could go someplace.

It's the same hand that had felt Max shudder that writes the note and leaves it front and center on Max's desk. That letter which details, well synopsized, what had passed between his ex-wife and Hal.

It's the same hand that holds up to Tex at the end of that day, both her four-week notice of termination of contract and the Will her dad had started to write.

'You think I care?' Tex said, holding up her letter of resignation. 'You think I'll miss you?'

'Yes,' she says. 'I know you will.'

'What's this?' Tex says looking at the second piece of paper.

'This is proof that you're wrong.'

Tex laughed. 'This, this scrap?' He rips it in two. 'Please Missy, you're going to have to do better than that.'

Four more weeks and she's out of here. She walks along the beam, heads towards the east supporting wall and sunrise, and turns to take the structure in. It's all about beautiful utility, that's what she's aiming for. Craft and usefulness and this is what she thinks as the square frame seems to slant into a rhomboid. A trick of sight, she thinks in that first second, and it's not until the girder beneath her tilts, turns really, that her stomach drops and churns, and she's shunted off, beyond the thin solid surface and into the air she fills, and she knows too many things come easily to her.

She's falling, remembering Bam's hands on the steering wheel of that Beetle and how Bam and her had to abandon the car after Bam had pumped the brake to no effect and how they drove into the corn and it's still slow motion as the car continues cleanly down the incline, cornstalks bending like twigs, like hair waving in the wind, the force of the out of control car and as Missy falls she knows she'll never have another encounter in the back of that car, of any car.

She knows her brother has cut too many corners, the whole of the architecture of the scaffolding twisting towards collapse and she and two of his men will be collateral damage, the first losses the Fremont firm has seen. And she knows god doesn't like a bragger, a girl who knows herself and the world too much, although he seems somewhat partial to assholes.

THE ALAMO

The house on the hill accepts the natural congregation that comes with a death, the natural convergence before migration. The Fremont girls arrive back, reacting to a change of wind across a map, phone calls from their sisters, the tilt of the earth, the devastation written all over a place most of them visit every day on the edge of sleep. Utah and Ari come from the southwest and Lou from Portland. Georgia, working her first catwalk in Paris as makeup artist, does not respond to any communication, paper or otherwise.

Rachel, Flo, Bam, the twins and Ginny have never left the house on the hill.

Betrayal, insolence, arrogance and meanness are one thing; willful liability, another. This is blindness. No one sees through this death clearly. None of them. No one eats. No one laughs. No balance. Missy. Why Missy?

Bam stays to the shadows waiting for the right time. Tex's car is ugly but it marks easily. His third car out of the company coffers. He walks from his car towards the back entrance of the office with his shoulders down, easy strides. Even now he is not afraid. He walks without hesitating. He doesn't look over his shoulder. He should be looking over his shoulder.

Bam's first punch is in the back of his neck. From behind. You only play fair with kids who play fair. You should only trust someone you know can be trustworthy. She's been a fool. He arches back and then doubles over. She turns him and shoves him against the wall. He'll last longer against the wall.

Right. Left. Her chest aches. Pleasure deeper than anything she's experienced so far. Shocking to acknowledge. Her fist hurts, his jaw is bony, not very giving, and his stomach has a toughness to it, like a coyote.

'Fight me you bastard. Fight!'

He does not make a sound. Does not raise a fist. Nothing.

'Haven't you learned how to fight yet?' she taunts him.

Tex grins, blood covering his front teeth, a nasty gash on his forehead. 'This the best you can do?'

Where does he get such arrogance? Any restraint she'd felt leaves. Left. Right. Left. Low. High. High. High.

For Missy. For me. For Flo. Another for Missy. For disrespecting Mom. For being stupid. For being mean. For being you, Tex. Just for being you.

He goes down, sliding down the wall where she'd pinned him. He'd not made much noise. A few peeps like a downed baby bird. She won't kick him. She bends down, her lips near his ear. She breathes. The calm. He breathes with her. False camaraderie. 'You killed her.' She holds nothing back with her last punch which knocks him out. She does not phone for help.

Bam touches her heart, runs a hand down her arm, a border. He's gone down, Missy. He's gone down. Violence solves nothing. She knows it. Solves nothing. But she's taken her brother down and it feels as good as she imagined it would.

He hears the footsteps behind him. He readies himself and then lets go of his fists. Take me out, he thinks. Make me pay. It's happening right here, to him. Just to him. The punches, the resistant nature of the wall, the sounds of his body abandoning him, her fury, and he knows there's a place she can reach if only she'd punch harder. Let go Bam, let go. Missy had been so small, such a beauty, she'd loved him. It's Missy who jabs his hip when he walks. This is what you could be, Tex, this is what you still could be. Harder Bam, he thinks. Is that the best you can do? This doesn't hurt enough, make it hurt more. It's swift though and silence falls first, then dark.

The blinds are down and he sits in the back office. Only one eye opens and his left hand feels broken. His right hand works well enough to search through all his papers about that building. He'd done what Missy had asked him to do. After the incident with Bam, he'd checked all the paperwork, and it wasn't in order. Not at all. That damn Nabon girl. He fired her and it took him almost a year, but he sorted every single detail. Any machine under question he pulled off site; he brought outside inspectors and engineers in to check all certificates and projects. Bill, the foreman, had become a bit sloppy and Tex had promoted a replacement from within the ranks. The build Missy was on had taken an extra eight days to get right because of problems with the ground and then with the fittings for the scaffolding. But it had been solid before they'd started work, he'd walked around with the inspector himself. He doesn't know what happened but when the police come he'll open his files. He'll make right what he's allowed to go wrong.

The church bells ring and Tex washes his face in the sink. Puts the only band-aid he can find over the biggest cut on his head, the one his cheek has started to scab and he hopes it'll hold. In heavy rain, he drives to the funeral.

The service has already started and his sisters and mother have their backs to him, umbrellas in a line against him. When he tries to get out of the car his legs will not support him. Such pain. He has never felt such pain.

All the Fremont women stand around the grave, in the pouring rain. Tex never shows up. The graveyard doesn't believe it, the house can't believe it, the girls can't believe it. The wimp.

After the funeral Bam goes straight into the house and places her hands on the map. 'We've been too generous. It ends here.'

Rachel is in the doorway, light and land behind her, and this place they have all been traveling towards is now beneath her feet. She gives a nod that only acknowledges what is already in movement.

The walls in the hall hiccup, exposing space between all the states; the glue, old and dry, allows corners and edges to ping off the wall.

Bam snaps her state from the wall. One or two of the girls gasp. Utah sways and she puts her hand up to cover the manic beating of her heart. She saw this in a dream. She puts her hand to the wall, then her cheek.

The girls take silence as permission and state by state they dismantle the map. Flo cries as she puts Colorado, New Mexico, Missy, and Georgia with her own state in the car. She's failed so many. Ginny and the Carolinas put theirs with them as well. The girls gather small items from the house and put them in pockets, and into the trunks of their cars and the flat beds of their trucks. Utah lifts the floorboards and packs her old notebooks in boxes and takes these, as well as the other papers she finds crushed there, away.

Only Texas is left. Flo steps forward. She's crying. It's a self-proclaimed lone star but it can't survive like that. She can't quite get a handle on his edges: they're tough and hard but wily. At the back by the wall her fingers have to reach to gain purchase, his state has started to erode but with a clean pull it's done.

'Look at this,' says Utah as she holds up a quilt she's found in his room: a single state, a silver star.

'That just about says it all,' says Flo.

Stitch by stitch they unmake the quilt and place the scraps in a pile next to his abandoned state. They draw a line on the front walk, with flour poured from a canister, and none of them step over it again.

Utah has an image of the house, the last time she sees it standing. As soon as she gets to what will be the base camp for her next excursion, her state leaning in the back of her truck, she sits down on a rock to sketch the house as it was when she left it: floorboard floorboard floorboard with stairs stairs stairs marching out the back of the page. Door door door, knob, counter counter counter fridge window window window. Each floor of the house gets a separate page. When she's drawing the miniature map far too small for any detail, a word she doesn't know comes into her head and repeats again and again. She looks it up in the dictionary she keeps in her glove compartment and then writes it in, repeating it in a finepoint hand from coast to coast, north to south: littoral littoral littoral. Between true land and true sea is the tidal sway, and in this place some things flourish.

Tex comes home and finds his state tilted at an angle, like a head in doubt or inquisition, on the front walk. A pile of quilting pieces and stuffing lie beside it: his prized quilt, dismantled. There's a faint line on the cement, wide and white. Pieces of cotton fly away in a lifting wind, stuffing looks like swirling snow. He sits down and nothing can make him enter the house.

The house creaks and sways. Hollowed of its rightful family, its own expected inheritance, and with only the slightest provocation from the wind, the house crumbles. When the dust settles, Tex picks up his state and crosses the line.

FAULTLINES

No one expects the death of a child, much less two. No one prepares you for one child to be responsible for the loss of another. No one expects to mourn children who remain alive.

Sudden change can have slow causes. Faults cause earthquakes, earthquakes cause tsunamis, gas emissions punch holes in the ozone that allow a heat up and melt down and this causes flooding in some places, drought in others. Resentment causes meanness; privilege causes stupidity. Movement in one place causes change in another: mountains push up as weather and gravity and erosion pull that same sediment back down. Catastrophe defines. Sometimes it's impossibly hard and carries a visible legacy. Sometimes the release of all that built up pressure creates ease of movement, belief, and decision making.

There is no moment in which Missy is not missed, no moment where she is not present. Her death does not cause doubt but rather clarifies. Rachel's cottage, a shed really, is the only house on their new property. Rachel and the girls cram in and the ocean brings the world to them in ebbs and flows. Within a week Flo keeps them moving forward, 'Let's build the big house.'

Rachel observes her daughters at dinner and sees that sometimes the past is not a void or a worrying presence, but sometimes is a lone star you visit at night and a brother you bring up in conversation often with a bittersweet missing which, although it turns quickly into rancor, the fact that you bring him to this place at all, holds a ghost-shadow of love.

FLO

Fabian did not wait all these years for Flo. Well, not really. He was a boy, after all, and then he became a man, not a saint. When Flo failed to throw pebbles at his window like he always dreamed she might, he married Mary Anne Chisholm, a good Christian girl, on a chirping spring day, the bride in white and the groom with a wide grin that took in all of his family and hers. Mary Anne had spark and intelligence and their marriage rode a curl of a wind of love and sensibility that would see most couples through. But at some point, just a few weeks ago, Mary Anne forgot what brought them together and rode a different, hotter wind to greener pastures tended by her new man, Mick Slavon, a civil engineer.

And Fabian remembers a girl. A powerful girl he once loved. When he visits his mom for the first time in years, she talks about the scandalous Fremonts the whole time, and how they'd just up and left with that disgraceful mother of theirs and now they live in a new house by the sea and how this was a scandal. Left that poor boy to fend for himself and how Flo and her sisters had been running a whore-house up on the hill and how Tex was the pimp and how they'd been laundering money for the NY mob and how, now that all the girls had left, the house has fallen down and how it's a disgrace to the neighborhood.

'And,' his mom says, 'that boy seems to be running a little bit wild with friends from the city. No good can come from that.' His ear aches, the pitch of his mother's voice like a fingernail on a chalkboard, and Fabian remembers why he'd left this place. 'Oh yeah,' his mom says, 'there are a few letters for you.'

One contains a coastal address and says yes to a very old invitation.

The new house is still under construction but finished enough to live in and Flo is standing at the front door because the wind had changed direction and that might be a good, or a bad thing.

There he is, parking in her driveway and walking towards her.

There she is. Standing outside her half-finished house.

Flo thinks there must be things they should say. She can't just take something like this as a given. Can she?

He takes steady strides towards her. She moves away from the door, to the edge of the steps. It's as far as she can make herself go. He stops a step or two below her. Looks at her.

'You look tired,' he says.

'You sure know how to make a girl feel good.'

He blushes. Looks down, mounts the last two steps so they are equal. Puts a hand on her hip, his thumb playing with a thin band of skin exposed between the top of her jeans and her shirt. Her body flushes. Melts out her toes and down the stairs.

'You're beautiful,' he says.

She rests her forehead on his shoulder. Her responsibilities are heavier than he'd expected but he adjusts quickly.

'Ms Flo Fremont,' he says. 'I am going to dedicate my life to looking after you.'

Even though she's still standing on her own two feet, it feels different, lighter, beautiful. 'With one stipulation,' Flo says.

'Anything,' Fabian replies, marking new borders on her skin.

'No children.'

'I understand.'

'And you do the cooking.'

And the man with the dark shining eyes will hold Flo so close that she'll forget, for a while, a luscious while, to take care of anyone else but herself.

The Carolinas take out a boat and they've gone to sea and docked at an island. These smart girls will also know how to get back.

Jon visits Rachel but doesn't stay long. One day, perhaps, maybe, when they're elderly rather than just getting older they'll live together and settle down. It's quiet, their love. Uncomplicated, true. And secondary, they both know it. Secondary to her love of her children, and to Jon's love of everything that's out there. Resistance causes friction, understanding the opposite. 'It's this easy,' thinks Rachel, 'to love and be loved.'

From a distance as they approach the mainland again, the Carolinas see their mother standing on the pier and for the first time they see a girl who swam a broad palm of sea when she was still a child, and they see all the Island held in her face (hinted at in their own), a history no one speaks of held in her brown eyes, and a logic in the magic of her maps.

LOW TO THE EARTH

Flo doesn't need to pee on a stick to know. But she does it anyway. A blue line appears. She groans. She paces back and forth in her bare feet on the tiled bathroom floor. Her hair sticks in clumps to the back of her neck, her shirt to her breasts and belly. It's noon and August and she's pregnant. She puts the lid down on the toilet and sits down with her elbows on her knees, her head in her hands. She exhales loudly. These damn Fremont genes, making mince meat out of two types of contraception.

She feels like weeping but the tears don't come. Already conserving water, already giving everything she has to this baby. When she finally stands it's almost evening and she's dizzy. So here she is, Florida Fremont Veracruz, in a low-slung house that spreads like a hand across the earth, tilting to the water. With child.

When she tells Fabian the news she makes her face peaceful to hide the devastation she feels. This gives Fabian just what he needs to pick her up and spin her around. 'Whooopppeee. Really? Oh, sweetheart I know you didn't want this, but now? How do you feel now that it's happened by accident?'

'Pregnant. I feel pregnant.'

He slows down a bit then, hearing her voice.

'I'm going for a walk, it'll all be fine when I get back.'

It wasn't quite true, but with each passing day the child she carries becomes more familiar. With the morning sickness, the tiredness, the aches, the restlessness in her legs, Flo has no idea how her mother had made it through twelve pregnancies, or ever thought fifty would be possible.

'I love this house!' shouts Ginny as she swings open the front door on Christmas Eve and drops her bags onto the floor, turns with her arms flung open, her head tossed back. 'Love this house!' Flo comes into the hall, Ginny rights herself. 'The shutters are gorgeous. Did you paint them?'

Flo gives Ginny a huge hug. 'No, Bam and Bud did, they'll do it every spring, that was the deal.'

'Their house looks like it's shaping up real good too.'

'She's being meticulous with that one. Even more than this one. No hurricane or tornado or wayward sibling will destroy that house. Personally, I'll be thrilled when they get that trailer out of the driveway.'

'I heard that!' shouts Bam from the kitchen.

'I knew you would.'

'Come in here and give me a hug Gin, I'm elbow deep in molasses sugar cookie dough.' Ginny hooks arms with Flo and they walk through. She kisses Bam on the cheek and rests a hand around her waist. Bam's hands are covered in dark dough and white sugar.

'Hey there you. How's that boarding school of yours?'

'You know. With the Carolinas there too, it's been fun. At school, they're working me hard. But I'm loving it. I get to read all day and argue politics and write about it.'

'I can imagine nothing worse.'

'And that my dear, might be why you build such great houses—cause you can't stand to be cooped up. In fact, I didn't know you knew how to bake.'

'I don't really. I'm just absolving Flo of domestic responsibilities.'

'Yeah, if that means I still have to watch everything you do so you don't burn the place down,' Flo says, sniffing the air.

'Damn!' And Bam goes to the oven; the cookies are dark but not yet burnt.

'So you're not keeping the trailer for the kids to use as a clubhouse?' asks Ginny.

'Not if I can help it,' Flo says.

'We'll see,' winks Bam, scraping the cookies from the sheet onto a cooling rack with noticeable grace. Kitchen utensils are just different types of tools.

'Enough of this small talk. Whip off that sweater Flo and give me your bump.'

It's with a fluid movement that she does so, and Ginny rubs her hands together to warm them and then lifts Flo's shirt to run her hands over her round belly.

She feels contours and heels and a swift kick to her hand. A wild, northern feel. A significant body of water curving up her west side.

'Michigan?'

'I think so. If no one gets the name first.'

'Well Utah's Kent is almost nine months old now, so is Ari's Idaho, and there's no other activity I can see.'

'I know. I'm just don't want to commit myself yet.'

'That's understandable enough.' Ginny soothes her hand up and down Flo's arm, 'I'll be here in a flash if you need me. You'll be in good hands.'

Flo tolerates the touch for as long as she can. 'I know,' she says quietly, and then she moves back a step. 'Gotta go pee.'

Bam slides the next lot of cookies in the oven and hands Ginny a warm cookie from off the cooling rack.

'What's up with her?' asks Ginny.

'That baby got through so many barriers you'd think it was a tank.'

'Is that all?'

'I have no idea. She's just plain old grumpy, all the time.'

'She worries me.'

'It's Flo, she'll be fine.'

'Will you let me know if anything happens?'

'Sure thing,' says Bam flicking on the oven light to check the cookies. 'When this batch is out of the oven do you want to go see my house?'

'I'd love to.'

'You'll have to imagine the roof.'

THE LONE STATE

No matter what the season, birds herald the dawn. Those damn birds. They arrived back after the house came down, the monstrous morning chorus. The racket, the disrupted sleep. Lou used to always be out here with Hal, and once he'd died she'd 'borrow' dad's binoculars from Tex.

'They are as good as any on the market,' she'd said and she pooh-poohed the new fangled roof-prism ones. At some point one of her temporary suitors gave her a pair of Leicas. Maybe it was because she was leaving, maybe it was because they actually were lighter and better, but she accepted them and the well cut leather and elasticized strap that crisscrossed its way on her straight, strong back. But that didn't stop her from also taking Hal's binoculars with her when she went.

Damn birds, Tex thinks. Like he has a target on his head. Even when he's only walking from the car to the garage he now calls home. Instead of following Lou to Portland, the things have stayed and multiplied, taken to nesting in the rubble. The Fremont yard actually attracts birdwatchers from throughout the state. Although the rarities have decreased over the years, the sheer volume of birds impresses the twitchers who abound at dawn and dusk.

One morning Sandra knocks on his door. Her eyes are red-rimmed. 'I don't know why it hit me today, but I miss Hal. And then I sat with that feeling for a minute and realized that, strangely, I miss your mother more.'

The dark of sleep still holds him but he turns away, he won't be the boy who cries for his mom.

Sandra touches his shoulder. 'What are you going to do now?'

'Something, I've got to do something.'

Tex carries his coffee to the edge of the yard. The year after Hal's funeral they'd planted some young trees and they've grown to a good height and even in the winter they protect the house from the plains' winds. Tex tosses the rest of his coffee over the fence and walks down to the office, stopping at Joe's for a morning paper. No big news. His office is neat and all the files are in order and it's only as he looks at it now he that realizes he's been preparing for this moment. After a long, drawn out investigation complicated by community factions, the police cleared him and the company of all wrong-doing in the deaths, and they are still trying to find the person they think tampered with the bolts of the scaffolding. There were signs of disturbance on the site, and it's considered an atypical collapse inconsistent with structural faults.

Two months later and his desk is even neater and three manila envelopes sit in front of him. Sandra sits across from him in a chair.

'Thanks for your help, Sandi. I couldn't have done it without you.'

'They're all fair offers for the firm and for the land. Good luck.'

The past is another country, this is not something to be carried with him when he goes. He calls his lawyer. 'If they create the bird refuge, we have a deal.'

He doesn't know where to go now. His sisters have been meticulous about not telling him where they are. Sandra won't budge either. He'll start his search tomorrow.

Back at home, Tex drinks a G&T and as evening sinks against the horizon, he nods off. And there in the orange and pink glow, and in the ever-darkening blue, he sees it for the first time: the Fremont family shining like a map of the USA at night, all black with a distinctive cluster of lights.

His hand relaxes and the glass drops and shatters on the concrete floor. Tex jolts awake. Suddenly he understands. His spends his days making up for years of failure and then spends long nights at this map.

TECTONIC

Beneath everything, plates float on a liquid core. It is on these plates we build our lives, our buildings. The Fremonts have built an entire country on this precarious foundation. Florida is a state particularly at risk.

It's an alarm, a scream. Directly in their heads. Bolted upright, feet on the floor before she can even find the words to tell Bud where she's going, Bam sprints in her bare feet across the short lawn that separates her from Flo. Rachel and Bam meet on the grass and race into the house.

'We're here Flo. Here.' The house as silent as the map. Flo is curled in a ball on the floor, the phone still in her hand, a thin anxious voice coming through the earpiece.

'Mrs Veracruz? Mrs Veracruz?'

Rachel listens briefly to this stranger's words and then hangs up the phone. She says nothing as she holds Flo. When the phone rings a few minutes later, Bam answers and tells the sisters what they already know.

Bam whispers into the phone. 'A semi,' she says, 'jack-knifed. Fabian never stood a chance.'

'It woke me up,' says Ari.

'It woke us all up.'

'I'll catch the first plane I can.'

'Bring everyone with you.'

'Of course. How is Flo holding up?'

'She's cracking up, Ari. What will it do to the baby?'

'It's a Fremont, it'll make it stronger.'

'Gotta go.'

'Tell Flo we all love her.'

'Flo, breathe.' Rachel says.

Flo gasps instead, paces. Hands in constant movement. Her face draws back into gauntness.

'I thought that I could sit back and relax a bit. Damn him. How dare he die. He promised...'

'Flo, breathe.'

'It hurts. Too much.'

'We're here,' says Ginny. The Carolinas and Bam mill about, not able to help.

Rachel stands in the doorway. 'Arizona and Utah are on their way.'

'I can't. Keep it together. Can't. Never have been able to. We had to leave Tex alone. Bam was right about him. Missy's dead, Cole too. Naomi and Georgia gone. How am I supposed to raise this baby right?'

'Because you and Mom raised us all and we've turned out okay.'

'But I couldn't keep you together.'

'We are, Flo. In our own way.'

'We've lost Tex. What if this is a wee lost soul of a boy? Will I lose him too?'

'You won't,' Carley says. 'You love them, they love you back.'

'I've always loved Tex.'

'We all do.'

'And it didn't matter. And Fabian. Gone.'

'Loving them matters,' says Rachel. 'It matters.'

'Flo, it's Paris,' says Georgia into the answering machine. 'I'll not be able to make it across.' A pause, vague party sounds in the background, her voice strong and then fading as if she's already turned her head away. 'What doesn't kill you, makes you stronger.'

Over the years her girls have brought Rachel seashells and oysters and pearls and grandkids. She has ocean ridges and trenches, sandbanks and rivers, icebergs and hot springs; she has painted a world of blue on her walls and has the real thing lapping against the sand below her cottage. She has trips planned, big trips.

When her son finally calls, she's ready for him. He's already tried her house phone and been forwarded to her cell. She takes the call in the backyard of Flo's house. His voice holds earth and reconciliation.

'Mom, it's me, Tex.'

'I know.' A tide comes in.

'I'm phoning because of Flo. Can I have her address? Please.'

'Tex, she's asked me not to do that.'

'Have you seen her recently? On the map?'

She sits down on a bench, looks out to the ocean. 'Tex. It's not your place. She's got her sisters. And me.'

'She needs all of us.'

'I'm not sure about that, Tex.'

'I am. I've been a fool.'

She tells him three lines of an address, and Tex wraps up the new quilt, with a few lines of a song he knows, and mails it with care.

Flo needs her sisters and her mom, and they arrive to hold her in place. Some wear black, some come just as they are, dressed in all the colors of the earth and sky.

Of course, those first few days are all a blur. The kids distract them; ensure that the house still knows laughter. When the quilt arrives from Tex, Flo shakes it open, the other girls whisper, and Flo gives a quiet nod and folds it away in a closet. She slips the accompanying note carefully into her pocket. With the quilt hidden and the note stowed, she comes back with an armful of paints and brushes that Rachel had brought with her.

'Let's get started,' Flo says and the Fremont women know it's time to do this thing they've been avoiding. On a wall built for the purpose, they outline a country, emphasizing all the bodies of water. It's a smaller scale than before but stretches further, is more precise.

'Be bold,' Rachel tells her girls. 'It's your map now.'

Their part of the map looks so small up on this new wall. When they've painted thirteen states and a small island off the east coast, they start in on the newer states.

'Room to grow,' Flo says.

They paint Wyoming, Alaska, Idaho, and Kentucky carefully. They take dibs on names: Minnesota, Nevada, California, Oregon, Vermont, Ohio and Maine. There is a tacit agreement that Michigan needs a strong, sure undercoat.

The plates have shifted and water and red-hot magma surge to fill the fissure. The very land they grew to rely on changes shape and on the edge of sleep the Fremont women see a state on the move.

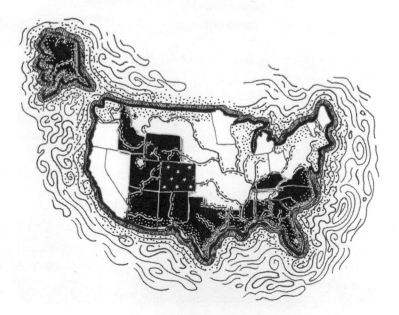

ACKNOWLEDGEMENTS

A huge thanks to all my family and friends who have contributed to the exuberance and substance of this book. A number of readers have been essential during the writing and editing and I am indebted to Jennifer Davis, Amanda Thomson and my dad. In the early days of the writing, I was obsessed with maps and I'm grateful to the students who took this interest in their stride as it sometimes directed our classes and the metaphors I used. I also want to thank Lesley and Leila at Kohl for choosing *Fremont* and handling it with such vision.

PGMJDX24

KOHLPUBLISHING

drawing a line under chick-lit ...

Kohl was born in a bar in Edinburgh in 2010. We, Lesley-Ann Dickson and Leila Cruickshank, often had difficulty finding books that were good reads, combining beautiful writing with thought-provoking ideas. We sought originality from books but often got the same stories over and over. We want to help people who, like us, are always looking out for the next good book but are often disappointed in the quest.

If you like great women's literature, are tired of chick-lit, and want something that captures your imagination, then you'll like Kohl.

We only publish books we love, so you can rely on our choices. We believe in supporting new writers, creating outstanding books, and listening to our readers. Visit www.kohlpublishing.com for exclusive deals, insightful discussions, and inspiring authors.

www.kohlpublishing.com

Follow us on Twitter @kohlpublishing

Like us at www.facebook.com/kohlpublishing